Brewed Awakening

Cleo Coyle

BERKLEY PRIME CRIME
New York

BERKLEY PRIME CRIME
Published by Berkley
An imprint of Penguin Random House LLC
penguinrandomhouse.com

ISBN: 9780451488893

Berkley Prime Crime hardcover edition / December 2019
Berkley Prime Crime mass-market edition / July 2021

Printed in the United States of America
1   3   5   7   9   10   8   6   4   2

Book design by Kristin del Rosario

Until one has loved an animal, a part of one's soul remains unawakened.
—Anatole France

This book is dedicated to two beloved cats, Cub and Mr. Fellowes, now gone to sleep, but forever alive in our memories.

ACKNOWLEDGMENTS

Brewed Awakening is our eighteenth Coffeehouse Mystery. As our longtime readers know, I write this series with my talented spouse, Marc Cerasini. Like every married couple, we have good days and bad days, but I'm thankful *every* day for the gift of Marc's partnership—in writing and in life.

The inspiration for this story began with a conversation. If our history as a couple were to be wiped clean, would we still be drawn to each other? How does "like" deepen into something more? When does love happen?

With two of our main characters on a path to be married, we decided to explore these questions within the plotline of this mystery and agreed the fulcrum of the tale would be memory loss.

Although Clare's story is fictional, we were inspired, through our research, by many remarkable true cases of amnesia, including a married woman whose traumatic accident resulted in forgetting her own husband—and believing her teenage daughter was still a toddler. In another case, a young teacher disappeared after going for a jog, and then reappeared, floating in New York Harbor, with no memory of how she got there or the weeks she went missing. (We could go on, but you get the idea.)

Other elements in *Brewed Awakening* were inspired by our decades of living and working in New York. While the Parkview Palace exists only in our imagination, you can visit many of the grand hotels that inspired its creation, including the Plaza (theplazany.com), the Pierre (thepierreny.com), and the Lotte New York Palace, formerly known as The Helmsley Palace (lottenypalace.com).

Our fictional Gypsy boutique hotel was also inspired by a real one: Paper Factory Hotel (paperfactoryhotel.com) of Long Island City, Queens, a uniquely modern inn that was literally transformed from a 100-year-old paper factory.

For coffee inspiration, we thank the folks at Hampton Coffee Company (hamptoncoffeecompany.com), an independent coffee roaster and retailer that pioneered micro-roasting on the East Coast, and whose dedication to freshly roasted joy is never short of admirable.

Our interaction with New York's Finest is always nothing but the finest, and we thank them for providing answers to our questions. For deviations from doctrine, we plead the author's defense—in the service of fiction, rules occasionally get bent.

Caffeinated cheers go to our publisher and the diligent crew who helped put this book into your hands. We are especially grateful to our editor, Michelle Vega, whose valuable input strengthened our story. Thanks also to editorial assistant Jennifer Snyder and production editor Stacy Edwards for keeping us on track; as well as to copyeditor Frank Walgren, our designers Rita Frangie and Kristin del Rosario, and our marketing and publicity team, Elisha Katz and Brittanie Black, for their essential contributions.

To the brilliant artist Cathy Gendron, we send sincerest appreciation for another spectacular Coffeehouse Mystery cover.

To John Talbot, our literary agent, we continue to treasure your patient support and consummate professionalism.

Last but far from least, we send love and gratitude to everyone whom we could not mention by name, including friends, family, and so many of you who read our books and send us notes via e-mail, our website's message board, and on social media. Your encouragement keeps us going, and we cannot thank you enough for that.

Whether you are new to our world or a devoted reader, Marc and I invite you to join our Coffeehouse community at our online home, coffeehousemystery.com, where you will find recipes, coffee picks, and a link to keep in touch by signing up for our newsletter. May you eat, drink, and read with joy!

—Cleo Coyle,
New York City

It's no use going back to yesterday, because I was a different person then.

—Lewis Carroll

PROLOGUE

~~~~~~~~~~~~~~~~~~~~~~~~~~~~~~~~

Two months ago

Nypd detectives Lori Soles and Sue Ellen Bass led a pack of uniformed officers through the door of my busy coffeehouse. Seeing their grave expressions, I feared something terrible had happened to Mike Quinn, and they'd come to deliver the grim news.

Despite my worries, I faced the women squarely.

"Detectives, how can I help you tonight?"

"Clare Cosi, we're here to place you under arrest."

With customers chattering around me, and the fire crackling loudly in the Village Blend's hearth, I assumed I'd heard wrong.

"Arrest me?"

Sue Ellen Bass, the more volatile of the pair, glanced at the small army of uniforms behind her and reached for the handcuffs on her belt.

"Did you think you could get away with grand theft?"

I blinked. "Are you kidding?"

"This is serious," Lori Soles said. "In New York State, stealing a police lieutenant's heart is a Class-A felony."

Suddenly the wall of uniforms parted, and there was

Detective Mike Quinn down on one knee. Wearing a rare smile and his best blue suit, he lifted a white ring box.

Time seemed to stop, the packed coffeehouse stilling with it.

Among the captivated crowd, I noticed the shaved head and grinning face of Sergeant Franco, the young detective my daughter was seeing. He was holding up his mobile phone, recording the scene for posterity—*and*, I suspected, for Joy to watch from her job in DC.

"Clare, I love you," Mike began plainly, "and I know you love me."

Opening the white box, he revealed a perfect diamond, its ice-blue color shining as brilliantly as the good in his eyes. Around the center, a circle of smaller coffee diamonds winked warmly in the glow of the firelight.

"I have something to ask you," he said. "And you'd better think hard about your answer. With these law officers as witnesses, it's going to be tough to change your story."

I nodded numbly, waiting for the words.

"Clare Cosi, will you marry me?"

My eyes blurred, emotions swirling, and my mind flashed back to the first time I saw this man, standing in my coffeehouse doorway, his expression haggard, jaw rough with stubble, trench coat stained and wrinkled. Never had I seen a soul more in need of caffeine.

But Mike hadn't come for coffee that day. He was there to inspect a crime scene; and, by the end of that case, he'd become a regular customer and eventually a good friend. Passion blossomed naturally between us. Trust wasn't as simple—at least for me.

My first wedding had led me into such cavernous misery that I'd been reluctant to step one foot back into that chasm. Mike had been battered by a bad marriage, too, but he was willing to try again, and I knew the reason. While the cop in him appreciated a friend and cherished a lover, what he valued more than anything was a partner.

As gun-shy as I was, I came to realize the painful cost

of *not* moving forward, which is why, in a voice choked with happy tears, I said *yes* to Mike's proposal.

Yes to a new partnership.

Yes to a new beginning.

Yes to another chance with another man, in so many ways, a better man.

I would take my time planning this wedding, a big one, with all our friends and family. This ceremony would be a true celebration, nothing like my first, when I was alone and pregnant, an anxious nineteen-year-old, half-desperate to be saved by a City Hall union to a peripatetic coffee hunter, little more than a boy himself.

Before me now, on one knee, was no boy. Mike Quinn was my rock, and I was his. How right this actual rock looked in his hand. Polished with patience, shimmering with certainty, fixed on an unending circle, it was the perfect symbol of what we shared together, and the years it took to make this moment. As he slipped it on my finger, I knew with complete conviction that I would love this man forever.

And this would be a day I'd never forget.

One

~~~~~~

I like coffee because it gives me the illusion that I might be awake.

—LEWIS BLACK

Two months later

I awoke in darkness, curled in a shivering ball. I'd been a restless sleeper since my divorce, and I assumed I'd kicked off the blankets. So why was something still covering my face? Heavy and stiff, it was definitely *not* my well-worn J.C. Penney comfort quilt.

A blaring horn and a string of angry expletives sat me up fast. A coat fell away from my face, and I blinked against a misty-morning sun peeking through naked branches.

Feeling dizzy, I rubbed my eyes before deciding—
This is no dream. This is real.

I tried to rise but my joints were stiff. My right arm was so numb that I had to shake it out. More troubling was the fact that somehow—and I could not for the life of me remember *how*—I wasn't in my nice warm bed in my cozy little bedroom in New Jersey. I was sprawled across a hard, cold bench in a public park, close enough to the street for me to hear a cabby cursing out the driver in front of him, which sounded an awful lot like Manhattan.

My suspicion was confirmed when I spied the towering arch of white marble that marked the start of Fifth Avenue.

I'm in Washington Square Park.

The triumphal arch gave me a triumphant rush of relief. I knew where I was—Greenwich Village, but . . .

"How in heaven's name did I get here?"

My baffled whisper emerged as a cloud of vapor.

Still shivering, I donned the coat that covered me. It fit perfectly, though it wasn't mine. I went through its pockets for a clue to its owner but found no ID or personal items, beyond a single right-hand glove. Its mate was missing.

The tan leather had a red-brown stain on the palm, about the size of a shot glass rim. *Blood.* I knew because I'd seen enough of it dried on clothing from scuffed knees and elbows after Joy's soccer matches.

I was tempted to start spit-scrubbing the stain but instead tucked the glove back in the pocket.

Rising to my feet, I felt wobbly and blamed the unsteadiness on my footwear. There was a theme here, because the high-end, high-heeled boots weren't mine, either—ditto for the cashmere sweater set and tailored slacks. If I hadn't been in public, I would have checked to see if I recognized my underwear!

Did I go on some wild shopping spree with my Jersey friends? If I did, where are they now? And why is it I don't remember? Cupping my hands, I blew warm breath into them and took a sniff. I detected no scent of alcohol. *Okay, so I didn't get tipsy and have a blackout.*

I sat back down on the cold bench to orient myself. While I retied my deconstructing ponytail, I realized my purse was nowhere in sight. I dug through every pocket, pants first and coat again. No wallet. No house keys. No car keys. All were gone.

I felt panic rising.

Okay, Clare, pull it together. You'll figure out what happened, but right now you've got to get home to your little girl.

With no watch on my wrist, I called out to a young man who was cutting through the park.

"Could you tell me the time, please?"

"Sure." He pulled an odd device from the pocket of his NYU hoodie. "It's six fifty-five, ma'am."

"Wow, that's really something you've got there."

He grinned, proudly displaying the black rectangle. Its glowing screen was crowded with colorful icons.

"I got it yesterday, first day of release," he said. "Everybody in my lab is jealous . . ." He rattled off a series of its "features," which sounded more like a shopping list in a foreign language. Then he cackled when all I did was ask if this amazing device would be made available to people like me.

"You're funny, lady. Give it a year. You can buy one used."

As he moved on, I took a breath and reassessed.

Okay, it's the crack of dawn. I have no money, no ID, no keys to anything. Panic began to rise again, until I remembered. This was the Village, my old neighborhood, and there was one place I'd always be welcome—

The Village Blend coffeehouse.

Even better, I could get some decent coffee there. In my experience, there weren't many problems a good cup of coffee couldn't help solve.

Two

As I started my stroll, a strange feeling came over me. The city's sights and sounds always energized and grounded me, but today I couldn't shake a creeping sense of displacement.

I'd moved out of Manhattan mere months ago, yet the city appeared to have changed impossibly since I'd packed up my young daughter and left. For years, Washington Square had suffered from neglect, its monuments scrawled with graffiti, its central fountain inactive. Now the white marble arch gleamed, the greenery was tidy, the paths newly paved, the fountain spraying rainbows in the morning light.

The sight should have cheered me. Instead the surreal sense of uneasiness only worsened as I walked. At the corner of West Fourth and Sixth Avenue, I saw the basketball court was still there, but the skeevy head shops, bodegas, and pizzerias around it had been replaced by slick storefronts and upscale eateries.

I tried to shrug it off. After all, New York never did stand still. The only constant in this town was change.

Crossing Sixth, I passed people with devices similar to the one that NYU student had shown me. They were staring, almost hypnotically, at their screens as they walked. Some were even talking into them!

Who were these people talking *to* at seven AM? And

what could they be talking about? Was there an advanced-technology convention at the university? Or was this some kind of rehearsal for performance art—it certainly looked bizarre enough to be an avant-garde spectacle.

I passed a convenience store with no magazine rack, just a colorful display for something called vaping. The only two newspapers on sale carried similar headlines:

HOTEL HEIRESS MISSING
MYSTERY AT PARKVIEW PALACE:
ABDUCTION OR MURDER?

The stories appeared to be about some wealthy woman named Annette Brewster, who owned the famous Parkview Palace hotel. She had disappeared days ago. Evidence pointed to foul play.

Staring at the headlines, I felt dizzy again, as if something was clawing at the edges of my mind, trying to get in. Then, whatever it was slipped away, like a dream disappearing as you wake.

Left only with a lingering frustration, I tried to shake my thoughts clear and suddenly remembered my young daughter, home alone. What was I doing wasting time on headlines that had nothing to do with me?!

Stepping up my pace, I made it to Hudson Street and felt an instant sense of calm at the sight of the Village Blend. Thank goodness nothing had changed there. The French windows were closed, but the blinds were open and front entrance unlocked.

I followed a pair of customers inside. Hearing the familiar bell above the door was reassuring; and the roasted coffee, freshly brewing, smelled like ambrosia. That surprised me—and, I admit, made me a little jealous.

I'd taken pride in my former work here as a master roaster. My mother-in-law said she'd never met anyone who had my touch with the Probat or talent for creating exceptional blends. Except her, of course, but right now Madame was in Europe with her second husband, Pierre.

I'd have to sample a few sips to be sure, but from the aroma (and the raves from the customers in line), I knew I'd been replaced. Madame had obviously found someone else who knew how to handle her son's specially sourced beans.

A line was forming at the coffee bar, but I didn't want to wait. I was anxious to call my daughter, so I approached a zaftig young woman wearing a blue Village Blend apron and black-framed glasses, which dominated her pleasant round face. She looked distracted, hurriedly setting up café tables for the day. (Tables that should have been set up by now—not a good reflection on the new management.)

"Excuse me," I said, tapping her shoulder. "I used to work here and I'm in a fix. May I use your phone?"

The young woman froze a moment, staring into space as if she'd heard a voice from the great beyond. Then she dropped the wrought iron chair, whirled around, and screamed.

Every person in the coffeehouse stared. Embarrassed, I stepped back, assuming I'd startled her.

What she did next more than startled me.

"Clare Cosi!" she shouted, giving me a smothering hug. "YOU'RE BACK AND YOU'RE ALIVE!"

I rolled my eyes. Would city people never change? Move out of Manhattan and you no longer exist? Sheesh!

"Omigod, omigod!" the girl kept chanting. When she finally broke her mother-bear clutch, I actually saw tears in her eyes.

What is wrong with this person?

I noticed her necklace displayed the name *Esther* in silver letters. "I'm sorry—*Esther*, is it? I assume Madame told you about me, maybe showed you my photo, but the joke's over, okay."

"Joke?" The baffled barista took a step back. "Boss, what are you talking about? This is no joke. You've been missing for days!"

THREE

~~~~~~~~~~~~~~~~~~~~~~~~~~~~~~~~~~~~~

I stared in confusion at the young woman named Esther. "I've been *missing*?"

She nodded emphatically. "We were sick with worry about you. We looked *everywhere* but there was no trace. We feared the worst. Now here you are, perfectly okay, talking about a *joke*. Are you saying your disappearance was some kind of prank?"

Before I could answer, another barista—this one male and wiry—emerged from behind the marble counter and threw his tattooed arms around me.

"Stop!" I cried, pulling away from the young man's apron. "I don't recognize you. Who are you?"

"See, Dante!" Esther smirked at him like a mocking sister. "I told you not to grow that beard. He's just trying to look cool for his big art competition next week."

"Sorry, Boss Lady. I should have waited and asked you," the young man said, sheepishly scratching his facial hair. "I wasn't sure you'd approve with all the catering we do. But Mr. Boss okayed it, since you weren't around."

I blinked. "Of course I wasn't around, Mr. Dante. I don't work here anymore."

Esther scowled. "You mean you're quitting? Is that what

the disappearing act was all about? So it had nothing to do
with the Parkview Palace murder—?"

"Murder?"

"Or maybe just an abduction," she said. "You would
know better than any of us—"

"Clare! You're back!"

Finally, the sound of a familiar voice.

Madame Blanche Dreyfus Allegro Dubois, the elegant
owner of this legendary coffeehouse, enveloped me in her
arms. "Thank God my prayers have been answered." Tears
choked her voice. "Oh, my dear child, I was beginning to
fear I'd never see you again. But I never gave up hope. Nobody did."

"It's good to see you, too . . ." I was buoyed by this reunion with my former mother-in-law, my mentor, and my
dearest friend. But I was completely confused by her over-
blown emotions. After all, we'd just seen each other a few
weeks ago.

"What are you doing back?" I asked her. "I thought you
were in Europe with Pierre."

Madame pulled away; her violet gaze, damp with tears,
began to study my face. As she did, I took in hers.

Matt's mother occasionally indulged in makeovers with
updates to her wardrobe, hairstyle, and cosmetics. Her taste
was impeccable, and the new looks always took years off
her age.

But not this time.

Yes, her tailored pin-striped pantsuit was chic, cut from
the finest cloth, and her blunt pageboy flattered her high
cheekbones. This time, however, she'd let her hair color go
completely silver. And whatever she'd done with the change
to her makeup had left her looking more wrinkled than I
remembered. Searching for reasons, I tensed.

Had some health issue reared its ugly head? Was that
why she'd come back to the States before the holidays?

"Madame, how are you feeling?"

"I was about to ask you that very question."

"She's lost her mind!" Esther declared. "She told me she's quitting the Village Blend. That's like quitting her family!"

"You can't quit," Madame said. "I've made this coffee-house your legacy."

"You have? When?" I shook my head. "I don't understand. I already quit. Months ago. The same day I left Matt . . ."

Legend has it that if you speak of the devil, he will appear. In this case, the legend was right. The bell over the front door jangled, heralding the arrival of one of the world's most talented coffee hunters, Madame's son, and my ex-husband.

Like mother, like child, I decided at the sight of him. It appeared that Matteo Allegro had remade himself, too. His usual shaggy hair was close-cropped now, and he'd grown a beard—full and dark around his straight white grin. With Matt, however, some things never changed. That deep tan, no doubt from some intrepid expedition in the tropical belt, was still in place, along with his obnoxious swagger.

"Damn, Clare, where have you been? I was afraid the next time I'd see you was on the side of a milk carton!"

It took every bit of my willpower not to lash out and slap him as he attempted to embrace me. I didn't want to resort to violence, but I did push free of his despicable grip.

"You've got a lot of nerve, trying to put your hands on me. And to answer your ridiculous question, I've been living in New Jersey, with an eleven-year-old daughter who adores you—and you've been neglecting!"

"What—?"

"Don't act like you haven't heard this before. You've only visited Joy twice since we split. She's just a little girl, Matt. What is wrong with you?"

There it was again! That expression of confusion.

"What is wrong with *you,* Clare?" His tone wasn't angry at all, just concerned. "We've been divorced for over fifteen years—"

Fifteen years? Matt kept talking, but he made no sense. Then that surreal feeling returned. The displacement I'd experienced, after opening my eyes on that park bench, flowed over me with disturbing force.

I took in the anxious looks around me: the worry on Esther's face; the confusion on Mr. Dante's; the absurdity of Matt's dopey stare. Even Madame appeared upset, almost frightened, and I realized I was as unnerved as they were.

That's when something went haywire, like a delayed reaction from a bar-crawl bender. The coffeehouse began to spin, and my knees went weak.

"I don't feel so good," I mumbled.

"Look at her face!" Esther cried. "She's gone white as milk foam!"

"Dante, call 911!" Madame ordered. "Clare needs medical attention."

"Good idea," I murmured as Mr. Dante pulled out one of those fancy devices everyone in the Village seemed to possess. Then I tried to grip the back of an empty café chair to keep from falling—and failed.

"Clare!" Matt cried, lurching toward me.

Before I hit the polished plank floor, he opened his arms to catch me. This time, I let him.

Four

∾∾∾∾∾∾∾∾∾∾∾∾∾∾∾∾∾∾∾∾∾∾∾

At the hospital, the staff put me in a room with a single bed and dull pink walls the color of Pepto-Bismol. The only decoration was one of those pain charts with rows of cartoon faces expressing levels of discomfort.

It wasn't long before I was visited by a smiling medical doctor. She asked me the same questions the nurse in the ER had asked, then the admitting physician—what day is it, what month, what year?

The only tough question was: "How did you end up on a bench in Washington Square Park?"

Yeah, right. Like I knew.

The smiling staffer gently suggested I might have been assaulted and could be suffering from physical trauma. A blow to the head might have induced "my confusion."

She scared me enough to submit to a thorough examination. And, wow, did she mean thorough.

Three nurses and the doctor—all women, thankfully—took every stitch of clothing from me, along with my last shreds of dignity. They searched my naked body, took blood, and probed places I'd rather not speak about.

In the end, they found nothing more serious than a quarter-sized bruise on the back of my neck, caused by a tiny puncture wound, or so the doc speculated. She asked me how I'd gotten that injury, and I told her I wasn't aware I had it, adding that it didn't hurt.

Next, the medical staff sent me hither and yon for body and brain scans. After that, it was back to my Pepto room. Through it all, I continually asked about my little girl in New Jersey.

"Is Joy okay? Who's taking care of her?"

The smiling nurse kept assuring me that my daughter was perfectly fine. Finally, she informed me that Joy was on her way to see me.

On her way? I thought. *But she's not old enough— unless my ex-husband is bringing her. Yes! That has to be it. Matt must be driving through the tunnel right now to pick her up . . .*

For the first time since I was admitted to this hospital, I smiled, deciding Matt must have taken my lecture to heart— the one about neglecting his daughter. Joy would certainly be happy. She always loved her alone time with Daddy.

The cheerful nurse gave me something to eat—a liquid diet, unfortunately. The tray included tepid apple juice, a tolerable beef broth, and a cup of completely undrinkable decaffeinated tea.

While I focused on my "meal," the nurse stepped out, leaving the door ajar while she spoke to someone in the hallway. I held my breath, cocked an ear, and listened as hard as I could. She muttered something about "a slow process of reality orientation to avoid emotional trauma" if the SPECT-CT scans "come up negative for injury or a disease of the brain."

I pondered that while another staffer walked in and cleared my tray.

There was no television for me and nothing to read, so I stared out the window until I dozed off. I didn't know how long I slept, but I sat up with eager hope when I heard someone come in.

I sank back again when I realized it wasn't my daughter, or even my ex-husband. The two men who came in were total strangers.

Flashing their badges, they introduced themselves as police detectives. I barely paid attention to their names. I was too startled and agitated.

The older cop was tall and broad-shouldered with sandy hair and a sadly wrinkled suit. The younger one was more muscular and wore a black leather jacket. With his shaved head and grim expression, he came off a little scary.

The haggard-looking older detective . . . well, he had a nice enough face and polite manners, but the way his glacial blue eyes kept staring at me made me want to jump out the window just to get away from him. He was acting as if he expected *me* to say something!

Finally, I did. "Where is my daughter, Joy? I want to see her."

"She'll be here soon," the sandy-haired detective promised.

His voice sounded hoarse, and those striking blue eyes never left me as he fumbled with a recorder. Something about his demeanor made me shy, and I pulled up the sheet to cover my skimpy hospital gown.

"Tell us, Ms. Cosi," the intense cop asked. "What is the last thing you remember?"

"Today or yesterday?"

This time the wannabe gangbanger spoke, his voice a low rumble. "How about we start with today, from the moment you got outta bed?"

Once again, I told the story of how I woke, not in my bed, but on a park bench in strange clothes with no knowledge of how I got there and no wallet, keys, or ID. I explained how I walked to my old employer's business to use the phone, and how two baristas I'd never met before acted as if they knew me.

"Then my ex-husband arrived, and I felt suddenly ill. An ambulance showed up, and here I am, in an ugly pink room being grilled by you, Detective—sorry. What was your name?"

"Sergeant Emmanuel Franco. You can call me Manny or Franco."

His gruff voice was like a low, woody reverb from a bass guitar. But it was the intense detective who kept drawing my eye. Rubbing the brown stubble on his square chin, he asked me to describe what I had done *yesterday*.

An easy enough question, but I strained trying to remember—and came up blank. "I can't recall," I finally replied. "Most likely, I tested a few recipes and wrote my In the Kitchen with Clare column."

"Do you remember talking to anyone? Or seeing anything that may have upset—?"

Before the intense detective could finish his question, a commotion broke out on the other side of the closed door.

"I need to see her!"

A young woman was arguing with others in the hallway. Her voice sounded frantic—and strangely familiar, though I couldn't quite place it.

"Wait! Don't go in there!" a man called. This voice I *could* place. My ex-husband had arrived.

"Stop her!" the doctor urged.

The door flew open and a woman in her twenties rushed into the room. She moved so fast, she eluded the grasp of the cheerful nurse *and* the young detective with the shaved head.

"Mom!" she cried, hurrying to my bedside. "I was so worried! You were gone for days!"

The young woman continued to speak, but nothing registered beyond her first word. *Mom?!*

I was about to tell this person that she'd made a terrible mistake. Then I blinked and stared. *Those green eyes. That heart-shaped face and chestnut hair. How odd,* I thought, *this stranger looks just like my daughter, only all grown up.*

"Joy!" The younger detective pulled her back. "This isn't helping!"

Joy?

As I anxiously searched those familiar green eyes—now filling with tears and an almost heartbreaking expectation—understanding dawned.

But understanding and acceptance are two very different things.

How could this person be my darling eleven-year-old? How could my child become a fully grown woman in just one night?!

Gasping for breath, I felt the world begin to spin.

"Mom! Mom!" Joy cried, hope turning to alarm.

The cheerful nurse, no longer so cheerful, hurried to my side. As she took my pulse, I slumped backward and heard my ex-husband groan.

"Well, so much for that slow process of reality orientation to avoid emotional trauma."

As I watched in dumbfounded confusion, the young cop with the shaved head put his arm around my impossibly *full-grown* daughter and guided her out of the room. Before they disappeared, the sandy-haired officer with the blue eyes called out to her.

"Don't worry, Joy. A specialist is coming to examine your mother. Everyone says he's one of the best. It may take time, but we'll get our Clare back."

As the Pepto walls burred and faded, I dizzily whispered—

"What do you mean, 'our' Clare?"

Five

〰〰〰〰〰〰〰〰〰〰〰〰〰〰

Madame

Ihe next day, Clare's condition had not improved, even after the arrival of a specialist to oversee her case. Several more days passed, and Madame Blanche Dreyfus Allegro Dubois grew anxious. She asked Detective Quinn to arrange a meeting with the specialist and wasn't at all surprised when her son insisted on joining them.

Blanche considered including her granddaughter, but she could see the girl was having trouble coping with her mother's memory loss. Better to speak with Joy after the meeting, she decided, and keep the consultation as unemotional as possible.

Leaving Clare at the hospital, Blanche, Matt, and Detective Quinn shared a cab uptown to the specialist's office. After genial greetings, the consultation began.

Dr. Dominic Lorca had plenty of charisma. Blanche could not deny that. His faint Portuguese accent, dark eyes, and curly hair completed the charming picture.

The display of celebrity patient photos on his office walls was obviously meant to impress. As a psychiatrist to the stars, Dr. Lorca often appeared on cable news shows as an expert on mental health. He had even worked with the NYPD on several baffling cases. That connection, Blanche assumed, was how Clare's gallant fiancé had come to know the man. The generous doctor even insisted on *donating* his services.

Still, Blanche wondered if Detective Quinn wasn't regretting his decision after hearing Lorca's directives for Clare's treatment. Her son certainly didn't care for the doctor's opinions, and he was quite vocal about it—

"Who are you to say I can't see Clare? She's my wife!"

"*Ex*-wife," Detective Quinn corrected. "As far as Clare is concerned, you two just split up because you cheated on her. Repeatedly."

Fuming (and, frankly, without a defense), Matt faced the doctor. "Clare and I worked out our differences. Nowadays we get along great—"

"It doesn't matter," Quinn went on. "Clare's lost those years. As far as she's concerned, you're persona non grata."

Before Matt could reply, Dr. Lorca cleared his throat. "I'm afraid the detective is correct, Mr. Allegro. In my examination of Ms. Cosi, she did not speak . . . *fondly* of you."

From behind his large desk, Lorca's demeanor appeared cool and professional. With palms together, his delicate hands formed a steeple, which he dipped to aim directly at Matt.

"You must understand, Clare's feelings toward you are quite raw. She is experiencing all the pain and negativity associated with your divorce, as if it had occurred only recently."

"Maybe," Matt replied. "But at least she knows who I am. Quinn here is nothing to her now. A complete stranger."

The unnecessarily blunt retort was obviously meant to wound the poor detective, but Quinn's death-mask expression failed to show it. Instead he focused his glacial gaze on the doctor.

"When can detectives schedule a second interview with Clare? She may not recall anything yet, but—as you already know—she's a witness to a major crime. I'm not in charge of that ongoing investigation, but I'd like to sit in on the questioning—"

Dr. Lorca silenced Quinn with a raised hand.

"The patient currently has no recollection of the incident you mentioned. Over the past few days, I tried several approaches, including hypnotic regression, but nothing broke through. Pressing her for answers now will only cause her distress. Any further questioning by authorities, therefore, must be done while I'm present—and you should not be taking part."

"I understand," Quinn said. "I admit, I have a conflict of interest in the case. But I do want to see her again—"

"No. I'm afraid that's out of the question. I intend to keep Ms. Cosi isolated from the life she has forgotten."

"Isolated?"

The doctor nodded. "She will either regain her memory on her own or evolve into an entirely new person, if her past life should fail to return."

Mike Quinn looked as if he'd taken a gut punch.

Matt folded his arms. "Did you hear that, flatfoot? She might be peeved at me, but at least she remembers we were married. *You*, however, are going to remain anonymous."

Quinn's jaw tightened. "If worse comes to worst, Allegro, at least I can try again with a clean slate. *You*, however, are going to remain a man she can't stand the sight of."

Blanche sighed. It was never a good idea putting two men who cared for the same woman together in a room. From a distance, it seemed romantic—Bogart and Paul Henreid loving Ingrid Bergman in *Casablanca*. But the reality was as messy as that King Arthur fiasco with Lancelot and Guinevere, which, if memory served, hadn't ended happily for anyone.

Before these two (apparently) grown men could inflict more emotional scars on each other, Blanche decided to speak up.

"Dr. Lorca, can you tell us anything more? Exactly what is wrong with Clare, from a medical standpoint?"

"She is displaying unique symptoms of what appears to

be a rare form of dissociative amnesia, which can be either transient or permanent. Right now it's far too early to know if she will ever regain her memories."

"How could this have happened?"

"I can only tell you that there are several causes of amnesia: disease, deficiencies, injury, including alcohol or drug abuse. Rarer, but just as real, are emotional traumas. I've seen Ms. Cosi's test results, and I can confidently rule out the physical issues."

Blanche's brow furrowed. "I still don't understand your isolation approach. If she's free of injury and disease, why can't she be released from the hospital?"

"Though she's healthy on a physical level, Ms. Cosi is emotionally fragile."

"Fragile? Clare Cosi?" Blanche suppressed a laugh. "I'm sorry, Doctor, but you don't know the woman like I do."

"That's just it, Mrs. Dubois. She's not the same woman. And consider this. If I released Ms. Cosi from the hospital, where would she live? She speaks of some little house in the New Jersey suburbs, but that property was sold years ago."

"She would live in the duplex apartment above our coffeehouse," Blanche insisted. "It's her home, after all."

"I doubt very much Clare would be able to function mentally. She still believes she writes a column for a defunct New Jersey newspaper. Her memory of managing your coffeehouse is so far in the past that your current staff would be unknown to her."

Matt spoke up. "And you think this is because of some emotional trauma? Something Clare saw or experienced?"

"According to the police, before Ms. Cosi went missing, a private security camera captured her witnessing a crime."

"And you think witnessing a crime was *novel* for my ex-wife?" Matt snorted, throwing a glance his mother's way. "Clearly, you don't know our Clare's history."

"Her history is no longer relevant, Mr. Allegro. If she doesn't regain her memories naturally, then Ms. Cosi's understanding of her personal history will be rewritten by Ms. Cosi herself. In the meantime . . ." The doctor made a show of looking at his watch. "I should have a bed for her by next week."

"What do you mean?" Quinn asked. "She already has a bed. She's been admitted to a Manhattan hospital."

"The hospital needs that bed for more urgent care. Since there's nothing physically wrong with Ms. Cosi, she'll be admitted to my clinic . . ." Lorca went on for a moment about the important research going on at his Lorca Institute for Brain Studies and Mental Health. "Once we've moved her upstate, she'll be in the very best hands."

"Upstate?" Quinn's calm façade was starting to crack.

"Yes, now that she's agreed to the treatment, we should have her there in the next few days."

"You can't just take her away!" Quinn stood up. "Clare Cosi is a witness to a felony. If the perpetrator suspects she can identify him, she might be in jeopardy herself."

"Do calm down. Ms. Cosi is under twenty-four-hour observation. She's certainly *not* in jeopardy. And I must insist you control your temper, or I'll be forced to call security."

"Call them!" Planting both hands on Lorca's desk, the detective loomed over the doctor. "From what we know, Clare was present during the abduction of hotel heiress Annette Brewster. Clare herself was missing for a week, and we have no idea where she was. It's probable she was taken, along with Mrs. Brewster, and she somehow managed to escape her captor—or captors if the man was working with others. With the perpetrator still at large, Clare's life could be in danger. We need answers, Lorca. And Clare deserves at least *a chance* to reconnect with the people in her life!"

"I'm her doctor, not you, Detective. And I'm not at all comfortable with this volatile display. I need you to *sit down* right now—or leave this office." He pointed to the door. "Your choice."

Quinn clenched his fists. "You're not taking her," he said, then turned and left, slamming the door behind him.

Blanche sighed. *So much for keeping the meeting unemotional.*

Lorca shook his head. "Sad to see such loss of control in

a grown man. And he's quite wrong. Ms. Cosi *will* be leaving the city for treatment."

"How long?" Blanche asked. "How long will she be in your facility upstate?"

The doctor sat back, hands steepling again. "Ms. Cosi is a fascinating subject, and I'll need time to observe her condition, evaluate her brain activity, and settle on a treatment protocol. It will take weeks, certainly. Perhaps months—"

"Months!" Now Matt stood up. "You're crazy!"

Lorca pointed to the door.

"I know, I know! My emotional display is making you uncomfortable." He folded his arms and sat. "Okay?"

Blanche took a steadying breath. She was beginning to feel as frustrated as the men she had brought with her, but she wisely tempered her response.

"Dr. Lorca, I realize you're doing what you believe is best, but I still don't understand. Why take Clare away from the people who know and love her?"

"The people who know and love her are also the people who will confuse and confound her efforts to regain her mental stability. Trust me. I am working toward the best outcome. This is the same technique I used in the Riverside Park case . . ."

Blanche had wondered when the doctor would get around to mentioning that famous incident, the one that had become the subject for the man's bestselling book, soon to be a cable TV movie.

Five years ago, a university professor and his wife had been walking through Riverside Park near their Upper West Side home when the woman was struck by a careless cyclist and sustained a head injury. When she awoke from a two-month coma, the woman had no memory of twenty-five years of marriage or her three grown children. In her mind, she was still married to her first husband and her eldest child was a mere toddler.

Most experts gave the family little hope that the woman they knew as wife and mother would ever recover her past. Then Dr. Lorca stepped in.

After a year of treatment, the woman made a partial recovery. The couple's public renewal of their marriage vows at the very location of the accident made international news.

"Will your 'treatment' be painful for Clare?" Blanche asked.

Lorca nodded. "At times. But I assure you, she'll be surrounded by a dedicated staff, and we'll be using cutting-edge brain-health supplements and anxiety-reducing drugs as needed in her therapy."

Matt scowled at the word *drugs*. "Does Clare herself have any say in your big plans for her?"

"I've discussed the situation with her, and she's agreed to be treated by me. Moreover, in my estimation, Ms. Cosi is a danger to herself. As her physician, it is legally my duty to decide what is best for her."

"May I see her?" Blanche asked as politely as she could manage. "Clare remembers me well, and in a very positive way. I don't see why I can't speak with her—at least to say goodbye for now."

"I'm sorry, Mrs. Dubois, but I can't allow it. I can't trust that you won't contaminate her."

"Contaminate her!" Matt cried.

"Confuse her with subjects or events that she won't recall. Just give it time." He forced a toothy smile. "Trust me."

As Matt slammed out of the room, Blanche followed, her thoughts in turmoil.

Clare Cosi—a person she loved like a daughter, the heir to her landmark business, mother to a devoted young woman, and fiancée to a worthy man—was about to be taken upstate to some mental institution and completely isolated from everyone who cared about her.

There had to be another way!

SIX

@@@@@@@@@@@@@@@@

WHILE Matt quickly left the building to "walk off" his frustration, Blanche stopped to talk with Detective Quinn. She spotted him in the corner of the marble lobby, finishing up a phone call.

"Why did you storm out like that?" Blanche demanded. "Why didn't you try harder to set Dr. Lorca straight?"

"Because he holds all the cards." Quinn rubbed his bloodshot eyes. "I just spoke with the hospital administrator. She told me Clare signed off on the doctor's care, legally agreeing to Lorca's isolation therapy."

"I can't believe she'd want that! Lorca obviously snake-charmed her."

"Excuse me?"

"Look at the man. He's tall, dark, and dreamy with adorable curly hair and an air of cool confidence. I'm sure he could sweet-talk any woman in Clare's confused and vulnerable state."

Quinn grimaced. "Whatever the reason, she agreed. It's done."

"You should have seen the opportunistic twinkle in Lorca's eyes when he spoke of Clare as being a *fascinating subject*." Blanche exhaled in disgust. "Subject of a new bestseller, most likely. And what exactly is this 'cutting-edge' drug therapy he's convinced her to try? Is our Clare about to become Lorca's personal lab rat?"

"I don't know. But what we think doesn't matter. As her physician, he's in charge of Clare's treatment—"

"Not if Clare requests a second opinion from another doctor."

"She's unlikely to, as long as he keeps her isolated from our influence. And if he deems Clare a danger to herself, then he's prepared to make a case for legal commitment."

"Why in the world did you get that man involved?"

Quinn blinked. "I didn't. Lorca came to me. He said he heard about Clare's case through a colleague at the hospital."

"I see. Well, I stand corrected," Blanche said. Then she paused and fixed a firm gaze on Quinn. "So what are we going to do now?"

"Pull every string we can. I've put in a call to the DA's office, another to the chief of detectives. Maybe, if we're lucky, the NYPD brass can use the witness angle to keep Clare in the city, even if she remains hospitalized."

"There they are!"

"Oh, no," Blanche whispered, hearing her granddaughter's voice. Turning, she saw Joy Allegro pushing through the office building's heavy glass doors.

Quinn frowned. "How much do we tell her?"

Joy waved excitedly as she hurried across the lobby. "Dad just texted me about the meeting. Why didn't you let me know sooner? I would have come!"

Blanche shot Quinn a warning glance. *Let me do the talking.*

Sergeant Manny Franco followed his girlfriend with concern in his eyes. Shaved head gleaming in the afternoon sun, he unzipped his leather jacket, and then stood stoically watching Joy hug her grandmother.

"How did it go? What did the doctor say?" Joy's voice was heartbreakingly hopeful. "Is Mom coming home today?"

"Not just yet, dear. The doctor doesn't think she's quite ready."

"When can I see her again?"

"Not now. But soon."

When young Franco exchanged glances with Detective Quinn, Blanche knew the boy had a hunch they weren't telling Joy the whole truth. Thank goodness the young man trusted his boss's grim silence and didn't ask questions.

As Joy's lips quivered and her eyes pooled with fearful tears, Blanche pulled her close. "No need to cry. The doctor told me that your mother is in perfect health and that everyone is very optimistic that she will be herself again."

"I want to see her!"

"We all do, but for now all we can do is be patient."

Joy swiped her wet cheeks with the sleeve of her jacket. "I feel so helpless. Isn't there anything I can do?"

"You can live your life," Blanche firmly advised. "Your mother is no longer missing. She's returned, and she's physically fine. We can all be thankful for that. In the meantime, you must go back to Washington—"

"No!"

"Yes. You have work to do. The Village Blend, DC, needs its manager. That's what your mother would tell you if she were here. That's what our Clare would want."

Blanche faced Franco. "My boy, why don't you drive Joy down to Washington? I don't want her to fly back all alone. Leave tonight—make it a pleasant road trip. Try to enjoy your time together. Maybe stay the weekend, too."

Franco glanced at Quinn, who nodded.

"Do as the lady says. The OD Squad owes you plenty of downtime. Get Joy settled and come back when you're ready."

"I'll call with updates," Blanche assured Joy in a farewell hug. "You'll see your mother soon. I guarantee it."

But even as she made the promise, Blanche wasn't sure how she could possibly keep it. Detective Quinn wasn't a fount of optimism, either. As Blanche watched Franco and Joy cross Broadway and head toward Central Park, Quinn checked his phone and cursed.

"The chief of detective's office should have called me back

by now." Quinn tucked the phone into his lapel pocket. "I'm going to One Police Plaza to force a face-to-face with him."

Blanche squeezed his arm. "Good luck, Michael."

To her surprise, Quinn managed a weak smile. "It's not over yet. I'll stop by the coffeehouse soon with an update. I promise."

Seven

~~~~~~~~~~~~~~~~~~~~~~~~~~

Detective Quinn kept his promise, though it took him until almost nine that evening.

Blanche spied his broad-shouldered form through the Village Blend's rain-streaked windows. Face twisted into a scowl, Quinn strode across Hudson looking as cold, wet, and battered as a piece of storm-tossed driftwood.

Blanche met the poor man at the door, helped him off with his trench coat, and hustled him into a warm chair near the brick hearth.

Esther was there in minutes with a steeping pot of a beautiful single-origin coffee from El Salvador with notes of brown sugar, ripe strawberry, and raisins. Matt had sourced it from a fourth-generation family-owned *finca* called *La Providencia* (providence). Clare had roasted it right before she disappeared; and since Blanche considered her return an act of providence, she prayed for *just a little bit more* as she gently pressed the pot's plunger and poured two generous cups. Quinn downed half of his before he declared—

"There's not a damn thing I can do."

"But you've been out of touch for hours."

"Believe me, I tried. I forced that face-to-face with the chief of detectives. He sent two female detectives to interview Clare. The questioning was done in front of Lorca, who refused to allow me in the room. The official line is that Clare remembers nothing about the night Annette Brewster was abducted, and Lorca is signing off on her memory impairment, which makes her useless as a witness."

Quinn shook his head. "I tried to circumvent the chief, insist we challenge Lorca's assessment and influence on Clare. The commissioner refused to consider it. After pointing out my obvious conflict of interest, he threw me out of his office. Then I went to the district attorney's office and got stonewalled. An assistant DA who works closely with my OD Squad tried to help. He confided the backroom reality. Lorca's been a valuable party fund-raiser through his celebrity connections, and there's no way the DA, the mayor, or his appointed police commissioner will cross the man. So that's it."

"What do you mean?"

"From my end of the puppet show, it's over. I'm out of strings to pull. In order to challenge Lorca, I'll have to hire an outside legal firm and take it through the courts."

"Won't that take forever? Weeks or even months? Meanwhile, Clare will be upstate, alienated from all of us, a drugged 'subject' of Lorca's next bestseller."

Quinn's body sagged. "Maybe it's been too long a day, but I can't help wondering . . ."

"What? Tell me."

He stared into his empty cup. "What if this 'treatment' is what's best for Clare? What if it's what she really wants?"

"Oh, please!" Blanche waved her hand. "That's your exhaustion talking." She picked up the pot and poured him a refill. "I know you, Michael. You won't give up."

"It's not a matter of giving up. We have to face reality." Quinn glanced away, his bloodshot eyes reflecting the rain-streaked windows.

"When I first saw Clare in that hospital room, and she didn't remember me, I told myself it would be okay. That even if her memories never came back, I would still have a chance to get *her* back, make her fall in love with me again. I mean, she's still Clare, right?"

He sampled his second cup. "I know that's not what you want to hear. You're probably hoping Clare will get back together with your son—"

"That's not true," Blanche assured him, but he looked so skeptical, she had to admit—

"All right, perhaps it was true once, but not anymore."

"And why would that be?"

"Because I was the cause of Clare's marital misery."

"That's ridiculous—"

"No, it's true."

Never in her life had Blanche thought she'd reveal this secret to another soul, least of all Michael Quinn. But these were extraordinary circumstances, and he not only deserved to know; he needed to.

"When I first met Clare, she was nineteen and pregnant with my son's child. She was also on her own. Her mother had abandoned her years before. Her grandmother, who raised her, had just passed away. My son wasn't much older than Clare, and far less mature, yet I insisted he propose marriage."

"You mean it wasn't his idea?"

"Matteo said he didn't want to be saddled with a wife and child, but I told him to marry Clare anyway. I suggested that if he truly needed time to sow more wild oats before settling down to a faithful union, then he should do so on his travels. 'If you must have flings, have them while you're out of the country, sourcing coffee,' I said. 'But marry Clare now, support your daughter, and you will always have a solid home to come back to. You may not appreciate that as a young man, but I promise you will one day.' I told him, as long as he never let Clare know about his 'global affairs,' I would look the other way."

Blanche reluctantly lifted her gaze. Quinn's expression remained unreadable.

"I convinced him for Clare," she said, "and for my granddaughter. I wanted the chance to take care of her and baby Joy. After the wedding, I happily taught Clare my business. Matt had no interest in staying put to run the Village Blend. This coffeehouse has become a landmark in the community, a legacy, a part of Village history. Too many New York businesses have gone the way of the dodo. I didn't want to see that happen to my beloved coffeehouse. I needed to pass it on to someone who would want—as much as I did—to keep the lights on, the fire burning, and the coffee brewing. Clare became that someone. So, I suppose, the unvarnished truth is that I pushed my son into marriage for my own sake, as much as Clare's and Joy's."

Quinn could no longer hide his disapproval. "You gave your son *permission to cheat*?"

"When you say it like that, it sounds shameful. And I suppose it was, if you look at my decision from a cool, judgmental distance. But you must understand, all those years ago, I was beside myself with worry. The situation felt dire, and it was the best solution I could muster for us all."

She paused to meet Quinn's gaze. "You know, Clare was as stubborn and headstrong then as she is now. She was determined to have her baby. If Matt didn't marry her, she was going back to Pennsylvania, and I couldn't bear to see her leave like that, pregnant and alone. Honestly, I held out hope that my son would grow into his roles as father and husband, that he would mature over time and eventually *want* to be faithful to Clare."

Blanche sighed. "Unfortunately, my son's nature is what it is. He's not content to stay in one place—or share himself with only one woman. Clare, on the other hand, will always want an anchored home and a faithful partner."

To Quinn's obvious surprise, Blanche took his hand in both of hers.

"Michael, you are that partner for Clare. Your steadiness gives her strength. And her goodness lifts your spirit. I've seen the understanding, admiration—and passion—in the silent glances between you. It reminds me of the love I once felt for Matt's late father. I've never come across two people more right for each other."

Quinn swallowed hard. "I can't bear the thought of losing her. But it seems so hopeless."

Blanche patted his hand and released it. "Go home and get some rest. It's my turn to take over."

"What are you going to do?"

She threw him a wink. "This old woman may not live in a shoe, but she knows how to pull strings, too."

EIGHT

∼∽∿∽∿∽∿∽∿∽∿∽∿∽∿∽∿∽∿∽

CLARE

I pulled the gray hair, separating it from my dark strands, and yanked it out. Then I stared at the reflection in the hospital's bathroom mirror, searching for more traces of the years I'd lost.

It was a waste of time.

I was still Clare Cosi, as far as I could see, though at the moment I couldn't see all that much.

My eyes, normally clear and bagless, were so red and puffy from crying, I couldn't tell if there were any new wrinkles. And I'd been frowning so long and hard, I could find no laugh lines around my lips—not even the ones I remembered.

I did discover more than one gray hair and wondered how I got them. Likely from raising a preteen daughter through the rough road of adolescence all by my lonesome— a daughter who, from my damaged perspective, had grown into her adulthood *overnight*.

I found it hard to hold that thought, to realize that my "little girl," Joy, was now a young woman who remembered all the intimate motherly moments I had obviously forgotten. I felt myself wishing I could speak with her now and with Madame, and even—

No! Not him! Not Matt!

I shook my head, trying to shake my volatile feelings. I simply could not reconcile years gone by with the raw pain I suffered at learning of his betrayals. Multiple, almost *routine* betrayals, from the moment he left me behind in New York for all those sourcing trips abroad.

The humiliation of his cheating felt too new, the cutting wounds of our breakup too fresh. But then—

What did it matter, anyway? Dr. Lorca insisted my recovery required isolation from anyone associated with the part of my life that remained a blank. Moving to new surroundings would help with my recall—at least, that was what the doctor assured me.

But that's not what you really want, whispered a little voice, deep inside.

"It's not?" I whispered back.

Why should you be alienated from your family—the people who love you—at a time when you need them the most?

"I don't know. The doctor *said* I should."

Running my hands through my tangled hair, I turned away from the confused madwoman in the mirror.

It's not that I didn't trust Lorca. He was so generous, donating his services, and easy to like, such an attractive and interesting man, so polished and charming. Not like that pair of detectives who spoke to me the other day.

The one with the shaved head and leather jacket looked downright dangerous. But it was the sandy-haired detective— the tall one in the wrinkled suit with the blue eyes—who made me the most nervous. I could still see his intense gaze staring at me as if I were guilty of some awful thing.

I shuddered at that memory.

Those female police officers, the ones who conducted the second interview, were far less intimidating. Ultimately, they accepted my testimony that I didn't remember visiting the Parkview Palace hotel or ever meeting its owner, Annette Brewster. And I certainly didn't see any sort of crime take place—not that I could recall.

Now I couldn't stop myself from thinking about that crime.

From their questions, it was clear I had been a witness to Mrs. Brewster's abduction—or maybe even murder—before I went missing, too.

"I'd like to know more," I told the policewomen.

They appeared willing to speak further, but Dr. Lorca quickly cut the interview short, and my questions remained unanswered, even by my own mind, which was unbelievably frustrating, especially since I *did* remember the headlines from the other day—

HOTEL HEIRESS MISSING
MYSTERY AT PARKVIEW PALACE:
ABDUCTION OR MURDER?

There was no TV in my room, so I couldn't learn more from the news. There weren't any clocks in here, either, and I didn't have a watch.

Those two female detectives—the friendly blond woman named Lori Soles and her pushier, dark-haired partner, Sue Ellen Bass—were the only outside contact I'd had with anyone since morning. Except the nurses. And Dr. Lorca.

Which means your isolation has already begun.

"Ms. Cosi?"

Hearing my name, I walked out of the bathroom to find my night nurse standing next to the bed, a placid smile on her face and a small white cup in her hand.

"Did you enjoy your dinner?"

"Not really. What's with the decaf tea? Can't a person get a decent cup of coffee around here? How about it? Will the nursing staff fix me up?"

"Sorry, Ms. Cosi. No stimulants are permitted."

"No coffee? Really? Not even a drop?"

"Once you're moved upstate, you can discuss your menu with Dr. Lorca."

"When will that be exactly?"

"Soon. Here you go . . ."

The nurse held out that small paper cup. Inside were two pills.

"What are those?"

"Something to help you sleep."

"No, thanks."

I climbed into bed and pulled the sheet over my legs.

She pressed the cup toward me again. "Dr. Lorca prescribed these. You'll have to take them—like you did last night."

"I'm not a fan of sleeping pills. I'll be fine without them."

The nurse lowered her voice. "Ms. Cosi, you can either swallow the prescribed medicine, or . . ."

"Or what?"

"I'll have to inject it."

"Over my objection?"

"Come now, Ms. Cosi, you've already agreed to the treatment. Now you'll have to trust the doctor's orders. Don't be difficult—"

With a slight turn of her head, she made eye contact with a shadow in the doorway. I hadn't noticed that shadow before. It belonged to a burly nursing assistant. As he stepped forward, I saw his beefy hands were carrying a small metal tray, and sitting on top, like a sundae's glistening cherry, was a hypodermic syringe, the sealed bottle of drugs next to it, all ready to go.

I blinked at the nurse. "Did I miss something?"

"What do you mean?"

"I mean, I have a memory-impairment issue. I'm not delusional. What's with the extra from *Cuckoo's Nest*?"

"I'm sorry. I don't understand your question, though I like birds, too. Just don't upset yourself, Ms. Cosi. We don't want to see you upset—"

She crooked her finger and the ox with the tray moved toward us.

"Hold on! I'll take your pills. I just have trouble swallowing, that's all. I'll need something to wash them down."

I pointed to the plastic pitcher I'd left on the wide window-sill. "May I have some water, please?"

"Oh, yes, of course!"

The nurse dismissed the ox and turned to fill a glass. That's when I dumped the pills down my neckline. When the nurse approached, I mimed swallowing the cup's contents and noisily drank the lukewarm water.

"Very good. Now, try to get some rest." Flipping off the lights, she headed out the door, her singsong voice echoing into the hallway. "Things will look better in the morning!"

Not with decaf tea, they won't.

After flushing the pills, I got back into bed, and punched my pillows. Then I turned my gaze from the darkened room to the lights of the city. One building was completely black, except for a single glowing window.

Was someone working late? Were they alone, like me?

Somewhere out there, beyond my hospital window, my family and friends were wondering about me. My daughter, Joy, was probably missing me. Madame, too. Maybe even those nice young baristas I met the morning I woke up on that bench—the ones who seemed so happy to see me walk into the Village Blend coffeehouse.

I closed my eyes. Somewhere out there, people cared about me, and a fresh hot pot of "stimulant" was brewing.

God, I'd give anything for a cup of it.

NINE

ᕙᕗᕙᕗᕙᕗᕙᕗᕙᕗᕙᕗᕙᕗᕙᕗᕙᕗᕙᕗᕙᕗ

MADAME

It was midnight at the Village Blend and the doors were locked for the evening, yet the lights and fireplace continued to blaze, the heat fogging the cold, rain-spattered windows.

A small group had gathered around a table near the brick hearth. In rapt silence, they sipped hot cups of coffee as they listened to Madame Blanche Dreyfus Allegro Dubois update them on Dr. Lorca's plans for Clare.

"So," Blanche said at the end of her talk. "What do you all think? Ideas?"

Blanche wasn't surprised when her hotheaded son spoke up first.

"I say we break Clare out of the hospital. If Lorca doesn't have her, he can't experiment on her. Meanwhile, Quinn and his overpriced lawyers can fix things on the crawl, you know, through our slow-as-molasses legal system."

Tucker Burton, the Village Blend's assistant manager, tossed back his floppy hair and nodded enthusiastically. "Breaking Clare out will be easy! I'll help!"

Tucker's reaction didn't surprise Blanche. As a passionate (albeit part-time) thespian, he always did prefer a bold production.

"Why do you think it would be easy?" Dante asked.

"Ever since that big charity Superhero Show, Punch and I have been hired to perform scaled-down versions for pediatric patients all over the city, and Clare's hospital is used to seeing my comings and goings. Last week, I walked through its lobby in my Panther Man costume and no one blinked an eye."

"But don't you think 'breaking Clare out' is a little extreme?" Dante argued. "What if this treatment of Dr. Lorca's is the right thing for her? Maybe Lorca is the Jonas Salk of head cases."

"You're a head case if you believe that," Esther scoffed. "I saw Lorca on one of those laugh-it-up morning shows. He spouted a bunch of pill-pusher platitudes and talked up his own brand of supplements for 'cognitive enhancement'— the man was so full of himself, his hubris added more pounds than the camera."

Dante folded his arms. "So now you're an expert in psychiatry?"

"No, tattoo boy, just full-frontal fakery."

Blanche cleared her throat. "Esther may be unnecessarily blunt, but she is right."

"About what exactly?" Dante said. "That I have tattoos? Or Lorca spouts pill-pusher platitudes?"

"Both," Blanche replied. "Earlier this evening, I asked my Gotham Ladies group for some urgent help, and they came through. One put me in touch with a practicing psychiatrist and professor at Stanford University who's had public disagreements with Lorca over his clinical work. Though Lorca's credentials are solid, those 'cognitive enhancement' supplements he peddles, for example, are not recognized by the medical community as achieving what they claim. He's made no effort to submit proper trials for peer review. What's more, given the fact that Clare suffers from no injury, disease, deficiencies, or physical trauma, the Stanford professor suggested an alternative, *drug-free* therapy that could help Clare."

Matt leaned forward. "Like what?"

"Like *aides-mémoires*."

"What?" Dante asked, scratching his beard.

"An aid to the memory," Matt supplied. "Such as?"

"First Clare must be made to feel safe and relaxed," Blanche explained. "Then sensory prompts can be tried to stimulate her memories. These stimuli might be found in sounds, smells, tastes, or even feelings. If we find the right keys, Clare's subconscious may release some or all of her imprisoned memories."

"That's the exact opposite of what Lorca is prescribing!" Matt threw up his hands. "How can Clare find this key when she's isolated from everything she knows?"

"She can't," Blanche said. "I believe our Clare's been misled and manipulated. I fear that smooth-talking doctor never mentioned any other type of therapy to her except his own. I would have to hear, from her own lips, that she doesn't want to see me—or even try reconnecting to her daughter, her work, or the life she's spent years building. But I can't. Not if I'm not permitted to see her."

"*Someone's* got to speak with her," Tucker urged.

"Please, let me break Clare out," Matt begged.

"No." Blanche was firm. "You cannot drag the woman, kicking and screaming, from her hospital room. Even if you could manage it, you'd be no better than a kidnapper."

"Then we're back to the slow boat of litigation," Matt griped.

"Why can't we just call her and talk to her?" Esther asked. "Get her to fire Dr. Quacker and walk out under her own steam?"

"Weren't you listening?" Dante returned. "A phone call from us isn't going to be allowed. Lorca has Clare isolated. He's about to move her upstate. And if she changes her mind and objects, he's ready to legally commit her."

"Then I'm one hundred percent with Mr. Boss," Esther said. "Why should we let Quacker get away with it?"

"Because we'll land in hot water if we don't."

"Well, I for one don't mind hot water." Esther raised her demitasse of espresso. "We wouldn't have a business without it."

"Doesn't bother me, either," Tucker said, "especially when it comes to helping CC. Count me in for the breakout."

"Slow down," Blanche interrupted. "Your intentions are noble, but your plan won't work. Not if Clare is convinced Lorca's treatment is her only way back to us."

Everyone fell silent a moment. Finally, Tucker spoke.

"Okay, people, how about this. Instead of breaking Clare out, we break Madame in."

Esther began to clap. "That's it!"

Dante nodded in agreement. Blanche praised Tucker for the idea. Only Matt stayed silent. After everyone settled down, he finally gave his caveat.

"I'm *only* in if we double our options."

"What do you mean?" Tucker asked.

"We sneak my mother into Clare's hospital room so she can have a talk. And if Clare decides to leave, we break her out, right then and there."

Tucker nodded. "A little costume change is all it would take to sneak her out of the building. No one pays attention if you're wearing scrubs."

"We should still plan a diversion," Matt insisted, "something to lure the floor staff's attention away from Clare's room."

"Oh, that's easy." Tucker waved his hand.

"What?"

"None of us may know the key to unlocking Clare's memories, but I know nurses. The key to Clare's escape is the Village Blend's pastry case!"

ten

TWO days later, Blanche was exiting the hospital's elevator. Peeking around a corner, she peered down the long, antiseptic-scented hallway.

On this rainy afternoon, all seemed quiet on the floor. Several nurses occupied the station in the center of the corridor, and a bored janitor mopped the shiny waxed floor. There were no doctors present, and no visitors, save for a bald, hard-faced man with a mustache and a tweedy brown sport coat.

Blanche easily spotted Clare's door halfway down the hall—it was the only one fully closed, and she prayed it wasn't locked.

Beside her, Dante Silva tugged at his green hospital scrubs. To calm his obvious tension, Blanche patted the young barista's tattooed arm. "I know you're nervous, Dante, but we can do this!" she said, doing her best to impersonate an octogenarian cheerleader.

"I'm not nervous," Dante informed her. "You forget, I'm wearing these so-called scrubs inside out, because the outside is covered with glue-on sequins." He scratched again. "And those shiny little buggers are rubbing me in all the wrong places!"

Blanche sighed. "It was all Tucker could come up with

on such short notice. He dug them out of his theatrical trunk. I believe they were used in a cabaret send-up of some soap opera."

"Glittery Hospital," Dante said. "Tuck already told me. Somehow that knowledge does not soothe the irritation."

"Grin and bear it. We can't have a medical doctor fiddling with his pants in public. And you had better pull down those sleeves, too."

"Oh, right," Dante said. "Esther warned me that she never met a doctor who had more skin art than a sailor with a drinking problem."

"Well, don't take her criticism to heart, dear boy. I find your tattoos fetching."

Five minutes passed. This time it was Dante who peeked around the corner. "Where is our diversion?" he wondered. "Ah, there he is."

On cue, Tucker emerged from a door at the far end of the corridor. Blanche and Dante watched him stroll up to the nurses' station and make the big announcement.

"Good afternoon, everyone! We've laid out a delicious spread on this floor's visitors' lounge, so come and enjoy! It's an array of goodies from the Village Blend menu." Tuck offered the nurses a flirty wink. "Our way of thanking you fine medical professionals for the care you've been giving our manager."

Tuck's volume went up a notch, to catch the attention of any staff members still working the rooms.

"Come and eat. We've got fresh-baked Blueberry Shortbread, Glazed Strawberry Scones, and warm Pistachio Muffins. *Plus* a whole vacuum pot of our famous Kona Peaberry, straight from the Waipuna Estate in Hawaii!"

Like the Pied Piper of pastry, Tucker led the delighted nurses to the snacks. Esther waved at the janitor to join the culinary conga line, and he happily set aside his mop to do just that.

"Let's give the staff a little time," Blanche cautioned Dante.

"I know the plan. When they're all busy noshing, we make our move." He raised a blue clipboard thick with official-looking papers. "I've got my prop."

Three minutes later, she nudged the young barista.

"It's showtime."

After warning Dante not to be nervous, Blanche suddenly felt butterflies in her own stomach. But there was no turning back. This was their last chance. Dr. Lorca was transferring Clare to his upstate facility in the morning.

So, side by side, Blanche and Dante walked around the corner, and literally crashed into a young nurse rushing out of a patient's room.

"Oh, excuse me," she cried, embarrassed. Then she noticed Dante's scrubs. "Are you new here?"

Blanche panicked. Though she kept a smile plastered on her own face, she feared Dante wouldn't be quick enough to think on his feet.

But Dante replied with an appropriate degree of hubris. "I'm Dr. Glitter . . . Kildare Glitter, Department of Psychiatry."

Blanche wanted to smack her forehead—or Dante's.

Fortunately, the nurse was too smitten to notice Dante's stammer, or his absurd moniker. Instead, her gaze was appraising.

"You're pretty young to be a psychiatrist," she observed, more impressed than suspicious.

"Top of my class at Harvard," Dante said, pouring it on a tad thick, in Blanche's opinion.

Dante glanced at the nurse's name tag. All charm, he offered her his hand.

"Nice to meet you . . . Nurse Fischer. I hope we meet again."

"Me too. Hey, there are refreshments in the floor lounge. Would you like to join me?"

"I've got to check on a patient," Dante replied, in a tone of genuine regret.

"Okay, I'll see you around, Dr. Glitter."

As the nurse departed, Dante smiled. "She's cute."

"And you're never going to see her again. Focus, my boy. Focus."

A moment later, they reached Clare's door. With Dante standing guard, pretending to read his clipboard, Blanche gripped the door handle. For a panicked second, she feared it was locked. But (*thank goodness*) the latch clicked!

"Wish me luck. Here I go . . ."

Eleven

~~~~~~~~~~~~~~~~~~~~~~~~~~~~~~~~~~~

Clare

Propped up on my hospital bed, I heard voices in the hallway but couldn't tell what was being said.

With a yawn, I turned the page on the book in my hand. I'd had a restless night. No dreams that I could remember. Rumbling thunder woke me. With growing despair, I watched the raindrops trickle down the windows. Then breakfast arrived—rubbery eggs, half a grapefruit, a sad piece of toast, and a tepid cup of water with a packet of Sanka sitting beside it. My spirits sank even further because, for me, a day without coffee (real coffee) was . . . well, *unthinkable*.

There would be no TV, radio, magazines, or newspapers, either. Books were the only thing I was permitted to read. A member of the hospital staff brought me a small stack of "approved titles" to choose from. Every one predated the twentieth century.

"You know, I do still remember a few authors other than Dickens, Austen, and the Brontës."

The young woman shrugged. "It's all I've got for you. Do you want one or not?"

I picked up *Jane Eyre* and began reading when a new RN came by with a new paper cup of pills.

Like a replay of last night, I asked what I was being given, and when I tried to reject the "something to help your nerves," I was again reminded that I had already agreed to the treatment in writing, and it was "Doctor's orders."

Once again, I played the diversion trick. But I knew, sooner or later, I would have to take the pills—or the injection.

I really wanted to believe the doctor knew best. The soothing way he described my treatment sounded safe and reasonable.

So why was I resisting?

Because, in the light of a new day, even a cloudy day like this one, I saw things in a new way. I was no longer shocked and confused by my situation. I wasn't happy about my mental state, but I understood the reality of it.

I was suffering from some kind of memory loss or block. My brain and body showed no signs of injury. There was no tumor. No disease. No deficiencies. Yet, for some mysterious reason, I could not recall fifteen years of my life.

A few days ago, I was confused and upset.

Today, I was curious. All I had were questions and I wanted answers. I was dying for answers!

I also wanted out of this isolation tank. I wanted to be with those I loved—especially Madame and my Joy, of course, even though she was a grown woman now, one I'd have to get to know. And I *wanted* to know everything: what kind of person she'd become; how her childhood and school years went; and, most of all, if I'd done okay as her mom.

Were there things Joy regretted? Had I let her down? Failed her in any way? Or was she proud of the mom she had and the job I had done raising her? Were we still a team, mother and daughter against the world?

As for Matt . . . honestly, I could live without seeing

him, *ever again*, but I did want to know about the other people in my new life, the ones who recognized me—

That young woman Esther with those tears in her eyes when she saw me standing in the coffeehouse. And the tattooed barista, the artist named Mr. Dante, who had hugged me with such enthusiasm.

Were there other friends I'd made who would miss me if I were to move upstate to a psychiatric facility?

What if I told Dr. Lorca that I had changed my mind about his treatment plan? Was it really my choice? Or was he only making me feel like it was? If I said no to Dr. Lorca and tried to leave the hospital, would I be—as indelicately as Matt might put it—"locked in a booby hatch" against my will?

Unsure what to do, I asked that little voice I'd spoken with last night.

Contact Madame, it whispered. *Find a way to reach her, and talk things over with her.*

Though she and I hadn't seen each other much since my divorce from her son, my mother-in-law has never been anything but totally honest, loyal, and loving to me. I knew I could trust her to help me make the right decision. Couldn't I?

I was about to give up on thinking and reading and just pull the covers over my head when I heard my hospital room door open and firmly shut again.

I turned, shocked to find my desperate wish had come true. The kind, familiar face that greeted me was like a shining sun parting the darkest clouds.

"Madame!"

Twelve

∿∿∿∿∿∿∿∿∿∿∿∿∿∿∿∿∿

PRACTICALLY leaping from the bed, I couldn't wrap my arms around her fast enough. She returned the hug with a tight squeeze. Then she tore herself away.

"We don't have much time," she said in a low, conspiratorial voice. "You're going to be moved upstate, isolated from your friends and family."

"I know!"

"Listen carefully, Clare. You don't have to be . . ." Madame described her discussion with another psychiatrist, a Stanford professor who did not agree with Lorca's approach to treatment.

"I'm glad you told me, because I've been having plenty of second thoughts. I don't want to go upstate. I want to stay with you and learn about my life. I want answers—and coffee! Can you help me get out of here?"

Madame's pensive expression turned to one of relief. "If you want out—*and* coffee—I'm here to help."

"You'll talk to Dr. Lorca for me?"

"No, dear. We tried that and got nowhere. Since the people who love you don't trust that man, we're taking our chances with a slightly unconventional approach to your problem."

"What kind of approach?"

"We're breaking you out."

"Out of this hospital?"

Madame nodded.

"When?"

"Right now, if you're game."

"Are you kidding? The sooner, the better, especially if there's an adult dose of caffeine in it!"

"Good! Then we can't waste any more time—" Madame tugged a bundle from her tote bag. "Change out of your hospital clothes and put on these scrubs. You'll need a disguise to get off this floor."

Happily, I took off my robe and hospital nightgown and unrolled the bundle. "Wait a second. These aren't real hospital scrubs. They're covered in sequins!"

"Yes, dear, I know. Just turn everything inside out!"

A minute later, Madame was putting on a large rain poncho and pulling the hood over her head. "Camouflage for the elevator and lobby cameras," she explained.

Then she tucked the last locks of my unruly hair under the inside-out surgical cap. Finally, she cut off my hospital ID bracelet with the tiny scissors on a Swiss Army knife.

As I straightened my "scrubs," she offered one last-minute instruction. "If anyone asks, you're a member of Dr. Glitter's staff."

"Dr. Glitter?"

Without further explanation, Madame was already out the door.

"Lead the way," she told a handsome young doctor.

I was about to ask if this was "Dr. Glitter" when I realized this was no doctor—it was Mr. Dante, the young barista who'd hugged me at the Village Blend. He was wearing scrubs, too, and from the way he was twitching, they were inside out and glitter-ized, as well.

The corridor was free of nurses, but our activity didn't go unnoticed.

A bald man with a mustache in a tweedy brown sport coat was sitting in the room across from mine. The room's door was wide open and the man appeared to be reading aloud to the patient in bed. I'd glimpsed this man several times before, in the hallway outside my room, and assumed he was a hospital volunteer, but the moment he caught sight of me, he dropped the newspaper and rose to his feet. He had a tough-looking face and his dark eyes were staring right at me.

Madame and Mr. Dante didn't appear to notice this man, but it didn't matter. Before I knew it, we were around the corner, and the bald man with the mustache was out of sight.

The three of us hurried down the hallway to join a small crowd getting into an elevator. I turned in time to see the bald man racing toward us, calling loudly for someone to hold the door. Madame reached out to stop it from closing, but I slapped her hand aside. As the car descended, I could hear him cursing.

"Why did you do that?" she whispered, careful to keep her head down, her face away from the elevator camera.

"Something tells me he's not just a hospital volunteer."

A few tense minutes later, we were moving across the crowded lobby and onto the sidewalk.

"What now?" I asked.

"We watch for our getaway car."

As we stood at the curb, a figure hurried toward us. Like Madame, this person (man? woman? I couldn't tell) was wearing an oversized rain poncho with the hood pulled up and his or her face directed down.

When this person reached us, I blinked in surprise, recognizing Esther, the zaftig barista with black glasses who'd screamed and cried when she saw me standing in the middle of the Village Blend.

Madame faced her with a frown. "Where's Tucker?"

"He's charm-schooling the nurses to cover our tracks. He told me to go, that he would be fine."

Seconds later, a black SUV rolled up and we climbed in. Behind the wheel, a broad-shouldered figure in a dark hoodie told us to hurry up and close the doors.

Oh, no, I thought. *It can't be . . .*

But it was. The driver's voice belonged to my lying, cheating ex-husband, Matteo Allegro.

"Strap in," he ordered, pulling away from the curb. "This is going to be a bumpy ride."

THIRTEEN

~~~~~~

"**S**TOP the car!"

I fumbled with my seat belt and the door handle at the same time.

"Clare, the car is moving!" Madame cried. "Do you want to get killed?"

"I'd rather be dead—or committed to a mental hospital—than ride in *this* vehicle with *that* man. In fact, if I stay, I probably should be committed because I could not possibly be sane!"

Madame's violet eyes were pleading. "Be reasonable. You can't just get out of the car. Where would you go? You have no money, no clothes."

"Clare! Please listen—" Matt's gaze found mine in the rearview mirror. "The bad stuff that happened between us was many years ago. I haven't done drugs in a decade, and since the divorce you and I have become good friends and business partners."

"Global amnesia or not, I find that *very* hard to believe!"

"It's true. Try to remember—"

"Focus on the road, son," Madame commanded. "We must stay ahead of rush hour at the Lincoln Tunnel."

"Lincoln Tunnel? Are we going to New Jersey? Are you taking me home—"

As soon as I said it, I checked myself. Dr. Lorca had made it clear that my life in New Jersey was in the past, completely over. Frustrated, I felt tears forming.

"Be strong, child." Madame patted my hand. "We have a plan to keep you safe and help with your memory. This is just a short diversion, so no one can find—"

Matt's curse silenced her. "Everyone, stay calm," he ordered, his gloved hands tightening on the steering wheel. "And for God's sake don't turn around."

Esther and Mr. Dante stopped short of doing just that.

"There's a cop car right behind us," Matt informed us. "I think these guys may have spotted my counterfeit license plates. If they call us in, we're sunk. I don't see us winning a high-speed car chase through Manhattan or—"

Matt went quiet when the NYPD patrol car activated its roof light and blasted the siren. No one in the vehicle took a breath until the police sped around us and up First Avenue, its siren fading as it went.

We all stayed quiet after that. Matt made a few turns and reached the Lincoln Tunnel well before rush hour. We made it through in less than thirty minutes, but we didn't stay on the highway. We took the first exit in New Jersey. Then we traveled through Weehawken and along the riverfront.

By now, the rain clouds had cleared, so we could see for miles when we passed Hamilton Park, site of that fateful Hamilton-Burr duel. With its view from the top of the Palisades, the park's landscape was striking. All around us autumn's colorful leaves swayed with the breezes while, across the river, Manhattan's fixed skyscrapers sparkled in the afternoon sun.

Soon we reached a residential area of large houses and expansive lawns. Two more turns, and we hit a narrow backstreet, ending on what appeared to be an unpaved driveway flanked by bushes and tall trees.

"What is this?" I asked.

"A local lovers' lane," Matt replied, "but it's too early for any action. The place should be deserted."

I sighed in disgust. "So, you were cheating on me in the States, too?"

Matt's eyes left the road for a second to meet mine. "What are you talking about?"

"This place. How many women have you brought to this so-called lovers' lane?"

"None. I've never been here before." Matt took one hand off the steering wheel to wave a crinkled piece of paper. "I followed this map."

"Oh, really? And who gave you this map? Anyone I know?"

"Our daughter."

"What?"

"Joy told me she came here in high school."

Dumbstruck and horrified at the same time, I suddenly lost my ability to speak.

"Don't worry," Matt went on. "She didn't lose her virginity here. That didn't happen until after she graduated."

"Too much information!" I cried, covering my ears.

"Sorry," Matt said. "But I didn't want you to think that I ever came here. Oh, bad choice of words. I mean—I never came here with a woman. I mean—"

"We *know* what you meant, son!" Madame declared. "Just drive!"

The SUV bounced along the narrow path until we reached a large clearing of dirt and grass, bounded by a battered chain-link fence. Only one vehicle was parked here, a dingy white panel van. Nothing else was in sight, except the trees around us and (beyond the fence) a view of the city skyline, rising up across the Hudson River far below.

Matt stopped and cut the engine.

"Everybody out! Stretch your legs."

"Then what?" I asked.

"Then we're all getting into that van."

Fourteen

⊚⊚⊚⊚⊚⊚⊚⊚⊚⊚⊚⊚⊚⊚⊚⊚⊚⊚

ESTHER frantically waved her hand, but Matt already knew her question—

"If you need a bathroom break, the bushes are over there."

"Excuse me? Do I look like Jane Goodall?"

"Rough it or hold it," Matt said, "your choice."

"Spoken like a guy who's spent the better part of his life in the wilderness."

"Hey, I brought towelettes."

He held out a few packets. Esther groaned, snatched them, and ran toward the brush. Then Matt unlocked the van and handed Madame a gym bag. She passed it to me.

"What's this?" I asked.

"I brought some of your things," she said. "Change out of those glitter scrubs and put on these clothes."

I found a cluster of bushes away from Esther. The area really was private. No people, no buildings, just the Manhattan skyline peeking through the swishing autumn leaves. I found it oddly comforting. Out of that suffocating hospital room, I could breathe again—and almost hear the sounds of the city over the whooshing Palisades wind.

When I rejoined the group, I was wearing jeans that seemed overly tight around my legs (the fashion now, apparently). Half boots with low heels were comfortable on my feet, but I was shivering slightly under the thin hooded sweatshirt.

"Goodness, Clare, you're turning blue!"

Madame, who'd exchanged her crinkly rain poncho for a belted cashmere coat, now wrapped me in a baseball-style jacket displaying the same Poetry in Motion logo emblazoned on Esther's T-shirt and matching jacket.

"What is Poetry in Motion?" I asked, pointing to the words. "A running club?"

"More like a running-your-mouth club," Esther replied, folding up her rain poncho.

"Tell me," I said. "I'd like to know."

She shrugged. "It's part of my urban outreach work. I'm not just a barista. I'm also a grad student at NYU."

"And a poet," Madame said.

"And a local rap artist," Mr. Dante added.

"I don't rap as much these days," Esther admitted, "though my fiancé does. That's how I met him. Anyway, I've been coaching inner-city kids who have an interest in the language arts. The Village Blend has been a big part of that."

I stared in amazement. "Am I a rapper, too?"

Esther laughed. "No, boss. But you've been a big booster for my kids."

"I have?"

"Sure! You've allowed us to host free poetry slams on the Village Blend's second floor. And you've helped us raise the money for trips to regional and national slams."

"That's . . . really nice."

"Yes, it is," Madame cut in, handing me a brown paper bag. Inside I found a blond wig and thick-framed black eyeglasses like the ones perched on Esther's face.

"Is it Halloween?"

"No. But you need a costume, and our Tucker came through with props. He's a firm believer in disguise. Given our situation, I can't say I disagree."

Tucker—whoever he was—certainly had the right idea.

With my chestnut ponytail pinned under the Goldie Hawn wig and with the glasses on my nose, I hardly recognized my own reflection in the van's side-view mirror.

While Mr. Dante changed clothes in the bushes, Matt wiped down the interior of the SUV we had abandoned.

"Just to be sure," he said. "No fingerprints."

Then my ex checked the small black device in the cigarette lighter, though he didn't pull it out.

"What is that?" I asked. "Did you take up smoking?"

"This is an Auto-Block. I've got one in the van, as well."

"What does it do?"

"Disables GPS tracking."

"I don't understand."

"GPS," Matt repeated. "That's Global Positioning System technology."

"Uh-huh."

He studied me. "How far back is your memory actually blocked?"

"Excuse me?"

"Here's a test. Do you still remember *Star Trek*?"

I folded my arms. "Captain Kirk, Mr. Spock."

"Okay then, the Auto-Block is like a cloaking device for modern satellite-tracking technology." As he spoke, he circled the SUV and began replacing the fake license plates with the originals. "A friend in Brooklyn lent me both vehicles. He'll pick up this SUV tonight. With these phony plates visible on all the traffic cameras that followed us through Manhattan, there's no way this will be traced to him, or to us. And the Auto-Block will leave no record of our travels."

"Still a schemer, I see. And you still have . . . *interesting* friends."

Matt shot me one of his trademark grins. Through his dark beard, it flashed even brighter. "Doing business stateside is the same as anywhere else on the globe, Clare. With the right connections—and cold, hard currency—you can acquire whatever you need."

A cynical view, but I didn't disagree.

Mr. Dante, sans scrubs, rejoined us, and Madame bagged all the old attire, the phony license plates, and the wiping cloth. Then we all boarded the dingy white van.

Matt resumed his role as driver with Mr. Dante riding shotgun, while I followed Esther and Madame through the sliding side door. There were no windows in back—making me wonder just why I needed a disguise—but there were plenty of seats, and the heater was running full blast (a definite plus).

As we all strapped in, Matt started the engine and adjusted the rearview until he caught his mother's eye.

"Where to?"

"Back to Manhattan," she said. "We have an important stop to make."

As we drove away, I thought over what Esther had told me—about her outreach with inner-city kids and the poetry slams on the Village Blend's second floor. Closing my eyes, I tried to remember *anything* that could have been part of what she'd described. But there was nothing.

I shook my head, frustrated at the blank.

"Were you trying to remember something?" Esther asked.

"It's like walking along a hotel hallway, but all the rooms are locked." I faced her. "You're really a poet?"

She nodded and, for a minute, glanced down in thought.

"Dark coffee's deep, so is your memory," she whispered. "Pour out the fear that leaves you blind. Try not to worry. No need to hurry." She squeezed my shoulder. "You'll find your New York state of mind."

Fifteen

~~~~~~~~~~~~~~~~~~~~~~~~~~~~~~~~~

A short time later, my state of mind was the same, though the *actual* state had changed.

After inching through the Lincoln Tunnel, we were back in New York, and (immediately) stuck in standstill traffic. That was when the argument began. From the sound of it, this discussion had started before I'd entered the picture.

"Okay, Mother," Matt said, "let's get this over with. Have you finally decided where we're going to stash Clare? And please don't dismiss my idea."

Madame let out an exasperated sigh. "I don't want Clare staying in a strange place. Remember what our Stanford professor said about finding keys to unlocking her memories? Don't you think we're better off finding them if she stays in a familiar place?"

"With familiar people," Matt added.

"Precisely."

"And that is *precisely* where the police will look for her," Matt said. "I didn't drive all the way to New Jersey to switch vehicles just to get caught now. My plan is better."

Madame pursed her lips. "I don't know—"

"Well, I do. The Hamptons house is perfect. Far from the city, but not too far. The summer people are long gone, so things will be quiet out there. And the address is untraceable to Clare. Even though Breanne left me the place as part of our divorce settlement, her name is still on the books as the owner."

"Wait a minute!" I cried. "Are you telling me that since we split, you managed to get married to someone named Breanne, break the poor woman's heart, get a *second* divorce, and end up with a place in the Hamptons?"

"It's not like that," he said.

"What's it like, then? Does Joy have any half sisters or brothers you're neglecting to tell me about? And likely neglecting!"

Gaze straight ahead, Matt remained stoically silent.

"Just forget about stashing me in your latest ex-wife's former love nest," I declared. "That is just twelve degrees of creepy."

"Everybody, please calm down," Madame insisted.

Suddenly, I realized that I was the only one who wasn't calm. Matteo refused to argue—the natural-born hothead wasn't even putting up a defense or blaming someone else for his misfortunes.

Hmmm . . . maybe he has changed. But that thought was immediately countered by another. *Not if he broke his marriage vows again, he didn't!*

As the crosstown traffic began to move, Madame picked up the discussion where it left off.

"You still think DC is a bad idea?" she asked. "I'm sure Clare would love to be reunited with her daughter—"

"And the Feds would love to grab her there," Matt returned. "Georgetown is practically the DOJ's rumpus room."

"I want to see my daughter," I said.

"You will," Madame assured me, patting my hand. "But you'll have to be patient for your own good."

"And Joy's," Matt added. "Helping you escape the way we did is bound to stir up trouble."

"So Joy is in Washington?" I asked. "Why? Does she work for the government?"

"No, she works for us," Madame said, "managing our second shop, the Village Blend, DC."

"There's a *second* shop? Really?"

"It was your idea," Matt said.

I turned to Madame. "I'm surprised you agreed, given your long-standing aversion to franchises."

"Yes, well . . ." Madame raised an eyebrow. "Let's just say there were extenuating circumstances. Anyway, you'll see Joy as soon as we have you settled somewhere safe. The question is where—"

"Clare can stay with me," Esther offered.

"Or me," Mr. Dante said. "I have two rooms I use for studio space, both with views of the High Line. I can move my paints and canvases out of one of them, easy."

I was genuinely touched. "Thank you both for the offers, but I can't accept—"

"Clare's right," Matt said. "She can't stay with any of you for the same reason she can't stay above the coffee-house, or at my warehouse in Brooklyn, or in my mother's Fifth Avenue apartment. The NYPD and *you-know-who* will surely sniff her out. I say the Hamptons, but I'm out-voted by a committee of one—"

As Matt paused to blow the horn at a driver about to cut him off, I asked who *you-know-who* was. Everyone fell silent. Matt glanced into the rearview mirror, but not at me. He made eye contact with his mother.

"You don't need to know that right now, dear," Madame said carefully.

"Fine." I sat back and sighed. My life was a puzzle with far too many pieces missing.

Matt's focus returned to the road. "Okay, then, Mother, while you're making a decision about where we should hide Clare, where am I supposed to take us?"

"To the Parkview Palace, please."

It was a good thing the traffic ahead of us came to a halt again, because Matt's head snapped in Madame's direction, his expression incredulous.

"Are you crazy? You're going to book Clare a hotel room?"

"No. We'll decide where to hide Clare later. Right now I'm taking her to the Gotham Suite. It's imperative that I retrieve something, and while I'm there, I want Clare to see the suite, too."

Matt's face remained baffled—an expression I was getting used to.

"It's the last place she visited before she disappeared," Madame explained. "Seeing it again might jar her memory."

"Can't it wait for a day or two?" Matt countered. "Someone might identify her."

"She's wearing a very good disguise," Madame argued. "And this is the best time to do it, before the police really start looking for her."

"And is there another reason we're returning to the scene of the crime," Matt asked suspiciously, "besides jarring Clare's memory, that is?"

"Let's just say I know something about that suite the police may not."

"How are you going to get in?" Matt pressed.

"I have a key to the private elevator. And because it's my year to chair the Gotham Ladies' Charity Committee, I also have a key to the Gotham Suite."

"You'll be spotted. Hotels have security cameras, you know."

"Cameras won't be an issue."

Madame's absolute certainty drew a puzzled glance from Matt.

"Why wouldn't there be cameras?" he pressed.

"There were cameras once at the Parkview. But not any longer."

"I don't know . . ." Matt drummed the steering wheel. "Are you sure bringing Clare is wise . . . I mean, going up to *that* suite in *that* elevator, after that *thing* happened with Annette?"

"Quit talking around me," I said. "Between the headlines I saw on the street and the police detectives' questions, I know everything that happened."

"I doubt that," Matt said.

"Yes, perhaps not everything," Madame agreed.

I sat back, silently admitting they were right. This trauma I supposedly experienced—whatever it was—remained buried in the same black hole as my other memories.

"All right, then," I said, facing Madame. "What happened that night? What am I missing, other than the last fifteen years of my life?"

With a deep breath, Madame began to tell me.

Sixteen

∿∿∿∿∿∿∿∿∿∿∿∿∿∿∿∿

"One of Annette Brewster's pastry chefs recently won a James Beard Award, and you expressed interest in meeting him. Annette surprised you with an invitation to a private cake tasting at her hotel."

"I knew Annette, then?"

"Not well," Madame informed me. "But she and I go way back, and I've bragged about your accomplishments for years. One day, she stopped by the coffeehouse, claiming she had a problem—don't ask me what. All I know is that she described her problem as 'personal and private,' and she wanted your help to solve it. But first, in a gesture of friendship, she wanted to help solve yours."

"With a *cake* tasting? Why?"

"That's not important," Matt said.

"No, it isn't," Madame echoed.

I could tell they were holding back, but I didn't want to waste time arguing. "Fine. What happened next?"

"At seven thirty that night, Annette Brewster picked you up in front of the Village Blend in one of her vintage cars."

"I saw you go," Esther cut in. "I remember because the ride was really cool, like an old James Bond car. Annette was driving, and there was no one else in the vehicle."

"So we went to the hotel," I said impatiently. "Then what?"

Madame shook her head. "There is more than one mystery here, I'm afraid. You see, the two of you didn't arrive at the Parkview Palace until nine PM."

"What happened in that hour and a half?"

"With no GPS in Annette's vintage sports car, the police only know that you drove to New Jersey and back. Toll scans at the Holland Tunnel registered Annette's license when you left and returned to the city. Unfortunately, you'd forgotten your smartphone—"

"I had one of those fancy phones?"

"Yes, dear. And Annette wasn't carrying one, so there were no GPS phone signals for the police to trace, either."

"Global-positioning technology in your *phones*? You mean these 'smart' telephones also tell authorities where you are and who you're with? There's no privacy in the future? What kind of world has this become?"

Matt snorted. "The kind where I had to hand out untraceable prepaid phones to everyone in this vehicle for our little adventure."

Mr. Dante waved his in the air. "I've got mine!"

"So Annette Brewster and I spent ninety minutes somewhere in New Jersey?" I mused aloud.

"It's a big hole the police can't fill," Matt said. "But then, in my experience, there are no rocket scientists on the NYPD."

Madame shot her son a look, as if warning him. Of what? I had no idea. Before I could ask, she continued her story—

"At nine o'clock, you and Annette arrived at the Parkview Palace. You rode the private elevator to the Gotham Suite, where Chef Tomas Fong was waiting. He hosted the tasting himself, which went on until about ten thirty." She paused. "After that, things turned tragic, for all of us—but for you especially, Clare."

"Go on."

"Annette had planned to drive you home. She escorted you down to the parking garage, where an anti-theft camera inside a luxury car captured you both walking into an ambush by an armed and masked assailant."

"There were no other surveillance cameras?" I pressed.

"Not inside the Parkview Palace. Annette had ordered them all shut down. She said it was necessary. Then she clammed up and wouldn't tell me why. The only useful camera footage the police could find was from that anti-theft device in a hotel guest's car—"

"And it didn't catch much," Matt cut in. "The recording only showed you and Annette confronted by an armed figure in an overcoat and ski mask. Then everyone moved out of camera range."

"How do you know all these details?"

Everyone fell silent.

"I know someone," Madame finally confessed. "He's, ah . . . Let's call him a source at the NYPD. He's not in charge of the investigation, but he talks to the detectives who are."

"I see." (All her life, Madame had attracted male admirers, so I wasn't all that surprised.) "He's a *special* friend of yours?"

"He's certainly a friend of our Village Blend," she said.

"Is he ever," Esther blurted. "He's also in love with—"

"Our *coffee*," Madame cut her off with a tight smile.

"Who isn't?" I said. "Don't worry. I get it. He's a cop who likes you, which is why he stuck his neck out and bent the rules. So when did you all realize I was missing?"

"Esther became worried when you failed to return to close our Village Blend that night. She called you several times, not knowing your phone was still in the duplex upstairs, where you'd left it."

Esther nodded. "I closed the coffeehouse at the regular time, and returned in the morning to open again because I was afraid you weren't around to do it. On my first break I went up to your duplex and found two very hungry cats—"

"Cats?" I smiled. "I have cats?"

Esther nodded. "Java and Frothy. Don't worry. The staff is taking turns caring for them."

Madame continued. "When you didn't show that night, and Esther couldn't reach you, she called me, and I called the Parkview. I discovered Annette went missing, too, so I phoned . . . our policeman friend."

"The next day, the cops found that surveillance video," Esther said, "and all heck broke loose. For a whole week, we were crazy with worry, and then you magically reappeared—"

"Safe, but not sound," Matt added as he pulled up to a red light. "A private security camera on Washington Square North caught you wandering into the park at four AM, but the police can't find any other clear footage that traces backward to show us where you came from. They canvassed the area but came up with nothing. Their latest theory is that you were dropped off by a vehicle, and they've been pursuing those leads, with nothing to show for it."

"Now you know as much as we do," Madame said, her gaze meeting mine. "It's not much, but it's enough for you to make an informed decision. So, choose, Clare. You can wait in the car with Matt, or you can come up to the suite and see what there is to see—and maybe get your memories back."

Hide from reality huddled with my ex-husband, or face the truth, no matter how painful it might be? I almost laughed. *It was no contest.*

"If Dr. Lorca is right, if my condition has been caused by some emotional trauma, then I want to face what happened."

Madame seemed pleased. "You and I will go to the suite. Everyone else can wait in the car."

"Hold on a minute!" Esther cried. "If Clare is going into that hotel, so am I. She might need more backup—"

"Then I'm going, too," Mr. Dante insisted. "I want to be there for her."

I should have been flattered, even honored that Esther and Mr. Dante seemed to care so much about my well-being. But the truth is, I was embarrassed, and a little ashamed, because I had no idea why they felt that way. To me, they were little more than strangers.

Taking in their concerned faces, I could see we must have been close once. I wanted to remember the reasons and feel that kinship again.

One memory did come to me in that moment, but it wasn't recent. My late grandmother, who ran a little Italian grocery store in Western Pennsylvania (and practically raised me in it) had a saying—

Walking with a friend in the dark is better than walking alone in the light.

I faced Esther and Mr. Dante. "Thank you," I told them sincerely. Then I looked at Madame and even forced myself to include Matt in the rearview. "Thank you *all* for caring."

Through the mirror, Matt's dark gaze held mine. "You're welcome," he said in a voice so quiet and mature, I hardly recognized it.

The expression in his eyes was different, too. I'd never seen him look at me that way, with such sad tenderness—and something else. Regret? Or was it hope?

A blaring horn startled us, and Matt tore his gaze away. The light had turned green.

"Okay, I guess it's settled." He hit the gas and turned the wheel. "Next stop, the Parkview Palace hotel."

Seventeen

~~~~~~

All of New York knew the Three P's: the Plaza, the Pierre, and the Palace.

On my coffeehouse manager's pay, I could never have afforded a stay in a luxury hotel like the Parkview Palace. But once, when Joy turned eight, and Matt failed to return from one of his many sourcing trips in time for her birthday, Madame gifted us "girls" an extravagant overnight stay in a gorgeous Palace suite facing Central Park.

The three of us enjoyed an early-afternoon high tea in the hotel's bright and lovely Sun Court. We took a carriage ride along Fifth Avenue, ending at FAO Schwarz, where Madame indulged little Joy in a toy-shopping spree. Finally, we decked ourselves out in brand-new dresses and dined among the rich and famous in the Palace's legendary oak-paneled Lords and Ladies restaurant, where Madame and I (and even our stately, old, iron-jawed waiter) sang a quiet but heartfelt "Happy Birthday" to our little girl.

It was a day like no other, and I was grateful the memory remained intact—so vivid, in fact, I could still remember the crunch of the candied pecans on the Parkview's famous Palace Salad; still taste the creamy, delicate sauce on its renowned Champagne Chicken; still see the peachy-pink blush on my daughter's cheeks; and hear the sound of her giggles as an entire fine-dining restaurant turned to smile at her. It felt as though it had happened only a year or two ago, instead of nearly twenty.

Once again, I was missing my little Joy.

Not so little anymore, said that voice, deep inside me. And I struggled to control my desperate desire to see her again, to find out everything I could about the years I missed. *Try to be patient. You'll see her soon enough.*

As we approached the hotel's address, I realized Matt was entering the property from its 58th Street side, far from the Oz-like golden front steps and elaborate Parkview Palace crest that faced Central Park South. The intricately carved columns and those world-famous "five gargoyles" would have been fun to see again, too. I still remembered Joy's eyes widening at the sight of that entranceway's majesty, designed to impress the hotel's well-heeled guests.

The back end of the Parkview was another story. Unremarkable office buildings flanked a gray loading dock and a very ordinary driveway, which led to the hotel's paid underground parking garage.

Below the street, the fluorescent glare was strong, making it easy to read the posted signs warning visitors that security cameras at the Parkview had been "deactivated" during renovations. "Increased patrols" were promised. In the meantime, the public was urged to "exercise caution."

"Is that why there are no cameras?" Matt asked his mother as he searched for a parking spot. "The hotel is under renovation?"

"That's the excuse," Madame muttered.

"Eureka!" Matt squeezed the panel van between a Saab and a Lexus, and we bailed out through the back doors. "Don't take forever," he warned. "I'm paying thirty-two bucks an hour to sit here."

"Soldier on, my boy," Madame replied, then began to lead Esther, Dante, and me across the underground garage.

Eighteen

~~~~~~

We followed Madame to a remote area marked for *Employee Parking*. On the way we saw a few clients of the hotel, but no sign of those promised security patrols.

Our trek ended in front of an ugly steel door in dented gray. It appeared to be a janitor's closet; but when Madame released the lock, the door opened into a tastefully appointed waiting area with a small private elevator.

Using the same key, Madame activated the elevator. As we filed into the mirror-walled car, I realized everyone was staring in my direction, waiting for me to exhibit a glimmer of recognition or explode into a psychotic episode.

In truth, I felt nothing, identified nothing, remembered nothing. Though I was told I'd been here before, I had no recollection of the experience or who had accompanied me here.

On the second floor, the elevator rumbled open to reveal a crisscross of yellow crime scene tape, which didn't make much sense to me.

"Why is there police tape here?" I asked. "Annette was accosted in the parking garage, wasn't she? Not up here."

"The detectives in charge of the investigation wanted fingerprints, DNA, and any other physical evidence taken from Annette's last known place of business—and that business was with you, Clare. I was informed the police completed their work here last week."

Without hesitation, Madame ripped the ribbons aside, and we stepped into a fashionably old-fashioned hallway with a polished hardwood floor, accented by a blue Persian area rug.

The entrance to the hotel's private Gotham Suite was marked by a plaque only partially obscured by more crime scene tape. Once again, Madame sent the yellow ribbons drifting to the hardwood. Finally, she unlocked the double doors, threw them open, and hit the light switch, illuminating the suite's main room.

The high-ceilinged space was designed for business meetings with a long, boardroom-type table dominating the room. A credenza, holding a computer with a large flat-screen display, was flanked by decorative wall panels (each carved with one of the Palace's five famous gargoyles). Tall windows, facing Central Park, lined one side of the room while framed artwork covered the opposite wall.

What surprised me, however, were the wedding decorations. A round table draped in white linen had been set up near the windows, where a banner with white bells declared, *It's Your Wedding Day!*

The arrangement on top of the table had been beautiful once. Now the flowers sagged from a crystal vase gone dry, stems bent from the weight of dead blossoms.

Beside the vase sat a bowl of brown and shriveling apple slices and a plate of salt-free soda crackers, ingredients that helped clear one's palate when sampling different pastries. This, I didn't deduce. Somehow I *knew* it, though I couldn't recall how.

I also knew, when sampling sweets, I preferred a liquid solution made with unseasoned polenta, the palate cleanser of choice for the International Chocolate Awards.

And how in the world did I know that?

With no answers forthcoming, I turned my attention back to the table. A binder of elegant wedding cake designs lay open with a dozen pastry stands set up around it. Each stand was topped by a glass dome with a mini cake sample beneath. All of the cakes were cut with several wedges missing. On a wheeled cart next to the table sat a pitcher of water and a drained pot of French pressed coffee.

"This is a lovely private tasting Annette arranged for you," Madame marveled. "Do you recognize anything?"

"Nothing, and I don't understand the theme. Was I catering a wedding reception? Who's getting married? Was it you, Esther? You mentioned a fiancé?"

Esther opened her mouth, but a quick glance from Madame shut it again.

"Was it my daughter?" *That must be it,* I decided. *Joy is getting married!*

"Don't speculate about future events," Madame warned sharply. "Keep your mind focused on the concrete details in front of you. These were part of your very recent past. Perhaps the key to unlocking your memory is right here. After all, everything is exactly as you and Annette left it."

"It couldn't be *exactly* as we left it—" I scanned the room. "There are no cups, glasses, dishes, or silverware. Any tasting would need them, yet they're all missing. The crime scene unit must have taken them, along with samples of the consumables, to be tested for drugs or toxins . . ."

Even as I said it, I wondered how I could know such things. Then I noticed Madame and Esther sharing a glance.

"What?" I said. "Do you two know why I know that? Have I been catering police banquets or something?"

"Or something," Esther said.

"That's not an answer," I returned.

"Don't let it upset you," Madame soothed. "From what I've learned about your condition, dissociative amnesia can wipe away autobiographical memories, yet leave the things you've learned completely intact. A person may remember how to drive a car, for example, but not recall how she learned, who taught her, or when."

"Like Jason Bourne," Mr. Dante said.

"You mean the Robert Ludlum character," I assumed, "from the Bourne books?"

"And the blockbuster movies," Esther noted.

"Movies?" I blinked. "There are Jason Bourne *movies*?"

"Forget it." Esther waved her hand. "Oops, sorry, no offense!"

"It's forgotten," I said. "Lately, it appears, I have a knack for it."

Esther smirked. "No dent in her sense of humor."

"Yes, she's still our Clare," Madame pronounced, and then narrowed her violet gaze on me. "Bourne is actually an apt reference. The professor I spoke with about your memory loss even mentioned him."

"Why would he do that? Bourne's story is fictional."

"But his condition was inspired by fact. Ludlum himself claimed the idea for Bourne came to him after he suffered a twelve-hour bout of amnesia. And many believe Ludlum borrowed the name of his antihero from a real man named Ansel Bourne, a preacher who suffered a famous case of amnesia in the nineteenth century."

"Was it like mine?"

"Not exactly. You can still recall your identity. Ansel's case was more drastic. He left his Rhode Island home in January for a trip to Providence. Somewhere in his travels, he lost his memory. He continued on to Pennsylvania, where he began living with another family and working as a confectioner using the name A. J. Brown. Two months later, A.J. woke up as Ansel again, not knowing where he was or what had happened to him. He still believed it was January."

"I can relate."

"Don't give up, dear. And don't let anxiety cripple you. Try to trust *what* you know. And understand that *how you know it* may be unclear until your memories return."

"Okay," I said, but once again I experienced that surreal dissociation between understanding a thing and accepting it. Madame's use of the word *until* was hopeful, too, but what if my memories never came back?

"Look on the bright side," Madame cheered. "Your instincts and observations about this scene were spot-on. My police source informed me that no toxins or adulterants of any kind were found in anything you and Annette consumed in this suite."

"So what's next?" I asked.

She turned to Mr. Dante. "I want you to go back to the hallway and keep watch. Alert us if you see or hear anyone coming from any direction."

"Why?" he asked. "What else are you going to do in here?"

"Something secret, my boy. Something I want as few to know about as possible. Now, hurry and do as I say."

As soon as Mr. Dante left us, Madame closed the double doors behind him and swiftly walked the length of the boardroom table.

"Do you know what she's up to?" I whispered to Esther. She showed me her palms. "No idea."

Nineteen

~~~~~~

As Esther and I watched in curious silence, Madame walked right up to the far wall, the one covered with artwork. She stopped directly in front of the two largest canvases, a pair of paintings hanging side by side in identical frames. The first featured the Parkview Palace itself.

Over the years, plenty of artists had painted this famous landmark, most of them focused on its posh grandeur. Such regal renderings always left me cold. But this painter saw the hotel with a romantic eye, capturing it at sunrise with soft hues at an angle that included a glimpse of Central Park along with a horse and carriage.

I took off my costume glasses for a closer view of the couple inside, lovers huddled together under a soft blanket.

Hanging beside the painting of the hotel, on a canvas of exactly the same size, was a portrait of an attractive young woman in a bold red dress. Her smile was warm, her generous figure and long blond hair as lovingly brushed by the artist as the hotel. I noticed the young woman in the large painting resembled the one inside the horse-drawn carriage.

"Who is the subject of this portrait?" I asked. "The lady in red?"

"Oh, that's Annette—before she became Annette Brewster. It was painted in the 1980s, when she was still Annette Holbrook. The companion piece *Parkview at Sunrise* was done back then, too."

"And the painter?" I looked closer. "Both of these works appear to be done by the same artist, but they're unsigned."

"Yes," Madame confirmed absently. "They were done by the same artist."

I asked *who*, but Madame was too distracted to reply. She had moved in front of the lady in red and begun fumbling with the picture frame.

"What are you doing?" I asked, putting my costume glasses back on.

"Be patient," she said, her fingers continuing to feel around the wood's carved flourishes. "I'm looking for a special—"

Just then, she must have pressed the right button because the portrait appeared to unlock itself from the wall. Madame swung it out on hinges to reveal a rectangular panel. Beneath the panel was a black screen, much like the ones on those fancy phones, only larger. She swiped the screen and it sprang to life.

"To ensure our privacy, Annette installed a custom surveillance system, independent of the hotel's security cameras. Her hidden cameras cover the Gotham Suite, the elevator, and the waiting area. The system is motion activated, so it should have captured images of the tasting. We can see if you were alone with the chef and Annette the whole time or if someone else—"

Madame groaned.

"What's wrong?"

"The system was deactivated and its memory erased." Madame closed out of the surveillance system and covered it back up with the portrait. "Let's check the office."

Esther made a show of looking around. "What office? Where is it?"

"It's here, Esther. Trust me and not your eyes."

But Esther's gaze wandered anyhow. "Hey, look at that!" she said, pointing to another piece of artwork on the wall.

"Is that an original Al Hirschfeld? And is that *you* in the drawing?"

Madame nodded. "It was done years ago, and a perfectly perceptive caricature of the Gotham Ladies it is. Al had such a long and brilliant career as a Broadway artist, and he was a sweet man."

I marveled at the piece. There were more than a dozen figures in the large drawing. "I don't know these women, do I? Apart from Annette Brewster, have I met any of these ladies?"

"You've met the oldest members, the leaders of the pack, so to speak. Let's see if we can jar your memory."

The first caricature Madame pointed out was a petite brunette with short, wavy hair. She wore a crooked grin and a full-length fur coat over a business suit. In one hand she held a knish, in the other a babka.

"That's Barbara 'Babka' Baum, Culinary Queen, originally of the Lower East Side, and owner of Babka's, the legendary New York bakery and restaurant on the Upper East—along with five new locations across the country, including the MGM Grand in Las Vegas. Of course, she's always been more than a restaurateur, as you discovered."

"I did?"

Madame sighed and pointed again. "The woman beside Babka is Jane Belmore, the last of a once powerful banking family. She's sweet but often wakes up on the prudish side of the bed. I do believe the term 'clutching her pearls' was coined for Jane."

Madame gazed at me expectantly.

I shook my head. "Nope. Nothing."

"Beside Jane is Annette, older here than in her portrait, of course, and between Annette and me—"

"The tall woman in gold?"

"Gold lamé," Madame corrected. "That's Nora Arany. She began as an assistant to my old friend, the late fashion designer Lottie Harmon. Remember her?"

"Only by reputation."

"Well, Nora learned *lots* from Lottie, I can tell you. Then she left to start her own design business, which took off after she became a fashion consultant to rock stars and then hip-hop musicians. Back then she was always bragging about her clients. Pat Minotaur, was it? The B-*vitamins*? M.C. Bammer? Do any of those names ring a bell?"

"Er . . . no."

"These days Nora creates athletic and yoga wear, bridal dresses, handbags, and gold jewelry. Her last name means 'gold' in Hungarian and she took it quite literally to the bank—investment bankers. Two years ago, she took her company public."

I gazed at the tall woman with the confident smile and platinum blond hair. She dominated the center of Hirschfeld's drawing, her caricature so broad, she was likely bigger than life in person, too. How could I forget a woman like that?

"Still nothing?" Madame asked.

"I'm sorry, but—"

Esther's call interrupted us.

"Hey, you two! There's a kitchenette through this door, and I spy a bag of beans on the counter. I can use the French press pot they left on the cart to make coffee for Clare. Maybe the taste of the blend will jar a memory or two."

"Coffee?! Oh, yes, *please!*"

Madame smiled. "I haven't forgotten our conversation at the hospital. Excellent idea, Esther. Be sure to clean the pot well—"

"I can help!" I offered, trying to move things along.

"Let Esther handle the coffee. You and I should check the office."

"Office? What office? I don't see any office."

"As I told Esther, trust me, dear."

A friend in the dark, I thought. *And, man, am I in it.*

"Lead on."

Twenty

~~~~~~~~~~~~~~~~~~~~~~~~~~~~~~~~~~~

I followed Madame across the room again, this time to the line of decorative wall panels flanking the credenza, the ones featuring the Palace gargoyles. When she pressed the gargoyle head on one of the panels, it swung inward like a door.

As promised, a tiny office was hidden behind the wall, but when Madame peeked inside, she gasped.

The room had been completely ransacked. The chair and the desk were overturned, and the contents of two filing cabinets had been dumped onto the floor. Someone had riffled through them. Files and loose papers blanketed the burgundy carpeting like autumn leaves in an indoor forest.

Madame dropped to her knees and began searching through the chaos. I crouched beside her.

"What are we looking for?"

"A black file with Annette's name on it—"

"What's in it?"

"Among other things, Annette's last will and testament. All of the Gotham Ladies have copies on file in this room."

"Why?"

"Let's just say we all try to watch each other's backs—ah, here it is."

Madame opened the file and leafed through the pages

inside. It contained documents and even a group of small art prints. But—

"The will is missing."

"Are you sure?" I pressed.

"Yes."

"What does it mean?"

"I don't know. Not yet. Help me up, dear," she said, still clutching the file to her breast. As she rose, the color art prints tumbled onto the floor.

"Would you get those, please?"

I gathered up the postcard-sized prints and tucked them into the pocket of my Poetry in Motion jacket. Once on her feet, Madame swept her hair back and finger-combed her silver pageboy.

"This is troubling, Clare. Not many people know about this office."

"The cops probably tossed it, looking for clues, don't you think?"

"Maybe. Maybe not. I see the private laptop computer Annette kept in here is gone, as well."

Esther poked her head through the door a moment later.

"A hidden office—how cool. But someone should really hire a secretary to straighten out the filing system!"

"What is it, Esther?" Madame asked.

"The coffee is brewing, and I found clean cups in the cabinet. But the refrigerator's empty, so we're drinking it black, no sugar. I couldn't find any cookies, either."

"Black coffee will do, Esther. This is a tasting, not a tea party."

Twenty-one

~~~~~~~~~~~~~~~~~~~~~~~~~~~~~~~~~~~~~~

I leaned forward in the chair and inhaled the roasted aroma rising from the cup. It took all of my self-control not to guzzle the entire thing down in one burning gulp. Instead, I tried to relax and concentrate on the tasting.

Before the coffee cooled too much, I took that first welcome sip. After swallowing, I took a second, deeper drink.

"It's quaffable," I said, keeping the disappointment to myself. For a crafted blend in a luxury hotel, this brew was one-dimensional and very ordinary.

"Anything else?" Esther asked. "Did the aroma or taste seem the tiniest bit familiar?"

"Sorry," I said, a little tired of apologizing.

I paused to take some fresh water while I waited for the coffee to cool and its flavor profile to change—and hopefully improve. Madame and Esther stood over me, watching with a mixture of hope and impatience.

I took that crucial next sip (okay, more of a gulp).

"Anything now?" Madame asked.

"It's . . . caffeinated—"

Madame rolled her eyes. "Oh, bosh, Clare. Don't hold back. Tell us what you *really* think."

"I think that this coffee is unworthy of a luxurious venue like the Parkview Palace hotel. I'm detecting a blend of

Sumatra and Colombian with buried notes of chocolate and walnut. But they botched the roasting and there is zero brightness for balance, no acidity at all, so it's flat and dull. I would have added an African, Kenyan AA or Yirg, or more likely one of Matt's specially sourced Central American beans for that missing top note. For a true premium blend, I might have included his Brazilian Ambrosia—and I would have roasted the single origins separately. This isn't one of ours, is it? *Please* tell me I didn't create this."

"You didn't. It's not Village Blend coffee." Madame set her own cup aside and studied me. "But your tasting displays advanced expertise. Do you know where you acquired it?"

"Of course! I worked for you the entire decade that Matt and I were married. You mentored me, taught me everything there is to know about coffee."

"I taught you everything I knew, Clare. But since then, you have far surpassed me. And you proved it just now. I only tasted a flat, dull blend, but you pinpointed the precise problems."

"Which means?"

"Which means there's no doubt now: We can absolutely tap into your accumulated knowledge. We've found a crack in the block to your memories. We're on the right track."

"If you say so . . ."

"I do." She smiled with satisfaction. "Matt wasn't importing the Ambrosia beans when you were married to him. His relationship with that Brazilian farm didn't develop until years after you divorced."

"Really?"

"Really." Madame nodded, and I felt hopeful as I finished the cup. I even poured myself another. Though the blend was mediocre, it was *real* coffee!

"Clare's Proustian madeleine could still be in this room," Esther declared. "I wouldn't recommend eating week-old wedding cake samples for *Remembrance of Things Past*, but maybe she should sniff a few. It might stimulate a cortex or three—"

"I have a better idea," Madame suggested. "After we leave, I'll have a friend order the same samples from the chef downstairs. Clare can taste them once she's settled—"

A sudden shout, muffled by the closed doors, halted her words.

"Hey!" Mr. Dante yelled from the hall. "Some guys are running this way. They're—"

His voice was replaced by the sound of a blow and a startled grunt.

"Dante!" Esther cried, rushing to the double doors.

Before she reached them, they burst open to reveal a trio of guards wearing identical blue blazers and gray slacks. The biggest one had immobilized Mr. Dante from behind, wrapping his thick left arm around the barista's throat while using the right to pin back the young man's hands.

Mr. Dante and his tormentor were flanked by a stout, older guard holding a truncheon, and a skinnier, younger guard, armed with a stun gun. Fortunately, he was pointing the gun at the ceiling and not at us.

Though these three men clearly meant business, they didn't intimidate Madame in the least.

"Release that boy immediately!" she demanded, her posture a tower of righteous indignation.

Scowling, the stout, older guard spun his truncheon once and dropped it into a belt loop. When he stepped in front of the others, I noted his badge read *Stevens*. His bulldog face was topped by thinning red hair. A jagged scar marred his ruddy cheek.

"You're trespassing, lady," he said. "All of you are trespassing—"

Madame squared her narrow shoulders and walked right up to him.

"We have a perfect right to be here. I'm this year's chairwoman of the Gotham Ladies' Charity Committee and this suite belongs to us!"

Stevens looked over the room.

"What the hell are you doing, having a tea party? This

is a crime scene. Didn't you notice the pretty yellow tape?" He snorted. "Are you completely batty or just senile?"

Madame's violet eyes flashed. "I'll brook no ageism from anyone, least of all from an overstuffed poltroon hiding behind a badge. Now, you tell that jackbooted thug to release my barista this instant! Then I want you all to leave these premises."

With an arrogant frown at Madame, Stevens shook off the order. Mr. Dante made a valiant effort to break free on his own—but the guard restraining him simply tightened his grip. The barista's complexion went from pale to purple.

That was when Madame strode right up to Mr. Dante's tormenter and slapped him in the face. "Release that boy, you fascist!"

Fearing the worst, I jumped in front of Madame.

"She's right," I argued. "This suite legally belongs to the Gotham Ladies. They pay good money for it. You have no right to harass us."

Stevens appeared to hesitate at my words—until he stared harder at me, narrowing his gaze on my blond wig and fake glasses, which didn't do much to convince him of our veracity.

"Step aside," he ordered. "I'm placing the old bag under arrest."

"She did nothing wrong!" I cried.

"She struck a member of my staff," Stevens shot back.

Now Esther stepped up. "She had good reason. Your rent-a-badge had it coming. He's harming our friend. And if he"—Esther pointed to said rent-a-badge—"doesn't *release* our friend, I am going to kick him where no man wants a boot to go—*ever*. Then you can arrest us all, and we'll sue!"

While the guard appeared distracted by Esther's tirade, Mr. Dante made his *Karate Kid* move. Pulling one arm free, he elbowed the guard's midriff hard enough to break the choke hold and escape. But the adrenaline-charged barista didn't retreat. Spoiling for a fight, he turned to face his bigger, bulkier abuser.

Before the guard with the stun gun could act, a woman's outraged voice broke through the chaos.

"Step back, Stevens! Call off your men. These people are friends!"

Twenty-two

⊚⊚⊚⊚⊚⊚⊚⊚⊚⊚⊚⊚⊚⊚⊚⊚⊚⊚

A woman in black hurried toward us. Statuesque and elegant, she made a sharp contrast to the bulldog guards, and she pushed through their ranks with regal determination, stepping between Mr. Dante and his uniformed foe.

"Blanche! My goodness! Are you all right?!"

To Madame's obvious surprise, the woman seized her shoulders and kissed the air around her silver pageboy.

"Victoria Holbrook?" Madame stepped back to take in the sight of the polished businesswoman in the sleek black pantsuit. "I can't believe it's you."

I tried to place the woman's age—fifties, sixties? Even with her auburn hair slicked back into a chic chignon, her ivory skin betrayed few wrinkles.

"It's been years since I've seen you." Madame continued to marvel. "Why, you haven't changed a bit."

"We both know that's not true," Victoria replied, though her wide blue eyes seemed pleased by the compliment. "And I can't apologize enough for this." She gestured at the guards. "Stevens here noticed the private elevator had been used and informed me he was going to check it out. I had no idea it was you!"

Victoria dismissed the security guards, but the one called Stevens took his time leaving. With a frustrated grimace, he shot Mr. Dante the kind of cold, hard stare a hungry wolf gives the lucky rabbit that got away.

Quickly stepping between the angry guard and his prey, Victoria asked Mr. Dante if he was all right. When he grunted in the affirmative, she directed us back into the Gotham Suite.

"What are you doing here, Blanche?" Victoria began. "You should have informed the hotel that you were coming. We could have avoided this unfortunate incident."

"I came to fetch our files for the Ladies' Charity Ball," Madame lied. "It's that time of year again."

I noted that Madame was not only dishonest, but she was careful not to mention the state of the ransacked office. Now her eyes narrowed suspiciously.

"What are *you* doing here, Victoria? Didn't you move to Vienna?"

"Yes, for a short time. But I came back to the States years ago—made a home on the West Coast. Lately, I missed life in Manhattan."

Madame shook her head. "I mean, what are you doing at the Parkview?"

"With Annette missing, I've stepped in to help out," she said. "Someone had to. Someone from the family, I mean." She leaned close to Madame's ear. "This place has been mismanaged for a long time. And with recent events, well . . . let's just say it's gotten much worse."

"Have you called on your niece to help?" Madame asked. "With Tessa's own successes in the hotel business, I'm sure she'd be an asset."

Victoria visibly tensed. "Annette wouldn't like that."

"But I thought Annette and Tessa were close?"

"They were, but . . ." Victoria seemed reluctant to reveal more.

"Tell me, please," Madame urged. "I'd like to help, if I can."

Victoria appeared to be fighting emotion—and trying to decide how much to say. With a polite nod to Esther, me, and Mr. Dante, she pulled Madame a few feet away.

Their backs were to us as Victoria began to talk in hushed tones. I signaled Esther and Mr. Dante to stay quiet and stepped a little closer to eavesdrop.

". . . and as you probably know, Blanche, my late brother's daughter used Annette's connections to get her hotel chain off the ground. But Annette confided in me that Tessa Simmons did something recently to upset her. I don't know what, but something led to a bitter argument. And given what's happened . . . well, I have a sick feeling Tessa—or perhaps someone close to her—is behind this whole ugly mess."

"By *whole ugly mess*, you mean—?"

"My sister's bizarre abduction, of course. I can't bear to think that it's anything worse than that. I've been waiting for a ransom note. I'm desperate for one, if you want to know the truth. I'll pay anything to get Annette back. But we've had no contact from anyone. *Nothing*. The police still haven't been able to trace a getaway vehicle . . ."

Hearing that, I thought about Matt's mobile machinations, and didn't doubt that motivated criminals could beat almost any surveillance system.

"The police have theories," Victoria went on, "but no solid leads, including no proof Annette and her captor crossed state lines. So there's no FBI, not yet, anyway. The case is still under local jurisdiction. And the NYPD detectives tell me your former daughter-in-law can't tell them anything, either."

"That's right," Madame replied. "Our Clare is back, but she was hospitalized with a damaged memory. We don't know if she'll ever regain it."

"You know what I can't stop thinking?" Victoria said. "If anything happens to Annette, Tessa is set to inherit the Parkview. What does that tell you?"

Madame expelled a breath. "Do you really think she's capable of murdering her own aunt? I never knew Tessa very well. I did meet her some time ago, at the opening of her first boutique hotel in Brooklyn. She seemed like a sweet girl."

"She was, Blanche. It's true, but she was barely out of her teens then. A lot has changed since she began that Gypsy hotel chain with her college friends. She's not so sweet anymore."

Victoria's voice turned anxious, almost fearful. "I admit, I have no proof. I wish I did, but I suspect Tessa wants control of the Parkview for gravitas, to prop up the reputation of those cheap, trendy lodgings she peddles. I conveyed my suspicions to the detectives on the case, but they seem convinced this is a revenge scheme on the Brewsters for past actions. I'm at my wit's end, Blanche. If there's anything you can think of to help—or if your daughter-in-law remembers something, *anything*—please let me know. I want my sister back . . ."

Her voice broke. As she wiped away tears, Madame took her hand and squeezed.

"I know it must be hard," she soothed. "You're right to step in and manage the hotel, despite the pressure on you. Someone must, until the authorities find out what really happened."

Victoria nodded, pulling a handkerchief from her pocket to dry her eyes. "You've always been so kind, Blanche. I—"

Just then, we all heard a ding. The sound sent tense anticipation through every one of us. The elevator we rode up in was about to deliver another passenger to the foyer.

Twenty-three

~~~~~~

Hurried footsteps came down the hall and a harried young man rushed into the suite. "Ms. Holbrook!" he began excitedly. "I got your emergency text in my car and drove here as fast as I could!"

Adjusting his horn-rimmed glasses, he looked us all over. "Are these the people that violated the police quarantine?"

Victoria looked embarrassed. "I'm afraid I overreacted, Owen. Thank you for coming, but it's just a misunderstanding."

"And who is this?" Madame asked.

"Blanche, I'd like you to meet Owen Wimmer, Esquire. He's the Parkview's legal representative. You can imagine he's been busy since Annette vanished."

The towheaded lawyer in a buttoned-down shirt and sweater vest couldn't have been more than thirty years old. Though small of stature, he displayed a great deal of intense energy. After barely acknowledging Madame, the lawyer faced Victoria and in one rapid-fire breath said—

"I have one question for you. And you know why. Was *Stevens* involved?"

"Yes." Victoria frowned. "He and two members of his staff restrained this young man."

Owen cursed and turned to Mr. Dante. "Are you all right, sir?"

"Sure, it was nothing," the barista replied.

The young lawyer frowned. "We won't stand in your way if you elect to file a complaint with the police."

"Forget it," Mr. Dante insisted.

Visibly relieved, Owen faced Victoria. "Stevens is a loose cannon. This is not the first incident. You should fire him—"

"I don't know if that's necessary. He's been at the Parkview for years. Without Annette here to agree, I don't feel comfortable making such a drastic personnel change, but I will speak with him."

"I'm sorry, but that's not good enough. We cannot have the Parkview subjected to any further legal jeopardy." The lawyer removed his glasses and cleaned the lenses with a pocket handkerchief. "I'd like to be the one to address Stevens and his staff—"

"I said I'd take care of it."

"Hmm, well . . ." Owen practically pouted. "You know best. I'll go, then."

Madame announced that we should be moving on, too.

Victoria apologized again to us for our rough treatment and requested that we leave by the front entrance, since the NYPD had ordered hotel management to seal everything off, including the private elevator.

"*And* because Owen is such a stickler," she added, practically rolling her eyes.

On our way out, I spied the young lawyer at the elevator, shaking his head as he fussily restored the crisscrossed police tape that Madame had torn off the door.

Then we turned the corner, and Victoria Holbrook led us down a wide, carpeted hall lined with suites. An ornate flight of stairs took us to the elegant lobby.

Before Madame exited through the bronze-and-glass doors, the woman in black rained more air-kisses down on her. "Don't be a stranger. The next time you visit, let me know. We'll have lunch in the Sun Court—my treat."

BREWED AWAKENING   93

Outside, buses, cabs, and cars crowded the street. The autumn wind, whipping along Central Park South, made the colorful leaves quiver, and me shiver. I pulled my Poetry in Motion jacket closer around me, glad I had the blond wig on my head for extra warmth.

Madame signaled for us to follow her lead. "Victoria expects us to leave so we'd better make a show of it."

She asked the doorman to call us a cab and, once we all piled in, informed the driver—

"We're only going around the block, to the hotel's garage entrance on fifty-eighth, but I'll be tipping you well."

"No problem, ma'am!"

Turning to Mr. Dante, she instructed him to contact her son. "Tell him to sit tight. We'll be there in a few minutes."

Mr. Dante nodded and pulled out his phone. "Too bad your friend stopped the fight," he muttered. "I know I could have taken that guy."

Esther shook her head. "Get over it, Rambo."

Twenty-Four

~~~~~~~~~~~~~~~~~~~~~~~~

Five minutes later, the cab lurched to a stop, and we piled onto the sidewalk next to the Parkview's garage.

Beep, beep, beeeeep!

The insistent car horn had us all turning to find a stylish woman waving at us from the window of an odd-looking SUV. Her long arm was flapping so excitedly, I thought she might actually lift the hunk of metal off the pavement.

"Whoa!" Dante gushed. "Look at that pimped-up G-Wagen!"

I'd never heard of the model. Heavily detailed in glittering gold, it looked more like a Vegas-ready Jeep with a shiny front grille about as subtle as the smile of a saber-toothed tiger.

The trendy contraption, which Mr. Dante informed me was a G-Class Mercedes, squealed to a dead stop in front of us. Then another screech assaulted our ears, this one through the driver's open window.

"Blaaaaanche! Sweeeeeetie! What a surpriiiiise!"

The car door flew open to reveal the driver, a striking older woman who reminded me a little of Carol Channing—with some Ethel Merman thrown in for volume.

Wrapped in a gold lamé car coat, she sported a platinum blond bob, highlighted with bright streaks of canary yellow, adding memorable shock to her already theatrical appearance. Her enthusiasm was dampened a moment as she detached herself from a tangle of bedazzled seat belts. Then she burst out of her luxury vehicle with a Broadway grin.

Once on her feet, her low-heeled booties—gold, of course—clicked across the sidewalk, running right up to Madame. With open arms, she lifted her friend off the ground in a big bear hug. And I do mean big. Compared to Madame (who stood taller than I did without shoes), the woman in gold was like a soaring statue in the flesh, literally enveloping Madame in her embrace.

I recognized her, not from memory, but because I'd just seen her caricature upstairs in the hotel's Gotham Suite. She was Nora Arany, former fashion adviser to rock and hip-hop stars, now a clothing and apparel designer—with an obvious fetish for all things gold.

In the process of greeting my former mother-in-law, Nora had completely abandoned her G-Wagen at the entrance to the garage ramp. With its door open and the keys in the ignition, the incessant *beep-beep-beeping* alert went completely ignored by the owner.

"Nora, what a delight to see you," Madame said, breathless from the clinch. "How have you been faring since our last Gotham brunch?"

Nora was positively giddy.

"I'm doing fabulously, Blanche. You won't believe this, but *The Crazy-Rich Cougars of Parma* are going to wear my apparel next season! I just sealed the deal this morning. The show's debut will coincide with the grand opening of my Cleveland store."

"That's wonderful," Madame replied, forcing a smile.

"You said it," Nora gushed. "With *The MILFs of Minneapolis* and *The Bickering Trophy Brides of Bridgeport*, I've got product placement blanketing half the country."

Madame struggled to suppress a visible shudder as Nora paused to take a breath. Meanwhile, a more conventional Mercedes pulled up behind Nora's. After waiting a millisecond (the median length of time a New York driver remained patient), he honked loudly.

Nora didn't appear to notice—or care. Instead, she pointed to the matching jackets that Esther and I wore. "I see you brought some of the Poetry in Motion people with you." As she said this, Nora focused her attention on me, her stare lingering long enough to make me sweat.

Can she tell I'm wearing a disguise?

"I'm sorry I missed your citywide poetry slam at Cooper Union last month," Nora said. "Being an angel donor, I hope I didn't offend you."

"Oh, no," Esther quickly replied. "We have one every quarter. You're welcome to see it next time—and thanks for your generous support, Ms. Arany!"

"It's nothing. Happy to." She fluttered her fingers. "What good is money, if not to support the arts!"

Finally, the impatient driver had endured enough. "Lady!" he shouted over the unceasing beeping from the G-Wagen's flung-open door. "Move your car!"

Nora narrowed her eyes at the outraged driver and turned to address Mr. Dante. "You there!"

The barista pointed at himself. "Me?"

"Yes, *you*, handsome boy! Be a *darling* and drive my car down to my designated spot. It's on the right after you go through the gate—" Gold booties clicking across the sidewalk, she reached out to shove a tip into his hand. "You can't miss it. Look for the sign with my name: Nora Arany . . ."

As Nora continued giving him instructions, Madame leaned close to me and Esther. "That's odd," she whispered. "Why would Nora suddenly have her own designated spot? Annette and Nora always act like friends, but we all know they can't stand each other."

"You mean they're frenemies?" Esther said.

"*Frenemies* . . ." Madame's gaze returned to Nora. "Is that what they call it now?"

"Historically, the term's been around since the 1950s," Esther noted. "Lately, it's made a comeback."

"It's a new word for me, too," I admitted.

"But a very old idea," Madame murmured.

As Nora returned to us, Esther smirked at Mr. Dante. "Here's your big chance to drive your dream car. Don't blow it."

Twenty-Five

~~~~~~~~~~~~~~~~~~~~~~~

ESTHER'S taunt proved prophetic. Or maybe it was simply the power of suggestion.

Grinning with excitement, Mr. Dante climbed behind the wheel. But his eagerness got the better of him. Leaning too heavily on the gas, he nearly slammed the luxury SUV into the garage's ticket meter.

Esther snorted, and Mr. Dante cringed with sheepish embarrassment. Then he quickly straightened out the vehicle, and drove down the ramp.

Fortunately, Nora was too busy chatting up Madame to notice any of it.

"So what are you doing at the Parkview, Blanche?"

"I needed the files for our annual Gotham Ladies' Charity Ball. Despite recent events, the rite of spring must go on."

"By recent events, you mean Annette's vanishing act?"

Madame's gaze narrowed. "Do you know anything about it?"

"Me? Nothing! It's a terrible business . . ." Suddenly, Nora's lips began to quiver, and she broke into a sob. "Poor Annette," she blubbered. "What could have happened to her? Will we ever see her again?"

I didn't think much of Nora's act. Madame wasn't impressed, either.

"Drop the show. You forget who you're talking to."

Pretending to dry her eyes, Nora waved a hand. "Oh, please. If I were Annette, I would have disappeared long ago."

"What do you mean?"

"I mean that rat bastard husband of hers made her life miserable for years. You know that—"

Suddenly we all heard a tinny voice singing. It was Shirley Bassey belting out the *Goldfinger* theme.

"My phone!" Nora exclaimed, snatching the device out of her gold-plated chain mail bag.

"Oh, shoot, I've got to dash!" she cried after checking the screen. "My Japanese buyer is inside the lobby, waiting—"

"Before you go," Madame said, "what can you tell me about the Gotham Suite's private office being ransacked?"

"Ransacked?" Nora shrugged. "Must have been a police search. Sorry, Blanche. We'll chat more another time. Mr. Ogata is very old-school, and he really wants to revisit the classic, classy Manhattan. That's why I'm treating him to drinks at the Parkview Palace—I mean, how old-school can you get, right? Then it's on to the Pierre. Of course, the Plaza and the Waldorf are half condo now, but they still have some of the trappings of the old days."

Nora leaned close to Madame. "I'm not looking forward to breaking the news about the Plaza's tiki room closing." She sighed. "He has such fond memories of Trader Vic's."

Before Madame could get another word in, Nora was dashing down the block. "Ta-ta!" she called, her booming voice barely fading into the traffic noise.

"And she's off!" Esther remarked. "What a character!"

About then, Mr. Dante emerged from the garage. "That Arany woman gave me a fifty, just to park her car!"

Madame grimly faced her barista. "Does she really have a *designated* parking spot?"

He nodded. "In the VIP section. Right beside a reserved slot for Tessa Simmons."

"Tessa Simmons," I repeated. "I remember that name."

"You do?" Madame looked hopeful. "From a past memory?"

"No, from upstairs in the Gotham Suite." I pulled Madame aside and lowered my voice. "Annette's sister, Victoria, mentioned her—and not in a good way."

"How do you know that, Clare?"

It was my turn to look sheepish. "I eavesdropped on your conversation. Victoria said she believes Annette's last will and testament names their niece, Tessa, as the heiress to the Parkview Palace."

"That's what Victoria believes, but I don't know that it's still true."

"What makes you think that?"

"It's why I wanted to see a copy of her will for myself. Before she disappeared, Annette told me she was updating it."

"And she didn't tell you why? Or how she was updating it?"

"No. At our last Gotham Ladies' brunch, I took her aside and reminded her that we ladies weren't sharing eggs Benedict and mimosas once a month for the calories and bubbles. We were there to help each other, when needed. She thanked me, but said she was fine. That her husband's recent death had opened her eyes—and changed everything. That's why she was going to update her will. She also confided quietly that she had 'put plans in motion' that I'd learn about soon enough."

"And then she was abducted?"

Madame nodded. "If you can remember anything, Clare, any details about that evening you spent with Annette, or about her abductor—and presumably yours—you could help us find Annette and clear this whole thing up."

"I wish I could remember, and not just that evening. I want all of my memories back—and my life."

"I know you do, dear."

"Hey, you two," Esther called. "I hate to interrupt, but do you really want to stand out here on the street, waiting for the next G-Wagen diva to throw her keys at Dante?"

"You're right." Madame glanced up and down the block. "Let's go."

Twenty-six

~~~~~~~~~~~~~~~~~~~~~~~~~~~~~

"**So?**" Matt asked, studying me as we piled back into the van. "Is she cured? How does she feel about me?"

"I still can't stand you. And I cannot believe I ever changed my mind about that."

"But there is a glimmer of hope," Madame noted.

"What does that mean?" Matt asked. "What exactly happened up there?"

Madame proceeded to tell him with Esther and Mr. Dante jumping in for color commentary. When they finished, Matt turned to me.

"So the coffee tasting helped unlock something inside your head? And the sensory keys might work, after all?"

"I guess so," I conceded. "But I need more answers. That's why I left the hospital, for answers—and coffee. What now?"

Matt shifted his gaze to his mother. "Decision time."

Madame frowned and looked away. She was clearly still struggling with the options from their previous discussion. "It's a shame we can't take Clare home, back to the duplex above the coffeehouse."

"That's a nice thought," Matt said, "but it can't happen."

"Why not?" I asked, the fight in me rising.

This ongoing debate about me—this *What shall we do*

with Clare?—was really starting to chafe. I wasn't some mental invalid, unable to function.

"So what if Dr. Lorca sends authorities looking for me! I'll simply tell them I changed my mind about the treatment. I'll tell them to leave me alone and send them on their way. What's wrong with that?"

Matt let the dust settle on my volcanic outburst. Then he calmly asked, "Do you know who the president is?"

"The president?" I blinked. "You mean . . . of the United States?"

"It's a basic question for reality orientation."

"I see."

"And what's your answer?"

"Is it a Clinton?"

"No."

"Another Bush?"

"You're guessing, aren't you?"

"Uhm . . ."

"Name the most recent movie you remember."

I bit my lip. "Was it a Robin Williams film?"

Matt turned to his mother. "You don't want to risk commitment, do you?"

With a shake of her head, Madame addressed her baristas. "Esther and Dante, listen carefully. When we're finished here, I want you to take separate taxis downtown." She handed them cash. "Give your drivers addresses that are near your apartments but not within sight of them. Then walk the rest of the way to your homes, change clothes, and go directly to the Village Blend to relieve the baristas on duty."

"What about me?" I asked.

"You're going to be driven to a safe place where you can take a little vacation."

My stomach clenched. "You're coming with me, aren't you?"

She reached out and took my hands in hers. "I'd like to, my dear child. I wish I could, but it's not a good idea. The authorities are going to come for you, and the first place they're going to look will be the Village Blend. I need to be there to answer questions. With luck, I'll be able to throw the bloodhounds off your trail. I've also got to find us an attorney, one willing to take our case and get us out of any legal jeopardy. We'll need to find a local psychiatrist willing to work with us, as well."

"You mean, work with me."

She gently squeezed my hands. "Be patient. If all goes well, you should be able to come back to the city in a few days, a week at most."

"And if all *doesn't* go well?"

"Let's focus on the positive, shall we?"

"I'll try . . ." I shifted my gaze to Esther and Mr. Dante. "Which one of you will be driving me to this hideaway house?"

Matt cleared his throat. "That would be *me*."

"You?" The man's dark beard parted with a smile so smug, I wanted to scream (and almost did). Given everyone's anxiety about my mental state, however, I forced myself to hold it together and just say—

"NO."

"That's the plan, Clare."

"I don't care. I am not driving to some strange house alone with you. There has to be another option. Esther?"

"Sorry, boss. I'm an Uber-subway kinda girl. Driving's not in my wheelhouse."

With pleading eyes, I looked at Mr. Dante.

"I'm sorry, too, but I don't know Long Island, let alone this Hamptons place Matt has in mind. I'm likely to get us lost. And it's a two-hour haul to get out there. I'm scheduled for an evening shift. I think I should keep the routine looking normal."

"Of course you should," Madame agreed. "And you'll be fine, Clare. I know my son would do anything to protect you. He only wants to help."

"You can trust me," Matt promised.

"Trust you?" I almost laughed.

"Come on, Clare," he wheedled. "This is a road trip. For all the terrible things you remember about me, there has to be one good thing you haven't forgotten."

"What?"

"I'm loads of fun on a road trip."

Twenty-seven

⊛⊛⊛⊛⊛⊛⊛⊛⊛⊛⊛⊛⊛⊛⊛⊛⊛⊛⊛

Ten minutes later, I was riding shotgun next to the last man I wanted to be with on this (or any other) planet.

While Matt guided our battered van through the heavy crosstown traffic, we sat in tense silence. Then we hit the Queensboro Bridge, and cars and trucks began moving around us like they'd entered the first lap of the Indy 500.

I checked the clock on the dashboard. "I'm surprised the congestion is letting up. It's not even six o'clock."

"It's Friday," Matt informed me. "In New York, rush hour starts earlier—"

"And ends earlier. Right, I remember that."

"But you didn't remember it was Friday, did you?"

"No . . ." I didn't like talking to Matt, either, so I reached forward to turn on the radio. He immediately turned it off.

"Not a good idea," he said. "Sorry, but you still aren't oriented to this time period. News on the radio may shake you up. Let's take things slow."

I sat back and folded my arms. "How about an oldies station? Do you still have those?"

Matt snorted.

"What's funny?"

"It's just . . . an age thing. I'll forever think of oldies as songs from the sixties. But 'oldies' these days means eighties music."

"That seems wrong to me, too—for an entirely different reason—but at least I'll recognize the tunes."

"Okay . . ." Matt turned to an FM station, currently playing Huey Lewis. "But I warn you, the second they go to a station break, it's off again."

"Fine."

I turned my attention to the scenery. By now night had fallen, and the East River was stretching out darkly below us. I'd crossed this river many times during our marriage to meet Matt's late-arriving planes at LaGuardia Airport.

I was so pathetic, so gullible, always so eager to throw my arms around my "darling" husband's neck and welcome him home.

What a fool I was.

I risked a glance in his direction, at that familiar masculine profile, the one I'd fallen so pathetically in love with, and felt the searing disgust over his betrayals rise inside me again.

Matt remained focused on the traffic, oblivious to my glare, which was probably for the better, since, as everyone kept telling me, my state of mind was out-of-date. Somewhere, in all the years that passed between us, I forgave my ex-husband. Now (apparently) we were not only business partners but close friends.

Yeah, right.

I returned my stare to the dark river, a fitting description of my present mood. I always thought of the undulating water as a black moat, separating the cloud-scraping castles of glamorous Manhattan from the rusty warehouses and worn-down row houses of working-class Queens.

Not anymore.

To my blinking astonishment, the Queens' side of the river had risen with sleek glass-and-steel skyscrapers that rivaled New York's poshest pillars. It looked so wrong to me, so out of place, but I couldn't deny the physical fact. Like a towering argument in Matt's favor, I saw the concrete evidence—

Things really have changed.

And Matt was right. It was all too much.

Feeling overwhelmed again and slightly unsteady, I turned my focus back to the "oldies" FM station, now playing (aptly enough) "Sister Christian" by Night Ranger.

Closing my eyes, I tried to calm myself further by remembering something pleasant from my past. This time I reached for a very old but beloved memory: baking crusty Italian rolls with my *nonna*, pans and pans of them, for her little grocery store.

I smiled as I turned the picture pages of childhood, seeing my grandmother alive again, happily teaching me how to proof the yeast, mix the sticky dough, and form those delicious rolls. I felt so grown-up and accomplished. How I loved working in her big, sunny kitchen through the years. I could still hear the radio playing upbeat music; smell the espresso brewing in the stove-top pot; and see my *nonna*, speaking in rapid Italian, praising my work and sharing some piece of amusing gossip that a customer or neighbor had told her.

I could nearly smell the goodness of those nut brown orbs baking, hear the crunch of the crust as I broke one open fresh from the oven and buttered its pillowy white interior, so tender and fluffy, the sweet butter dripping from my fingers and chin as I took my first bite—

My stomach growled. "Matt, have you got any food in this jalopy?"

"No. Are you hungry?"

"Starving."

"I could eat, too, but stopping is a bad idea. I don't want us spotted." He thought a minute. "We could hit a drive-through."

"Do you know of any in this part of Queens?"

At the next red light, Matt consulted his prepaid phone.

"Really?" I said. "Your *phone* will tell you where to find a drive-through?"

"Convenient, isn't it? And in more ways than one."

"What do you mean?"

Once again, he flashed that infuriating smile. "You'll see."

Twenty-Eight

~~~~~~

"An eight-piece bucket, please," Matt informed the dented speaker.

"Just the chicken?" the tinny voice asked. "Or the whole meal?"

I grabbed my ex-husband's still-hard biceps. "I'm *literally* starving."

"The meal."

"Sides?"

I was about to recite a list when Matt held up his hand and shot me a familiar amused look—one I usually saw in the bedroom: *Don't worry, Clare. I know what you like.*

The food came out hot and fast. Matt handed me the paper sack. I hurriedly opened it, ready to shove my face inside with all the polite refinement of a horse greeting its feed bag.

"Hold on," Matt commanded as he returned the van to Queens Boulevard. "Don't eat yet."

"Are you kidding me?!"

"Look, this isn't just dinner, okay?" Matt said, taking a quick right. "You could make a mental breakthrough with this food."

"A mental breakthrough? With *Kentucky Fried Chicken*?"

Matt nodded vigorously as he made another right, lap-ping us around the crowded residential block. "Be patient, Clare. I need to find a legal spot for us to park and eat."

Easier said than done. Zero spaces were free here; both curbs were packed with cars and vans, all of their bumpers kissing.

"Can't you just double-park? We won't be long."

"I don't want to risk some drive-by flatfoot with a ticket quota getting suspicious."

My stomach growled again, and I groaned. The tempting smell of freshly fried chicken was cruelly taunting my saliva glands. "I'm dying here. Can I at least eat a biscuit?!"

He grabbed the bag from my lap and dropped it into his. "Control yourself."

"You wouldn't say that if you saw my last hospital meal!"

A few minutes later, we were passing the KFC again. This time we crossed over the wide, busy boulevard and motored down a much quieter cross street. Seeing a shadowy shoulder, Matt pulled over.

"We're nice and secluded here . . ." He killed the engine with satisfaction. "Perfect, huh?"

"Perfectly creepy."

On one side of the road, I saw nothing but dingy brick warehouses, their garages shuttered for the night with pull-down doors of accordion metal. On the other side, a stone wall stretched as far as I could see with tangled brush below and tree limbs hanging above.

"What's on the other side of that wall? A park?"

"Sort of."

I tried to remember the last map of Queens I'd consulted out of boredom on a taxi ride to the airport. I recalled seeing a large green space adjacent to Queens Boulevard, but it wasn't a park—

"That's a cemetery!"

"It has a lawn. And trees."

"There are graves in there!"

"You want me to find another spot?"

By now I was drooling.

"Forget it," I said. "If I don't eat soon, I'll be giving up the ghost. Then instead of driving me to the South Fork, you can dig me a bed on the other side of that wall."

"You know, I forgot how overly dramatic you used to get."

"Excuse me?"

"You're acting like you did right after we divorced. Impatient, argumentative, accusatory. You're much more mature now."

"Are you *trying* to get slapped?"

"That's your *hanger* talking."

"My what?"

"*Hunger* plus *anger* equals—"

"I get it. But if you don't hand over some sustenance pronto, I'm going to hang you."

Twenty-nine

〜〜〜〜〜〜〜〜〜〜〜〜〜〜〜〜〜

At long last, Matt passed me the sack of food. My hand was barely in the bucket before he cried—

"Wait!"

Oh, for the love of—

"I want you to close your eyes before you take a bite."

"Why?"

"Just do it."

The car was plenty dark already, but I humored my relentlessly annoying ex-husband and let the world go black. Then I clamped my salivating maw around the juicy, breaded meat and (finally!) ate.

Matt obviously did the same because his next words sounded garbled, presumably around a mouth full of Original Recipe.

"Now, listen," he said. "I want you to think about those old Kentucky Fried TV commercials, and the colonel in the white suit, and the eleven secret herbs and spices. What do you remember about that?"

"Just that you used to joke about them being secret and whether I could detect them . . ." As I finished chewing and swallowing, I realized this wasn't a guess. It was something I knew.

"Go on," Matt coaxed.

"All three of us joked about it. Me, you, and our daughter. *Chef Sherlock*, that's what Joy called me."

"And how is that sharp palate of yours doing? Can you detect any of the chicken's herbs and spices now?"

I took another bite, chewing more slowly.

"Thyme, black pepper, oregano . . ."

"That's three," Matt confirmed.

"Don't be impressed," I said. "Those are typical spices in brand-name poultry seasonings. Thyme, black pepper, and oregano along with sage and some other spices. But I'm not tasting the usual sage—or rosemary or nutmeg. This chicken breading has a different flavor profile."

"What else do you taste?"

I lifted the chicken to my nose and inhaled. Took a few more bites, letting the warm morsels roll around every taste receptor in my head.

"Garlic, basil . . . paprika . . . and celery, or more likely celery salt . . ."

"Keep going."

"Dried mustard . . . a bit of ginger. I'm also getting a tinge of MSG, which I doubt was in the original Sanders's recipe. But, hey, in fast food, MSG makes everything better."

"Anything else?"

"White pepper. That's the real secret ingredient here— one you wouldn't expect—and it's used to great effect."

"You did it, Clare. You named them all."

"Oh, please. How could you possibly know that? It's a corporate secret."

"Open your eyes."

A bright light nearly blinded me. It was Matt's phone, shining in the dark van like a small, flat searchlight. On the screen was an article from the *Chicago Tribune*.

"A few years ago, a *Trib* reporter went down to Corbin, Kentucky, to do a report on the birthplace of KFC. Colonel Sanders's nephew showed him an old family scrapbook. Inside, the reporter found this—" Matt scrolled down to the picture of a handwritten list of eleven herbs and spices.

"The KFC company refused to confirm its authenticity, but copycat cooks say it's the real deal."

"Okay, fine, but I still don't understand why fast-food fried chicken has anything to do with my situation."

"Like I said, you tell me. Close your eyes again. Try to picture where you were the last time you tried to guess those chicken seasonings. Can you see it?"

"Yes . . ."

The memory was there. Just like that. No revelation, shock, or surprise. It felt as if I'd walked into a room in my head and observed a painting on the wall. Nothing about the artwork was new. All along it had been there. I simply hadn't noticed it for years.

"Go on," Matt said.

ThIRTY

"WE were at a picnic in a park. You and I were there together . . ."

I saw Matt in my memory as clearly as my *nonna* on those mornings we baked together in her kitchen. He had cleaned himself up for the visit with me and Joy: close shave, trim haircut, new shirt, a subtle cologne. He was deeply tanned from a sourcing trip, looking muscular and attractive.

"Joy was there, too, a young teenager—thirteen. Oh, my God, Matt, that picnic was a few years *after* we divorced! Part of the years I can't remember!"

"You're doing great. Do you know how we got to the park?"

"You showed up at my Jersey house, unexpected. You got back early from a *finca* in Central America and you had some time on your hands. So you drove out to see us and bought a bucket of chicken on the way. You wanted to have a picnic with Joy and me. I remember how you finally persuaded me."

"How?"

"You said something funny about fried chicken as a peace offering in one of the countries where you source coffee. That sounds crazy. Can that be right?"

"It's right. I made a friend in El Salvador who served as a gang mediator. He told me that before they start their peace talks, the rival leaders always sit down to a meal of fried chicken from *Pollo Campero*. I figured, *Hey, why not bring the tradition north?*"

He laughed softly, and I felt something inside me soften.

"Of course, back then," he went on, "there were no *Pollo Campero* restaurants in Jersey, let alone the tristate area. But KFC was close enough."

"Close enough to pacify a hostile ex-wife, you mean?"

"Like I said, you tell me. What else do you remember, after I showed up with the bucket?"

I closed my eyes and concentrated.

"You drove us out to a nearby park, and I spread a blanket. I brought a cooler with homemade lemonade . . ." The images were rolling out quickly now.

"As we ate, you challenged me to name the eleven herbs and spices in the chicken. Joy thought that would be a great game, and she joined you in egging me on. I had fun doing it. For the next year or so, she called me Chef Sherlock and kept asking me to guess the ingredients whenever we ate out."

"What happened after the picnic? Do you remember?"

"Joy begged you to drive us to the shore, and we went. We spent the rest of the afternoon hanging out at the beach, and when Joy was off shopping for souvenir T-shirts and seashell jewelry, you and I got ice-cream cones and talked. It was the first time, since we'd split, that we had a really long talk about Joy and our lives, and our little daily problems, and we watched the clouds change colors over the ocean as the sun set and . . ."

When my voice trailed off, Matt knew why. "You remember the kiss?"

"*Kissing*, you mean. Once we started, we didn't stop. I'm surprised I let it happen."

"Why? At that point in our relationship—our divorce relationship—things were going well. I was doing everything you asked to help you and Joy, and you appreciated it. Not that you wanted to get back together, but you were starting to forgive me, and you admitted you were missing . . . you know."

"No. Missing what?"

"The good things we had. Our friendship. Our love of the coffee business. Our chemistry."

"You mean our physical chemistry?"

"You can't deny history, Clare. We were good together, especially in bed."

"And? Did we ever . . . you know, make love again, after the divorce?"

"Oh, yeah. We did that night, and several more times in the years that followed."

I shook my head (in lieu of smacking it). "I can't believe I slept with you after we split. Why would I do that?!"

"Why not? You might have hated me, but you still loved me."

"That makes no sense."

"Of course it does. Down deep, you know it does."

"Sorry, but sitting here now, I don't feel it."

"Maybe not now. But you did . . ."

He sat back, studying me in the shadowy van, his big brown bedroom eyes doing their best to remind me of a double *ristretto*—warm, sweet, and hard to resist.

"You know what might help?" he asked.

"What?"

"Since your memory responds well to sensory stimuli, what if we played out what happened that night?"

I stared at him in disbelief. "You want me to go to bed with you?"

"We could start with a kiss?"

"Don't push your luck."

"Just think about it. We have a long drive ahead. The house where we're going is peaceful and secluded. We can take our time getting to know each other again—"

A flashing red light cut Matt short. The pair of us sat in tense stillness, until the NYPD patrol car flew by our van, silent as the grave.

"No siren," I said absently. "Probably a 10-31, crime in progress . . ."

I marveled at my own words, confused by this sharp, sure knowledge. I looked at Matt.

"Where did I learn that?"

"No idea," he said.

But I could tell he had *some* idea. His whole demeanor had changed. He was frosty now, less friendly.

"Let's get out of here," he said.

Then the engine turned over, and we were on our way.

Thirty-one

MIKE

"Got a minute?"

Lieutenant Michael Quinn looked up from a desk buried in paper to find Detective Anthony DeMarco loitering in his office doorway. A quick glance at the wall clock told him he'd been at it nonstop for five hours.

"Come on in, Tony."

"Burning the eight-o'clock oil again?"

"The work piles up . . ."

That was Quinn's response, not the whole story.

He'd been stealing daylight hours away from his job with attempts to help the woman he loved. There were repeated face-to-face appeals to the Annette Brewster investigating officers (uptown), the DA's office (downtown), the chief of detectives, and the deputy mayor—with little to show for his efforts.

His colleagues still didn't see Clare Cosi as a credible witness. Nor did they see her as a candidate for protective custody. With her written consent for treatment, she was legally in Dr. Dominic Lorca's care, and that was safe enough, as far as the NYPD was concerned.

Not as far as Quinn was concerned.

After a barrage of inquiries, he had secured a consultation appointment with a well-respected (and extremely pricey) law firm. That meeting, in which he hoped to use legal pressure to set Clare free, wouldn't happen until Monday. Tonight was Friday, which meant this weekend would be the longest of his life.

Not that it mattered. There was no Clare to go home to.

And, anyway, all that stolen time from the job meant hours of catch-up, primarily with paperwork. People were another matter. Quinn had command responsibilities. Despite his personal problems, he would always try to support his people. Now he sat back in his chair and loosened his tie.

"What can I do for you, Tony?"

DeMarco looked frayed around the edges. He was on cleanup detail after a batch of bad fentanyl-laced heroin hit the Tremont section of the Bronx. From the anxious expression on the young man's face, Quinn guessed there was more bad news.

"The medical examiner confirmed an overdose death. It's that teenage girl I found on Montgomery Street."

Despite near-numbing exhaustion, and the sad reality of what had become his OD Squad's routine business, Quinn felt a stab of emotion. *Five people in the hospital, one dead—and just a kid.*

His frustration had been building for days. Now Quinn just wanted to rage. But he checked himself, and made sure his reply was calm, measured, managerial.

"It could have been worse. That was good work catching the dealers so quickly. Who knows how many lives you saved?"

"I know one I didn't," Tony muttered.

"You can't save everyone . . ." It was a trite response. Quinn knew it, even as he said the words.

He remembered Clare serving that same mush to him one night.

"You can't save everyone, Mike."

"That's a trite expression," he'd snapped back to her, regretting the words as soon as he'd said them. He'd been feeling bitter over a lost cause, taking it personally, like DeMarco was now.

Before he could even begin his apology to her, Clare forgave him. Seeing the pain in his eyes, she put a hand on his cheek, brushed her lips across his, and whispered—

"Just because it's trite doesn't mean it isn't true."

Unlike his first disastrous relationship—with an immature woman who never understood, never forgave—Clare was relentless in her love and her belief in his goodness. Her steely faith in him never failed to keep him propped.

He could still hear her soft voice in his ear; still see her smiling that unsinkable Clare smile, filled with a level of stubborn optimism that he'd never encountered before (not in this city).

Well, trite or not, words wouldn't change a thing. Not for the men in this office. He felt as helpless as DeMarco.

If I could just hold her again . . .

Quinn felt a black shadow descending—until he realized Detective DeMarco had been speaking.

"Sorry, Tony, my mind wandered."

"I was saying we've got another problem. The DA wants to press homicide charges against the dealers, but there's a risk."

He handed a sheet of paper to Quinn.

"The teenage victim posted this on social media hours before she overdosed. You'd better read it."

Quinn cursed. "This could be construed as a suicide note."

"And the defense will happily use that interpretation to pressure the prosecutors into reducing the homicide rap to a lesser charge—manslaughter or crim. neg."

Quinn rubbed his tired eyes. "Nobody wants that, but you can't suppress what you found in discovery."

DeMarco sighed. "Yeah, that's what I thought you'd say."

"Just turn the information over to the DA. If they want to take their chances hiding exculpatory evidence during the plea process, it's on them."

"Okay." DeMarco nodded. "By the way, Lieutenant, may I also say you look like crap."

Quinn smiled weakly. "You trying to sweet-talk me? Or just get on my good side?"

"If you need fuel, Sergeant Perez made a fresh pot of joe. I can grab some for you."

"Of Perez's swill? Thanks, but no, thanks."

DeMarco laughed. "Yeah, we all missed Franco this week. Where did that punk learn to make such great coffee?"

"It's the company he keeps."

Quinn's phone buzzed. He checked the screen. "I'd better take this."

"Already gone," DeMarco called as he left the office.

"Quinn speaking."

"Lieutenant, we have a problem—" The voice belonged to Detective Lori Soles. Her tone was all business. "It appears your fiancée flew the coop."

Thirty-two

~~~~~~~~~~~~~~~~~~~~~~~~~~~~~~~~~~~~~~

Quinn sat up in his chair. "Clare's missing?"

"Relax," Lori said. "She left the hospital of her own free will, on her own two feet. But we believe she had some help, and we're about to interview the prime suspects."

"Where?"

"Meet me and my partner at the Village Blend as soon as you can."

Quinn shook his head. *Leave it to the Blend baristas to break out their beloved boss.* Then he tensed. *God, I hope Allegro wasn't part of it. Given Clare's vulnerable state, the last thing she needs is that operator trying to manipulate her.*

"I'll see you in twenty," Quinn said, ending the call.

After clearing his desk and checking on the last of his people still on duty, he grabbed his coat and walked the short distance from the Sixth Precinct station house to the Village Blend.

He was surprised to find the front door locked, and the *closed* sign in the window. But the lights were still on, and Quinn could see people moving around inside. He knocked firmly, and waited. A few moments later, Esther Best practically ripped the door off its hinges.

Instead of the usual genial greeting, she pushed up her

black-framed glasses and regarded Quinn with open suspicion.

"So, Lieutenant. Are you playing the good cop or the bad cop this evening? I hope you're the former, because we have an annoying surplus of the latter."

Quinn raised an eyebrow, and she jerked her thumb in the direction of two female detectives, sitting stone-faced at a table by the blazing hearth.

"Grab a chair, Lieutenant. This won't take long . . ."

Detective Sue Ellen Bass, dressed in a navy blue suit this evening, her dark hair scraped into a ponytail, spoke in the same faux-friendly tone Quinn liked to use himself when starting an interview with a suspect.

Her blond partner, Lori Soles, equally tall and similarly dressed, took a sudden interest in her laptop.

Known in the department as the "Fish Squad," Soles and Bass were liked and respected by their peers. They were usually on friendly terms with Quinn. Tonight, neither detective would meet his eyes, which instantly set off alarms.

As much as he wanted to ask questions and demand answers about his fiancée's whereabouts, Quinn understood that he was on the wrong end of the interview for that.

Keeping his mouth shut, he took a seat at the table.

To his left sat two members of Clare's staff: Dante Silva and Esther Best. To his right sat the shop's venerable owner, Clare's former mother-in-law, Madame Blanche Dreyfus Allegro Dubois, looking as poker-faced as the pair of detectives. There was no one else in the shop that he could see.

Lori cleared her throat. "Okay, let's get started."

Ⴑhirty-three
∿∿∿∿∿∿∿∿∿∿∿∿∿∿∿∿

Lori turned her laptop screen to face the group.

"This is elevator footage shot at the hospital earlier to-day. That shorter woman in the crowd is Clare Cosi. As you can see, she's disguised as a member of the hospital staff."

The herky-jerky footage of a crowded elevator abruptly switched to lobby-camera footage. The woman in scrubs proceeded out the front door, followed closely by someone in a rain poncho, hood up, face down. A graphic circle had to be drawn around Clare and the other person, because the lobby was so crowded that individuals coming and going were not easy to identify.

The next jump was to a traffic-cam view of an intersection, the closest one to the hospital entrance. Quinn watched what he surmised was Clare (aka "woman in scrubs") standing with two other figures (one also in doctor's scrubs, the other drowning in a large rain poncho with the hood up). They were joined by a fourth person (also well camouflaged by a rain poncho).

Because the footage was focused on traffic, the lens so far away, and the figures facing away from the camera, no one's identity was revealed, even when magnified at the end of the video presentation.

The recording ended after the four figures boarded a black

SUV, which proceeded north on the avenue. A different ground-level-camera shot from a few blocks uptown revealed the make, model, and license plate of the fugitive vehicle.

Lori closed the laptop, and Quinn felt the detectives' eyes on him.

"Lieutenant Quinn," Lori began. "What do you know about this?"

"Nothing. I'm just learning about it now."

Lori and Sue Ellen exchanged glances. Lori spoke next.

"We made a note of the time stamp on the camera and checked with the desk sergeant at the Sixth. You weren't in the precinct when this went down."

"I had business at the DA's office."

"Coincidental timing, Lieutenant."

"They'll confirm it." Quinn gave her two names to check with, and she jotted them down.

It was Sue Ellen's turn to look skeptical. "And you know nothing about this?"

Quinn's instinct was to fold his arms, but he fought it, forcing his body language to remain relaxed and open.

"Look, I don't deny I have issues with Clare's treatment. I don't believe she's getting the best medical care, and I'm going to use legal means to change that. There's also the issue of her involvement in an open case."

"You mean the alleged abduction of Annette Brewster?" Lori said.

"Yes. The department sees no value in Clare's testimony, given her state of mind, but she *is* a witness, and I believe she should be in protective custody. That said, I had absolutely nothing to do with her leaving the hospital today."

Quinn could feel some of the tension melt away. He could tell the detectives believed him.

"We'll follow up with the DA's people," Lori muttered. Then she and Sue Ellen both shifted their stares to Madame.

"We also found out something interesting when we interviewed the nurses on Clare's floor," Sue Ellen said. "It seems the staff was *distracted* from their usual duties by a coffee-and-pastry feast provided by the Village Blend."

Thirty-Four

~~~~~~~~~~~~~~~~~~~~~~~~~~~~~~~~~~~~~

DEAD silence filled the shop. Mike held his breath to keep from groaning. Then Lori leaned in for the kill.

"A check of the hospital log has *you three*"—she stabbed her finger at Esther, Dante, and Madame—"along with your colleague Tucker Burton, signed in as visitors."

Madame replied with a polite smile. "There is no designation for 'servers' on the visitor forms. So, we listed ourselves as 'visitors,' even though we weren't permitted to see Clare."

"Why the big spread?" Sue Ellen demanded.

"The coffee and snacks were simply our way of thanking the staff for the thoughtful care they were giving to our shop's manager and master roaster."

Sue Ellen tossed her dark ponytail. "And while the food was being served, Clare Cosi managed to walk out of the hospital in a disguise and hitch a ride with a passing SUV? That's one hell of a coincidence, don't you think?"

"Not at all," Madame sniffed. "Last year, when my friend Jane Belmore had surgery in that very same hospital, we thanked the nurses for her care with a sumptuous spread of coffee and pastries."

"And did this Jane Belmore use the distraction to escape the ward?"

Madame's violet eyes flashed. "Of course not!"

"What about her disguise?" Lori pressed. "Who provided Ms. Cosi with the surgical scrubs and hat?"

Madame blinked innocently. "It's a hospital, Detective. Aren't scrubs part of the milieu? Could she not have grabbed them out of a supply closet or obtained them from a member of the hospital staff?"

Lori fell silent a moment, then turned her focus to Esther and Dante.

"Do either of you know who joined Clare on the sidewalk? Any ideas?"

"Why ask us?" Esther loudly blurted, as if offended by the question. "We were there to serve coffee. How would we have time to help anyone escape? I could barely keep up with demand. Those nurses are fiends for caffeine! And free pastries! You should have seen them gulping our Kona Peaberry and shoveling Pistachio Muffins down their pieholes—"

Quinn bit his cheek to keep from laughing.

"What say you, Junior?" Sue Ellen narrowed her eyes on Dante. "You were at the hospital. What did you do after you were done, and before you reported here for work? That's a couple of hours unaccounted for."

"It's no mystery what I typically do when I'm not pulling espressos. I'm at home painting," Dante said. Then he folded his tattooed arms and stubbornly refused to utter another word.

Though Quinn wanted to stay silent, he knew this crew was in deep. The Fish Squad had placed Madame and her people on the scene. It was only a matter of time before they tightened the snare.

On the other hand, he was willing to bet Lori and Sue Ellen were less interested in slapping cuffs on a couple of baristas than in simply finding Clare Cosi and returning her to the hospital.

Either way, Quinn decided it was time to divert their attention.

"Why not focus on the vehicle?" he suggested. "You traced the SUV's plates, surely?"

"They're fake," Sue Ellen said. "The license number belongs to a retired grade-school teacher in Schenectady. She drives a silver Honda Civic, not a black SUV . . ."

"What about traffic-cam footage?"

"We put in the request," Lori said. "Traffic should have their route traced for us sometime tomorrow."

Sue Ellen nodded. "It's only a matter of time before we catch up to our fugitive."

Madame nodded her encouragement. "With you two on the case, I have no doubt. After all, everyone here wants what's best for our dear Clare."

"Then help us find her," Lori urged. "Whether you like it or not, she is legally in Dr. Lorca's care. In his statement to us, he characterized her condition as *a danger to herself and others*. She must be found and hospitalized."

Madame took a breath and let it out, giving the impression she was trying to decide whether to share a valuable piece of information. Finally, she said—

"I *do* have an idea of what might have occurred."

Quinn didn't doubt it.

Thirty-Five

~~~~~~

"Go on," Sue Ellen said. "We're all ears."

Madame shifted uneasily. "While I feel compelled to tell you, I don't wish to cause trouble for my son."

"Say your piece, Mrs. Dubois. Let us decide if anyone is in trouble."

"I believe it's *possible* that Matteo had something to do with all this. He has plenty of friends around the city, and the globe, for that matter, who are always willing to help him."

"Where is your son now?" Sue Ellen asked, eyes brightening.

Quinn recognized the look—a solid lead was like a shot of caffeine.

Madame's reply was hesitant. "I'm not sure *exactly* where he is at the moment. But . . . if I were you, I'd check his Brooklyn warehouse. It's certainly a good place to hide someone."

Quinn smelled a rat. He knew Madame too well. The members of the Fish Squad were being played. It was obvious to him, but it wasn't his job to straighten them out.

Sue Ellen remained wary. "If you really want us to believe Clare isn't here, then I assume you'll have no objections to our thorough search of these premises?"

"None at all," Madame assured her. "I'll be happy to show you whatever you like."

The two detectives stood up. "Let's go."

Madame led the detectives toward the back staircase, taking them down to the basement. The coffeehouse included a second-floor lounge. The third and fourth floors contained a private duplex apartment, which was where Clare resided. The full tour would take at least twenty minutes.

Quinn sat back and released a breath.

Esther observed him. "So? How do you like being on the hot seat for a change?"

Quinn folded his arms. "It would go down better with a cup of coffee."

Dante immediately stood. "What would you like, Lieutenant? I'll be happy to get it."

"Anything, thanks."

"How about a red-eye? You look as though you could use a shot in the dark."

"I guess I could."

Esther leaned forward, presumably to say something else—

"Don't," Quinn advised. "Don't say anything else to me. Don't say anything else to them." He pointed in the direction of the shop's back stairs.

"But I was only going to tell you—"

"I don't want to hear it. I know it's hard for you, Esther, but for once in your life, just sit there, twiddle your thumbs, and keep your mouth shut."

W̰ʜ̰ɛ̰ɴ̰ Soles and Bass returned, empty-handed (no surprise), they gathered up their laptop and coats. Madame handed them a card with Matt Allegro's warehouse address on it.

"We're going to Brooklyn," Lori announced.

"I'm going with you," Quinn said, rising.

"Oh, no, you're not," Lori returned. "Let us handle this, Lieutenant." Then her eyes scanned the rest of the people at the table. "Can I trust you all not to warn Matteo we're coming?"

Dante nodded.

"I won't tell," Esther said, crossing her heart.

Quinn faced the detectives. "Allegro will get no warning from me. I'd rather Clare were in the hands of Dr. Lorca than her lying, cheating, ex-drug-addict ex-husband. If you catch Allegro with Clare, punch him in the eye for me."

"We'll let you know what we find," Lori promised as Esther unlocked the front door and let them out.

When the distaff detectives were gone, Madame laid a gentle hand on Quinn's shoulder. He turned to find her smiling.

"You played those two very well, Michael."

"Me? You played them like a Stradivarius. Now, stop fiddling around, and tell me what the hell is going on."

Thirty-six

~~~~~~~~~~~~~~~~~~~~~~~~~~~~~~~~~~~~~

"**I** broke Clare out," Madame confessed. "She *wanted* to go. Clare no longer trusted Dr. Lorca for her treatment—and they were depriving her of coffee!"

"Do you know where she is now?"

When Madame nodded, Quinn felt a measure of relief, but only a small one.

"Look, I've got to make a show of leaving the coffeehouse in case Soles and Bass are watching. I'll walk back to the precinct. Then I'll double back. Meet me upstairs."

It didn't take long for Quinn to complete the show.

As he approached the coffeehouse again, he saw that Esther and Dante had reopened for the Friday night crowd. A line was already forming at the espresso bar.

Good. Everything is back to normal.

Quinn moved around the building to the alley. Clare had given him a key to the shop's rear entrance so he could slip in after hours. Once inside, he took the back stairs, two at a time. He had a key to the apartment, as well, but decided to knock.

The door opened immediately.

"Come in, come in!"

Madame waved him into the living room, sat him down on the sofa, and poured him a hot cup of coffee. She had already poured one for herself, and settled into the antique chair near the hearth, where a low fire was burning.

As he drank and sat back, Java and Frothy hurried into the room, happy to see their favorite male human again. While Java rolled around Quinn's big shoes, Frothy jumped up next to him on the sofa to take swipes at his loose tie.

Quinn felt a tug inside him, too, as if Clare should have been here with them, playing with the cats, talking about her day, asking about his.

"I'm glad you did it," he said, snatching his tie back from the determined cat's claws. Frothy looked miffed, until Quinn began making it up to her, rubbing her ears and scratching her chin. Then the purring began and the rolling around—a fluffy white ball, half on his lap.

Madame smiled at the sight of man and cat. "I'm glad we did, too."

"How was it done exactly? Will traffic cameras be able to trace your getaway vehicle?"

"Only as far as New Jersey . . ." She described the license plate switch and vehicle swap once they reached a secluded area, clear of public and private cameras.

"How is Clare? Her mood? Her memories?"

"Her mood is good. Her memories are still blocked, but there is a glimmer of hope. She's responding to sensory stimulation . . ." Madame described their success with a coffee tasting. "She's not sure why she knows things, but she does. Her mind can recall recent knowledge, even though she can't tell you how she gained it."

"That's something." Feeling encouraged, he took another hit of the coffee. Smooth and earthy, bright and balanced, perfectly roasted. It had to be Clare's.

"What about our acute police problem?" he asked.

"You mean those nice lady detectives?"

"I assume you sent them on a wild Allegro chase."

"Yes, of course. When Detectives Soles and Bass get to Brooklyn, my son's warehouse manager is going to reluctantly tell them that his boss mentioned he was heading down to the Village Blend, DC, to see his daughter for the weekend."

"That will buy us time, but not much. Where exactly is Clare? I assume you sent Matt to Washington as a diversion and Clare in the opposite direction. Is she on a train to some friend in New England?"

"No, Michael. Clare is not on a train. And my son is not traveling to DC tonight."

Watching Madame squirm, Quinn took a tense breath. "Don't tell me—"

"They're together," she blurted, pulling the tooth in one hard tug. "At the moment, Clare and Matt are on the road, just the two of them, driving to his ex-wife's house in the Hamptons. He was given the property as part of their divorce settlement."

"I'll need the address," Quinn said, rising so rapidly that Frothy nearly rolled off the sofa.

"Take it easy," Madame said as he gathered up the offended cat and set her gently on the carpet, next to Java, who began licking her *mroowing!* head.

"How can I take it easy? He's alone with her!"

"It was the only way. There's nothing to worry about. The property where they're headed is still listed as owned by Breanne Summour. My son's name is not attached to it, and he left his mobile phone in Brooklyn."

"That's not what worries me."

"I understand. But I fully assumed you would be joining them out there. I'll give you the address, as soon as I'm finished packing Clare's things."

"And how long will that take?" he asked, checking his watch.

"Almost no time at all." She pointed to Clare's large gym bag. "There are clothes, shoes, and toiletries inside. Please take them to her."

"What else is there to pack?"

"Only one thing. Come with me . . ."

ȚHIRȚY-SEVEN

∾◌∾◌∾◌∾◌∾◌∾◌∾◌∾◌∾◌∾◌∾◌∾◌∾

Quinn followed Madame up the carpeted staircase and into the master bedroom. It was Clare's favorite room in the duplex.

Back when Madame managed the Village Blend, she lived in this apartment. Then she married importer Pierre Dubois and moved out, but kept this duplex as a guest residence. Using a bit of Pierre's money, she redecorated the place with (in Clare's words) her "romantic setting" on high.

"It's like a little piece of Paris tucked into a West Village Federal-style walk-up . . ." What Clare loved even more than the French doors, window boxes, marble bath, and antiques were the treasures on the walls.

Throughout the duplex, priceless original paintings, large and small, covered every inch of free space. There were sketches, too, including framed doodles on napkins and scraps of paper—all from artists who'd frequented this landmark coffeehouse.

Most were unknown to Quinn, but a few were names he recognized: Andy Warhol, Basquiat, even Edward Hopper (one of Quinn's favorites), who'd sketched the Village Blend at a café table three floors below.

Given her fine-arts studies, Clare was the perfect curator of this eclectic collection. She not only chose older works to rotate into the public shop, but invited new artists to display—and, like Dante, if they wanted to sell their art to admiring customers, right off the Village Blend's walls, even better.

"I'll just be a moment," Madame promised, moving toward the dresser.

"That's fine," Quinn said, lingering in the doorway.

The hearth was dark tonight, the room drafty. The cold emptiness seemed appropriate without Clare here.

He could almost see her stretched out between her cats on the four-poster bed. She always looked so beautiful sleeping in the firelight. As that haunting image came back to him, so did the memory of the last time they'd made love . . .

"**D**on't panic," Quinn whispered into her soft chestnut hair. "It's only your fiancé—"

He'd been on the job downtown until the wee hours, supervising a coordinated sting operation with the DEA. Using the keys she gave him, he let himself into her apartment. Then he slipped into bed, as he often did when he worked this late.

Brushing aside her hair, he planted kisses on her neck while his strong hands gently caressed her body. She moaned, still groggy, then turned, surprising him by hungrily fastening her mouth to his, uncaring that his five-o'clock stubble sanded her cheeks and chin.

She once said of all the tastes she'd savored and defined in her life, his was still the most powerfully unique. Words failed her in describing the "mysterious sensory chemistry" of his kiss—

"There is nothing like the taste of you, Mike Quinn."

Unlike Clare, he couldn't stop remembering their time together. If her condition didn't change, those sweet memories would become a bitter curse. He'd feel more alone than ever.

"Here it is . . ." Madame moved toward him with a familiar white box.

He knew what was inside. Opening the lid, he lifted out the perfect ice-blue diamond. *"I love the color,"* Clare had told him. *"It reminds me of your eyes, and all the goodness I see there."*

Around the center, a circle of smaller coffee diamonds glowed with warmth, despite the shadowy chill in the room. These little gems, she said, were like all the special people in her life. She said she loved Quinn all the more because he understood and honored the relationships she treasured. *They're part of who I am.*

"The ring is hers, of course," Madame said. "But I don't think you should give it back until she's ready."

Quinn forced the question. "Do you think she'll ever be ready?"

Lifting her wrinkled hand, she touched his cheek. "We have to think so, don't we, Michael? Now, go find the woman you love, and do all you can to bring our Clare back to us."

Thirty-Eight

~~~~~~~~~~~~~~~~~~~~~~~~~~~~~

Clare

THE world around me looked dark, but it smelled like heaven—

Coffee! Oh, coffee!

Eyes closed, I inhaled deeply.

Earthy. Nutty. Sweetly roasted.

"Nice way to wake up, right?" It was Matt's voice.

Opening my eyes, I realized I was still in the getaway van. The air was freezing, my neck was sore, but a hot cup of bliss was *literally* under my nose. Matt was in the driver's seat. His strong hand was holding the cup. After ten years of marriage, he knew what would rouse me—and *arouse* me. (The latter was what worried me.)

I took the cup and thirstily drank.

"How are you feeling?" he asked.

"I had the strangest dream."

"Good dream or bad dream?"

"I'm not sure."

"Was I in it?" he asked.

"No." I rubbed my sore neck. "Where are we? I remember Queens. Then we took the Long Island Expressway. I must have nodded off for a few minutes."

Matt snorted. "More like ninety."

"Sorry."

"It's okay. After all you've been through, you needed the rest."

"And this miraculous coffee? Where did it come from? Don't tell me you bought it at a gas station."

"Close—it's a *converted* one. Look behind us."

I did and saw a brightly lit building a short distance away. "What is that?"

"Hampton Coffee Company. They have a few locations out here. That's the Water Mill store. I'm one of their green bean suppliers. They roast their own, like we do. What do you think?"

"Are you kidding? After the torture of decaf tea and Sanka, it's liquid ecstasy." I drank again. "Are your Ugandan beans in this blend?"

He nodded.

"I *remember* this coffee . . ." I closed my eyes, took another sip. "You helped the tribe get a washing station, right?"

"That's right, Clare. That's good."

When I opened my eyes again, Matt was smiling, white teeth flashing attractively in his dark beard. He started the engine. "We're not far from our destination, but I figured you'd appreciate a cuppa *real* coffee."

"I did, but wait!" I gripped his shoulder. "One's not nearly enough!"

He laughed. "You think I don't know you? I bought two pounds of whole beans. I'll make more at the house."

"How far is it?"

"Ten minutes."

Thirty-nine

∽◎∽◎∽◎∽◎∽◎∽◎∽◎∽◎∽◎∽◎∽◎∽◎∽

Matt smoothly swung the big van around. It was a deft U-turn for the narrow lane, but then his driving always did impress me.

After years of muscling off-road vehicles around the coffee belt's muddy mountains, treacherous rain forests, and edge-of-cliff death roads, a few dark, narrow lanes on Long Island weren't about to faze the guy.

Ahead of us was Montauk Highway. Cars and trucks were zooming in both directions. With no stoplight to slow traffic, it looked intimidating to me, but Matt easily got us across and onto a road called Deerfield.

This was another lonely stretch, lined with trees and open land. The occasional high row of groomed bushes indicated estate property, and then came the thick trees again.

"This rural run is giving me the creeps," I said. "Whoa!"

A Lamborghini with high beams nearly blinded us as it flew by.

"Idiot," Matt muttered.

There were no streetlights along these two narrow lanes, just a yellow line to follow. Matt had to switch to high beams to illuminate the dark turns—but at least *he* clicked them off when another car appeared!

I gripped my cup for caffeine courage. "Given the wealthy set's penchant for parties, alcohol, and fast cars, I'm guessing there are a lot of accidents on these Hamptons roads during the summer season."

"Yes. Lots."

"It's not uncommon, then," I said. "The way Annette Brewster's husband died out here, in an auto accident."

Matt gave me a funny glance. "Is that something my mother told you? I mean, about Harlan Brewster?"

"She did mention that Annette's husband was dead."

"Did she tell you how he died?"

"No, Madame didn't. I just know."

"Concentrate. Try to remember. How did you learn that? Who told you?"

I closed my eyes, shutting out the van's headlights while I sipped more coffee. A female voice came back to me, but it wasn't Madame's. It was Annette's. I recognized the voice as Annette Brewster's!

"Matt, I can't tell you *when* she told me, or even what she looked like at the time, but I can hear Annette's voice. I know it's her!"

"That's good, Clare. Keep going." Matt noticed my eyes were shut. "Do you see *anything*?"

"Just a table covered in white linen."

"Sounds like the cake tasting on the night you disappeared. Don't stop. What else do you remember about your conversation with Annette?"

"Coffee," I said, eyes open again. "We talked about her hotel's coffee. I wouldn't call it swill or mud or anything. I mean, it was *drinkable*, but a place like the Parkview Palace should be offering guests something of much higher quality. Something like this . . ."

I lifted the excellent Hampton blend and paused to enjoy more of it.

"What else did you discuss? I'm betting you pitched Annette on our Village Blend coffee, right?"

"Yes, I did—" Another car came rocketing toward us,

high beams bleaching the dark road in a flash of blinding white. Matt cursed and I tensed, holding my breath until it zoomed past.

"Sorry. Go on," Matt coaxed. "Did your pitch work? Was she interested in switching coffee suppliers?"

"Yes and no."

"I don't understand."

"Annette said her husband, Harlan, insisted they use Driftwood Coffee because the execs of the national chain spent a fortune at the Parkview—corporate meetings, suites as perks for franchisees, that sort of thing. Harlan reciprocated with an exclusive contract for their product."

"So, Annette planned to continue honoring that relationship?"

"No. She said *everything* changed with Harlan *finally gone*—and she emphasized those words, as if she were happy about it. She said, if it were up to her, she would dump Driftwood, but she wasn't in a position to make any deals."

"But she's the owner," Matt said, puzzled.

"She said I should talk to the *new owner* of the Parkview. She encouraged me to make a pitch when the time came. She thought the Village Blend could easily get the contract."

"New owner? Are you telling me Annette was planning to *sell* the Parkview?"

"Yes."

"Are you sure, Clare? Nothing like that has been in the news. My mother never mentioned it."

"I'm sure."

"Then who's buying Annette's hotel?"

"I don't know. She wouldn't tell me. She said it was too risky to reveal the details of the deal, and she swore me to secrecy."

Matt went silent a moment. "She said the word *risky*?"

"Yes."

"And it was after your conversation that she was abducted. Can you remember *anything* about the crime? Concentrate, think."

I tried once more, but there was no anchor, nothing to

guide my mind, and I felt myself falling into the now-familiar shadowy wooziness that preceded a blackout. I immediately opened my eyes.

"I'm sorry. I don't remember," I said, staring at the road.

"We know it happened. The cops have the picture of Annette and you and a ski-masked goon with a gun."

"So everyone keeps telling me. But I don't recall it—though I did *dream* about a man with a gun."

"When?"

"When I fell asleep here in the van."

Matt sat up straighter behind the wheel. "Clare, this could be it. Your dream could be the breakthrough you need."

"You think so?"

"You just shared a recent memory of Annette."

"That's true."

"Tell me about this man with a gun. Describe him . . ."

I took a breath, closed my eyes.

"He's tall and broad-shouldered, but I can't see his face."

"Because he's wearing a mask?"

"No. I can't see his face because it's deep in shadow."

"What's he wearing?"

"A blue suit. In my dream, when he took off his jacket, I saw his gun. It was in a leather shoulder holster, strapped across his white dress shirt. The man was walking along a city sidewalk. He turned a corner and suddenly he was in the woods, looking for me among the dark trees. He called my name over and over. His voice was so sad. He kept begging me to answer him. I wanted to cry out . . . but I couldn't."

I opened my eyes. "That's it. What do you think?"

Matt sat in silence, gaze fixed on the road.

"I know it's an odd dream." I chewed my lip. "Do you have any idea who that man might be?"

"No, Clare. No idea."

Forty

~~~~~~

Mike

"So, does she remember you yet?" Sergeant Franco asked.

Quinn barely heard the question. The gas station's pay phone was pressed to his ear, but it did little to drown out the rumble of the highway traffic. As he leaned against the warm hood of his car, the wind from a passing semi buffeted him.

"I just told you. Clare has fled the hospital. She's a fugitive."

"Yeah, and I naturally assumed *you* had something to do with that."

"So did the Fish Squad," Quinn responded, "until they moved on to more likely suspects."

"More likely suspects?" Franco said. "That must mean Madame Dubois and her merry band of baristas—with some larcenous help from Joy's father, I assume." He paused. "Is Clare with them now?"

Through gritted teeth, Quinn answered, "Not *all* of them."

"I take it from your constipated reply that your fiancée is alone with her ex-husband."

"You always were a smart detective, Franco."

"I also take it that you're about to get between them—"

"As fast as possible."

"So, what do you want from me, boss?"

"Two things. First, I want you to break the news to Joy about her mother's hospital escape. Tell her there's no reason to be alarmed. Clare is safe, and Joy will see her soon. If she wants to help her mother, she should not come to New York. Tell her to remain in DC, and act like she knows nothing about Clare's hospital breakout."

"Why do we even have to tell Joy?"

"She'll find out. The Fish Squad has been led to believe that Joy's father is driving Clare to Washington. Soles and Bass won't take the time to travel down there. They'll reach out to locals to search the Village Blend's DC shop and Joy's residence. Tell Joy to demand a warrant. That will stall them. Then get out of their way. They're obviously going to come up empty."

"Okay," Franco replied. "And you don't have to worry about Joy coming back to Manhattan. She's up to her neck in work. Plus she's got me here to keep her warm—"

"Not anymore. Sorry, pal. That's my second favor. I have comp time coming to me, and I may need to take it. That means I want you back on the job on Monday to run the shop."

"Will do, *jefe*. No worries." Despite his words, Franco *sounded* worried. "I assume you can't tell me where you are, or where you're going?"

"The less you know, the better. I don't want you giving false statements to the DC badges. Avoid the situation completely, if you can, and leave Washington before they get to Joy."

"I'd rather stick around to make sure things go smoothly."

"That's your call."

"Don't worry. I'll keep my lips zipped."

"And I'll be back at the Sixth as soon as I can." Quinn popped the thermos sitting on the hood of his car and poured the last dregs of the Village Blend coffee into his travel cup. The parting gift came from Madame. Now he wished he had more.

"Any instructions for the team?"

"No, we're good. Next week should be a quiet one. And you know the job well enough. But if you—or any of our people—need me, then text or call. I'll get right back to you."

"You mean you're keeping your mobile with you?"

"Yes."

"They can track you, you know?"

"Of course. I have a plan."

"Fine. Just tell me what to do next week if *other people* start looking for you," Franco said. "And by other people, you know I mean the Fish Squad."

"Soles and Bass can contact me anytime. I'll be happy to talk with them. But this is the last time you and I will speak openly about Clare. I'm at a pay phone. In the future, I'll be using my mobile—and any discussions will have to be strictly work related. Got it?"

"Got it."

"One last thing. Once you know the DC badges have come and gone—empty-handed—I want you to text me."

"In code, I assume."

"That's right. Tell me *your friends have left*. And if you need to refer to Clare, she's *your cousin*, okay?"

"Okay, and, Mike—"

"Yeah, Manny?"

"I really hope you win her back. I was just warming to the idea that we might be in-laws someday."

Quinn nearly dropped his cup. "It ain't over till it's over."

Franco laughed. "I never really understood that saying."

"It means I'm not giving up on the woman I love. If her memories of me don't come back, I'll be doing whatever I can to get history to repeat."

"Good luck with that, brother. I don't envy you."

"I don't, either. But thanks, just the same. Right now the odds aren't in my favor, and I can use all the luck I can get."

Forty-one

~~~~~~~~~~~~~~~~~~~~~~~~~~~~~~~~~~~

Clare

THE road was dark, and Matt had gone quiet. I almost nodded off again until he slapped the steering wheel and cursed in a foreign language. I *think* it was Portuguese.

"What's wrong?" I asked.

"I went too far." He pointed at a lighted sign, dead ahead.

"Deerfield Farm?"

"That's my landmark. When I see the farm's sign, I know I've missed the turn."

He swung the van around again. This time his U-turn wasn't as deft as before. He nearly smashed the front bumper into a tree. Cursing again, he straightened us out and hit the gas.

Ever since I told him my dream, about the man with the gun, his mood had gone south.

"Is something bothering you?"

"No."

"Are you *hangry*?"

"Change the subject."

"Okay, then, what do they grow at Deerfield Farm? Do they have a farm stand? I could eat."

"It's a horse farm, Clare—stables, training, riding lessons. It's one reason why my ex-wife bought the house at this location."

"She was an equestrian?"

"No. I don't think she even liked animals. The CEO where she worked played polo out here, and she wanted to fit in with his horsey set."

"By learning to play polo?"

"Learning enough to talk the talk. You know, understand what the hell the boss and his trophy wife were babbling about at cocktail parties when dressage and forelocks entered the conversation."

Matt slowed the van to make the correct turn. As he did, the headlights flashed across a dark green street sign: Edge of Woods Road was aptly named. Other than the pitch-black path in front of us, I saw nothing but trees and more trees.

"Aren't there any houses around here?"

"Are you kidding? These woods are filled with them. Expensive ones with pools, Jacuzzis, and tennis courts."

"Where are they?"

"Behind the timber. You don't think wealthy people want the unwashed general public gawking at their properties, do you?"

"Some do."

"These don't."

I drained the last of my coffee and studied Matt's profile, trying to reconcile my memories of the man I'd married with this Hamptons dweller.

"I don't get it," I said.

"Get what?"

"The Matteo Allegro I remember was more at home in a tent or a tribal village than in a tax shelter. What are you doing with the horsey and Lambo set? It must have been this new wife of yours—"

"Ex-wife."

"You must have fallen hard for her."

"I wouldn't put it that way."

"How would you put it, then?"

He shrugged. "Bree liked to travel as much as I do. The money made things nice, and she had a lot of it."

"Was this Bree person an heiress? Or a fashion model or something? Would I recognize her name?"

Matt hesitated. "Breanne Summour is her name, and she was—"

"The famous magazine editor?!"

Matt nodded. "We weren't married very long."

I shook my head. "I'm glad I wasn't there."

"But you were. You catered our wedding at the Metropolitan Museum of Art. You did an amazing job, too. You don't remember anything about that?"

"Not a thing."

"The truth is, Clare, if it wasn't for you, Bree and I might not have gotten married at all."

Once again, I doubted my sanity. Only this time I was wondering about my state of mind before I had lost my memory. Had I been completely mad, catering Matt's high-society wedding? Was this amnesia an improvement?

"All I remember about Breanne Summour is that I was freelance writing in New Jersey, to make ends meet. Most of my work was for trade magazines and local papers. At one point, I decided to take a chance on myself and submit a piece to a national publication. The first place I pitched was Breanne's magazine. Did I ever tell you that?"

"No."

"It was a great little article on trends in U.S. coffee consumption. The *New York Times Magazine* ended up publishing it. But she rejected it, and she was pretty nasty about it."

"Join the club. Breanne rejected me, too, *and* she was pretty nasty about it."

"Why in the world did you think marrying her was a good idea?"

"At the time, I figured I could use the support. Not just financially." He slowed the van and made another turn. "Do you really want to know?"

"I'm listening."

FORTY-TWO

~~~~~~

"**AFTER** you and I split, Clare, I thought I'd feel free, unburdened."

"That's certainly the way you acted, relieved to be rid of us."

"That's not true! I always loved you and Joy, and I never stopped. It was the obligation of being a husband and parent—all those expectations put on me—that I was relieved to be free of."

"Matt, that's what it *means* to be in a relationship! You have to be willing to compromise. Accept expectations from people who love you—"

"Stop. I know that now. *Listen.* Will you just listen? It didn't take long before I realized what I'd done. I no longer had you and Joy to come home to. Whenever I came back from my sourcing trips, I started to feel lost. And, well, lonely. The kind of lonely that no amount of partying or traveling can fix . . ."

He glanced at me. "I tried, many times, to rekindle what you felt for me, but—" He looked away. "It was ruined. I ruined it. And I've been living with that regret ever since."

My ex-husband's quiet words were moving. I knew he was sincere, but he wasn't telling me anything I didn't already know. In many ways, Matteo Allegro was a good man. He just wasn't the kind of man who should be married. That was why I was shocked to hear he'd tried it again, and I told him so.

"Like I said, Clare, I wanted someone to come back to, a place to hang my Akubra. You made it clear that you wanted to move on. And when I met Bree, she and I worked as a couple. For a while, anyway."

"Were you unfaithful to her? Like you were with me?"

"She agreed to an open marriage."

"I see. And how did that work exactly?"

"We had an understanding. My . . . uh . . . extracurricular activities could only take place outside of the country—and never close to anyone she knew. As long as I was back in New York when she needed me as an escort to parties or formal functions or whatever, she was happy. The way she put it to me was that she'd reached an age where having a spouse was an asset in her social and professional circles. It looked good for her stability and squelched unwanted gossip."

"I don't believe it."

"What?"

"You were a trophy husband!"

"You know, Clare, that is incredibly insulting, and I'd argue the point, but—" He shrugged. "I guess I was."

"I'm sorry. I'm not trying to insult you."

"I know you're not. In all honesty, I did complete Bree's checklist: good in bed; expert travel companion; dressed up nice for parties; cool profession—even if it didn't earn me the kind of bank the top dogs here throw around. That fact never did sit well with her."

"So you served a purpose for each other."

"We did."

"Then what went wrong?"

"We had fun. And then we didn't."

"Deep."

Matt smirked. "Are you mocking me?"

"Yes."

"Good. That's more like the old you than the older you—if you know what I mean."

"I do."

"And?" He gave me a sidelong look. "Are you feeling any differently toward me?"

"Yes. I admit I am. But only because of your honesty. You really have matured, Matt. I can see that. Unfortunately, I still feel like I belong in New Jersey, that Joy is waiting for me to cook her dinner, and I'm behind schedule on writing my column."

"Your column? Oh, you mean the In the Kitchen with Clare thing?"

"That's right."

"You actually haven't written that in years. And the paper you wrote for went out of business."

Great. I glanced out the window, but there was nothing to distract me from my own anxious feelings of disappointment and displacement. Not in this dismal darkness.

"Should I find another oldies station?" I asked.

"No need."

After making one last turn, Matt slowed the van.

The tree line was so dense here that I couldn't see beyond it. Finally, a narrow gap appeared between two thick trunks. Matt hit the brakes, and steered us into that dark gap.

"Is this it?" I asked. "Are we there?"

He answered me with an enigmatic smile. "Almost."

FORTY-THREE
❧❧❧❧❧❧❧❧❧❧❧❧❧❧❧❧❧❧

THICK woods crowded us on either side as we rolled down a long black driveway. Then the van's high beams illuminated a clearing. The bright light unattractively blanched the manicured grounds. Finally I saw the house.

On this cloud-covered night, the moonlight was muted, shrouding the three-story structure in shadow. Looming large, its dark silhouette looked less than inviting. I said as much.

"It's a beautiful property," Matt assured me. "With the landscape lighting off, you can't tell. But when no one's here, the darkness makes it invisible from the road."

"Do you have a security system in place?"

"Of course." He pointed to his prepaid phone on the dashboard. "I control it through an app." At my obvious confusion, he added, "An application on the smartphone."

"If you say so."

"Don't worry, Clare. You'll be comfortable here—once we get the lights *and* the coffee on." His white grin flashed in the dark. "Let's go."

AFTER parking the van, he tossed me the two bags of whole-bean coffee and unlocked the house. The night air was cold. Shivering on the porch, I couldn't wait to hurry inside.

When the interior lights came up, I stepped back, surprised by the main room. Matt called it a "great room," which was an accurate description—if only in sheer size.

The open layout boasted a three-story ceiling, soaring up to reveal gallery-style floors at the second and third levels. Their open hallways were guarded with polished wooden railings.

"Impressive, right? You'll love it in the morning. There's so much light . . ."

He strode across the great room's floor, skirting the cream-colored sofa to activate the sleek gas fireplace. Flames leaped up, adding a sudden burst of color to the otherwise stark white space—but almost no warmth. And, man, was it cold in here!

"Your walls are so naked," I said, looking up.

"Bree took the artwork. I'll find other stuff. Maybe you can help with that?"

"I don't know . . ." I shook my head, considering the emptiness. There certainly was a lot of it.

"The kitchen is at the other end." He pointed to where a freestanding marble bar served as a divider. "You've got Viking appliances in there and a breakfast nook farther back."

He turned again and swept his hand across the line of French doors. "As you can see, there's a large deck that extends this living area, and a heated pool farther out in the yard. It's closed for the winter, but feel free to make use of the sunken hot tub. It's right there on the deck."

I nodded and looked up again, straining my neck to find the top of the cathedral ceiling. "How many bedrooms are up there?"

"Six, along with a study, and a master bedroom suite with its own luxury bath, fireplace, and private deck."

"Nice."

"You take the master suite on the second floor. I'll sack out in the room next to it."

"No, you should have the master bedroom."

"You're my guest. I insist. I want you to be comfortable."

"In this place, I don't see how I can't be." I brought the two bags of coffee into the kitchen, checked the giant fridge, and revised my statement.

"Matt, there's *nothing* inside!"

"I know—" Leaning one jean-clad hip against the counter, he studied my face. "It's been empty a long time, Clare. And I'm hungry, too."

I got the impression my ex-husband was talking about more than food. When he spoke again, I heard hope in his voice.

"Now that you're here, maybe we can fix that. What do you think?"

I took a moment to choose my words carefully. "I think I don't know you. Not the you that gives tours of his Hamptons McMansion. I also think I'm not myself, and we should give this—whatever *this* is—some time." I pointed to the bags of Hampton beans on the counter. "I'm willing to start with coffee."

"For you and me, that was always a good place to start." He smiled. "Okay."

"And a shower. I could *really* use a nice, hot shower."

"Alone, right? Just kidding."

Forty-four

꘎꘎꘎꘎꘎꘎꘎꘎꘎꘎꘎꘎꘎꘎꘎꘎꘎꘎

If I were going to sketch a picture of my mind, I decided it would look like the walls in this pretentious summer house. Stark white paint covered with frame lines, faint markings where pictures once hung.

My memories were haunted by ghosted works, too, frames with nothing inside. Something had been there once. I knew it. But I couldn't see it.

With resolve, I counted my blessings instead. People in my life sincerely cared about me, including (as hard as it was to believe) my ex-husband. He seemed to have faith that my memories would return.

I had to admit, if my memory block was a waiting game, this house—even as vacant and hollow as it felt—made a vast improvement over that hospital room.

After my shower request, Matt took me up to the second floor, and showed me the master bedroom suite. The walls were as bare as the great room, but the king bed looked comfortable.

He turned on the bedroom's gas fireplace, which made the large space seem a little cozier, and the bathroom was practically a mini spa with a teak floor, a walk-in shower/steam bath, and an odd, bucket-shaped bathtub made of hammered copper that Matt called a "Japanese soaking tub"—the name was to be taken literally. You weren't supposed to bathe in it. You entered after showering yourself clean, and then you simply soaked.

"It's very relaxing," Matt promised.

"I'll try it tomorrow," I said.

Tonight, I didn't want to be on my own. I wanted to shower quickly and learn more about my life. That was why I'd left the lonely hospital, to find connections—and coffee, which Matt went downstairs to make.

After my steamy "simulated rain" shower, I wrapped a bath sheet around me and blew my hair dry.

"I have something for you!"

Matt's voice came from the next room—the bedroom. I tensed. *What is he doing back up here in the bedroom?!*

After a few minutes of silence, I peeked out of the master bath. Matt was gone. But he had left a few things behind. Laid out on the bed were a fluffy white terry-cloth robe; a pair of his sweatpants; one of his T-shirts; and a pair of his boot socks. He had also left a mug of freshly brewed coffee on the dresser. I picked up the mug and inhaled the rich, earthy warmth.

Ahhh . . . It smelled like ambrosia. I drank deeply and immediately felt more grounded.

A few minutes later, I was dressed in Matt's comfy clothes, including the oversized tee, the thick socks on my feet, and the robe, which I'd wrapped tightly to keep me warm in this big, chilly house.

"Hey!" he called enthusiastically from the kitchen. "Feel any better?"

"Yeah. But the house is still cold."

"I know. The great room is great for summer. Not so much in fall and winter. Give it time. You'll warm up."

"Are you cooking?" I asked, even though it was obvious. Matt's hoodie was off, his shirtsleeves were rolled up, and there were pots and pans on the stove.

He shrugged. "You said you were hungry."

"Yes, but what could you possibly be making? Stone soup? Your fridge was bare."

"But not the cupboards."

Walking into the kitchen, I peered into the deep pot. A full pound of dried spaghetti was boiling in a small sea of salt water.

On the burner next to it, Matt was warming a skillet. Sipping my coffee, I leaned against the center island and watched him pour in generous glugs of olive oil, then use his cupped palm to add spices to the pan: garlic powder, rosemary, basil, oregano, and freshly ground black pepper.

"I know what you're making," I said.

"You remember?"

"*Cacio e Matteo,* right?"

It was Matt's version of *Cacio e Pepe,* a popular Roman pasta dish. Literally it translates to "cheese and pepper," and the ingredients were just that: Pecorino Romano cheese and ground or crushed black pepper, along with the pasta, of course.

When doing it the Roman way, I'd use the hot, starchy water from the pasta pot to help melt the grated cheese. Together they magically conjured a kind of quick sauce, right in the bowl.

My grandmother taught me the tricky maneuver, but Matt could never manage it. After we split, he tried to make the dish on his own, but instead of a smooth sauce adhering to the pasta strands, he only created a gloppy mess. His solution was to throw out the traditional version and improvise his own. This included a number of other ingredients that, once I tasted them, I happily approved of—and Joy announced she preferred.

"Wasn't it Joy who christened the dish *Cacio e Matteo*?" I asked.

"Yes, she did—about a year *after* our fried chicken peace talks. You still remember that, right?"

"Yes, Chef Sherlock remembers."

"Then you're retaining the recovered memories. Good, Clare. We have to keep it up."

"Fine. But first, let's eat."

FORTY-FIVE

∾∾∾∾ ∾ ∾ ∾ ∾ ∾ ∾ ∾ ∾ ∾ ∾ ∾

Matt told me where to grab the plates and silverware, and I set up everything on the marble-topped bar dividing the kitchen from the great room. Then I settled myself into a cushioned bar chair, propped my elbows, and became slightly hypnotized watching Matt finish his *Cacio.*

"I'm impressed," I told him after my first bite.

After stirring in the flavor-infused olive oil, he'd tossed the spaghetti with a patience that surprised me. Then he added the cheese, taking the time to coat all the strands.

"Where did you get the Pecorino? Your fridge was empty."

"After Bree cleared out her things, I found a huge hunk of it left in there. I couldn't bear to toss it, so I grated and froze it."

"You really perfected this dish."

"Red pepper flakes are my new add-in." He sprinkled some over his serving.

"I'm game." I reached for the jar.

He pulled it back. "I'd rather you eat the version I used to make for you and Joy. It might help with your memories."

I didn't argue; the food was too good to waste time doing that. Then we both tucked in, putting conversation on hold as we entered a bilateral food trance.

"I really miss her," I said when my trance finally lifted.

"I know how you feel."

"No, you don't. It's a disturbing state of mind, not to know your own daughter."

"So nothing more is coming back to you? Nothing at all?"

"Like what?"

"Close your eyes," Matt suggested. "Tell me—I don't know—about the last strong memory you see of Joy."

"You and I shared fried chicken with her at a park near my New Jersey home. Then we took her to the shore."

"What's Joy's age in your mind's eye?"

"Thirteen." I opened my real eyes. "Why can't I remember more?"

Matt appeared confounded. "In the van, we were able to progress your memories forward with guided sensory stimulation. Then, when you drank the Hampton Company coffee, you remembered a conversation with Annette Brewster—but nothing else about your life."

"Why don't you just *tell me* more about Joy? Despite whatever I apparently know about this crime I witnessed, it's my own daughter I'm desperate to learn more about. Do you have any pictures of her?"

"Of course I do, but I think it would be better if we tried to coax your own memories to come back naturally, like we did with the fried chicken."

"What do you suggest? A Big Mac? How about a Dunkin' Donut?"

"Calm down."

"Just show me one picture! What can it hurt?"

He scratched his dark beard. "I don't know."

"You won't be shocking me, Matt. She rushed into my hospital room, remember? I've already seen her as she is now, all grown-up. Just show me a photo of a happy memory. Maybe it will jar mine. *Please?*"

With a resigned sigh, Matt brought out his prepaid smartphone.

"I transferred some stuff from my regular phone. I should have something for you . . . Okay, here's one . . ."

He turned the phone screen toward me. Joy's pretty face was beaming into the camera, her chestnut hair pulled into a neat ponytail. She was holding a half-sheet pan of freshly baked croissants and wearing a chef's jacket.

"Matt, why is she in chef's whites?"

"This is a picture of Joy when she was in culinary school."

"In Manhattan?"

He nodded, naming the prestigious school.

"Oh, my goodness, I'm so happy for her! Did she graduate with honors?"

Matt looked away. "I'd rather not tell you. I'd prefer you remember what happened during those years."

"Oh, no. Was it something bad?"

"Focus on the photo. Try to remember."

"Nothing's coming."

"All right. I have another idea. I'd like you to trust me on this, okay? I want to give you some physical stimulation."

"Physical?" I blinked. "What are you proposing?"

"I want to make love to you."

FORTY-SIX

~~~~~~

I stared blankly at my ex-husband. When we were parked in Queens, he had said something about sleeping together, but I didn't think he was serious! Now he leaned closer.

"You know how good it is with me, Clare. Think of it as a kind of medicine."

"Let me get this straight. You want to have sex with me for *medicinal* purposes?"

"Me? No. I want to *make love to you* because I miss you. Because I want to be close to you. Because I want to hear you cry out with pleasure, like you used to with me, all night long."

"Matt—"

"You, however, should let me make love to you because you'll enjoy it. It's the ultimate sensory stimulation, and it may bring back more of your memories."

"You mean, all the years I missed seeing my daughter grow up?"

"You didn't *miss* them, Clare. You simply can't remember them. You were there for Joy, every step of her journey to adulthood. You were a wonderful mother, and your daughter loves you like crazy."

"She does?"

"Of course she does!"

I wanted to cry. "You don't know what a relief that is to hear."

I rubbed my eyes and then my neck. It had been a very long day and my back was still sore from that nap in the van.

"Here, let me—"

Matt gently swiveled my bar chair around and placed his warm hands on my shoulders.

"Your muscles are tight. Try to relax. Close your eyes . . ."

At this point, my knots had knots, but Matt's strong fingers were as patient in massaging me as they were in tossing his *Cacio*. Slowly, tenderly, he worked on releasing the stress in my molecules. There could be no objecting; it was too delicious—and I felt my resistance weakening.

"Just answer me this," I murmured, letting my head loll from side to side. "How would sleeping with you help me remember the lost years with my daughter?"

"The last time we made love wasn't that long ago. It happened when Joy was still in culinary school in Manhattan."

"Go on."

"You and I were alone together in the duplex, above the Village Blend. You called her mobile phone for some reason and a drunk boy answered—total asshole. He was at some club and implied that Joy had gone off with her girlfriends to a restroom to do drugs—"

"Drugs!"

"Take it easy. Before the night was over, our daughter was back in her apartment, safe and sound, and she called you to assure us that everything was fine. But until that call, you and I were pretty upset."

"And after she called?"

"To say we were relieved is an understatement. We were together in a foxhole that night, terrified and tense—and then everything was fine again. It was late; our guards were down. You said something that made me laugh, and before we knew it, we were . . ."

Matt's mouth kept moving but he was no longer talking. Sweeping my hair aside, he pressed his warm lips against my neck. Then he was caressing my jawline, my cheek. Finally, he turned the chair.

The kiss was deep and sweet. I did my best to relax into it. When I lifted my arms to embrace his hard shoulders, he whispered—

"Let's go upstairs."

My body was certainly amenable to Matt's suggestion. My limbs and lips would have followed the man to any bedroom in this ridiculous house. But something deep inside me resisted.

"What is it?" he asked as I broke away.

"I don't think we should be doing this. It doesn't feel right."

"Okay . . ." He pressed his forehead against mine. "You've had a long day. I understand."

"I do want my memories back," I assured him. "And your sensory approach did work before. But making love is a big step. Maybe we can try again tomorrow?"

"Whenever you're ready. We have total privacy up here, and all the time in the world."

I sat back. "But that's not really true, is it?"

"What part?"

"The time part. You said I was there for Joy when she was growing up, and I hope to God I was. But I need to *keep* being there for her. How can I let her go through a wedding without her mother?"

"What?"

"How must she feel? Getting ready to celebrate one of the most memorable days of her life and having a mother who doesn't remember her aging beyond Girl Scouts and middle school."

"Clare, you're mistaken."

"No, I'm not. Everyone is trying to keep me from knowing, but it's obvious she's getting married."

"Married? To that shaved-headed mook she's seeing? Oh, hell no. Over my dead body. You're wrong. They are *not* engaged."

"I don't know about any mook. I know that I was tasting

wedding cakes at the Parkview. No one seems to want me to know the truth. But it had to be for Joy's wedding. Nothing else makes sense."

"Listen to me. The cake tasting wasn't for Joy. It was for—"

Matt stopped so short, I thought he had choked on his own tongue.

I waited for him to finish, but his incomplete sentence stayed that way. Even after his strangled words echoed through all three stories of this great room's ceiling.

"Well?" I said at last. "Who was the tasting for? Who is getting married?"

Matt's abrupt silence continued, but his expression was communicating plenty. He looked more than disturbed. He looked downright guilty. And I made the obvious assumption—

"Are you telling me, before the print was dry on your second divorce, you and I were planning to get *remarried*?!"

"God, no. It wasn't *me* you were planning to marry."

I blinked. "So you're saying I was tasting cakes for my wedding? My own wedding?" Matt's deep frown seemed to confirm it, but I had to hear the words. "Answer me!"

"Okay, yes!" He put his hands up, as if he'd been unfairly backed into a corner. "You were selecting a cake for your own wedding because you're the one who's engaged to be married. And the man you're engaged to isn't me."

My jaw went slack. Then my mind began to (for lack of a better word) race. Like me and Matt on the scary roads that led to this hollow Hamptons hideaway, my thoughts couldn't see a place to turn. Or maybe they simply didn't want to arrive at a disturbingly inevitable address.

Finally, after what felt like hours, though it was more like seconds, I gathered the courage to ask what had to be answered—

"If you're not my impending groom, then who is he? And *where* is he?"

FORTY-SEVEN

~~~~~~

MIKE

"FILL the thermos, would you?"

"Of course, sir."

After years of drinking Clare's blissful brews, Mike never thought he'd find a coffee shop as good as the Village Blend, but he'd been driving for nearly ninety minutes since his last stop, and he needed a break.

Like a caffeinated beacon, the bright glass windows of the Hampton Coffee Company beckoned him off Montauk Highway. Skeptical of the quality, he ordered a small take-out cup of their Water Mill blend. Why not? It was the name of this location. After a few beautiful sips, he went right back to his car to retrieve the empty Village Blend thermos.

After paying the bill, Mike hit the restroom, and headed back out to the parking lot. It felt good to stretch his legs. The cold air felt good, too, bracing him awake. Frigid and fresh, it smelled faintly of saltwater. No surprise, given the roiling Atlantic was less than ten minutes south, the placid bay nearly as close in the other direction.

Nice address, Allegro . . .

Mike knew many of the residential properties around the South Fork were worth millions. Clare's ex-husband had done well for himself with his coffee importing and trading, but not *this* well. Sure, the guy had recently inherited some money, but it was his talent with the ladies that got him this address.

As Mike drank the coffee, he mused about the punch in the nose Allegro would give him if he recited that truth to his face—

"What you did, Allegro, was remarry and divorce well."

With a resigned sigh, Mike checked his mobile.

No texts, no messages. Thank goodness.

The DC badges weren't likely to follow up with Joy until business hours tomorrow. In the meantime, he would locate Clare tonight, and try to make some sense of this bizarre situation.

Mike had great affection for Clare's Village Blend family, especially Madame Dubois, but he couldn't stop mentally smacking himself in the forehead over their conduct.

What the hell were they thinking? Breaking her out of that hospital, like the Scooby-Doo gang. And here I am, playing right into it . . .

What else could he do? He couldn't let Soles and Bass apprehend her like some criminal. They'd just drag her back to Lorca. He'd rather take his chances on keeping her free. With a little luck, they could dodge the badges long enough to crack her blocked memories—and the Annette Brewster case.

Mike drained the paper cup and headed for his car. The streets around here were darker than an MTA subbasement. Most of these houses wouldn't be marked or even visible from the road. He'd have to rely on his GPS to locate Allegro's lair—and that's exactly what it was.

For years, Clare's ex-husband had tried to get her back. It was no secret how much he wanted her. How could he resist this attempt to manipulate her back into his bed—or, God forbid, his life?

Well, buddy, not without a fight.

Mike slammed the car door and started the engine. He might make some wrong turns and U-turns, but he was determined to take his own turn at fixing this mess and winning Clare back.

Forty-eight

~~~~~~~~~~~~~~~~~~~~~~~~~~~~~~~~~

Clare

Days ago, I woke up on a cold park bench, asking myself how I'd gotten there. Tonight, I was asking myself the same question. Only this time I was sitting in a great white room with a ceiling as high as a wedding chapel and an ex-husband as sullenly silent as a corpse staring at his own grave.

How I arrived at this Hamptons address was no mystery. What I needed to know—what I was desperate to know—was how I'd gotten to *this place in my life*?

I was engaged to be married, and this was *news* to me.

Dozens of questions were flooding my brain—

Where had I met my alleged fiancé?

How long had we been together?

What made us fall in love?

And what could possibly have possessed me to say *yes* to another wedding in this lifetime? Was I deluding myself, making another stupid mistake? It seemed I was. After all, where the heck was this guy?

What kind of man would allow his fiancée to be spirited away by Matteo Allegro for a weekend in the Hamptons?

And what did that say about this person's affection for me, not to mention his intelligence quotient? Was I engaged to a gullible idiot?

The biggest question in my mind, however, the one looming largest (and scariest), was the one I'd already asked my uncooperative ex-husband—

"If you're not my impending groom, then who is?"

After a full minute of caustic silence, Matt finally said: "If you can't remember on your own, Clare, I'm not going to tell you."

I stared at Matt in a kind of low-level shock. "Have we entered another dimension? Don't you understand? As long as I'm betrothed to a man I can't remember, I'm effectively engaged to a complete stranger."

"Then maybe you shouldn't be engaged to him."

I blinked. "Did you actually *say* that? How could you be so presumptive? So arrogant!" I sprang off my chair. "I knew I shouldn't have agreed to come out here with you. I knew it!"

Pacing the great room, I spat invectives like machine-gun bullets. Since Matt couldn't get a word in, he simply sat on his bar chair, arms folded, jaw clenched, taking the hits.

"How could you lie to me again? How?!"

Taking a breath, I waited for an answer. It came in a surprisingly calm voice.

"I never lied to you, Clare."

"A lie of omission is still a lie. You manipulated me for your own ends, your own benefit, just like you did during our marriage!"

"No! Back then, I was young and stupid. Tonight, what I've been doing is trying to help you restore your life, or at least your memory of that life."

"Without remembering to even mention I was engaged to another man?"

"That's right, because *you* didn't remember him." Matt rose up off the chair. "But you remembered me."

As he stepped closer, I backed away. "Are you . . . trying to confuse me?"

"Of course not." Seeing my retreat, Matt stopped moving. "What's going on between us isn't complicated. Not if you understand a simple fact." Standing firm, he met my gaze. "I still love you. I know deep in your heart, you still care for me, which means this memory loss of yours could be our second chance."

Our second chance? All of a sudden, I was out of comebacks—and energy. Like a deflating balloon I sank into the cloudlike cushions of the overstuffed sofa, wishing they could spirit me away.

Seeing the fight go out of me, Matt got the wrong impression. Feeling encouraged, he took a step closer, then another, but slowly and cautiously, as if he were approaching an unpredictable cheetah on the African veldt.

What will she do? Lash out? Bolt? Both?

Personally, I was leaning toward *both*. I might have grown tired of fighting, but I was still furious with Matt's obvious intentions to manipulate me. He claimed he was simply trying to help me regain my memories, but his decisions were still all about him and what he wanted.

What if I *had* slept with him? How would I have felt in the morning if I'd suddenly remembered, *Oh, that's right. I'm engaged to be married to (insert name here).*

"Clare, you're tired," Matt purred, inching closer. "It's been a long day. How about a drink? Gin and ginger will take the edge off. Then we can go upstairs, relax, and—"

"I don't want alcohol. And I'm not going upstairs. I want to leave this house. *Right now.* There must be a hotel around here somewhere."

"That's a terrible idea. Remember, we're trying to keep you hidden."

"Then drive me back to the city."

"It's too late for that, and I'm too tired—"

"Give me the keys to the van. I'll drive myself."

"That's crazy. Look . . ." Hands up, he backed off. "How about if I get out of the house? Right this minute. How about that?"

"You're going to a hotel?"

"No . . ." He pulled on his hoodie and zipped it up. "There's a twenty-four-hour supermarket on Montauk Highway. I'll take my time, buy us some food for the weekend, some staples for the pantry—"

"How is that going to solve our problem?"

"For one thing, it will give our argument a rest. You'll have some privacy. Go upstairs to the master bedroom. When I get back, I won't disturb you. Lock the door, if it will make you feel better, and I'll see you in the morning. You'll see things differently after a good night's sleep. If not, we'll get you out of here. Or maybe we'll have Joy come for a visit. Would you like that?"

"Yes. I would."

"Good, great. That's a step in the right direction. Okay, I'm going . . ."

Seconds later, I heard the door firmly shut. Then the van's motor started up and slowly faded down the long driveway.

The house went quiet after that, and I would have climbed the stairs to bed, but I had too much adrenaline coursing through me. So I washed the dishes and cleaned the pans. It didn't take long, less than ten minutes—

That was when the doorbell chimed.

Matt must have forgotten something, I assumed, his wallet most likely. Easy to do when you're hurrying toward the exit in a desperate attempt to keep your ex-wife from fleeing your house. The doorbell was obviously his way of warning me that he was back sooner than expected—either that or he'd forgotten his house key, too.

Without bothering to glance out the peephole, I yanked open the door to find a man standing in front of me.

He was not my ex-husband.

Forty-nine

ꙮꙮꙮꙮꙮꙮꙮꙮꙮꙮꙮꙮꙮꙮꙮꙮꙮꙮ

The stranger was tall, over six feet, with sandy brown hair, and a rumpled trench coat hanging from his broad shoulders.

"Hi, Clare," he said, expression guarded.

He looked haggard, as if he'd been through a battle, and rough stubble darkened his square jaw. But his ice-blue eyes were sharp, and they stared at me with spooky intensity.

"Oh, my God!" I cried. "You're that detective, the one from the hospital!"

I tried to slam the door in his face, but this guy was ready. Using his body as a wedge, he forced his way inside.

Time to make like a cheetah and bolt!

I ran toward the steps, planning to lock myself in the master bedroom. Unfortunately, the physics of Matt's oversized socks on a highly polished wooden floor didn't resolve in my favor. I went down hard, right on my sweatpants-covered assets.

"Son of a bunny!"

"Are you okay?!"

Hands flailing, I warned him away. "Don't touch me! I'm not going back to that hospital!"

"Take it easy—"

The rumpled detective extended his hand, but I got up under my own steam. Retying the robe over Matt's sweatpants and T-shirt, I attempted to regain what was left of my dignity. Head held high, I faced him squarely.

"I mean it. I no longer want Dr. Lorca's drug treatment. I'll hire a lawyer, if I have to, but I'm not going back!"

"Good, because I'm not here to take you back."

"You're not?"

"No. I came to help you, Clare . . ."

Clare. The way he said my name—so personal, so familiar—made me uncomfortable. Ignoring the feeling, I stood my ground.

"What exactly do you mean, you came here to *help* me?"

"I have some of your clothes and shoes and things." He pointed toward the half-open front door. "They're in my rental car. Madame packed them."

"Madame? How do you know—Oh, wait. Of course! I'm so sorry. I should have remembered!"

"You *remember* me?"

"I remember Madame saying something about a friendly cop sharing information with her. You're him, aren't you? The friend of the Blend?"

He swallowed hard. "I'm a little more than that."

"What do you mean?"

"I don't know how to break this to you, Clare. To be frank, I'm not sure if I should. Let's just say it's important that you know I'm here for you. That I'm in your corner . . ."

As the detective's voice trailed off, his guarded cop expression began to melt into something more human. I could see the sadness in his blue eyes. It wasn't pity for me. It was more personal, a kind of tender pain, like heartache.

That was when I began to get a clue.

I still didn't know who this man was, but given Matt's reluctant revelation, I deduced *what* he was.

"You're a stranger to me," I warned, backing up a step. "I don't remember any history with you."

"I know that." He raised his hands, palms up. "Like I said, I came to help you. Not pressure or upset you . . ."

His words sounded sincere, and his voice was certainly kind. "So you're really the one? I mean, the man I'm supposed to . . . ?"

The detective waited patiently for me to finish. But I

couldn't get the words out. *Maybe if he just came out and said it.*

I rubbed my forehead. "I don't want there to be any confusion, okay? I'd like to get things straight in my mind and shake this bizarre sense of . . . I don't know what!"

"Tell me what to do."

"I want you to say it. State it out loud. Are *you* the man I'm supposed to . . . you know . . ."

"If you mean *marry*, the answer is yes."

With a deep, brave breath, I stared hard at the stranger's square-jawed face and searched my mind for any memory of him, some reason why he would want to drive all the way out to the South Fork in the dead of night, or look at me with such forlorn affection. But I felt nothing, other than pity for the poor guy.

On a rational level, I understood what was happening. On another level, however, I felt as though I'd walked through Lewis Carroll's looking glass.

Some *other* me had met this man and fallen in love.

Some *other* me had agreed to marry him.

So where was this woman? Was she ever coming back? Would she be able to repaint all the pictures missing in my empty frames—or only *some* of them?

One thing did come back in that moment, an almost crippling sense of displacement. It returned in a powerful rush, just as it had when my grown daughter ran into my hospital room.

Suddenly, I had trouble breathing. My skin turned clammy and my heart began to race. The stranger didn't appear to notice my changing state from gobsmacked surprise to dead-cold shock. Still focusing on my request that we *get things straight*, he took a step closer.

"I'm Mike Quinn, your fiancé," he said, extending his hand, as if we were being introduced at a cocktail party. "Nice to meet you."

It was the last thing I remembered before the great white room began to spin. Then everything went black.

Fifty

~~~~~~~~~~~~~~~~~~~~~~~~~~~~~~~~~~~~~

"Where am I?"

"A safe place . . ."

I felt a soft bed under me. Warm covers over me. There was a fire crackling somewhere, and something squeezing my arm, then a whoosh of air, and the tightness released.

"Your blood pressure's better." The deep voice was quiet but firm. "You're doing well."

Looking up, into the man's eyes, I lost my tongue for a moment. Azure blue like that you didn't see every day. "Who are you again?"

"A friend. A good one. You're safe with me, Clare. Just close your eyes and rest."

"Ressst . . ."

Fifty-one

⚭⚭⚭⚭⚭⚭⚭⚭⚭⚭⚭⚭⚭⚭⚭⚭

I was warm and comfortable, nestled in a floating feather-bed cloud, until a vocal thunderclap of clashing male voices broke through my cushioned quiet.

"YOU?! What the hell are you doing here? Where is Clare?"

"Calm down, Allegro. She's upstairs, and she's fine."

"Are you crazy?! Just showing up like this?"

"You want to talk crazy? Let's discuss what *you* did—"

Yawning, I opened my eyes and quickly scanned the empty bedroom. The door had been left wide open. A chair had been pulled next to the bed and an EMT jump bag was sitting on it. That was when I remembered the blood pressure cuff on my arm and the deep, tender voice telling me I was safe.

That same deep voice—not so tender anymore—was now arguing with my ex-husband downstairs. Their noisy discussion echoed up through the great room's high ceiling. The acoustics were perfect for eavesdropping, which is exactly what I did . . .

"You broke the law," the stranger said. "You took her out of hospital care, spirited her into seclusion—"

"Don't give me that crap," Matt returned. "I was in Lorca's office, right there with you. You heard that jerk, telling us how he was going to isolate Clare, take her upstate, pump her with who knows what kind of drugs. You're the one who stormed off. I'm the one who *did* something about it."

"To what end?"

"What do you think, Quinn? To help restore her memory."

"Selectively, though, right?"

"What is that supposed to mean?"

"It means, if I hadn't shown up here, your primary focus would have been on restoring Clare's memory of her feelings for you and no one else—"

"How did you find us?" Matt demanded, changing the subject a little too fast.

"Your mother gave me the address."

"My mother!"

"That's right. She didn't want Clare left alone with you. Your own mother. What does that tell you?"

"It tells me not to believe a word out of your lying cop mouth. You'll say anything in an interview room to coerce some poor joker's confession. Why should I believe a word you say?"

"Because you know my history with Clare, and you're well aware of your own."

"History isn't the problem tonight, flatfoot. It's current events."

"What's that supposed to mean?"

"Half the NYPD knows that you and Clare are engaged. Did you take precautions coming here? Or are you leading a SWAT team to my doorstep?"

"Don't be ridiculous."

"What I'm trying to be is *careful*," Matt said. "Answer me this. Do you have your personal mobile on you?"

"Yes."

"Then they can track you!"

"Take it easy. I have a plan. Believe me, I'm not letting anyone take Clare back to that hospital."

"That's right because you're leaving. Now!"

"I'm not going anywhere, Allegro. She needs to be medically monitored."

"Medically monitored? Did I miss something? You claimed she was fine!"

"She is fine. Now."

"You'd better explain—and fast."

"She wasn't feeling well, so I carried her upstairs to lie down."

"Not feeling well? That sounds like your typical stinking load of flatfoot spin. She passed out, didn't she? Didn't she?!"

"What Clare experienced was a mild form of shock."

"For God's sake! What the hell did you say to her?"

"After I arrived, she was close to guessing who I was, but felt confused and disoriented. She thought it would help if I told her the truth."

"And what did you say? Let me guess. Good evening, Clare. Nice to meet you. I'm your fiancé."

"Something like that."

"You really are an idiot."

"And you're anything but trustworthy. She deserves better."

"That's it. You're outta here!"

"Forget it. I'm not going."

"This is my house."

"That's the point. I'm not leaving Clare to believe her own fiancé would abandon her to her ex-husband."

"Then I'll have to physically remove you."

"Don't be stupid."

"You don't think I can do it, Quinn? Try me!"

"You *do* know I'm armed."

"So? What are you going to do? Shoot me? I don't think so."

"Back off, Allegro. I mean it. Or I'll power-cuff your ass to your hot-tub railing."

"STOP IT! RIGHT NOW!"

Hearing my shout above them, the two men froze. Then they looked up to find me glaring at them from the second-floor gallery.

"Stay where you are!" I commanded. "I've heard just about enough! I'm coming down to sort this mess out."

Fifty-two
༺੭੭੭੭੭੭੭੭੭੭੭੭੭੭੭੭੭੭༻

WHEN I reached the two men, Matt looked me over. "Are you okay, Clare? Should you be out of bed?"

"I'm fine. And wide-awake, thanks to both of your big mouths."

The two men looked sheepish. *Good,* I thought. Given the way their animal-kingdom-level "discussion" was going, sheepish was a vast improvement over pigheaded.

I faced Matt. "Where are the groceries?"

"In the van."

"Would you bring them in? And take *plenty of time* putting them away. It will give us some privacy."

"Excuse me?"

"I want to talk to this gentleman." I tilted my head in the direction of the stranger. "And I'd like to do it without you butting in. So move it, please."

Folding my arms, I waited for my ex-husband to leave. When he finally clomped away, mumbling in what sounded like Haitian Creole, I turned to the stranger.

"Let's sit down . . ."

By now the detective had removed his rumpled trench coat. I suggested he take off his suit jacket, too, and make himself comfortable beside me on the sofa. When he did, I couldn't hide my surprise at the sight of the leather shoulder holster strapped across his dress shirt.

"I'm sorry," he said, seeing my startled reaction. "I'd take this off, too, but I honestly don't trust your ex-husband. I'd rather stay strapped for a while, if you don't mind."

"I don't mind . . . It's just that . . . I had a dream about a man wearing a gun like that."

"I hope it was me."

"I couldn't see the man's face, but he was looking for me."

"That's what I'm doing here, sweethear—I mean, Clare."

"If you're going to call me sweetheart, I should at least know your name."

"You don't remember? I did tell you when I first arrived."

"I'm sorry, but things got a little fuzzy before I . . . you know—"

"It's Michael Quinn . . . Mike."

"Mike," I said, trying it out. "Nice to meet you."

"I'd say the same, but the last time I did, you went down like a sack of rocks."

"Sorry about that."

"Stop apologizing. You have nothing to be sorry for. This situation would feel overwhelming for anyone."

"So you took care of me after I blacked out? You carried me upstairs?" When he nodded, I asked about the emergency medical gear I saw in the bedroom. "I thought you were a police detective. What are you doing with an EMT kit?"

"Before I joined the PD, I was a New York firefighter. I've got the skills, so I carry the jump bag. You never know." He shrugged his broad shoulders. "On top of that, the sort of work I do for the department sometimes requires acute response."

"What do you do exactly?"

"I'm the head of a special unit tasked with investigating criminality behind overdose cases. I also carry a naloxone kit. All my people do—" At my questioning look, he explained, "It's a countermeasure for opioid overdose, that is . . . when we reach them in time."

"I see . . ." I said those words because I *did* see, or at least I was beginning to. There was more to this rumpled detective than ice-blue eyes and a morose demeanor. "I have more questions. Is that okay?"

"Shoot."

"Not with that, I hope—" I pointed to his gun.

"Still the same Clare."

"Well, that's good to know. I mean, who wants to find out that life beat the sense of humor out of you?"

"That's how most of us feel on the job. Gallows humor is pretty common at crime scenes."

"Oh, I'm sure you're a laugh riot."

"Let's just say I appreciate a joke. Telling them is another animal."

"Then the whole stand-up-comedian thing is a pipe dream?"

"Funny," he said, though he didn't laugh. He was too tense for that, but he did loosen his tie and quip: "I particularly appreciate the drug reference."

"I thought you might."

"Any other questions for me, Clare?"

"Seriously? How did someone like you meet someone like me? Wait. Let me guess. Matt overdosed and you came to the rescue with your supercop kit?"

"No, although the first time I met your ex-husband, circumstances were—let's just say, less than convivial."

"Then how did you and I meet?"

"At the time, I was newly assigned to your local precinct. Your Village Blend was the scene of an accident that turned out to be a crime. I was the detective on the case."

"Did you solve it?"

"Actually, Clare, you did."

"Really? How?"

"It's a long story. Maybe you'll remember it."

"Maybe . . ."

As we continued to talk, I studied the man's weary face.

I thought his sandy brown hair was cut too short, but I liked the solidity of his jaw, shadowed with bark-colored stubble. I could see he was tired, yet his glacial eyes were still admirably sharp. And I liked his creases: the crow's-feet and frown lines. He'd obviously been through hard times, and I liked that, too.

I didn't like that he was so stiff. Even when we joked around, he remained guarded. Maybe it was occupational habit. Maybe he didn't trust me enough to reveal his feelings. Either that or he didn't trust himself.

After a few more questions, I finally asked the big one, at least in my mind—

"Are we sleeping together, Mike?"

His eyebrows lifted. I had surprised him with the question. His answer was a quiet nod.

"And I'm supposed to be in love with you?"

"Yes. Madly."

"Is that so?" I made a show of looking him over. "Must be your inner qualities."

He smiled, the first time tonight. I liked it. My own smile, in response, must have encouraged him because he shifted uneasily before asking—

"Do you think you could . . . I mean, is it possible you might fall for those 'inner qualities' again?"

"Let's put it this way. From what I've learned so far, I'd *like* to remember you."

"And if you don't?"

Now it was my turn to shift. "Honestly, Mike, you seem like a nice guy, but you're still a stranger to me."

His disappointment was palpable.

"Don't be discouraged," I told him. An impulse to touch his hand flowed through my body, but my mind pulled back. Instead of reaching out, I made a fist. "Can we give it more time?"

"Of course," he said, forcing a weak smile. "That's why I'm here."

FIFTY-THREE
∾∾∾∾∾∾∾∾∾∾∾∾∾∾∾∾

"**ARE** you two about finished *getting acquainted*?"

Matt was done putting away the groceries and (apparently) maintaining his patience. Like a centurion defending his fort, he strode across the room and planted himself in front of us, hands on hips.

"It's late, Quinn. Time for you to go."

I stood up. "Is that necessary? You have enough bedrooms in this colossus to open a B and B."

"He's not staying here, Clare. He's got a phone on him that could lead the police to you."

"I overheard that discussion, and he told you he has a plan."

"I don't believe him."

"Well, I do, and I've made up my mind."

Unfortunately, Matt had made up his. He wasn't backing off, and I'd have to think fast. So I did—

"Do you want me to leave with him?"

"What?!"

"If he goes, so do I."

(Honestly, I wasn't going to leave this house at this hour with an effective stranger, but I was out of ideas.)

Turning my head, I sneaked a wink at Mike, just so he knew I was bluffing. The detective's response was a raised eyebrow, which I took as some kind of Spock-like code for fascinated amusement.

Matt didn't see my wink and—thank goodness—believed my con. Grumbling again, this time in Spanish, he acquiesced.

A small victory, but a victory.

In deference to my ex-husband (who was, after all, our host), I suppressed my smile, though I couldn't quell the joke—

"Looks like you'll be staying with us, Detective Quinn. Welcome to *La Casa* Allegro."

A short time later, I was back in the big corner bedroom. Astonishingly, the detective was sleeping right next door. *That* had taken some angling.

"I have EMT training," he told Matt. "I should be closer to her in case she needs help. And, Clare, you should leave your door open. I'll do the same."

"Then I'm keeping my door open, too," Matt proclaimed. "Don't try anything cute, Quinn. Remember, you're no better than a stranger to her."

"Yes, I know." He turned to me. "Don't worry, Clare. I won't touch you unless you need medical help—or you ask me to." This time Mike Quinn slipped me the wink. "Okay, Allegro?"

Matt's grunt was his version of approval. (Clearly, he hadn't seen Quinn's wink.) Then we all retired to our assigned bedrooms.

Before long, I was burrowing under the covers, trying to keep warm. The house was still chilly, and I was restless. Turning over, I faced the gas hearth, though it didn't offer much heat.

Like the rest of this place, it was set up for show more than substance, which, come to think of it, sounded like my ex-husband's second marriage.

Staring into the dancing flames, I tried to imagine what a relationship with a man like Detective Quinn would be like. I could see he was intelligent, mature—and he even got my jokes. He also clearly cared for me; or, at least, the "me" I used to be. But he was so obviously repressed, so stiff.

He seemed surprised when I asked about our sex life. His quiet nod was unreadable—and he certainly didn't want to prolong the discussion. Then again, my hostile ex-husband wasn't far away. Who could blame the guy for wanting to prevent World War Three?

Still, this match seemed odd.

Detective Quinn was so different from what I was used to. Where Matt was hotheaded and passionate, the detective seemed calm and deliberate. Was he like that in the bedroom, too? Was there *any* heat under that cool blue exterior? Or was he just a big human version of this McMansion fireplace?

I couldn't deny I was curious to find out. Certainly not tonight, and not in *this* house, but Matt did say physical stimulation might help my memories, and who was I to stand in the way of a neurological experiment?

Turning over again, I stared in the direction of the open bedroom door. The woods outside were dark and quiet, the house like a tomb, save for a distant, rhythmic rumbling. It was Matt. He was already asleep, snoring up a storm.

Well, I'm glad someone is getting some shut-eye.

With our host unconscious, an imp in me considered tiptoeing into the next bedroom. I had more questions for Detective Quinn—and I couldn't help wondering what the man looked like out of his bureaucratic blue suit.

With a sigh of frustration, I grabbed a pillow to hug. I didn't have the nerve. What would I say to the man? "Hi, Mike, just passing through." Even worse, what if he misinterpreted my arrival in his bedroom in the dead of night—and my ex-husband woke up?

For heaven's sake, I told myself, *don't make things worse. Shut your mind and get some rest. Detective Quinn was obviously exhausted. He's probably fast asleep, just like Matt. He's certainly not lying in bed thinking of you!*

FIFTY-FOUR

~~~~~~~~~~~~~~~~~~~~~~~~~~~~~~~~

MIKE

SHE'S *still Clare.*

Lying awake in the dark, Mike smiled, marveling at that outstanding discovery. He hadn't known her all those years ago, raw from the pain of her broken marriage, but the circumstances didn't matter. She was still the woman he loved. When she had quickly flipped the tables on Allegro, then flashed him that secret wink, he wanted to grab her and kiss her.

Her memories might be blocked, but her quick, curious mind and dry sense of humor were still there. Her lively green eyes were as beautiful as ever, and still noticing the littlest things.

Sitting next to her downstairs, he'd used every ounce of control not to touch her or scare her with his racing thoughts and emotions.

Earlier in the evening, when she'd passed out on him, and he'd taken care of her, making sure her vitals were strong, he imagined her waking up and remembering him, inviting him to join her in bed. He fantasized pulling her to him, enjoying a deep, long kiss, tugging off her clothes, and—

Punching the pillows, Mike propped himself up, clasped his hands behind his head, and exhaled hard. He'd never get to sleep if he didn't stop thinking of her, right there in the next room.

With the house so quiet, he held his breath, listening for any sign of her stirring or calling out. All he heard was Allegro snoring.

At least someone is getting some shut-eye.

For the third time, Mike checked his mobile. There was nothing new from anyone, including Franco or the Fish Squad. This weekend would be a challenge—on many fronts—but he was grateful for one thing. Tonight, Clare had stood up for him. She was back on his side. That was progress, though not enough.

Outside the window, tree branches swayed in the moonlight, casting odd reflections on the walls and ceiling. That was what he was to Clare now, a vague impression, a mental shadow. It was devastating the way she looked at him, a real gut punch to be treated as a stranger.

Mike had years of experience responding to human traumas—from tragic to absurd. He was familiar with the effects of dementia and brain damage. But this bizarre form of amnesia was something he'd never encountered.

Lorca said he'd tried hypnosis, with no result. If more therapies failed, Mike knew what task was ahead of him, but—

How do you make a woman who once loved you fall in love again?

Thinking back on his years getting to know Clare, he could remember things they'd said and done, but he couldn't say exactly when or why her feelings for him went from platonic "like" to something more.

He needed to discover that place again. He had to, because he couldn't take losing her. Life would go on, but not the way he wanted, not the way it could have been.

"Don't be discouraged."

Hearing her voice in his head, Mike closed his eyes.

Back when he was a young cop, he had played the field a bit, but he'd been far from a playboy. When a gorgeous young model became enamored with him after he'd arrested her stalker, he thought he was the luckiest guy in the world. But she'd glamorized his job, and he'd romanticized their relationship. His buddies on the force had, too, slapping his back with envy.

Once he married Leila, reality set in. Mike went from being her knight in blue to a "square-jawed bore." There were too many long hours and sad stories for her liking, too many tough guys from hard walks in his world.

Eventually, Leila left him for a new husband, after a series of affairs with the class of men who had less baggage and more bank. The whole marriage had scorched his soul, left him feeling less of a man, dead and buried.

It was Clare who'd resurrected him. From the beginning, she admired his vocation instead of shunning it. She was always happy to lend an ear or a piece of advice. She genuinely loved the city and her job serving its people, the ones he also served—and swore to protect.

There were bad days. Lots of them. New York had a sunny side, but most of what Mike saw was an ocean of urban despair. These past few years, whenever cynicism sank his spirit, Clare's faith showed him a way back to the surface. How could he lose that light?

"Don't be discouraged."

Were Clare's words a sign that her memories of him were still intact? Still reachable? He hoped so. As sleep finally overtook him, he let that hope become his dream.

FIFTY-FIVE

~~~~~~~~~~~~~~~~~~~~~~~~~~~~~~~~~~~~~

MIKE Quinn slept in.

After his endless, stress-filled Friday, it felt good to saw away half of Saturday morning. When he finally stirred (10:47 AM, according to his mobile), he showered, threw on an NYPD T-shirt and sweatpants, and headed downstairs. That was where he found her, yawning in the mansion's large kitchen, head bent over some appliance on the counter.

"Good morning, Clare."

"Oh, hi! Hello . . . I mean, good morning . . . Mike."

She was blushing.

He tried not to smile too wide at her reddening cheeks. Or bend down for a kiss. Or tell her how good she looked in her favorite blue jeans and how that sweater always brought out the deep green of her eyes. All those things, which came naturally to him, were now sadly wrong. Instead, he approached the woman he loved like he was an aloof professor with hands behind his back.

"What are you doing?" he asked.

"Trying to figure out this odd coffeemaker of Matt's."

"You're kidding."

"It's a model I've never seen before—"

Curling a lock of chestnut hair around an ear, she described the machine as appearing to be an autodrip, but with features that made no sense to her, including a lidless filter on an open Chemex-type carafe.

"I *think* it's an electric pour-over machine. But the whole point of pour-over coffee is the *manual* control of the pour. I don't get it."

Mike scratched the rough stubble on his chin. (He'd been so eager to see her again that he'd skipped his morning shave.) "It's hard to believe any coffee contraption could stump you. I've seen you work the most complicated espresso machines."

"You have?"

"Something called a Slayer?"

"I don't remember that one, but espresso machines in general I understand. And I've deduced how to *operate* this thing. What I don't understand is the *brewing philosophy* behind it."

"Every problem has a solution."

"And the most obvious one is to wake up our host."

"Naw, let Allegro get his beauty sleep. I have a better idea. How about you and I investigate alternatives?"

"Such as?"

Mike began opening cupboards. It took a minute, but he found what he was looking for on a high shelf. "Here we go. A French press."

Clare tilted her head. *"You* know what a French press is?"

"That surprises you?"

"I would have pegged you for a convenience-store-coffee kind of guy."

"Bodegas, actually. Remember those blue-and-white paper cups with the Greek design?"

"The Anthora?" she said, putting water on to boil.

"Excuse me?"

"That's what the design is called. Back in the 1960s, a paper cup manufacturer wanted to create something that would appeal to the Greek-owned coffee shops—they were all over New York at the time. 'We are happy to serve you,' right? That was the motto on the cup—"

"And on my patrol car, come to think of it, another version of it, anyway."

"I don't recall the NYPD serving coffee."

"No, but we drank enough of it to keep the shops in business. I practically lived on it when I was in uniform, the younger model of me."

"This model's not half bad." She looked him up and down, and threw him a cheeky wink.

Now *he* felt like blushing.

Clare smiled. "Was the younger model of you that different from this one?"

"This one's a lot wiser. Otherwise, not much different in the things that matter."

"Oh, I already guessed that."

"How?"

"Let's see—" Her fingers ticked off a list. "Number one, the way you talk about your work. It's obviously part of your identity. Two, you carry an EMT jump bag in your car, you know, just in case you casually come across a civilian having a heart attack. Three, your haircut is vintage police academy. Shall I go on?"

"Be my guest. But I'll need coffee first. Lots of it."

"You read my mind." She rolled her eyes. "Or what's left of it."

Yep, still Clare, he thought. How could he not love this woman?

She was about to grind the beans when he stepped in and took the bag from her hand.

"Sit down, let me."

"You know how?"

"Guess who taught me."

"Oh . . . okay."

"Don't sweat it. I taught you a few things, too. But not in the kitchen . . ."

When his captivated gaze found hers, her blush came back. Mike couldn't stop himself. The back of his hand lifted to brush her cheek. She immediately backed away.

"Sorry," she said.

"No, I'm the one who's sorry. I need to take things slow. I keep reminding myself, but . . ."

"Don't be discouraged," she said again.

He smiled. "We detectives wouldn't get very far if we gave up easily."

"I don't give up easily, either."

"No, you never have—and I'm counting on that."

Fifty-six

෴෴෴෴෴෴෴෴෴෴෴෴෴

As Mike Quinn shared coffee with Clare, the rhythm of their relationship resumed so beautifully, it almost felt like a normal morning, until—

"Hey, you two, what's going on?" Matt strode into the kitchen in jeans and a T-shirt, bluntly asking, "Is she cured?"

"No," Clare returned without blinking an eye, "but that slab of bacon you bought is. Why don't you tactlessly ask it?"

As Quinn suppressed a laugh, Matt put up defensive hands. "I just thought with the pair of you playing footsie down here, something might have, you know, been kicked loose."

Quinn wanted to kick him. "Dial it down, Allegro. We're getting to know each other again."

With a shrug, Matt retreated to the kitchen counter, where he began futzing with one of his high-end appliances. "Just tell me the truth," he said. "Was there any *funny business* last night, after I fell asleep?"

Quinn risked a peek at Clare to find her already peeking at him. When they awkwardly glanced away, Matt cackled.

"You two look like a couple of teenagers in your parents' house."

"Only you would think that," Clare said, "given your maturity level. But it isn't that simple."

"It was until *he* showed up."

Quinn was about to respond (and not politely) when Clare cut in—

"Are you making coffee over there? I was wondering about *that thing* on your counter—"

The eye roll she shot Quinn, before jumping off the bar chair, made it clear she didn't care all that much about Matt's mystery machine, but *acting* like she did might defuse the mounting tension.

She was right. Like a neglected kid, Allegro appeared pleased to have his ex-wife's focus back on him. As the coffee talk ensued, Quinn felt his pocket buzzing. He pulled out his mobile and read the screen.

The text was from Franco:

My friends arrived. With papers.
They didn't see my cousin.
No worries. Already gone.

That was fast, Quinn thought. *Too fast.* He weighed whether or not to tell Clare and Allegro the bad news. At the moment, they were in the weeds over the particulars of automated pour-over.

". . . and the copper-coil heating system maintains the temperature throughout the brew cycle," Matt droned on. "Not only that, the showerhead evenly saturates the grinds like the manual method."

Clare shook her head. "Won't it flood the bed?"

"No, that's the beauty of it. The showerhead *pulses*, allowing perfect blooming."

"I still don't get the rationale."

"Because your memory loss doesn't take into account the latest trend in the coffee business. Manual pour-over became so popular with high-end-coffee consumers that shops began to feature slow bars."

"*Slow* bars!" Clare gawked at her ex. "I'm sorry, but on what planet do coffee drinkers wait for pour-over? New Yorkers can't wait three minutes in line without complaining."

Reluctantly, Matt confessed that she had announced these same reservations when he insisted they try a slow bar at the Village Blend.

"And?" she asked. "How did it go?"

"Ultimately, nobody had the patience for it."

"I was right? You admit it?"

Matt shrugged. "Even I lost patience with my manual pour-over. That's why I bought this automatic."

"Espresso bars were created so customers *wouldn't* have to wait for their coffee—you know that. The machine itself was invented to speed up service." She glanced around. "Why don't you have an espresso machine here?"

"I moved it to the warehouse in Red Hook. That's where I spend most of my time when I'm in New York."

"I see, well . . ." Clare patted his shoulder. "I'm sure slow bars work in resort areas. Waiting for water to gradually seep through ground beans is probably a Zen experience—in the land of hot tubs and pool parties."

"Don't knock the pleasures of anticipation." He waggled his eyebrows. "You always enjoyed it in foreplay."

Hearing the change in subject, Quinn cleared his throat, *loudly*.

"Excuse me. I thought you two might like to know. I received a text message from my second-in-command."

"Who's that?" Clare asked.

"You met him at the hospital, Sergeant Franco."

Clare's face froze. "You mean the young cop with the shaved head and leather jacket?"

Quinn could tell she wasn't a fan—and decided *not* to mention his relationship with her grown daughter. Unfortunately, Allegro couldn't keep his big mouth shut. He immediately started ranting about Franco being a "mook" and how he was looking forward to the day Joy came to her senses and gave the poor sergeant the heave-ho.

"Are you finished?" Quinn asked.

Allegro folded his arms, and Quinn turned to Clare, who looked scared out of her wits.

"Don't listen to your ex-husband. He has his own history with Franco and reasons for disliking the guy. But Franco is a good man. He's been a real friend to you, and you've been one to him. Despite your ex-husband's objections, Joy has great affection for Franco and the feeling is mutual."

"Really?" Clare sounded skeptical. "And I've had no objections to their relationship?"

"Joy's history has been rocky. She's had negative experiences with men, but never with Franco. You were thrilled to know she chose to be with a good guy like him. You've been holding out hope they'll make a commitment one day."

"As in marriage?"

"Not long ago, you told me you were having mother-of-the-bride fantasies."

Allegro's groan was highly audible. Quinn ignored it. Thankfully, so did Clare. Still a little wary, she nevertheless nodded, apparently willing to accept the situation—at least for now.

"What about this message from your sergeant?" Clare asked. "What's his news?"

"The DC police paid a visit to Joy this morning with a warrant to search her home and business. They were searching for you."

"What!" Clare and her ex cried together.

Matt looked ready to kill. "You'd better explain, Quinn."

"Calm down, and I will . . ."

Fifty-seven

ooooooooooooooooooooo

Quinn quickly recounted the Fish Squad's visit to the Village Blend, and Madame's bright idea to send them on a wild Allegro chase to Washington, DC.

"Great! Just great!" Matt began to pace.

"She had no choice," Quinn told him. "Soles and Bass added up the obvious. They came to your coffeehouse, expecting a lead, and your mother gave them a credible one. She bought us time."

"Well, the clock is ticking now," Matt said. "We need to get her memory back."

"I'm right here," Clare said.

"Okay." Matt faced her. "We need to get *your* memory back. Or the NYPD is going to deliver you right back to the hospital."

"Take it easy," Quinn stepped in. "Piling on stress isn't going to help. You've got coffee on. Let's all sit down and have some."

The three of them moved from the marble bar to a sunny corner of the large kitchen, where a breakfast nook with a cushioned banquette was tucked against the mansion's tall windows.

Matt filled their mugs with coffee. Quinn sampled the excellent brew and nodded. He had to give it to Allegro; the man knew his trade.

"We have to find more keys for Clare," Matt began.

"Keys?" Quinn said.

"Sensory stimulation to unlock her memories."

"Like the chicken?" Clare said.

"What chicken?" Quinn asked.

Taking a seat, Matt recounted the KFC experiment. He also reminded Clare of her breakthrough after her first taste of the Hampton Coffee in the van ride. She responded by reminding him that it all started with her visit to the Parkview hotel's Gotham Suite.

"So we need to find more memory aids for her," Quinn said, summing up, "preferably ones that highly stimulate her senses."

The table went quiet as they all began to ponder a next step. Quinn caught Clare peeking at him several times and blushing. *That* intrigued him. Before he could pursue what was on her mind, Matt spoke up.

"Why don't you try baking something?"

Clare arched an eyebrow. "Is that because you're hungry?"

"I could eat. But the truth is, you love it. You do a lot of it, and it could bring you back to yourself."

"You're not wrong," Clare admitted. "I grew up baking with my grandmother, and it always relaxes me."

"That's good," Quinn agreed. "Anything that makes you feel safe and comfortable will help. So what do you feel like baking?"

"I don't know . . ." Clare gazed out the window in thought. "At this point, my memories of baking are all about my grandmother—and my daughter, of course, teaching her recipes in our Jersey kitchen. Can either of you remember what I baked, say, in the last few weeks?"

"Your Apple Cobbler Cake," Matt immediately suggested. "You made that for a staff meeting before you disappeared. I had a piece, and it was great. You mentioned you wrote about it in one of your old columns. A few ingredients, magically whipped together into a breakfast cake, something like that—"

"I have a better idea," Quinn cut in. "Since that recipe goes back years, it's not a good anchor in Clare's mind. But the morning before she disappeared, she baked something special for the two of us."

"I did?" Clare leaned closer. "What was it?"

"Your shop's pastry case recently added glazed Blueberry Cream Cheese Scones. They were so melt-in-your-mouth tender and such a big hit, you wanted to try a version using strawberries. You baked a sample batch for the two of us. They were amazing, Clare."

"*Strawberry* Cream Cheese Scones?" She licked her lips. "*Mmmm.* Were they glazed, too?"

Quinn nodded. "I remember you used sweet juices from the macerated strawberries to help flavor the glaze and color it pale pink."

Clare's eyebrows lifted. "You know what *macerated* means?"

"I learned it from you. You used vanilla and sugar for the process."

"Then you watched me make the scones?"

"Of course. Watching you cook is a beautiful thing. I feel guilty sometimes, because you make us meals so often. When you let me, I treat you to restaurants, but you usually prefer to stay 'Cosi at home'—that's how you put it."

He smiled and she returned it.

"That sounds nice. Just the two of us?"

"And Java and Frothy. Those are your cats. I start a fire in the living room, and you start dinner in the kitchen. I enjoy talking with you at the end of the day, so I mix us drinks, or pour glasses of wine, and we decompress together. I even help, when you let me. The truth is, Clare, whatever lights you up lifts me, too . . ."

As she listened to Quinn, Clare leaned closer and closer. "Strawberry Cream Cheese Scones," she repeated, her expression growing softer. Then her lips parted, and Quinn almost thought she was going to kiss him, until Matt peevishly pointed out—

"Strawberries are out of season."

"So what?" Quinn said, unable to unglue his gaze from his fiancée. "I've seen Clare use frozen blueberries in muffins. Can't you get frozen strawberries around here?"

"I'm sure we can find fresh," Clare said almost dreamily. "Just like Matt's coffee beans, berries are shipped here from farms in other countries so we cold-weather dwellers can enjoy some variety in our produce year-round."

Matt folded his arms. "Clearly, you have no memory of the *locavore* movement."

"The what?"

Matt appeared to relish breaking the mood completely with a mini lecture on the California origin of the movement, along with its philosophy, and the general attitude it reinforced among those who thought of themselves as foodie elite.

"And what attitude is that?" Clare asked.

"Eating produce out of season is frowned upon."

"I get that, and I like using seasonal produce, too. You get the best pricing that way. It's also commendable to encourage people to use farmers' markets and support local producers. But"—her eyes narrowed into a look Quinn knew well—"until I move to California and have a citrus tree in my backyard, I'm not giving up oranges, lemons, limes, bananas, avocados, coffee, and all the other fresh fruits and veg that don't happen to grow anywhere near this region. I'd rather not give up their health benefits, either. My guess is that most families in this country, including low-income families in urban areas—not to mention the hardworking people in the grocery industry, who've labored to develop trade practices that provide year-round variety for our diets—are of the same opinion."

Quinn almost felt sorry for Allegro. He didn't know what hit him.

Swallowing his smile, Quinn addressed Clare. "Why

don't you and I take a drive to find some berries, fresh *or* frozen? We can get some air, stretch our legs—"

"You think that's wise?" Matt asked. "I think she should stay hidden."

"I have a good disguise," Clare said. "And I'd like to get out."

"She'll be fine," Quinn agreed.

"How do you know?" Matt challenged. "With that mobile phone on you, your flatfoot pals can trace you to this area."

"That won't happen. I have a plan."

"So you've said, but I haven't heard it."

"You don't need to."

"Is that right?"

"That's right!"

"We'll see about that!"

Fifty-eight

~~~~~~~~~~~~~~~~~~~~~~~~~~~~~~~~

Clare

I shook my head, watching the men argue. The word *pig-headed* came to mind again, though this morning they were acting more like alpha dogs. The yapping became so intense, they failed to notice the light knocking at the front door.

Happy for a reason to get up from the table, I left to investigate. Of course, I checked the peephole first (I'd learned my lesson last night). Then I pulled the door open for a visitor I recognized.

"Are you Barbara 'Babka' Baum? One of the Gotham Ladies?"

"Hah," cried the elderly queen of retro cuisine. "Amnesia or not, I knew you'd never forget a gal like me!"

The sunny autumn morning was temperate, with only a slight chill left over from the night before, and Babka had dressed appropriately, in tan slacks and a hand-embroidered sweater under a tailored jacket. Stylishly thin, her jewel-studded glasses dangled from a spangled necklace. Stepping over the threshold, she removed her chic sun hat, to expose wavy hair rinsed mahogany brown with tasteful salon highlights.

"Nobody forgets me, Clare, because I'm unforgettable," Babka declared. "Why, even my ex-husband says I'm impossible to forget—as much as that bastard would like to!"

Suddenly, I heard Madame's voice in my head—

"Be careful, Clare. Babka takes offense as easily as she offends."

I could not recall the time or place of that warning, but I heeded Madame's advice and allowed Babka to think that I fully remembered whatever we'd experienced together. The truth is, Madame's remarks about her old friend were about all I recalled—that and Al Hirschfeld's lighthearted drawing of her hanging in the Parkview's Gotham Suite.

As short as I was, the petite Babka didn't have to stoop to cup my head between her hands or kiss both cheeks. Stepping back, hands on hips, she gave me an appraising once-over.

"Clare, you look darn good for someone who's not right in the *kop*!" She tapped her head with a finger.

"Err . . . thanks. You look good yourself."

The legendary New York restaurateur and businesswoman struck me as part swaggering CEO, part meddling grandmother. As I ushered her into the great room, she chattered on about maintaining a vacation home in East Hampton—at least twice the size of Matt's—where she staged lavish summer parties.

Hearing our approach, the battling bulldogs finally noticed we had a guest. Babka's smile brightened considerably when she saw the men.

"Look who's here! Your rogue ex-husband *and* your big, hunky fiancé." Babka clapped her hands and grinned. "I've got to hand it to you, doll. You sure do know how to recuperate!"

"It's not as pleasant as you might think," I muttered.

"Hey, you two!" Babka called to them. "I got a hired limo full of cakes out there. Fetch them, would you? And tell the driver he can go. He's already on my tab, so don't waste good money tipping him."

I blinked in confusion. "Cakes?"

A minute later, Detective Quinn was walking through the door carrying four circular bakery boxes bearing the Parkview Palace seal. They were neatly stacked and tied together with blue ribbons. Matt followed with a three-cake stack in each hand.

"Clare, you've got to smell these," he said excitedly.

"Smell them!" Babka cried. "Clare and I are going to taste every single one!"

"There are *ten* cakes here," Quinn observed.

Babka nodded. "According to Chef Fong and his staff, they represent his spin on some of the most popular wedding cake tastes in America."

"Chef Fong?" I said, registering the meaning of the Parkview logo. "Is this the wedding cake sampler from the hotel's kitchen? The same cakes I ate on the night Annette went missing?"

"It was Blanche's idea," Babka explained. "She thought tasting these cakes might help with your memory problem. I've got to say the whole idea sounds meshuga to me, but what do I know? I just shill fancy knishes." She tossed her sun hat on the table. "Of course, Blanche wanted to bring these herself, but—"

"She couldn't," Matt said. "We know."

"Then you also know she's worried about the police watching her for suspicious activity. You think she's a little paranoid? I don't know! What do I know?"

We all glanced at one another.

"Well, that's why she sent me. I ordered the cakes myself, told them they're for a relative having a wedding at my East Hampton house."

"Good thinking," Quinn said.

"How did you get here so quickly?" I asked.

"Easy!" She snapped her fingers. "I choppered in!"

"Well, I'm a big fan of cake for breakfast," Matt announced, "so I'm going to sample every one of them, too. Just give me a few minutes to brew more coffee."

Quinn followed Matt into the open kitchen, where they

resumed arguing in loud whispers. For the second time that day I regretted not hiding the knives.

While Babka and I made small talk, Matt brought out dishes, mugs, silverware, and even linen napkins. He spread the boxes out on the long marble counter and we seated ourselves on the cushioned bar chairs.

Detective Quinn seemed excited, too, but for a different reason. He whispered that he was hoping for a break-through. The intimate combination of his deep voice at my ear with the warmth of his breath brought heat to my face.

My head swam a little, and I stepped away quickly, feeling embarrassed by my body's reaction—and then feeling terrible at the sight of Quinn's crestfallen face.

"Cake time!" Matt said, proudly pouring his coffee. "Which one do we try first?"

Fifty-nine

❧❧❧❧❧❧❧❧❧❧❧❧❧❧❧❧❧❧

Each pretty blue box held a mini layer cake made with six-inch pans. Matt took over serving the sample slices, one cake at a time, and he started with the basics.

Chef Fong's simple, elegant Vanilla Bean Cake was delightfully delicate, though we all thought the fondant was too thick and sweet. The Deep Chocolate was rich with a bittersweet sophistication, and its icing tasted just right.

The Luscious Lemon was too tart for my taste, even with the buttercream, which the chef had peppered generously with zest.

Babka agreed. "Ah, it's making me pucker like an octopus!"

Matt tried each cake with us, giving his opinion, rather loudly. Quinn sampled them, too, but didn't say a word. His mood appeared to have soured worse than the lemon cake, and his stone-faced mask was cemented back in place. Was it because I'd shyly put air between us again? Or was Matt annoying him? Or was it something else . . . ?

Cheer up, Detective, I wanted to tell him. *I don't like seeing you this way.* But I was reluctant to say something so personal in front of Babka. Instead, I refocused on the food.

Savoring each forkful of cake, I tried to detect some memory associated with the tasting. I noticed Quinn pensively watching my reactions. Once again I disappointed him. Nothing came to mind.

Babka, on the other hand, was thoroughly enjoying the exercise. "What's next?" she asked.

"Bananas Foster," Matt said. Babka made a skeptical face but took a sample anyway.

I was wary, too, but pleasantly surprised. The vanilla filling, as rich as ice cream, lifted the banana cake to another level. So did the frosting, a spreadable version of the buttery sauce poured over an actual Bananas Foster with notes of dark brown sugar, cinnamon, and dark rum.

"Do you like it?" I asked Quinn.

He nodded. "It's good—"

"Next is the Carrot Cake," Matt interrupted.

"I know plenty who love it," Babka said. "Personally, I prefer my vegetables in a salad or a side, not dessert."

The Red Velvet was excellent, but like the Carrot Cake, I thought the cream cheese frosting would be too heavy after appetizers and dinner.

The Grand Marnier Cake was grand but overpowering while the Royal Elderflower Cake, a copy of the one served at Prince Harry and Meghan Markle's famous wedding, was a delicate beauty.

The Ginger Spice was layered with flavor and the sweet molasses nicely offset the peppery spices, but I agreed with Babka when she proclaimed it "not right for a wedding."

Then came the rustic Italian-style Chocolate Hazelnut Cake with its chocolate-hazelnut frosting. I swooned a little. Quinn stayed quiet, but I could see him nodding with approval after each bite.

"You like it, too, don't you?" I quietly asked the detective as Matt busied himself getting another sample.

Quinn nodded, appearing pleased that I cared what he thought, and I finally, stupidly realized: *This was supposed to be our wedding cake. How awful must he feel that I'm not remembering that?*

I was about to apologize to Quinn for the sad situation when Matt broadly announced—

"This one looks promising!"

Chef Fong's Prosecco Cake was indeed the best yet. He'd filled the tender layers with white chocolate and raspberry mousse, and covered the cake with a silky champagne frosting. I had to have a second forkful, and so did Babka. Matt went crazy, as well, and even the stoic Quinn had seconds.

Despite all the sensory stimulation, not one flavor evoked a buried memory. By the time Matt opened the final box, everyone had pretty much resigned themselves to the fact that the tasting was a bust.

Matt didn't even announce the last flavor. He just plunked the cake on a plate and dropped it in front of me. Everyone had eaten enough by now, and I was the only one who sliced off a chunk with my fork and stuck it in my mouth.

Pure bliss followed.

This was Chef Fong's famous Coffee and Cream Cake! As I savored the delicate layers of coffee-laced chiffon, filled with sweetened whipped cream, and finished with an amazing mocha buttercream, I felt the tiny hairs on my arms begin to tingle.

Suddenly, I was jolted by the memory of Chef Fong's proud expression as he described the creation of this cake to me. The coffee he used was not from Driftwood, the Parkview's less-than-inspiring vendor. Instead, the chef had sourced a fruity East African bean, sold by a cooperative under the name *Ladha Nzuri* ("Good Taste" in Swahili). He home-roasted the beans himself, especially for the cake.

Frowning at my long silence, Babka misconstrued the reason.

"*Bupkes*, eh, kiddo?" She patted my arm. "My sympathies."

I couldn't reply because I was experiencing the most intense rush of memories yet. They flooded my head, drowning my consciousness, until I feared I was going to black out again.

Meanwhile, the men resumed their bickering.

"Of course the tasting was a bust," Matt said accusingly. "Because Quinn was here."

"Me?" the detective blurted. "I hardly said two words—"

"That's what I meant. You were here, but you weren't any help at all. Why didn't you say something? Help guide her?"

"Because you were doing enough talking for the three of us!"

"What's your problem, flatfoot? Feeling threatened?"

Quinn stepped up to Matt and poked his finger into my ex-husband's chest. "Why don't you do me a favor, Allegro, and—"

"A favor!"

I cried out the words and everyone went silent.

Quinn turned to me. "Clare? What is it?"

"That's why Annette staged the cake tasting for me. She invited me to the Parkview because she wanted to ask me for *a favor*!"

Sixty

~~~~~~~~~~~~~~~~~~~~~~~~~~~~~~~~~~~~~~~

Silent seconds seemed to stretch as everyone stared at me with eyes bigger than the cakes we'd sampled.

"What kind of favor?" Quinn pressed, gaze intense.

"A strange one," I said. "Give me a moment . . ."

Closing my eyes to block out distractions, I tried to make sense of the whirling bits of memory. Finally, the kaleidoscope in my head coalesced, and I was back in the Gotham Suite.

I smelled the array of cakes, the sweet apple slices, the fresh roses in the vase. I heard Fifth Avenue traffic through the windows overlooking Central Park and Chef Fong and his assistant tinkering in the kitchenette.

"It was near the end of the tasting," I told Babka, Matt, and Quinn, my eyes still closed.

"I'd chosen to go with a traditional stack cake in three tiers. I wanted Coffee and Cream at the bottom, Hazelnut in the middle, and the Prosecco Cake on top—"

Matt interrupted. "These details aren't important—"

"They are to her," Quinn snapped. "Let her talk."

I swallowed hard to keep from tossing my cakes, and I wondered whether my wooziness was partly induced, not just by the visions, but the amount of sugar I'd just consumed!

"Go on, sweetie," Babka urged. "What else do you remember?"

"After I chose my wedding cake flavors, the chef and his assistant left, and I was alone with Annette Brewster for the first time. That's when I pitched her on our Village Blend coffee, and she opened up about the death of her husband, and the real reason she'd invited me to the Parkview Palace."

I rested my elbows on the marble bar, afraid I'd fall from the high chair. Squeezing my eyes even tighter, I saw Annette as she appeared that night.

The elegant hotelier didn't look very different from the thirty-year-old portrait I'd seen in the Gotham Suite. She was still shapely in a tasteful black dress, and her large blue eyes, soft blond hair, and high sculpted cheekbones were striking.

Madame told me that back in the 1980s, Annette could have been a fashion model. That night, I thought she had all the glamour and poise of a middle-aged movie queen. Her hair was pulled back in a French braid, showing off her slender neck. Her décolletage might have been daring for some women over sixty, yet it appeared natural and right for her.

Finally, I heard Annette's voice, speaking as clearly as if she were in this room . . .

"CLARE, I'm going to tell you something that very few people know, and I need you to keep it that way. The Parkview Palace is under a cloud, and I want out. That's why I'm selling it."

"What's your definition of a cloud?" I asked.

"The worst storm you can imagine, and it may already be too late to stop it." She took my hands in hers. "The next thing I'm about to tell you is an even greater secret. I haven't told anyone, because I can't trust those around me, not even members of my family."

I assured Annette that her secret was safe with me.

"My husband's death was no accident—though the Suffolk County police ruled it one. Harlan made enemies. Some of them were our neighbors in the Hamptons. Others were ruthless people in powerful positions. He didn't care. With his money and connections, he thought he was invincible. And he was, until four months ago."

"What can I do?"

"I know your reputation, Clare. I know you've helped people in the past. Now I'm in trouble, and I'm hoping you'll help me." Annette bit back tears. "I *need* to know who killed Harlan."

"You have no idea?"

"We weren't close anymore. Harlan and I had been living separately for years. He had his own place downtown in the Mews, while I lived here at the Parkview. We only saw each other at social engagements, or in our summer home in the Hamptons."

"Why didn't you ever divorce?"

"The split would have been a disaster for our finances. So we agreed to live separate lives." She shook her head. "It's not for love that I care who killed that bastard—it's fear. I'm worried the person who killed Harlan will be coming for me next."

"You should trust the police with that worry."

"I can't—for many reasons. For one, I have no real evidence. And my suspicions are based on . . . well, frankly, things I do not wish law enforcement officials to know about. Harlan's dead now, but he engaged in activities that the media and the papers would have a field day with, if they ever found out. I don't want to hire private investigators for the same reason. I don't trust them. But I trust Blanche, and she trusts you. For years, she's bragged about your accomplishments. All I'd like you to do is ask around, see what you can find out about Harlan's so-called car accident. Come to me with whatever you discover. If you think we should go to the police, then we can go together."

ABRUPTLY, I opened my eyes. Blinking against the glare, I found myself back in my ex-husband's Hamptons house, and realized it was Detective Quinn who caught me before I slid off the chair and onto the floor.

Matt and Babka stared at me, mouths gaping. But no one was more shocked than yours truly.

"I told Annette I'd do it. I said I'd learn all I could about her husband's death. Now why would I say a stupid thing like that? Did I wake up in an episode of *Murder, She Wrote*?"

Detective Quinn and Matt exchanged strange glances but said nothing. It was Babka who spoke up—

"That's what you've been up to, kiddo. Over the past few years you've been doing a helluva lot more than roasting and serving coffee. You've been helping out friends, family, and people in the community when they needed it. In the process, you've also helped the police put some bad people away."

"I have?" Unsure how I felt about this revelation, my gaze fell on Detective Quinn. "Are *you* the reason? Did you turn me into some coffeehouse version of Jessica Fletcher?"

Quinn shook his head. "It was all you, Clare, from the start."

"You're just like I was when I ran my East Side place," Babka said with a proud smile. "A buttinsky—in a good way."

"Clare is also a natural detective," Quinn added. "And I think she's capable of helping to solve this crime, too—"

"Wait a second!" Matt said. "This is not her business!"

"What if Harlan Brewster *was* murdered?" Quinn argued. "And what if the person who did it came after Annette, as she feared?"

"Frankly, I don't give two burps about Annette Brewster," Matt returned. "The person I care about is Clare—"

"Hold on," I interrupted. "I'd like to help Annette, if I can."

"Look at it this way, Allegro," Quinn said. "If we find out what really happened to Annette Brewster, we might find out what happened to Clare, and that might help her fully regain her memories."

Matt waved a hand. "My advice? Worry about yourself, Clare, not some rich hotel diva—"

"No," I said firmly. "I agree with Detective Quinn. We should investigate Harlan Brewster's death."

"Don't listen to this guy," Matt spat. "It's just his inner cop talking."

"It's reason and logic talking," Quinn countered. "I'm already here in the Hamptons, which is where Harlan Brewster died. I can at least start looking into it."

"Not without me, you don't," I said. "It's *my* life that got screwed up over this. And I'm the one who promised Annette I'd help. So you're not doing a thing without me. Got it?"

Matt sighed and shook his head. "And she wonders how she got involved in snooping."

Sixty-one

~~~~~~~~~~~~~~~~~~~~~~~~~~~~~~~~~

My head was still spinning, but the questions wouldn't stop. So I took my first sleuthing step, realizing many of the answers were probably right here next to me.

"Babka, you've been Annette Brewster's friend for years. What can you tell us about all of this?"

She tapped her chin. "I don't know. Some of it sounds fishy."

"Fishy? What part?"

"The part where you 'remember' Annette telling you she's selling the Parkview Palace. It was built by her family in 1885 and passed down through generations. Are you sure you didn't dream the whole thing up, Clare?"

Great! I thought. *You lose your memory and people think you're crazy. Then you get some of it back and people still think you're crazy!*

"That's what Annette told me," I insisted. "There are things I don't recall, sure. But I do remember that."

Pausing to think, Babka repeated Annette's words. "Under a cloud? If Annette really used those words, she was probably referring to the lawsuits—"

Detective Quinn perked up. "Lawsuits? What kind of lawsuits?"

Babka looked uncomfortable all of a sudden and theatrically threw up her hands. "Any kind of lawsuits! If you're in business, you get lawsuits. They come like flies to a *lekach*. Slip and fall. Damaged property. Failure of service. Failure of product. You name it."

"But you can't remember anything *specific*?" I pressed. "Come on, help us out here."

Babka went silent. Finally, she admitted, "Okay, maybe one. The one about the cameras. Annette was pretty upset about that suit—"

"Cameras?" Matt said. "You mean the security cameras at the Parkview? Is a pending lawsuit the reason they're off?"

"The *threat* of a suit," Babka said with a nod. "Annette was in the middle of settling it to keep it all from going public. She discovered her husband was using the security cameras to spy on guests. She worried someone on the hotel staff, maybe even the security staff, was helping him."

"Why would Harlan Brewster spy on his own guests?" I asked.

Babka shrugged. "She said it was some income scheme of his. That's all I know."

"Income scheme, huh?" Quinn rubbed his jaw.

"What do you suspect?" I asked.

"A lot of famous people frequent that hotel. Harlan could have used the camera images for some form of extortion. When people like that misbehave, it's usually worth something to news outlets. If Annette's husband had no scruples—which is what it sounds like—he could have made a small fortune on his own version of 'Catch and Kill' stories."

"What's a Catch and Kill story?" I asked.

"A tabloid-type publication asks for money to keep a story from seeing the light of day—things like football stars abusing wives or girlfriends or politicians hiring escorts from a service that deals in underage sex trafficking."

"Good Lord," I said, and turned to Matt. "We need to find out more about Harlan's car crash. Is there a paper out here? Something that covers local news?"

"The *Hamptons Ledger*. Come on, there's a computer in the study."

A few moments later we were all packed into the sunny, half-empty room. The bookshelves were as barren as the spindly modern desk, which didn't hold much more than a personal computer.

Matt navigated to the news website. Unfortunately, the *Hamptons Ledger* published only a single article about the so-called accident that took the life of Annette's husband. The location and time of the crash were listed, along with an interesting sidenote.

"There was a witness to the accident," Matt read. "But no name is given."

"They do say the witness was *uncooperative*," Quinn said, reading the text over Matt's shoulder.

"What do you think that means?" I asked.

Detective Quinn's blue eyes shifted to me. "Most likely, it means this person didn't wish to speak with the police."

"Then we've got to find this witness." I turned to Matt. "Are there any other places that report the local news? Maybe they'll have the witness's name."

"Well," Matt said, "for real Hamptons news, sprinkled with innuendo, gossip, and borderline libel, you don't read the *Ledger*. We're going to Facebook."

"That's an odd name for a news site," I said.

Matt shook his head. "It's a social media platform, Clare."

"A what?" I looked at Detective Quinn and back at Matt.

"Facebook is a site where people create a public page all about their lives," Matt explained. "They write up a profile of themselves, and post pictures of friends and family, news about jobs, vacations, kids—"

"You said it was public, for anybody to see?" I asked, perplexed.

"You can lock down your profile, so only friends and family see it, but plenty of people go public with their pages for more friends and likes—"

"Likes?"

Matt nodded. "You post something trenchant or witty, and your friends hit an emoji to show their reaction."

"Emo-what? Is that Japanese?"

Matt waved his hand. "Don't worry about it."

"Do I have a Facebook page?"

"You never took the time to create one, though you asked Dante to make a pro page for the Village Blend."

"How much do you have to pay for this service?"

"It's free. Facebook makes its money with display ads, and also by selling users' personal info to marketers."

"They sell your personal information? And that's legal?!" I cried, horrified, and then I remembered I had woken up in a world where your mobile phone can tell government authorities where you are and what you're doing at all times.

Matt shrugged. "There are opt-out buttons and site warnings galore, but these days, life online is basically a trade-off. People give up their cherished illusion of privacy for cherished illusions of convenience and popularity."

While I mulled that over, Matt tapped the computer.

"This is the Facebook home for Hamptons Babylon, the official web page for a content farm of advertorials that also reposts news items and gossip columns about anything having to do with the Hamptons community. And let me tell you, this page's postings were required reading when I was married to Breanne."

"You turned up in a gossip column?" I asked, surprised.

"Sometimes. But only because of Breanne being mentioned." Matt visibly paled. "Man, I dreaded those days. The snark was always nasty, and she'd either throw a tantrum or pout all week, or both—Here! I found something."

He pointed to a news item that someone named Roberto had posted about Harlan Brewster's accident. Roberto's comment about the story read:

I heard it was Galloping Gwen who had her eyes on the road when Harlan met that tree. True?

"Is Roberto talking about the uncooperative witness?" I asked.

"There are more comments under that posting." Matt pointed. The first comment came from a woman named Valerie:

Yes and not surprised, given their festering feud.

Valerie's comment gathered a number of little blue "thumbs-up" icons. Then at least six people asked "What feud?" and begged for more info. A woman named Justine made things clearer:

The Prescott/Brewster Feud was the Hamptons's own Hatfield and McCoys. Now it's over, with only two casualties—and no shootings, as far as I know!

"The Prescott they're talking about is Gwendolyn Prescott," Matt explained.

"I've seen her at parties," Babka said. "Mrs. Prescott is an amazon."

"She's certainly athletic," Matt said, "and well known among the horsey set. Galloping Gwen is what the locals call her because of how we always see her whenever we drive by her place—on the back of one of her horses. She owns Deerfield Horse Farm and Stables."

"So you actually *know* this person?" I assumed.

"Only because of Breanne. She—"

"Took riding lessons at Deerfield," I finished for him. "You mentioned that last night. But what's this 'feud' with the Brewsters?"

Matt shrugged. "No idea."

"Me, either," Babka added. "Nothing specific, anyway. But I *can* tell you that Harlan was a piece of work. The man had an ego the size of Montana. He cheated regularly on Annette, and he made plenty of enemies. Why *exactly* Gwen Prescott had a grudge, I couldn't tell you."

"I'm going to Deerfield Farm to find out," Quinn said and turned to Babka. "Why don't you come with me and ask her yourself."

Babka shuddered. "What do I look like, Ben-Hur? Horses are for Cossacks. And the stink of their plop wrecks my palate for a week. Count me out, Detective, but you have fun."

Quinn turned to leave. I blocked his way.

"Where do you think you're going?"

"First, I'm getting into my suit and tie. Then—like I said—I'm heading over to Deerfield—"

"Not without me, you're not!" I said. "Didn't you read the article? That woman wouldn't talk to the police. And if you flash your badge, she's not going to talk to you."

Quinn arched an eyebrow. "So *you* want to talk to her?"

"Sure. Matt says he knows her." I turned to my ex. "You can make the introductions."

Matt put up his hands. "I'm not going anywhere."

"Come on, please? You claim you want to help me. Prove it."

After a little more arguing (and cajoling), Matt finally sighed, agreeing to come with us for the interview on one condition. "As long as *he* doesn't dress like a J.C. Penney mall store mannequin."

Quinn opened his mouth to object, but Matt was ready—

"You've gone undercover, right? Dressed yourself well, or maybe like a gangbanger?"

Quinn nodded. "Sure, both."

"Then you already get it, because high society in the Hamptons has a lot in common with criminal gangs. You have to look like you belong, or they will never accept you. And if you're not accepted, then to them, you might as well be dead."

Sixty-two

"**N**o way!" Matt cried an hour later. "We are not driving to Deerfield Farm in a rented Toyota Corolla."

"Now you're going to complain about my car?" Quinn griped.

The three of us were standing in the driveway: Matt, Quinn, and I. By now, Babka was long gone, and I was back in my blond wig and fake glasses. The afternoon had turned unseasonably warm, with birds chirping happily among the autumn leaves. Unfortunately, the chatter on the ground wasn't quite so happy.

"You've already pointed out that my clothes were inappropriate," Quinn told Matt. "You stopped me from shaving, and made me dress like a beach bum—"

"Out here, an off-the-rack suit is like a cross to a vampire," Matt lectured. "The Hamptons elite instinctively recoil at the sight of one. But in my polo shirt and chinos, you almost look tony. The celebrity stubble is a must."

My ex-husband was right. The detective looked quite dapper out of his wrinkled suit.

"Okay, it's not perfect," Matt conceded. "Your haircut's still dorky and your big flat feet won't fit into my deck shoes. Let's hope Gwen Prescott thinks those clodhoppers are some sort of fashion statement."

Quinn spun the car keys in his hand and pocketed them.

"If my car isn't good enough, I take it we're riding in your rattletrap getaway van?" Quinn paused. "Yeah, that will sure impress the smart set."

Matt's grin was as smug as his reply. "I'll show you what will impress."

He led us to the nearest of the twin garage doors and pressed a button. The door rolled up and the interior lights sprang on to reveal a sleek black-and-chrome ride, gleaming in luxury-car glory.

"I give you this year's model of the Mercedes-Benz S-Class, fully loaded."

Silence followed. Cars didn't interest me much, but Quinn had the opposite reaction. He was speechless for a moment. Finally, he said a single word.

"Nice."

"I have this until the lease runs out at the end of the year, and Breanne stops paying," Matt explained with (I had to admit) admirable honesty. "It's good to get some use out of her before I'm forced to give this baby up."

Detective Quinn didn't reply. He was too busy ogling the fawn brown leather interior and the space-age control panel. I could see Quinn was impressed. Matt could see it, too.

"You want to drive?"

Quinn blinked. "Sure."

I breathed a sigh of relief as Matt tossed Quinn the keys. It appeared my ex-husband was about to bury the hatchet.

"Get behind the wheel and I'll brief you," Matt said. "Some people find the technology in the S-Class a bit challenging."

"Please," Quinn replied, close to rolling his eyes. "I drove a sector car for years—in Manhattan, with advanced-pursuit training. And I've driven high-performance vehicles on undercover assignments. I *think* I can handle this wagon just fine."

Quinn adjusted the seat and started the car. A moment later he gently rolled it out of the garage.

"I can feel the power under that hood," he said, nodding.

"It's a convertible. Pop the roof."

It took a moment, but Quinn worked it out. With the top down and the sun at our backs, Matt closed the garage door. I climbed into the backseat. To my unhappy surprise, Matt jumped in beside me.

Only then did the detective realize that Matt had tricked him into the role of chauffeur.

"Drive on, Quinn!" he commanded, ramming home the point. "Take a left at the end of the driveway, another left at the first crossroads, and push on until you see the sign to Deerfield Farm."

I had seen that sign the night I arrived, but I never imagined I'd be visiting the place—or looking for clues in a murder investigation. I was a little nervous about this "undercover" act, but eager, too.

Because of the balmy temperature, I'd left Esther's Poetry in Motion jacket hanging in the bedroom closet, though Matt probably would have objected to my wearing it, anyway. At least he approved of the lovely sweater, comfortable jeans, and low boots that I'd found in the bag Madame had packed for me—and Detective Quinn had delivered. Apparently, the future me was making enough extra dough to spend on clothes that were good enough to pass muster in these parts.

Minutes later, we turned onto the estate's long, curved tree-lined driveway. The forty-acre horse farm had been professionally landscaped, with natural jumps interspersed with open pastureland, dense wooded areas, a large natural pond, and lots of cross-country trails.

Though I was able to glimpse the ultramodern stables, the paddocks, and riding trails through the colorful autumn trees, the feel of Deerfield Farm was very private and secluded—much as I imagined the Hamptons used to be in the days when Jackson Pollock painted masterpieces out here, before the arrival of old money, nouveau riche, tourists, and celebrities.

We parked in the small lot and followed the signs to the Main House. Aggressively modernized to provide all the twenty-first-century amenities, the nineteenth-century farmhouse appeared to be the centerpiece of the sprawling property.

A member of the staff informed us that Gwen Prescott had been riding most of the afternoon but was expected to return at any moment. I was glad for the delay since it gave me time to enjoy the magnificent view from the Main House's expansive front porch.

When I saw two stable hands scrambling ten minutes later, I knew the rider galloping up to the house on an ebony stallion was Deerfield Farm's owner. Seeing her approach, Detective Quinn moved toward the steps. Matt stopped him with his hand.

"Where are you going?"

"To question the Prescott woman on what she saw," Quinn replied.

"And you're going to flash your badge?"

"If I have to."

Matt rolled his eyes. "That will get you nowhere. Let me do the talking."

Sixty-three

〰〰〰〰〰〰〰〰〰〰〰〰〰〰〰〰〰

"Mrs. Prescott, what a delight it is to see you again."

Ignoring Matt, the statuesque woman dismounted and stroked her steed's powerful neck. The horse nickered and pricked his ears at Matt.

In her boots, Gwen Prescott stood as tall as my ex, but not quite as tall as Detective Quinn. Though I'd placed her in her mid- to late forties, the owner of Deerfield had an athlete's physique and dressed youthfully, in formfitting riding tights, knee-high leather boots, and a long-sleeve polo shirt bearing the Farm logo. Streaming out from the back of her baseball cap (also emblazoned with the Farm logo) was a glossy black ponytail nearly as long as the one on her horse.

As a stable hand led away the stallion, the woman belatedly acknowledged our presence.

"Mr. Summour. I haven't seen you since last year's Fourth of July soiree. How is Breanne?"

"I wouldn't know. We've been divorced for several months."

"Pity. Your first divorce?"

Mrs. Prescott's half smile told me she was already aware of the answer, but asked anyway.

"Second." Matt shrugged. "That's how it is in love and war."

Mrs. Prescott nodded once. "I've found love and war are often the same thing, Mr. Summour."

"It's Allegro now. I'm back to using my maiden name," Matt corrected good-naturedly.

"So, Mr. Allegro, what brings you to Deerfield Farm?"

Matt wrapped his strong arm around my waist and pulled, until we were hip to hip.

"Well, my new fiancée, Clarissa Clark, would like to take riding lessons in the spring, so I thought we should sign up early."

The woman met my gaze. "Have you ridden before?"

"She hasn't been on a horse for many years," Matt jumped in. "My driver, Quinn, is an excellent equestrian, and offered to freshen Clarissa's skills. But really, I didn't want the love of my life around a guy like that, if you know what I mean—"

Matt threw a knowing wink at Mrs. Prescott.

"I feel my fiancée would be better served by a feminine touch, so here we are."

Gwen Prescott's curious gaze never left mine. "What sort of riding are you interested in, Miss Clark? At Deerfield Farm we have over a dozen paddocks of various size, and miles of riding trails. We teach dressage, eventing, show jumping—"

"My driver, Quinn, is an *excellent* show jumper," Matt interrupted.

Detective Quinn winced, but said nothing.

"But I don't think Clarissa is interested in competition. Are you, dear?"

I shook my head.

"Cross-country, then," Gwen Prescott advised. "It's quite popular with our casual riders—"

"Yes," I said. "That's what I'm looking for. I have this romantic notion of riding along wooded trails at night."

Gwen Prescott frowned. "I'm sorry. We have miles of

trails, through woodlands and pastures, but they aren't lighted, so night riding is not part of our services."

"But there *is* night riding here," I insisted. "I read about it in the local paper—"

"We never advertised such a service," Prescott countered. "Experience is required to ride in the dark. One misstep, and both the horse and the rider could be injured."

"But someone from this farm was riding at night four months ago," I pointed out. "The police reported this person witnessed a fatal accident but was uncooperative."

Gwen Prescott's gray eyes flashed. "I was not uncooperative. That's a libel spread by the *Ledger*. I told the police exactly what I saw—everything I saw. They simply didn't believe me."

"We're talking about the Brewster crash?" Matt said.

Gwen Prescott sniffed. "If I had known it was Harlan Brewster in that vehicle, I wouldn't have bothered to call an ambulance."

Cold, I thought. "What did you see, Mrs. Prescott?"

Her face clouded with suspicion.

"I'm sorry to be so curious," I said with earnest sincerity. "The truth is, the police didn't convey many details to Annette Brewster about her husband's death. She and I are friends. And she asked me to find out what I could."

Mrs. Prescott paused to consider my words. But her expression remained guarded, and the silence stretched between us, until I softly added—

"Please understand. Annette was estranged from her husband, but he was still her husband. As a widow, she simply wants answers. She needs closure."

At the word *widow*, Gwen Prescott's tight expression appeared to loosen. She didn't warm up exactly, but there was definitely a crack in the ice. Holding my gaze, she took a breath, and finally said—

"Well, Miss Clark, all I can tell you is the accident happened about a quarter mile along what we call the West Trail—" She pointed to a narrow dirt path that led into a wooded area. "When I landscaped the farm, I chose to exploit the land's natural features. I made sure the West Trail crossed a small rise that happens to overlook the highway."

She pulled her eyes from the trail to face me again.

"On the night of the accident, I'd just crested that hill when I saw the headlights on the road."

She paused, remembering. "The car was moving erratically, swerving from lane to lane. Then it suddenly sped forward, increasing in speed until it struck a hundred-year-old oak tree that borders my property."

"Sounds like a typical accident out here," Matt said.

"What did the police *not* believe?" I asked.

"It was something I witnessed after the accident that the police dismissed. You see, Miss Clark, I saw someone flee from the wreck. The person was holding a flashlight and the beam was all I could really make out, but I watched that column of light move farther and farther away, until it disappeared around the bend."

Gwen Prescott gave a signal to another stable hand. The man began to saddle a tawny colt with a blond mane and a spirited gait.

"I called 911 and waited on the trail for the police to arrive. By the time they reached the scene, the person with the flashlight was long gone."

"And the police didn't believe you saw anybody?"

"They said it could have been a bicyclist, or someone out for a walk. They insisted that Harlan was alone in the car. They said it was unlikely a passenger sitting beside him could have survived the crash—which was a mercy, I guess."

"What do you mean?"

Mrs. Prescott's expression darkened. "Harlan Brewster was alone in the car when he died, which means that on the last night of his miserable life, that man was not able to destroy another innocent young woman."

SIXTY-FOUR

~~~~~~

Mrs. Prescott's admission was a great help. Now I could easily and naturally ask her questions about the "festering feud" people were gossiping about on that Facebook page.

I cleared my throat. "I've heard rumors about Harlan Brewster, but you sound like you're speaking from experience."

Mrs. Prescott sneered. "Look up Dana Tanner on that damn Hamptons Babylon page."

"I don't understand."

"Dana was my niece. She and Harlan met at a summer party. She was curious about the Parkview Palace and its history, so he invited her to lunch at his hotel. Dana took the train to Manhattan a week later—and vanished."

I felt the tiny hairs pricking on my arms.

"She was missing for two days before a neighborhood watch group found her wandering in Prospect Park. She was without her purse and phone, and in some sort of shock. At first, Dana couldn't remember the events surrounding her disappearance and she didn't know how she got to Brooklyn. But within hours, she began to have disturbing flashes of memory. My niece swore something had happened to her—some sort of assault, she said, though she couldn't recall any details. Needless to say, my sister was frantic to find out the truth. Flora had lost her husband earlier in the year, and now something terrible had happened to her daughter."

"Did Flora tell the police?"

"Yes, but the evidence was inconclusive. Apparently, there were bruises on her body, but Dana had showered and changed clothes after the incident, though she had no memory of doing so."

"Did she lose any more of her memory," I asked, still tingling with goose bumps, "besides the events surrounding the assault?"

Mrs. Prescott looked at me strangely.

"Why, yes," she replied. "Dana couldn't remember anyone she met in college, or even her time in college. My sister found expert psychological help, but eventually Dana was institutionalized upstate."

Mrs. Prescott's eyes narrowed. "After several weeks, Dana left the care facility without her doctor's approval. Another patient said she was missing her mother, who had fallen ill, and was going to catch a train home. But instead of catching the train, Dana jumped in front of it."

Mrs. Prescott bit her lower lip. "The poor girl was only twenty."

"Was there an investigation?" I asked. "What did Harlan Brewster say?"

"Brewster claimed that Dana never showed up for their lunch date. He had time-stamped surveillance tapes to prove it, showing him having lunch alone, which was odd, and I've always been skeptical of that evidence. But because there was no real proof an assault happened, no physical evidence that could be recovered on her clothes or body, and the victim had a spotty memory, the police investigation was sidelined. It led nowhere."

"Except to a feud," I said. "Or perhaps a vendetta?"

"My sister was delighted to hear of Harlan's demise, naturally, but if you are insinuating that she had *anything* to do with Brewster's death—"

"Of course not, Mrs. Prescott. It was an accident. I didn't mean to imply—"

My apology was interrupted by Detective Quinn, who spoke for the first time.

"The accident happened along the highway that runs parallel to your farm, correct?"

"Yes."

"Can you give me directions?"

Mrs. Prescott pointed to the newly saddled tawny colt. "Take Sprite, follow the West Trail for a quarter mile or so, and you'll see the highway when you get to the top of the rise. The damage to the oak is still quite visible—"

"Oh, no, Mrs. Prescott," Quinn quickly replied. "I won't trouble you by borrowing a horse. I can check the accident scene from the road."

"But why bother?" she said. "Your mount is ready— unless you prefer Western over English? Mr. Allegro did say you were an expert rider. Is that not correct?"

"Hop on, Quinn," Matt goaded, practically snickering. "Check out the trail. Tell us what you see, if that horse doesn't throw you first."

Detective Quinn was on the spot, and I felt sorry for him. But when our eyes met, he surprised me with a wink.

"Okay, Mr. Allegro," he said, "if you insist."

While the stable hand stood by, Quinn took hold of the reins with his left hand, placed the same hand on the saddle, slipped his foot in the iron stirrup, and expertly swung his long leg over the horse. Settling in gently—and quite comfortably, I thought—he deftly turned the colt. The detective rode in a small circle for a moment, in total control of his mount.

Then, with a gallant wave, Quinn galloped off, following the West Trail at a brisk pace until he vanished among the trees.

"You were right," Mrs. Prescott said to my gaping ex-husband. "I thought you were taunting the man, but Mr. Quinn is clearly an accomplished rider."

Sixty-Five

~~~~~~~~~~~~~~~~~~~~~~~~~~~~~~~~~~~~~~~

We returned to the car after "Clarissa Clark" signed up for cross-country riding lessons starting next May. Thankfully no deposit was required, because Miss Clark was going to be canceling.

Detective Quinn, wearing a self-satisfied grin, still held the car keys and got behind the wheel. The roof was down, so Matt jumped into the backseat, sliding aside to make room for me.

I surprised them both by getting into the front seat beside the detective.

"So, what did you deduce from the crime scene?"

"That Harlan Brewster is one unlucky bastard."

"Hey," Matt interrupted, "what are you two talk—"

Quinn gunned the powerful engine until it drowned out my ex-husband's voice. Then he threw the vehicle into gear, raced out of the parking lot and down the long driveway to the main road.

"Why was Harlan unlucky?" I cried over the sound of rushing wind.

"I'll show you."

Instead of turning toward Matt's place, Quinn went in the opposite direction. We drove beside an area of pastureland for a few minutes. Then he slowed down along a desolate stretch of road.

"There," he said, pointing. "That's where it happened."

The damage to the tree was substantial. Though the tree was still standing, a ragged chunk of its trunk had been ripped away, leaving a splintered yellow hole. Studying the area, I noticed something else.

"This is the only tree around in this pasture, the only solid obstacle, in fact. If Brewster's car had gone off the road anywhere else, it would have plowed through grass until it ran out of steam and stopped."

I faced Quinn. "It's almost as if Harlan *aimed* for the tree."

The detective's response was an approving nod. I hardly noticed because my mind was racing.

Did Harlan commit suicide? I wondered. *Was he drunk? Did he simply pass out behind the wheel? Was it possible someone else was actually in that car like Gwen Prescott claimed?* I had no answers—but then I wasn't a professional.

"What does it all mean?" I asked.

Eyes on the road, Quinn shrugged. "I don't know yet."

"Really?" (Suddenly I didn't feel so bad.)

"We don't have enough facts."

"Then we should find more," I said. "Where shall we look first?"

"I have an idea. It's a place that won't give us any answers, but it will provide us with a lot more facts."

"Hey," Matt cried, leaning over the front seat, "what are you guys talking—"

Quinn hit the gas, throwing Matt backward. My ex finally gave up trying to join the conversation, folded his arms, and sulked.

At a stop sign, Quinn fiddled with the GPS device on the dashboard.

"What are you looking for?" I asked.

"The local police station."

THE "local" police station was more than a twenty-minute drive from Deerfield Farm, in a picturesque town called Southampton Village.

Located along scenic Windmill Lane, the law enforcement headquarters resembled a Tudor-style leisure station at a national park more than any police facility I'd ever seen. The modern building even had its own stone sign and a long driveway lined with faux-Victorian lampposts.

Detective Quinn found a spot in the busy lot. There were police cars, civilian SUVs, even an official-looking truck with a tow and a boat attached.

"Time for me to do the talking," Quinn told us.

"I won't say a word," I promised.

"No, you won't, because you're staying right here," he said, raising the convertible roof. Despite my disguise, Quinn explained I was still a wanted woman, and even suburban cops can have sharp eyes.

Then Matt and I both watched Quinn stride across the parking lot and through the glass doors.

"You never mentioned Quinn knew how to ride a horse," Matt complained.

"Don't put that on me, buster. You're the one who tried to humiliate him. And don't forget, for all intents and purposes, I just met the man. For all I know, Detective Quinn spent time in the NYPD Mounted Unit before he took over his special squad."

Turning my back on Matt, I faced the police station again. No more than a minute later, the glass doors opened and a male figure stepped into the sunlight, but it wasn't Mike Quinn.

"What's he doing here?!" I whispered and ducked my head under the dashboard.

"Who? Clare, what the hell are you—?"

"Shh!" I hissed. "See the guy who just came out of those doors? Describe what you see."

Matt stared for a moment. "He's middle-aged, stout—built like a fireplug—with thinning red hair, ruddy skin, a jagged scar on his cheek, and bad taste in clothes. I mean, who wears a burgundy corduroy suit? Maybe he was a tough guy once, but he's gone to seed. Too many beers and doughnuts. I'm guessing he's a retired officer, maybe a PI, or a rent-a-cop."

"Bingo on the latter. His name is Stevens. He's the security chief at the Parkview Palace, and one of the guards who confronted us at the Gotham Suite."

Matt tensed. "What's he doing all the way out here?"

"I don't know. But he was very suspicious of our crashing the crime scene. On top of that, one of his guys worked over Mr. Dante pretty good—and he tried to arrest your mother."

"Do you want me to punch his lights out?" Matt asked. "I know we're in front of a police station, but if he threatened my mother—"

"Just watch him. See where he goes."

Matt groaned a moment later. "The man's streak of bad taste continues. He's driving a neon yellow Nissan Juke."

I peeked over the dash to watch the little yellow car turn onto Windmill Lane and speed away.

"All clear," Matt said.

Breathing again, I sat up.

"What was he doing here?" we asked in duet.

"Could he be working with the police, trying to find me?" I wondered worriedly. "Maybe he saw me, your mother, Esther, and Mr. Dante pretend to leave the hotel in the cab, and then turn up again in the parking garage. He could have had one of his staff follow your van out to the Hamptons and report back to him."

"If he did, I doubt he's specifically looking for you, Clare. But it is possible he's trying to find out more about where the van ended up and why." Matt tensed. "And if he's out here, then it's also possible he'll turn up at my place with questions."

That stopped the conversation dead in its tracks. Before it was resurrected, Detective Quinn was back.

Sixty-six

~~~~~~

"BILL Piper, the sergeant on desk duty, answered the 911 call the night Harlan Brewster died—"

Detective Quinn climbed into the driver's seat, talking rapid-fire the whole time. Clearly, the man was in supercop briefing mode.

"Along with the eyewitness account, the sergeant let me see Brewster's accident report, the coroner's report, and the toxicology results. Harlan wasn't legally drunk, but he'd had a few before he got behind the wheel. The official cause of death is blunt-force trauma. His airbag deployed properly, but Brewster wasn't wearing a seat belt or a shoulder harness, so the bag did more harm than good. Also, Harlan was a short man, and children and small adults tend to get hurt the worst when airbags deploy."

"So," I said when he finally drew breath, "there's *nothing* suspicious about it?"

"The sergeant said this type of thing is not uncommon among the summer crowd."

"What about the person running away? Galloping Gwen seemed awfully certain about seeing a flashlight come out of that wreck."

"No mention in the accident report. The cops obviously

didn't believe Mrs. Prescott." Quinn shrugged. "That's the whole story from this station."

"Not the *whole* story," I said.

"What do you mean?"

I told Quinn about spotting Stevens in the parking lot. I shared as many details as I could remember about my tangle with him in the Parkview's Gotham Suite, including the conversation I overheard between Madame and Annette's sister, Victoria Holbrook. I also shared my suspicions—and fears—about why the hotel security chief was out here in the Hamptons, far from his limited jurisdiction.

Quinn's reaction was surprisingly subdued. He even made an effort to dial back my rising panic. "Calm down, Clare. From what you just told me, Annette's sister—"

"Victoria."

"—is running the hotel where Stevens works. You said this woman is desperate to find her sister. We know Annette and Harlan have a house out here, right?"

I nodded. "That's right."

"It makes more sense that Stevens is out here on Victoria's behalf, looking for clues to Annette's disappearance, and not necessarily for you."

"Or"—I gave Quinn my own version of the Spock eyebrow—"maybe he's doing the same thing we're doing, looking for Harlan's killer."

"Maybe," Quinn said. "Speaking of which, we have one more stop to make—"

"Wait a second, flatfoot!" Matt cried. "Weren't you *listening*? If this Stevens guy really did track our van from the hotel, then he's going to show at my place in Water Mill."

"What's your solution, Allegro?"

"Drop me back at the house. Then you and Clare can take that rental car out of my driveway and to your next stop. I want no evidence that anyone is at home but me if this little piggy turns up on my doorstep with questions."

Quinn shot me that wink again. "Good team work, Allegro. Sounds like a plan."

Sixty-seven

〜〜〜〜〜〜〜〜〜〜〜〜〜〜〜〜

Our next stop, after dropping off Matt, was the home of Flora Tanner, widow and mother of doomed Dana Tanner.

"Sergeant Piper gave me her address," Quinn said.

Obviously, Quinn thought Mrs. Tanner was a suspect, although I was the one who had used the word *vendetta* back at Deerfield Farm. Clearly, the man's detective mind was running on the same track.

"Do you think Dana's mother killed Harlan," I asked, "or somehow engineered his death?"

"We're going to find out" was his reply.

The Toyota hatchback was cramped compared to Matt's luxury sports car, but it forced me to sit closer to Quinn, and I found the situation—to borrow his word—*nice*.

We drove toward East Quogue but turned onto Lewis Road before reaching the town. Passing the entrance to the Westhampton Dwarf Pine Plains Preserve, we made a right onto a woodsy road lined with gated homes partially hidden behind shrubbery and ivy-covered stone walls.

"That's the place."

Quinn drove through open wooden gates, once white-washed but now weathered and pockmarked by peeling paint. The house—a three-story Victorian at least a century old—suffered from the same sort of neglect. Even the paved driveway leading up to the house was cracked and pitted.

As we climbed the creaky wooden steps to the front door, Quinn leaned close and whispered, "Let me do the talking . . . partner."

I flashed him the Spock eyebrow again.

Quinn rang the doorbell three times before we heard the lock on the windowless door click. It opened slowly, to reveal a frail, middle-aged woman gripping an aluminum walker. She wore a housecoat, no makeup, and her dark hair was a tangled nest.

"Forgive my rudeness," she said, her words garbled by a partially paralyzed tongue. "My brother's not here to answer the door, and it's difficult for me to get around."

"No apologies necessary," Quinn replied. "Are you Flora Tanner?"

The woman tried to focus on Quinn's face. It was clear from her sagging features that she'd suffered a stroke and was still recovering. Finally, she drew a pair of thick-lensed horn-rimmed glasses from her pocket, put them on, and looked up again.

"Yes, I'm Flora Tanner. And you are?"

"Detective Michael Quinn, New York City Police Department." Quinn displayed his badge. "And this is my partner, Detective Clark. We're here to talk about your daughter's case."

The woman scoffed. "What case? You people didn't find enough evidence, remember?"

"We may reopen the investigation," Quinn said.

"Why? The bastard's dead."

"You're talking about Harlan Brewster?" I asked.

The woman stared at me for a moment. Then she turned on her walker. "Come in, sit down," she called over her shoulder.

The house had a faint musty smell, and with the curtains drawn against the waning late-afternoon sun, the interior was shrouded in shadow. Flora Tanner led us to a large living room with an ancient stone fireplace, cluttered antique cabinets, a worn couch, and a threadbare lounge chair, which she immediately occupied.

After an uncomfortable moment, Quinn and I sat on the couch.

"Why did you two detectives come here?"

Quinn cleared his throat. "New evidence has surfaced, Mrs. Tanner. Another case involving memory loss similar to your daughter's. This incident is also connected to the Parkview Palace."

Flora Tanner sighed heavily. "What do you need from me?"

"Please tell us what you remember about the events surrounding Dana Tanner's alleged assault."

She objected to the word *alleged* and said so. Then, for the next fifteen minutes, Flora Tanner related her daughter's story. There was nothing in her version we hadn't heard from Gwen Prescott back at Deerfield Farm. But Dana Tanner's amnesia after she'd gone missing and the regression to memories of a time years before were both eerily familiar.

With some bitterness, Flora Tanner related her frustration with the district attorney's office, which ultimately refused to pursue a case against Harlan Brewster.

"I knew he was responsible. Ask around. That man had a bad reputation. I may not have proof, but as a mother I *know* Brewster is the reason my daughter is dead."

Sixty-eight
~~~~~~~~~~~~~~~~~~~~~~~~~~~~~~~~~~

FLORA Tanner brushed away a tear.

"What more can I tell you?" she asked, her voice breaking.

This woman obviously hated Harlan Brewster, and likely celebrated his death, as her sister hinted. But it was also obvious that Flora Tanner was physically incapable of harming the man—unless she hadn't been impaired at the time of Harlan's death, this past June.

I cleared my throat. "Ma'am, if you don't mind my asking, is your illness serious? Have you had the condition long?"

"I had a stroke, Detective Clark, in the spring of this year. It was my second stroke because I stopped taking my medications. I spent the entire summer in a rehab facility. The doctors say I should be fine, if I stay on my medication. And my brother is seeing to that."

I glanced at Quinn, who nodded his encouragement at my questioning. Was he thinking the same thing I was? If Mrs. Tanner had been in rehab the entire summer, she wasn't in a position to cause Harlan's accident, but she could have engineered it with someone else's help. Her brother? Another relative or friend? A direct question like that would certainly get us thrown out of the house. Fortunately, I thought of a less volatile line of pursuit, and jumped in.

"Again, if you don't mind," I asked gently. "I'd like to go

over what happened to your daughter after the incident. Your sister mentioned a specialist and an upstate mental health facility?"

"Yes. The facility belonged to Dr. Dominic Lorca."

Lorca? The name sent a chill through me. I noticed Quinn visibly tense.

"I didn't trust that celebrity doctor," Flora continued. "But I didn't have a choice."

"I don't understand," I said.

"No, I guess you wouldn't."

"Please explain it to us, then."

"Well, Detectives, the people who maintain summer homes out here tend to be very rich. But many of us who've lived in this region all our lives are not. I didn't have medical insurance for myself or my daughter. And I couldn't afford treatment for her, not unless I sold this home and the land it's been on since my great-grandfather bought it. I wasn't going to do that, so I considered begging a loan from my sister or taking a mortgage from the bank. I was weighing my financial options when Lorca came to me, offering to treat Dana without a fee. I jumped at the chance."

She sighed again. "But you get what you pay for, as they say. I'm certain that quack did more harm than good."

Quinn leaned forward. "You say Dr. Lorca came to you?"

"The doctor knocked on my door a few weeks after the assault. I thought my prayers had been answered. Three months later, I buried my Dana beside her father in Southampton Cemetery."

"Did you ever see or speak with Harlan Brewster after the incident with your daughter?"

Her laugh was bitter. "We didn't travel in the same social circles, Detective Quinn."

"But Gwen Prescott told us your daughter met Mr. Brewster at a beach party," I countered.

"That beach party was hosted by Harlan Brewster. I'm told a lot of pretty young girls got invited to his parties. Pretty girls get invited to a lot of parties out here. That's how my sister, Gwen, married so well."

Flora Tanner hung her head, as if she were suddenly too exhausted to support it.

"I had my first stroke last fall, a few months after I lost Dana, so I don't socialize much these days—though I'm told the lights are still blazing at Harlan's house."

I blinked. "Excuse me?"

"Harlan's house is open," she insisted.

"How do you know?" Quinn asked.

"My friend Mary works for a service that delivers my groceries. For the past three weeks, she's been delivering groceries to the Brewster house."

"But Harlan's dead and Annette Brewster's missing," I said. "Who would be staying there?"

"I only know what I heard" was Flora Tanner's mumbled reply.

After that, she seemed more fatigued than ever. So tired that she could hardly keep her eyes open.

Quinn and I exchanged glances.

"Thank you for your help, Mrs. Tanner." Quinn rose. "If there's any change in the status of your daughter's case, I'll be sure to let you know."

She bade us goodbye, and we showed ourselves to the door.

"Dana Tanner's case sounds a lot like what happened to me," I said as we stepped off the porch, "including the timely arrival of Dr. Dominic Lorca."

Quinn nodded. "Lorca muscled in on the Tanner case the same way he did on yours. He could simply be an opportunist, looking for another research subject or bestseller topic. Or . . ."

"Or? What do you suspect?"

"I don't know. But my gut tells me there's something more here than coincidence."

"Me too, but how can we possibly investigate Lorca?"

"Very carefully. Believe me, I know from experience. The celebrity doctor has powerful friends."

I was about to open the door to Quinn's rental car when a dirty green pickup truck rumbled through the gates and pulled up beside the Toyota—so close I was forced to press myself against the car to avoid getting smacked.

Ernest Landscaping was painted on the truck's door, along with a phone number. The vehicle's bay was packed with tools, a pile of tin signs with the Ernest logo, and a pair of lawn mowers.

"What are you doing here?" The voice was male and very annoyed.

I heard a door slam and a big man in grass-stained overalls came around the truck. His long, dark hair was wrapped in a bandanna like a Barbary pirate's. His angry eyes were focused on me, but Detective Quinn quickly intercepted him before he got in my face.

"Are you Ernest?"

"Who's asking?"

The detective flashed the badge and introduced himself. The bandanna man's attitude adjusted appropriately.

"Yeah," he said, scratching the back of his neck. "I'm Ernest . . . Ernest Belling. Flora's brother."

Quinn nodded amicably. "Yes, Flora told us how you're taking care of her. You're doing a good thing, Ernest."

The man's face softened. "All she's got left is me."

"Well, you sure are doing your best, while maintaining your career at the same time. I suspect you do a lot of work for the summer crowd. Are you still busy in the fall?"

"Planting and pruning is nearly year-round, Detective Quinn—"

"But not many of the summer people are out here now, right?"

"Not many, no."

"Flora mentioned the Brewster house is open," I said, jumping in. "She said someone is staying there."

Ernest grunted. "Flora says a lot of stuff about Harlan Brewster. Sometimes she curses him out as if he were standing in front of her. Sometimes she thinks he's still alive. I don't want her thinking about that man anymore. It upsets her too much. Anyway, Flora is in no position to know. She hasn't been out of that house in weeks, except for trips to the doctor. I wouldn't put much stock in her crazy talk."

I was about to counter that Flora had heard about the Brewster house through a local gossip, but a glance from Quinn silenced me.

"I don't think you came here to ask me about my business," Ernest said, his anger flaring again.

"No, we didn't," Quinn said. "We came to inform your sister that new evidence has emerged, and the NYPD might reopen her daughter's investigation."

"Oh." Calmer now, he nodded. "That's good, I guess."

The groundskeeper's gaze traveled to the front door, then back to Detective Quinn.

"I've got to check on Flora. It's time for her medicine."

"We won't hold you back then, Ernest," Quinn replied. "Thanks for your help."

Sixty-nine

~~~~~~~~~~~~~~~~~~~~~~~~~~~~~~~~~~~~~~~

"**I** thought Ernest was going to tear my head off when he got out of that truck."

"I handled him," Quinn replied, gaze on the road.

"Bandanna Man claims Flora is touched in the head, but I don't buy it. Flora's body was frail, but her mind was just as sharp as yours or mine—well, maybe not *mine*, but you get what I mean. I heard no 'crazy talk' from her."

"We'll know soon enough."

"How so?"

"You and I are going to the Brewster estate. If it's occupied, as Flora claimed, they're likely members of the domestic staff. If we're lucky, one of them was around on the night Harlan took his last ride. We can find out if he was alone, where he was going, his state of mind—"

"Didn't the local police already investigate that?"

Quinn shook his head. "They treated Harlan's death like a routine traffic accident."

"Maybe it was routine," I said. "On the other hand, Galloping Gwen's flashlight story certainly seemed credible."

"I agree," Quinn replied, "though there was no blood or anything to indicate someone was sitting next to Harlan during the crash."

"What about the backseat?"

"The backseat." Quinn fell silent a moment. "That's a thought."

"Care to share it?"

"I saw something once as a rookie. There was a high-speed chase along the FDR Drive that ended at a road construction site where the perps slammed into a concrete abutment. The car was totaled and the pair in the front seat died instantly. But a girlfriend cowering on the floor in the back walked away. Someone from the Traffic Division told me her position in the car saved her."

"You're saying someone might have been crouched in the backseat?"

"I'm saying it's possible."

Quinn fell silent after that, and I gazed out the window. The sun had set, clouds were moving in off the ocean, and the rural roads were becoming as dark and scary as the night I arrived. Things didn't get any better on the drive to the Brewsters' estate.

Quinn saw the address in the police report, but even with GPS we made two wrong turns on the narrow two-lane blacktop and wasted twenty minutes before we finally saw the brush-covered stone sign that read *Sandcastle*.

The wrought iron gates were closed and locked. Had we come in daylight, we might have assumed the place was empty. But it was night, and we could clearly see the glowing windows through the trees.

"I can't wait to find out who's at home," I said.

"Yeah, you're still Clare," Quinn replied with barely suppressed amusement.

"What's that supposed to mean?"

"Never mind. Just don't set your expectations too high. It could be some hired house sitter who never met Harlan and doesn't have a clue how to answer our questions."

But for once Detective Quinn was wrong. When he pressed the intercom button, a familiar male voice answered.

"May I help you?" Despite the electronic distortion, I knew I'd heard this man's inflection before—and recently.

"Is this the Brewster residence?" Quinn asked.

"It is."

"To whom am I speaking?"

"Owen Wimmer. I'm the Brewsters' attorney. And you are?"

"Detective Quinn, New York Police Department, and my partner—"

I frantically shook my head and waved my hands. Then I dived under the dashboard (no mean feat in a compact car).

"—*isn't* with me now. I'd like to speak with you, Mr. Wimmer."

"Oh, yes. Come in, come in," Owen said eagerly. "I'd like to speak with you as well, Detective."

The lock clicked, and the iron doors opened automatically.

I didn't utter a sound until we were on the long driveway leading up to the sprawling house. Then, in a whisper, I explained how I'd encountered the young lawyer before, at the Parkview Palace, and that he was sure to recognize me. I was even wearing the same blond wig and big glasses, minus the Poetry in Motion jacket.

Wily Quinn then appeared to channel Odysseus and come up with a solution as sneaky as the Trojan horse.

"When I get out of the car, you do the same, but crouch low and stay hidden until I get inside the house. I'll distract the lawyer while you have a look around the place."

"What am I looking for?"

"Signs that anyone else is present in the house: a domestic, a cook, a guest. We can try to interview them separately later, see if they can offer any information. Wimmer will likely disarm the security system to let me in, but I wouldn't touch the windows or doors anyway. Just peek through them."

I was nervous but tried not to show it. "Will do, *partner.*"

As we drove closer, I couldn't help admiring the mansion, which had great, old character. It was built in the same Italianate architectural style as the Parkview Palace, minus the gargoyles and about fifteen stories. The exterior was lit by spotlights that sprang to life as we moved along the drive.

Quinn parked with the passenger side facing away from the house. When he opened his door, I popped mine, and we closed them together. Then he sauntered to the brilliantly lit front entrance, and I ducked into shadows behind the Toyota, and waited.

The night was a lot cooler than the afternoon, and my sweater was now woefully inadequate. I longed for that cozy Poetry in Motion jacket to ward off the chill.

Quinn hadn't even reached the top of the steps before the ornate front door quickly opened. No domestic staff here. The diminutive lawyer—dressed in the same casual style as Quinn (in Matt's clothes)—greeted the detective personally. The two shook hands, spoke briefly, and then Owen Wimmer invited Quinn inside.

The moment the front door closed, all the exterior lighting went out, plunging me into near-total darkness.

Seventy

⟨⟨⟨⟨⟨⟨⟨⟨⟨⟨⟨⟨

Mike

MIKE Quinn thought the interior of Sandcastle was grand enough, but cold and impersonal. There was no warmth in Owen Wimmer's handshake, either, which Mike conceded was typically lawyerlike—cautious and noncommittal.

Despite his casual Hamptons attire, Wimmer came off as intense rather than relaxed. In Mike's experience, that was lawyerlike, too. He wore his horn-rimmed glasses on the end of his nose, making him appear as if he'd just finished perusing texts on jurisprudence; and his thin, reedy voice struck Mike as perfectly capable of delivering legal threats in a nonthreatening tone.

Unlike most lawyers Mike knew, however, Owen Wimmer was full of surprises.

"You're here about Mrs. Brewster, I assume?" Wimmer said. "Are there any new developments?"

"That depends," Mike replied carefully. "What are you doing at Sandcastle, Mr. Wimmer? With the owner of the hotel and your client missing, shouldn't you be in Manhattan?"

"I'm doing the same thing you are, Detective. I'm looking for leads and evidence."

"Leads concerning Annette Brewster's abduction?"

"Of course!" Wimmer said. "As I recently told your colleagues in Manhattan, I believe Harlan Brewster was murdered, and it's likely the same party took Annette. Now that I'm finishing up my digging out here, I believe I can point to several more suspects, as well."

"That would be very helpful, Mr. Wimmer."

With a self-satisfied smile, the diminutive lawyer turned on his heels. "Please follow me, Detective Quinn, and I'll show you what I've discovered."

OWEN Wimmer led Mike to a study that might have been orderly once, but now looked as though it had been ransacked.

Drawers were pulled out of desks and credenzas, their contents dumped into separate piles on the hardwood floor. Stacks of papers covered the surface of an antique table, with many ending up on the floor around it.

Mike noticed a pair of white cotton gloves—the kind Crime Scene Unit techs used to gather evidence without smearing fingerprints. Beside them was a thin stack of clear Mylar bags, each containing a sheet of paper and an envelope.

"Harlan was obsessive about keeping correspondence, but not so conscientious about filing it," Owen complained. "I found locked drawers stuffed with mail going back a decade. But it's the letters Harlan received in the months before his death that most concern me."

Owen reached for that stack of Mylar-sheathed correspondence.

"Like this one," he said, passing it to Mike.

The envelope was postmarked three months before Harlan's demise, and was mailed at the Old Chelsea Station on West 18th Street. There was no return address.

The single-page missive appeared to be produced by a standard computer printer, and the message was simple:

What you stole from me I can never get back.
But I will kill you before you do it to another woman.

Owen took back the letter and handed Mike a handwritten message this time. The writing was frantically scrawled on yellow notebook paper in bright red ink. The author was so full of rage, pen holes were torn in the cheap stock.

The threats included "hope you die in a car crash" along with a string of free-associated obscenities that even caused the hardened cop to wince.

"That one is especially ugly and perhaps prophetic," Wimmer said. "And the threats didn't all come from the United States. The next one arrived from overseas."

Sent airmail from Rouen, France, the note was printed on thin white stationery. Its message was short and as menacing as the others:

I paid you the money. Where is the evidence?
Send it immediately or harm will come to you.

"It's not signed, of course. None of them are."

"There are more like these?"

"At Victoria Holbrook's request, I've been searching everywhere I can think of, including this property. I'm almost finished. I'll bag up everything I find here and turn it over to the NYPD on Monday for forensic analysis."

"That's good, Mr. Wimmer. Good work."

"Thank you."

Mike's sharp eyes noticed a second pile—not swathed in Mylar, but neatly stacked, unlike the messiness surrounding them. The top correspondence bore a law firm's letterhead.

"What are these?"

"Legal matters, which I believe are also pertinent to the case."

The first was a cease-and-desist letter ordering Harlan Brewster to stop "demanding additional recompense" from their client "beyond what has already been paid." The client, Mike noted, was a first-string tackle on an NFL team.

The second letter, from a Beverly Hills, California, law firm, made a similar demand. There was also a demand "for any and all copies of the recording (or) recordings." Mike recognized the client's name, too. He'd seen her many times on the big screen.

The third was also a cease-and-desist order, and the client represented was a well-known politician, a name Quinn could have sold to the tabloids for a tidy sum.

"I've already given the NYPD a few similar threatening letters to follow up on—the ones I found among Harlan's papers in Manhattan. I hate doing this, Detective. The Brewsters deserve their privacy. But in the cause of full disclosure, I'm turning over whatever I discover."

"These communications appear to implicate Harlan Brewster's involvement in criminal activity."

Owen Wimmer nodded grimly. "We're past worrying about Harlan's reputation now. Annette is missing, her life may be in danger, and we've got to find out what happened to her, no matter where that investigation might lead."

Seventy-one

~~~~~~

CLARE

WHEN the exterior lights went out, I *should* have waited until my eyes adjusted to the dark. But I didn't know how long Detective Quinn was going to be inside that big house, so I moved immediately.

I didn't get far.

On the walking path that circled the expansive house, my low-heeled boot caught on a loose paving stone. I sprawled face-first into a mass of decorative shrubbery.

"Son of a bunny!" I hissed (not too loudly).

I sat up spitting mulch—but again, I didn't get far. My blond wig was tangled with a small metal sign on a three-foot post. I had to do all sorts of contortions to free it. Even in the darkness, the glow-in-the-dark letters on that sign were easy to read:

ERNEST LANDSCAPING

Now isn't *that* interesting. Making a mental note of my discovery, I was on my feet again, this time proceeding with a little more caution.

Though most of the ground-floor windows were curtained or shuttered, I did find one that was partially open. This window looked into a vast stainless steel catering-type kitchen. The area was bathed in subdued lighting, with no signs of activity, and I could have easily climbed through the window, but Quinn had warned me not to mess with the windows or doors, so I moved on.

Circling a hot tub large enough for eight, I negotiated a gauntlet of lawn furniture and passed a massive stone barbecue on the vast patio.

In the back of the house, the woods that surrounded Sandcastle ran nearly up to the walls. The stone path ended, and I probably would have turned back, but I noticed a lot of light reflecting off the trees. Steeling myself, I pushed through the branches and stepped between bushes until I discovered a wall of windows.

On the other side of the glass, I spied a large virgin white living room with a fireplace and wet bar. The room seemed showy and sterile. With no art on the walls or sculptures dotting the room, there was almost nothing to give the space personality.

The only adornment in that bleached wasteland was a line of five decorative panels along one wall, each featuring the likenesses of the five Parkview Palace gargoyles.

I was about to turn back when I heard a branch snap behind me. Alarmed, I whirled to find two eyes staring at me through an ebony mask!

Seventy-two

~~~~~~

T**HE** pair of eyes staring at me became four, then six, and finally eight. I was surrounded!

Luckily, the raccoon family I'd stumbled upon was as spooked as I was and quickly moved on. Heart pounding, I stayed frozen like a female mannequin, until the sound of the animals crashing through the woods faded into the night.

I'd had enough of stumbling around in the dark, freezing and being threatened by local wildlife. It was time to return to the car. But on my way, I spotted a second stone path, illuminated by a pool of light from a window.

You're in for the penny, Clare. Might as well go for the big bucks.

Unfortunately, the window's glow emanated from an empty hallway. Nothing to see there. But I noticed another lighted window along the path and moved toward it. When I peeked inside, I saw an absolute wreck of a room. It reminded me of the ransacked office in the Gotham Suite. Inside, Detective Quinn and Owen Wimmer stood beside a crowded desk, poring over documents encased in clear plastic.

The window was sealed tightly, so I couldn't hear a word being said. But within a minute of my arrival, the men were shaking hands again, and I realized the lawyer was about to escort Quinn to the front door, which meant I had to get back to the Toyota as quickly as possible.

I took the rest of the stone path at top speed, and a seemingly endless trip it was. I ran past a sunroom attached to the main house, a small but vibrant greenhouse, and the dark waters of a reflecting pool.

Not another soul was in sight. No staff. No visitors.

Finally, I raced across the driveway to the detective's rental car. I'd just dived behind the Toyota when the exterior lights sprang on and Quinn exited the house.

Inside the car, he made sure I was aboard before he started the engine. It wasn't until we drove through the gate that I crawled out from under the dash, shivering.

"I roamed around in the dark and found nothing," I told him, hugging myself in the cold car. "Other than a curious sign."

"What sign?"

"Our friend Ernest, the friendly landscaper's sign."

"Ernest Belling does the landscaping for the Brewsters? That is curious."

"It could be an old sign," I conceded. "Still, it's a connection worth pursuing, don't you think?"

"I agree," Quinn said, turning the heat on full blast. "You look like you're freezing. Do you want me to grab a windbreaker from the trunk?"

"Don't bother. The car's already warming up."

"Let's get you back to the house."

"Fine, but tell me what you discovered. What did the lawyer say?"

"Plenty. For starters, Wimmer thinks Harlan was murdered, too. He doesn't know much about Harlan's Hamptons life—apart from being invited to the house as a guest for a party or two. He says there's a fixer out here, an attorney, who Harlan consulted, but Wimmer doesn't know who."

"Is that why Wimmer came out here? To track down the fixer?"

"No. As the Parkview's attorney, he says his primary

concern is finding Annette. That's why he came out, looking for any evidence of a vendetta against the Brewsters."

"Did he find anything?"

"Are you kidding? It's a cast of thousands. Harlan had enemies way beyond that little Hatfield and McCoy feud. And I was right about extortion. From the cease-and-desist letters I read, Harlan was heavily involved in using the hotel's surveillance cameras to record embarrassing or possibly criminal behavior by his wealthy and famous guests for purposes of blackmail. Until his death, Harlan hid the activity from Annette and Wimmer, who looks a bit frantic now that he's uncovering it."

"How could Harlan get away with it?"

"He didn't, did he? From the dates on the letters, it appears this was a fairly recent endeavor. He must have been desperate financially. And you heard the sum of his character—he was a reckless, selfish, egocentric man."

"A cruel one, too, if he really did abuse that young woman. He probably got off on it." I shuddered and shook my head, wishing any of this would shake some awareness loose of what had happened to me—and Annette.

"So what now?"

In the dim dashboard lights, I saw Detective Quinn's blue eyes brighten. "There is one more line of investigation worth pursuing, and that mystery directly involves you."

Seventy-three

ᘓᘓᘓᘓᘓᘓᘓᘓᘓᘓᘓᘓᘓᘓᘓᘓᘓᘓ

By the time we got back to the house, a storm was brewing outside and in. We found Matt at the kitchen stove, making stew—and stewing. Before we could say a word, he announced (somewhat sarcastically) that absolutely *nothing* had happened while we were gone.

"No Stevens. And no NYPD SWAT team, though I'm *still* expecting them, thanks to the flatfoot here."

The detective and I exchanged glances. It was obvious we were in for a tense dinner.

"Food's ready," Matt declared. "Are you two hungry?"

"Starving," Quinn and I said together.

"What are you? A duet now? Set the table in the corner nook. You know where everything is."

A few minutes later, Quinn and I slid onto the cushioned bench in the kitchen. Rain began to streak the dark glass behind us as Matt ladled stew into our bowls. Then he plopped down a basket of warm rolls and tortillas and dropped into a chair across from us.

I dug in and swooned a little with memory. "This tastes like your famous Coffee Beef Stew. You used to make it for me and Joy when we were married, right?"

"That's right," Matt said a little shortly.

"It's not exactly the same, though, is it?" I already knew

it wasn't, but I thought the question might draw him out and warm him up—or at least take the edge off his bad mood.

"What you're eating is my stripped-down version of the *Carne con Café*," Matt informed me, voice still tight.

"That's the recipe you brought back from El Salvador. The one with Mayan roots. What's in this version?"

"Chunks of beef, veg, stock, coffee. I prefer this version when I'm in a hurry. What do you think, Quinn?"

"There's coffee in this?" he asked, incredulous.

"Damn right. I use the coffee to tenderize the beef cubes before browning. Whatever the meat doesn't soak up, I pour into the pot."

"Gives the stew a rich, earthy flavor, don't you think?" I gushed.

"Works for me," Quinn said when he came up for air again. "It's pretty amazing, Allegro. Thanks."

"I'll tell you how you can thank me—both of you. Give up this sleuthing nonsense."

"Excuse me?" I said, dipping a torn tortilla into the beautiful beef broth. "What's that supposed to mean?"

"It means Harlan Brewster was a bastard, and I'm glad he's dead. Whether he died accidentally or someone whacked him, I don't care. I care about *you*, Clare. You're the mother of my daughter and a partner in our business. One I count on. I brought you out here to protect you and help restore your memory. I don't see how uncovering a dead man's ugly scandals will help."

"That's because you haven't heard what we discovered after we left you," I calmly informed him.

Matt set down his spoon and leaned toward Quinn. "Are you happy now? Thanks to you, she's got blocked memories *and* impaired priorities."

Quinn put up his hands, and I slammed down my fist.

"Don't you dare patronize me. Suddenly, your own intentions in bringing me out here were all pure as virgin snow, right? Well, good for you. Now, why don't you try opening your ears and listening!"

"Easy! Take it easy," Detective Quinn counseled. "Let's

all calm down. You have any wine, Allegro? I think we all need to unwind, decompress, okay? We'll work this out."

Matt threw down his napkin, along with a few angry words in Spanish. But he did as Quinn suggested, uncorking a reserved Chianti with notes of black cherry and oak, which were (not unlike me, frankly) bold enough to stand up to the other strong flavors at this table.

As we all continued eating—and drinking—the tension in the air began to subside.

"All right, tell me," Matt finally said, refilling his wineglass. "What did you discover?"

I spoke first. "Remember that young woman, Dana Tanner, the one Galloping Gwen told us about? She went missing the day she was supposed to have lunch with Harlan. Then she turned up with partial amnesia and ended up committing suicide—"

"What about her?"

"We spoke with her mother, Flora Tanner. Guess who contacted the family, out of the blue, with an offer to treat Dana at his upstate clinic, free of charge."

Matt put down his wineglass. "Not Lorca."

"The same," Quinn said. "Dr. Dominic Lorca."

"Coincidence?" Matt asked. "After all, the man does research and writes books. Maybe he aggressively seeks out interesting cases."

"Maybe," Quinn said. "But something doesn't smell right."

"So what?" Matt challenged. "You found some facts. Big deal. What can you actually do about it?"

Detective Quinn pulled out his mobile phone. "Like Clare suggested, open your ears and listen . . ."

Quinn made a call to his second-in-command at the OD Squad, Sergeant Franco. After a few pleasantries, he placed the call on speaker and asked the sergeant to put together a report.

"Search for records, over the past twelve months, of missing persons who reappear with memory impairment. Do a separate search for crime victims or witnesses who report memory problems in the course of the investigation.

And pull any and all records where a case mentions Dr. Lorca or his clinic."

"What are you looking for?" Franco asked.

"I'll know it when I see it."

"O-kay. I'm on it."

"I also want you to tap our contacts at the hospital where 'your cousin' was being treated. Find out who called in Lorca. I want a name."

"Right. Anything else?"

"One more thing. Run background checks on Ernest Belling, Flora Tanner, and any incidents involving Ernest Landscaping." He gave Franco their address.

"That all?"

"Keep in touch. I'll do the same."

When the call was over, Matt shook his head. "What do you think you'll find?"

"I can speculate, but I'd rather be patient and see what Franco dredges up from the database."

"Sounds like you're just fishing," Matt said.

"Detectives go fishing all the time," Quinn replied. "And I can tell you from experience, you can't catch a thing without patience."

I laughed. "Patience is not one of my ex-husband's virtues."

"Can't argue there," Matt said, lifting his glass in toast. "Speed is my style."

"Spoken like an ex–cocaine addict," Quinn noted.

"No, spoken like a current caffeine addict." Matt rose from the table. "You people want coffee? Or shall we open more wine?"

"More wine," Quinn and I said together.

"Better be careful, you two. *In vino veritas*."

"What's that supposed to mean?" I asked.

"In wine lies the truth."

"I know the Latin," I said. "What I don't know is your meaning."

"My meaning is that stone-cold sober, you and the Eagle Scout have been pussyfooting around each other. Getting tipsy lowers inhibitions. You may not be ready to handle that."

"I'm not planning on getting drunk," I said. "Are you, Mr. Eagle Scout?"

He smiled. "I'm an Irish cop. I think I can hold my drink."

As Matt continued *vino*-ing, however, he refused to shut his *veritas*. "I still believe *he's* putting you in jeopardy by being here." Matt waved his glass at Quinn. "Any second now his mobile's going to ring and—"

The timing couldn't have been better. Or worse. Quinn pulled out his vibrating phone and raised an eyebrow.

"Lori Soles is calling."

"Who is that again?" I asked.

"One of the two detectives tasked with trying to track you down."

Great, I thought. "Are they here? In the Hamptons?"

"Let's find out."

Seventy-Four

〰〰〰〰〰〰〰〰〰〰〰〰〰〰

"I'm going to put Lori Soles on speaker, so we can all hear what she has to say. Don't make a sound," Quinn warned, "either of you."

We nodded and Quinn answered the call. "Good evening, Detective Soles. Have you found Clare?"

"Not yet," Lori replied. "Washington, DC, was a bust, but we've got eyes on the daughter. We also tracked the getaway vehicle to New Jersey. We lost it there, but believe they could still be in the state."

"Jersey is where Clare used to live. That's a logical place to look."

"We think so, too. Allegro might have taken her to stay with old friends. So we're checking with Clare's known associates."

"Look, I'm on Long Island right now, pursuing leads in another case, but I want you to keep me informed. I'd like to know where that bastard took my fiancée. Does Allegro have his mobile on him?"

"No. That would have been easy, right? He left it at his Brooklyn warehouse, which we also searched with no luck. Sue Ellen and I are waiting for him to use a credit card."

"That's what I would do."

"So you have no other leads for us, Mike?"

"I feel good about the Jersey search."

"Okay, then. Keep in touch."

"Will do, Lori."

The call ended, and Matt and I stared at Quinn.

"I don't believe it," Matt muttered.

"It's called hiding in plain sight. If I had left my mobile phone in my apartment, and it went unanswered, I guarantee you it would have set off an alarm of suspicion. But here I am, relaxed and available for consultation—with a perfectly normal explanation, if they should happen to ping my phone for its location. Okay?"

"No. Not okay," Matt said. "You heard her. She and her partner are still aggressively looking for *me*—along with Clare."

"That's true." Quinn leaned forward. "So if you really want to help your ex-wife and the mother of your daughter, here's how: The police are waiting for you to use your credit card. I say use it—far away from Clare."

"You want me to leave my own house?"

"Look, Allegro, your mother was the one who gave you up to the police. Right now the smartest thing you can do for everyone involved is lead a wild-goose chase. Go north. Use your credit card and move fast to a new area. When you get nabbed, and you will, *you don't know anything about Clare Cosi.*"

Matt thought it over, but not for long.

"Okay, I'll do it," he said. "It shouldn't be difficult. At this point in my life, police interviews are a cheap form of entertainment." He paused and studied me. "What do you want to do after I leave? You're welcome to stay. This house is a good place to hide."

In more ways than one, I thought. "I don't really want to stay here, but—" I looked at Quinn. "Where could I go?"

"How about back to New York?" he said. "To your Village Blend?"

"What?" This time Matt and I were the duet.

"Hide in plain sight, remember?" Quinn said. "I have an appointment with a law firm on Monday afternoon. If they agree to take Clare's case, we can start our legal fight. In the meantime, we can continue working on restoring her memories. Clare, you already have a disguise. So use it. Stay in your apartment and act the part of a Village Blend barista taking care of her boss's cats."

"It's not a bad idea," Matt reluctantly conceded. "Since she has breakthroughs with sensory keys, then she probably should be back in the home she loved. Do it, Clare. It may turn out to be your best chance to reconnect with who you were before you went missing."

"I have to admit, I'm a little nervous about going back. But I agree. It's a good plan."

Matt put down his wine and stifled a yawn. "I'm done in. I'm heading up to bed now. Take care of the dishes, will you? I'll be up early, crack of dawn, if I want to catch the first ferry. Be sure to lock up and set the alarm when you go. I'll leave a key and the pass code."

"Wait," I said, catching him as he headed for the stairs. "You'll really be gone by morning?"

"I wish I could stay with you, Clare, but it's clear I can't. I'll do the best I can to buy you time."

"Where exactly are you headed?"

"Connecticut first. And then Rhode Island. After that, I guess to Massachusetts, Vermont, and Maine."

"You probably have an old girlfriend or four you can look up, right?"

"Hell, you know me. If I can't find an old one, I'll charm a new one." He shrugged. "Don't worry, I'm happiest when I'm traveling."

"I know you are. Before you go, can I tell you something?"

"You're asking, but you'll tell me anyway, right?"

As he folded his arms and waited, I took a breath, hoping I'd say this right—

"Matt, this place, this Hamptons Babylon, it's not who you are. My memories of you—the fearless coffee hunter and global explorer—aren't about a man who lived his life for status or money. The guy I remember would rather sleep in a tent under real stars than in a McMansion next to the Hollywood kind. And you know what? Except for being a terrible husband, he's not a bad guy. In many ways, he's a fairly awesome human being."

Matt grunted, looked away—at the stark walls and pretentious ceiling—and, instead of arguing, quietly nodded. He seemed a little sad when his gaze returned to mine, but a more genuine expression was there, too, one I hadn't seen since we got here.

Stepping close, I opened my arms and gave him a hug. "Thank you, Matt Allegro. I mean it. Thank you for loving me."

"I always will. Remember that." He squeezed me tight and kissed my cheek. Then he let me go.

"Take care of her, flatfoot."

"I will."

"Good night, Clare. I'll see you soon—I hope with better memories."

"Me too."

Seventy-Five

~~~~~~~~~~~~~~~~~~~~~~~~~~~~~~~

The house seemed very quiet after Matt went to bed. All his agitated energy went with him. In some ways, it was a relief, but not in others.

My ex-husband had accused me and Detective Quinn of "pussyfooting" around each other. It galled me to admit it, but Matt was right. I kept my low-level anxiety to myself as Quinn and I busied ourselves clearing the table and cleaning the kitchen.

Then there was no more busywork.

When Quinn suggested opening another bottle of wine and relaxing together on the couch in front of the fireplace, I decided to be honest with him.

"I'm still feeling a little nervous around you."

"Really? But I thought we got along well today . . ." He paused. "Can you tell me why you're feeling nervous?"

"No. I'm sorry," I said because now I was feeling shy—and that made me a little angry. Shyness was weakness, and I didn't want to be weak. Steeling myself, I tried to explain.

"When we were working together as partners in the car, it felt comfortable and right—a little exciting, too—but alone, like this, you make me uncomfortable."

Once again, Detective Quinn's crestfallen face tore me up. And that was when I realized—

"It's the expectation," I confessed. "I know you can't help it, but I can sense you wanting more from me, wanting me to be something that I just can't be, not yet. Maybe not ever again."

Quinn closed his eyes a moment. Then he regarded me.

"I understand what you're saying. But do me a favor and put that aside a minute. Other than your anxieties over my expectations, you do know you can trust me, right?"

"I do—if only through logical deduction."

"Deduction?"

"There is no way on earth my ex-husband would leave me with you if he didn't trust you. And there is no way Matt would trust you if you hadn't earned that trust over time. So it's logical that I should trust you, too."

"It's logical in your head, but what do you feel?"

Once again, I found myself dumbfounded by the glacial blue of the man's eyes. Or maybe it was the way those eyes were staring at me—with such sad, sweet affection. Not for the first time, I was genuinely sorry that I didn't remember any history with him.

With regret, I looked away, at the cold rain streaking the dark windows, and told him the hard truth—

"I don't have enough experience with you to feel much of anything, Mike. So I think we should just go to bed—I mean in our *separate* bedrooms."

"I knew what you meant, Clare."

The detective scratched the stubble on his chin. "All right, then. Go upstairs. Do whatever you can to relax. I'm heading to bed, too. But if any memories come to you, please don't feel nervous or shy. Wake me up and let me know."

"I will. Good night."

Seventy-six

~~~~~~

D₀ *whatever you can to relax . . .*

Not so easy in a freezing-cold bedroom.

On the way to my posh igloo, I climbed the mansion's staircase. Quinn didn't follow. Instead, he pulled out his phone and headed for the sofa. I got the feeling he'd stayed behind to give me privacy as I went up to the second floor.

A considerate man, I thought, and for that, I was grateful—and a little more trustful.

Cresting the stairs, I noticed Matt's door was now firmly shut. For some reason this made me melancholy. My ex-husband was no longer the man for me, but he was the only man I could remember being a part of my life, including my love life.

With a sigh, I opened the master bedroom door and began to shiver with more than regret. Earlier today, I had cracked a window for fresh air. But the drop in temperature and the wet storm winds killed any coziness in the large space.

I hurried to shut the window and turn on the gas fireplace. The chill was so strong that I grabbed Esther's Poetry in Motion jacket from the closet. Pulling it on, I felt something inside. Reaching into a pocket, I found a small stack of postcard-sized art prints.

"Where did these come from?"

My mind went blank. Then I remembered—and this memory was recent: When Madame took me up to the Parkview's Gotham Suite, these prints had fallen out of Annette Brewster's private black folder—the one from which her last will and testament was suspiciously missing. I had gathered the cards off the floor and forgotten to put them back. Until now, I'd never taken the time to examine them.

As I shuffled through the six images—beautiful, witty, wistful images—I wondered why they held such significance for Annette. These paintings, reproduced on the small cards, were quite accomplished, but I'd never seen them in books or magazines, or even heard of the artist.

"James Mazur," I read on the back of all the cards, along with a gallery address in Paris, and the name for each painting written in English and French.

The first, titled *Unexpected Kindness*, showed a cold, rainy day on a Paris street. A sad, defeated old man, caught in the downpour, displayed surprise when a smiling young woman offered him an umbrella.

Two more paintings included one of a quiet, dusky Paris street with the only light coming from the golden glow of windows and a standing streetlamp; the companion painting showed the same location alive with activity at midday, flower boxes overflowing with color.

A fourth painting, *Parting*, portrayed a scene on a lonely train platform of two lovers kissing goodbye. The fifth, *Waiting*, featured a young waiter in an apron, leaning against a café doorway, gazing with open infatuation at his only customer, a stylish woman sipping her coffee, oblivious to her admirer as she absently stared out the window.

Finally, *Sunset Basket* depicted the lush French countryside. In the foreground sat a picnic basket filled with bread, cheese, fruit, and wine. In the distance, an older woman rode an old-fashioned bicycle toward a silver-haired gentleman gathering wildflowers.

The narratives of Mazur's work reminded me of Hopper, but with a much softer, more romantic approach to his subjects. In fact, the style and palette were exactly like the duet of paintings I'd seen hanging in the Gotham Suite—one depicting the Parkview Palace with the horse and carriage out front; the other a portrait of Annette Brewster. I remembered those paintings were unsigned.

But why?

That surreal feeling began creeping through me again. I was sure I knew more about these paintings. But my mind's blank walls carried only vague shadows and empty frames.

I shoved the cards back into my jacket's pocket. I felt so alone tonight, so disconnected and displaced, staring at Matt's empty walls.

Do whatever you can to relax . . .

Detective Quinn's deep voice came back to me. It was a comforting voice with good advice, and it chased away some of the shadows.

"Okay," I whispered to myself. "Enough wallowing. Time to get out of this frigid room."

Moving to the attached bath, I ran the shower until steam fogged the mirrors. Then I stripped down and washed up. Toweling off, I spied the Japanese soaking tub, and remembered Matt had encouraged me to try it.

What the heck? I thought. *It's my last night here.*

After filling the oversized copper bucket, I slipped into the warm water, closed my eyes, and uttered one word—

"Nice."

A state of deep, natural relaxation overtook my muscles, mind, and spirit for the first time in . . . I wasn't sure how long.

I had started the week on a park bench, moved to a hapless hospital bed, a getaway car, and a strange house in the Hamptons. Was it any wonder high anxiety was my constant companion?

Now I let it all go and just . . . drifted . . .

As I listened to the rain beating on the window, that stormy Paris street of Mazur's *Unexpected Kindness* came back to me, but not from the small cards.

I remembered admiring the original canvas of the work,

and it was glorious. Annette was with me. She was talking with great affection about James Mazur. She *loved* James. All her life she'd loved him. And she loved him still.

We were standing in a warehouse, Annette and I, looking at all six of Mazur's paintings. This was *Tessa's* warehouse, I realized. Tessa Simmons, Annette's niece!

Suddenly, I felt woozy and the rest of the memory flowed over me with the force of an Atlantic windstorm.

Seventy-seven

⦿⦿⦿⦿⦿⦿⦿⦿⦿⦿⦿⦿⦿⦿⦿⦿⦿⦿⦿

MIKE

He heard her voice, calling him.

"Mike! Mike!"

"Clare?"

At first he thought he was dreaming. Rubbing his eyes, he realized this was no dream. She was here, in his bedroom, excitedly telling him—

"I remembered. I remembered!"

In the shadowy darkness, he felt the mattress sink a little as she sat down beside him. The storm was churning outside. Suddenly, lightning flashed. In the heaven-sent light that streamed through the window, Mike saw her and his breath caught.

Her chestnut hair was loose and damp, her lips slightly parted. She leaned over, smelling fresh as the rain, and—turned on the lamp.

Her terry-cloth robe had been hastily tied. As she moved, he caught glimpses of her bare curves. His physical reaction was automatic. He tried to fight it, but it was only natural, given the situation, and he hoped it wouldn't matter, because if her memories of him were finally restored, then he'd gladly pull that robe off completely.

"What do you remember?" he rasped expectantly.

"Jersey City."

Mike swallowed hard. It took him a moment to control his almost painful disappointment. She wasn't here to make love. She was trying to tell him about a memory—one that didn't include him.

"Jersey City?" he repeated, as he began propping himself up.

"Yes, that's where Annette Brewster took me last week, before the wedding cake tasting . . ."

Clare's excitement about her recovered memory had cured her shyness with him. When he sat up completely, bare chested, he thought that would change. He expected her to blush again and put distance between them. But she didn't. Her expression was more curious than embarrassed. He could almost feel her gaze running over his shoulders and chest before returning to his eyes.

Now her own voice sounded a little unsteady. "It was the night Annette asked me to look into her husband's death. Before we went to her hotel near Central Park, she drove me to a warehouse in New Jersey rented by Tessa Simmons."

Quinn rubbed his stubbled jaw. "And who is Tessa Simmons?"

"The young CEO of a boutique-hotel chain. Tessa is also Annette Brewster's niece, the daughter of her late brother . . ."

As Clare focused on the memory, her robe opened a little more, revealing a glimpse of bare thigh. Quinn shifted on the bed, trying not to be distracted—and failing miserably.

"Annette took me to the warehouse to show me six very special paintings by an artist named James Mazur."

"Paintings? Why is that important?"

"Annette told me she knew the artist when they were young. She said James was the only man she ever really loved, and that soon they would be reunited . . ."

According to Clare's memory, Annette had lost touch

with James Mazur decades ago, when he moved to Paris without her. She first met him during her daily walks in Central Park. He was always there, painting beautiful canvases. They fell in love quickly, but her father had other plans for Annette. The eldest Holbrook child—Annette's brother—was supposed to take over running the Parkview, but he and his wife died tragically young in a small-plane accident, leaving their only child Tessa an orphan. Annette's mother passed away soon after, and Annette's father heavily pressured her to break off her relationship with James and do what was expected for the good of her family—learn the business she was now destined to inherit.

"Annette said she always regretted letting James go. When her father died of a stroke a few years later, Harlan was suddenly there to seduce and romance her. After they were married, she discovered he wasn't the man she thought he was.

"As the years went by, she found her joy in running her family's landmark hotel and taking care of Tessa. Then, two years ago, Annette had a breast cancer scare. She beat the disease, but while she was fighting, she told Tessa about her great love, about James, and how she always regretted not moving to Paris with him. That's when Tessa secretly undertook the task of searching for the mysterious painter."

"Did she find him?"

"Yes, a few months ago. Tessa was organizing an art show for the opening of her first Gypsy hotel in France when she located him. James never married. And he never forgot Annette. When he learned of her lifelong torch for him, he invited her to stay at his home in the French countryside. With Harlan dead, Annette was finally going to live the life she wanted. She said her niece, Tessa, was helping her heal her wounds and remake her world, and she would soon be reunited with the man she loved.

"Don't you see, Mike? It's possible the whole abduction was an elaborate *hoax*. A trick designed to get Annette out from under the ugly legal tangles that Harlan left her with. To set her free!"

Clare laid her hand on Mike's arm, oblivious to the dev-astating effect that her lightest touch was having on him. Another flash of lightning came before a rolling boom of thunder. Startled, Clare realized how far her robe had parted and quickly pulled the terry cloth more tightly around her. As she retied the robe's belt, Mike made a val-iant effort not to notice. Expression steeled, he pretended he was too busy contemplating her theory to be fighting the powerful impulse to pull her close. Glancing away, he fo-cused instead on the rain beating against the glass.

"I don't know, Clare . . ." Massaging the back of his neck, he struggled to clear his head. "The official diagnosis on your state is emotional trauma. The assumption is . . . you witnessed something so upsetting that your mind blot-ted it out, along with years of memories. That doesn't sound like a hoax to me—"

"Dr. Lorca was the one who claimed I suffered an emo-tional trauma, but I don't trust Lorca anymore. And neither should you."

Mike didn't disagree with her, so he remained silent.

Misreading his doubtful expression, she frowned. "You don't believe me, do you? You don't think Annette arranged her own disappearance?"

"It's not that I don't believe you. It's certainly a possibil-ity. It just seems so outlandish."

Her green eyes flashed. "Why don't we simply *ask* Tessa Simmons? If we pressure her, I'll bet we can tell if she's lying."

"Maybe."

"And while we're on the subject of Tessa," Clare contin-ued, "there's something else you should know . . ."

"What?"

"Annette's sister, Victoria, claimed Tessa and Annette had a bitter argument. But I don't remember Annette men-tioning anything negative about her niece. Do you think Victoria is trying to cause trouble for Tessa?"

"Why would she want to do that?"

"Most likely reason? Because Tessa was set to inherit

the Parkview. With Harlan dead and Annette missing, maybe Victoria wants her family's hotel for herself. Casting doubt on Tessa might give her a way to challenge the will."

Mike considered the angles. "Do you think Annette's sister could be behind the abduction?"

"I don't know. Victoria seemed genuinely upset when Madame spoke to her, almost desperate to find her sister. It could have been an act. Or maybe Tessa was the one acting—to gain Annette's trust. Really, anything is possible at this point, including my theory that Annette herself arranged her own abduction to escape her legal troubles."

"Which means Tessa Simmons is either a savior or a villain." Mike paused to deliver his next words as gently as he could. "I'm sorry to say this, Clare, but you have to consider the possibility that your own memories could be faulty."

"That's *why* I want to meet Tessa. I need to decide for myself."

"And where do we find her? Europe?"

"If what I just remembered isn't a false memory, then she's here in New York right now, staying at the brand-new Gypsy hotel in Long Island City, Queens. That's what Annette told me because she invited me to meet Tessa at the art show."

"Let's check it out . . ." Quinn reached for his phone. He navigated to the Gypsy website.

"You're right. There is an art event at the Queens hotel this weekend. According to the site, twenty local artists are represented in a competition to help decorate the new hotel—and one of them is your tattooed barista."

"Mr. Dante?"

When Mike nodded, Clare conveyed another memory, one that came after she woke up on that park bench. Apparently, Esther had teased "Mr. Dante" about growing a beard to look more hip for an upcoming *art competition*.

"Lend me your phone," Clare demanded. "I'll call him and find out if he knows Tessa. He can introduce us."

"It's late," Mike countered. "This can wait until morning."

But Clare was a bundle of energy now. Mike figured the rush of memories had given her hope that more would come. He just wished she would try to recover more memories about their own history.

She seemed to read his thoughts.

Without warning, she leaned over and gave him a quick kiss. It was little more than a peck, but it was the first physical sign of affection she'd shown him all weekend.

"Annette could be just fine," she said, eyes bright, "and Tessa might know where she is. The whole mystery of Annette's disappearance could be solved tomorrow with a simple happy ending. And then you know what?"

"What?"

"I can concentrate on getting the memories of our life back."

Mike lifted an eyebrow. "Did you just say *our* life?"

With a short laugh, she reached out and touched his rough cheek. "Yes, Mike. I did."

Closing his eyes, he kissed her palm. When he opened them again, he was relieved to see her smiling.

"Looks like you were right, after all," she said softly, before bidding him good night and slipping out the door.

"Right about what?"

"I really can trust you."

Seventy-eight
∽✺∽✺∽✺∽✺∽✺∽✺∽✺∽✺∽✺∽✺∽✺∽✺∽✺∽✺

Clare

By the next afternoon, we were packed up and driving back to the city. The stormy weather continued to plague us through the rural South Fork, all the way across the suburban sprawl that composed the rest of Long Island.

As twilight descended, we hit the Queens Borough boundary and were soon approaching the densely populated urban neighborhoods near New York's East River. Despite the gloomy weather, once I saw the Manhattan skyline, shining through the murky shadows, I was filled with a sense of well-being. It felt like a homecoming, even if I couldn't recall every memory about this particular home.

I was also feeling good about Mike Quinn—in more ways than one.

During the long drive, we agreed to set our personal issues aside and simply enjoy each other's company. As Quinn's wiper blades continued their steady beating, we reviewed the facts of the Annette Brewster case.

I knew Quinn was dubious of my "hoax" theory. But he'd gamely agreed to join me in speaking with Annette's niece. Earlier today, he'd arranged a meeting with Mr. Dante, using some cagey text messaging.

> I need your help. I want to meet the woman running your art show, Tessa Simmons. Can you introduce me and our mutual friend?

Mr. Dante texted back that he didn't know Tessa personally, but he would find out what he could and text back again soon with a plan to meet, which he did.

Once we got there, I was prepared to take the initiative, shake the woman's hand, and ask her point blank if Annette Brewster was with her old flame, James Mazur, in Paris.

Of course, if I was wrong, and Tessa had something to do with Annette's disappearance, then seeing her again might trigger some of my buried memories.

This could be dangerous, I had to admit.

If Tessa was guilty of masterminding her aunt's abduction to speed up her inheritance of the Parkview Palace (or the fortune it would create upon its sale), she would likely recognize me, even in disguise.

But a certain NYPD detective would be there, too. He was my backup. And I trusted him. Now all I had to do was *get* to the Gypsy hotel, a destination that seemed in doubt.

"Mike, did you miss the turn to Long Island City?"

"What makes you think I'm lost?"

"The skyscrapers. They're suddenly everywhere. Did we cross the bridge? Are we already in Manhattan?"

"Look at the signs."

We were still in Queens, but this part of the borough, near the river, looked very different from what I remembered. A few days ago, driving with Matt, I *had* noticed the rising skyline as we crossed the bridge. But here at street level, the visual impact was much greater, almost overwhelming.

In a little more than a decade, this ignored industrial waterfront neighborhood had become a sleek, bustling extension of Manhattan's Midtown—with a short subway ride in between.

I was awed by the ultramodern structures around me, some branded with the names and logos of corporations I recognized (and others I didn't). Tall, needle-thin apartment buildings rose up among them, like stalagmites with windows.

"I can't believe the transformation. Did I wake up in some kind of *Blade Runner* future?"

"Depends on which *Blade Runner* you're talking about."

"There's another one? I'll have to rent it."

"You mean stream it."

"*Eesh.* Change the subject."

Seventy-nine

∾ ⓢ ⓢ ⓢ ⓢ ⓢ ⓢ ⓢ ⓢ ⓢ ⓢ ⓢ ⓢ ⓢ ⓢ ⓢ ∾

Ten rainy minutes later, we arrived at Tessa's hundred-room boutique hotel. Her latest addition to the Gypsy chain was located near the East River, but it wasn't part of the glittering new Long Island City skyline. Instead, Tessa had converted a century-old paper factory.

The blocky ten-story structure was dwarfed by the soaring skyscrapers around it. But I preferred this funky industrial building—a creative tribute to saving a piece of the old neighborhood's history from the wrecking ball.

Now that night had fallen, the brick-and-glass façade was bathed in a pretty blue glow, sparkling with laser stars. Quinn pulled into the hotel's adjacent parking lot, and we entered the lobby.

This vast ground-floor space was taken up by a line of trendy shops facing the street and a large ballroom that opened up onto the lobby. The hotel's public areas were loud and crowded, filled mostly with the under-thirty set, boisterous and casually dressed.

As I stripped off my wet rain poncho and brushed droplets off my blond wig, I admired the décor, a combination of bohemian shabby chic and rust-belt retro with reclaimed factory equipment converted into functional furniture and eye-catching sculptures.

The ceilings in the hotel were well over twelve feet, a preserved feature of the old paper factory's design. It allowed plenty of room for the colorful murals on the lobby walls, including a free-spirited rendering of the Gypsy logo—a laughing barefoot girl riding a bird.

Quinn tapped my shoulder. "It's almost time to meet Mr. Dante."

"Almost," I said, and pointed to a touch-screen display, much larger than the phone screens I'd seen everyone using.

Creatively framed like an antique mirror, this screen was freestanding near the reception desk and displayed information about the hotel and its amenities. Curious, I scrolled through the list: room service, "hot" yoga (?), a "detox" spa, tour "guidance," a rooftop bar with something called "artisanal cocktails," and—

"What the heck is a complimentary Wi-Fi?" I asked Quinn.

He raised a Spock eyebrow. "What do you think it is?"

"A trendy new energy drink?"

"Nope."

"Japanese therapeutic massage?"

"Three's a charm."

"I've got it—a futuristic form of hi-fi?"

"Close," Quinn said when his phone buzzed. Pulling it out of his jacket, he checked the screen. His amused expression vanished.

"It's a text from Lori Soles." He glanced around. "I need to find a quiet spot to call her back, or the Fish Squad may get suspicious."

"Go ahead. I'll be okay."

Before parting, he bent down and *almost* gave me a peck on the cheek—habit, I guess. But he quickly thought better of it and backed off. Then he gestured to the wide-open double doors across the lobby.

"I'll meet you and Dante at the bar, as soon as this call is over. Shouldn't take more than fifteen minutes."

"No problem. Take your time."

EIGHTY

〰〰〰〰〰〰〰〰〰〰〰〰〰

The large ballroom space was packed with artists and their guests, admiring the display of paintings and sculptures. A circular bar, made from recovered industrial parts, was set up in the center of the room.

Some kind of synth pop was playing—I didn't know whether the speakers were hi-fi or Wi-Fi, but the music was fun and upbeat and the sound quality was impressive.

Since I was supposed to meet Mr. Dante at the bar, I headed straight there and quickly spied him sitting on a stool, sipping (I assumed) one of those "artisanal cocktails."

"Mr. Dante!" I called.

The tattooed barista froze and scanned the crowd around him. With my blond wig and big glasses, I wasn't easy to recognize, so I caught his attention with a wave.

"There you are! We've got to move and move now," Mr. Dante said frantically.

"Calm down. Let's sit for a few minutes and you can fill me in on—"

"No," he said. "There's no time. If you want to talk to Tessa Simmons, we've got to go *now*."

"But Detective Quinn is busy on an important call. Can't we wait fifteen minutes?"

"Tessa could be gone by then. It's now or never."

This isn't the plan. Not at all!

I thought I'd have time to check out the art show—and gather my courage to speak with Tessa. I reminded Mr. Dante of the plan he'd texted us during our drive. He was *supposed* to take me *and* Detective Quinn behind the scenes, to some back office, where he said Tessa could usually be found all evening long.

"Not tonight," Mr. Dante informed me. "Her assistant just told me that she decided to have an early dinner with a business associate, and then she's going home."

"Where?"

"I don't know where she lives," Mr. Dante said.

"No! Where is she having dinner?"

"Upstairs, at Nostalgia, the rooftop bar and restaurant."

"Let's go."

Mr. Dante took me to a dedicated elevator in the lobby that went straight up to the restaurant. Just as the doors began to close, we spotted a man who looked disturbingly familiar. He wasn't in his burgundy corduroy suit tonight or his security uniform. But I instantly recognized the grumpy, stout fireplug with the thinning red hair, ruddy skin, and jagged scar on his cheek.

Mr. Dante scowled. "Isn't that one of the assholes who roughed me up at the Parkview?"

I nodded. "That's Stevens, the security chief—and he's in the wrong hotel."

Not only that. It was the second time this weekend that I'd run into the man. The mathematical odds for chance coincidence were falling fast.

Eighty-one

~~~~~~~~~~~~~~~~~~~~~~~~~~~

Mike

"What's going on, Lori?"

Mike Quinn steeled himself. He was standing in front of the Gypsy hotel, and it was raw out here. Drizzly wind gusts were rattling the awning and whipping his trench coat, but it was the only quiet spot he could find to return the detective's call.

"I wanted to give you a heads-up," Lori said. "Sue Ellen and I won't be searching for your fiancée anymore."

"You're letting Clare go?"

"No, the opposite. The chief of detectives doesn't want us reaching out to other jurisdictions. We're turning our files over to the FBI tomorrow afternoon."

Mike cursed.

"Sorry, but those are the orders. After all the running around we did, Sue Ellen is fit to be tied about the decision. And I have more bad news."

"Tell me."

"Over drinks tonight, a friend of yours and mine who's close to the Major Case Squad confided that your fiancée's bizarre hospital breakout has made the detectives on the Annette Brewster case *consider* taking another look at her."

"You can't be serious." Mike closed his eyes. "They think Clare is involved in Brewster's abduction? Come on, you *know* that's crazy."

"Crazy or not, the theory is gaining momentum. Some of them think it's plausible that she left the hospital because she's faking her memory loss and knows more than she's telling."

"For what reason?"

"The speculation on Clare's motives vary. There's a theory that she took a payoff to set Annette up. And another that she struck a deal with the perpetrators who were holding her, agreeing to stay silent for a bribe—or because they threatened her in some manner, scaring her into silence—which is one answer to why they let her go."

"Lori, you know Clare. You don't believe any of this, do you?"

"It doesn't matter what I believe. The plausibility of it alone could make her a person of interest. Even worse, if they *do* decide to pull the trigger on Clare, the brass will have a horrendous conflict of interest problem on their hands—and it's *you*."

"They're trying to make *me* the problem? Are you kidding? Sounds more like they've got no results, so it's cover-your-ass time."

"Look, you know Sue Ellen and I believe Clare is a victim in all this. That's why I'm warning you. The chief of detectives is sweating bullets. He doesn't want to catch any political heat. So he's going to the commissioner tomorrow to discuss whether or not they should turn over the *entire* Annette Brewster investigation to the Feds."

Quinn watched the rain falling and suddenly felt the sky was, too. He was silent for so long, Lori assumed her signal had cut out.

"Mike? Are you there?"

"I'm here."

"You okay?"

"Sure. This is nothing I can't handle."

"If you think so," Lori said, but her tone was full of doubt.

"Thanks for the heads-up."

Mike ended the call staring grimly into the unsettled night. Despite his own calm assurances to Lori, he was filled with dread. He and Clare were already caught up in a bad dream. FBI involvement could plunge them into a genuine nightmare.

Once that bogus theory—that Clare was "faking" her memory loss—was conveyed to the FBI, ungodly pressure could be put on her for a "confession" of her involvement in Annette Brewster's abduction, or any "knowledge" of the perpetrators who had engineered her disappearance.

An ordeal like that would give a stable person a mental breakdown, let alone someone who was struggling with memory loss. And after it was all over—after they got nothing useful from the woman he loved—she would be placed right back in the hands of Dr. Lorca, in an even more distressed state than he'd found her. She'd be drugged and isolated again, taken from everyone who cared about her.

Even if he were to hire the best attorneys, the FBI could decide to press a circumstantial case against her or make an argument for commitment. She could end up remanded to a mental institution for years.

Mike could see no clean way out of this, not unless Clare could come up with some useful memories about the details of her abduction.

Or Annette Brewster was found.

Eighty-two
∿∿∿∿∿∿∿∿∿∿∿∿∿∿∿

Clare

"Do you think that Stevens jerk is looking for you?" Mr. Dante asked as we rode the elevator north.

"I don't know," I said. "But I don't want to miss Tessa."

When the elevator doors opened on the rooftop level, my breath caught. The wall of windows facing Manhattan's shimmering skyline made a spectacular sight and so did the restaurant's floor. The restored factory planks had been painted with intricate stencils, forming colorful patterns, all of it lacquered and laminated to protect the designs from foot traffic.

"Come on!" Mr. Dante waved me forward and together we bypassed Nostalgia's seating hostess.

"We're going straight to the bar," he told her with a charming smile.

Mr. Dante spotted Tessa far from the windows, in a quiet corner, near the distressed-wood bar that hugged the restaurant's back wall. Excited, he pointed her out with a sharp nudge to my ribs.

"That's Tessa Simmons, and she's with familiar company."

I didn't recognize Tessa. But I certainly knew her lamé-wrapped companion: the Golden Girl of Fashion, Nora Arany.

"Should we approach Tessa now?" Mr. Dante whispered.

"Let's get a drink and spy a little first."

I was relieved to discover the young, bearded bartender was *not* too cool for school. He had a welcoming smile and took my order right away. The "artisanal cocktails" were posted on a digital chalkboard, and I chose a gin drink, aptly named the Daisy Fay.

Luckily, Nostalgia's bar also featured a wall-sized tavern mirror—the kind that allowed old-time Western gunfighters to watch their backs, and modern-day barflies (and barista buttinskies) to people-watch the room behind them.

Our seats were very close to Tessa's table, and the mirror offered a good view of the young CEO. While I waited for my drink, I studied her reflection. Tessa appeared to be in full bohemian mode tonight, wearing a mishmash of clashing colors, accessorized with scarfs, dangling feathered earrings, and an entire Slinky's worth of bracelets. Her yellow hair hung in two long Alpine braids bound by ribbons knotted tighter than bondage straps. Her face seemed tight, too, with large blue eyes circled by dark makeup.

Sadly, I found nothing familiar about Tessa Simmons. I felt no tingle of recognition, no wooziness signaling an oncoming flashback, *nothing*. Hearing her voice, I was sure I'd never met the young woman.

Tessa had been doing most of the talking since I arrived, and her soft voice was a strain to hear over the room's background noise. From what I could decipher, she was forming a limited partnership with Nora.

When Nora finally spoke, it was a huge relief. The first time I'd encountered the Golden Gotham Girl, her voice was so loud, it carried over the traffic sounds on Fifth Avenue. Compared to that, penetrating the noise level in this bar was a cinch.

"Tessa, honey," Nora said, after downing an entire martini in two thirsty gulps. "Whatever you wrote into that little contract is fine with me, as long as I get a Fifth Avenue store on the ground floor of the Parkview Palace."

"You'll get that and more, Nora. Within eighteen months, the hotel will be fifty percent co-op, with apartments selling in the millions per. On top of that immediate windfall, you'll get a percentage of the Parkview's future revenue for your investment. And there *will* be revenue. The old style of hotel keeping espoused by Aunt Annette and Aunt Victoria is over. My way is the future. That's why I bought the Parkview Palace."

Tessa bought the Parkview? I thought in surprise. *But why buy something when you're about to inherit it?*

The simple answer was that you *wouldn't*—certainly not if you were planning to abduct and/or murder the person who was *willing* the hotel to you.

"I've got big bucks invested in the Parkview," Nora said. "I hope you're right about the money."

"I'm never wrong," Tessa said boldly. "According to projections, you'll double your investment within three years."

"Well, that's something to celebrate!" Nora cried, demanding another martini.

But when the waitress returned with her cocktail, it took only one sip to stoke Nora's anger. "Can you imagine how much revenue I lost because of the years Annette kept me out of her hotel? She always had a reason, too. My fashions weren't the right fit for the Parkview's clientele. My designs were too urban, too young, too trendy—like there's something wrong with that!"

During her rant, Nora knocked a water glass off the table. It broke with a tinkling sound.

"Relax, Nora," Tessa soothed as she signaled for a busboy to clean up the glass. "Give the past the slip. Try hot yoga. It worked for me. That and deep meditation got me through my divorce."

Nora waved her off. "You want to know the real reason Annette kept me out? It was because I slept with her damned husband."

EIGHTY-THREE

～～～～～～～～～～～～～～～

"**You** did what?!" Tessa seemed as shocked as I was.

"Take it easy," Nora quickly replied. "She and Harlan were estranged at the time, living completely separate lives. He and I were seated next to each other at some charity dinner. We were laughing it up over something or other, and I said to myself, 'What the heck? I've never slept with a randy munchkin before!'"

Nora's laugh shook half the room. She paused long enough to take a second swig of her cocktail, and Tessa shook her head.

"No wonder Aunt Annette was annoyed with me when I told her about taking you on as a partner. She refused to say why, but she was livid."

"Hey, it's not like I was the only one of Annette's friends Harlan screwed. Instead of holding a grudge against me, Annette should have looked closer to home—and family."

Now even Mr. Dante was shocked. He and I exchanged a silent glance. *Holy cow*, I thought, in *martini veritas!*

This time, Tessa didn't appear shocked by Nora's words, as much as curious. "What exactly are you referring to? Who in my *family* slept with Harlan?"

Like the amps in *This Is Spinal Tap*, Nora's volume was

permanently set on eleven. So when she spoke "quietly" to Tessa, I could still hear her.

"When your aunt Victoria fled to Vienna, she claimed she was pursuing a career in classical music. But the real reason she left was because she wasn't so thin, if you know what I mean."

Tessa grimaced. "Are you saying what I think you're saying? That I've got some long-lost cousin, adopted by some unknown Viennese couple?"

"You probably do. I mean, if Victoria wanted to get rid of the baby bump, she didn't have to go all the way to Vienna to do it. My money is on the adoption. Anyway, I heard that after she moved back to the States, Victoria took up with Harlan again. And this wasn't some fling, either, like it was years ago—before he went after Annette. He and Vickie supposedly had some love nest, right here in the city, for her secret visits."

The waitress delivered yet another martini and Nora went back to downing it in two gulps.

As a busy busboy cleaned up the broken glass, Nora moved on to rather mean-spirited gossip about other members of the Gotham Ladies. Before long, she went from inebriated to incoherent. The Golden Girl was as drunk as a skunk!

The waitress noticed and approached Tessa. "Should I call a car?"

The CEO shook her head. "Let's get Ms. Arany a room."

The waitress returned with confirmation, and with help from the bearded bartender, Nora was soon on her feet and moving again.

"I need to lie down!" she announced to the restaurant.

"We've got a bed for you, Nora," Tessa said. "You can rest as long as you like."

After the fashion designer was escorted out, making an unsubtle pass at the "handsome boy" bartender as she went, I expected Tessa to leave, too. Instead, she sat down and pulled a phone from her bag.

"Do you want me to introduce you to Tessa now?" Mr. Dante whispered.

Before I could answer, the restaurant's hostess approached Tessa's table.

"Toby Mullins is here," she said. "He says he has an appointment to see you."

Tessa nodded. "Bring him over."

A minute later, a familiar tweedy brown sport coat appeared in the mirror above the bar, and I nearly choked on my Daisy Fay. At last, I knew the identity of that mystery man at the hospital, the bald guy with the mustache who tried to follow me when I bolted for the elevator.

His name was Toby Mullins.

And it appeared Tessa Simmons knew him, too.

EIGHTY-FOUR

~~~~~~

THE situation was infuriating but there was nothing to be done.

Toby Mullins and Tessa Simmons were the quietest couple in the bar. From the moment he sat down, their heads were together, their faces somber as they chatted in whispers. It was obviously a serious and sometimes emotional conversation.

And I couldn't hear a word of it.

There was a long moment when Tessa and Toby were both huddled over his mobile phone. What they were looking at and what they were whispering about remained a mystery to me.

"Do you recognize that man?" I quietly asked Mr. Dante.

"No," he said. "Should I?"

"When I was in the hospital, I saw the guy outside my room *several* times. And when he noticed me leaving with you and Madame, he tried to follow us."

"Why?"

"That's what I'd like to know, along with why Tessa Simmons is so interested in what he has to say."

Finally, Mullins rose, and so did his voice.

"I'll keep you informed," he said with confidence. As he tucked his phone away, she said something quietly to him.

"I will," he replied. "Now I'd better get started. It's a long drive and the roads can be treacherous."

I elbowed Mr. Dante. "He's driving somewhere. That means he's heading to the parking lot."

"Do you want me to follow him?"

We both acted nonchalant until Mullins passed us.

"*I'm* going to follow him," I said, scooping up my rain poncho.

Tessa was someone I could catch up with again. My questions for her could wait. But Mullins was someone I knew little about. And since the man had been *spying* on me at the hospital, it made me much more interested in getting answers from him tonight.

I whispered to Dante, "You know where to find Detective Quinn. Tell him I'm following a bald man with a mustache named Toby Mullins, and that he should meet me in the parking lot, pronto!"

I hurried to the elevator, slipping into my poncho as I moved.

The car hadn't arrived yet, and a small crowd had gathered in the waiting area. I mingled with a group of young people, their gazes glued to phone screens.

Keeping my head down, I entered the elevator with the group, which included Toby Mullins. Mustache Man never even looked in my direction. Like everyone else in this phone-fetish future, his attention was completely focused on his small screen.

Mullins didn't leave through the lobby's main exit. He went to a pair of doors that led directly to the parking area. I gave him a few seconds before I followed—only to get blocked by a dozen raucous partiers entering the hotel through a door that was clearly marked *Exit Only*.

Finally, I pushed through the mob and then the doors. Without slowing, I rushed into the cold night.

In the brightly illuminated parking area, misty droplets shimmered like pearls on the cars around me. There was more fog now than rain, but the air was still heavy and damp.

I was determined to follow Mullins, and I wasn't about

to do anything stupid. I wouldn't attempt to approach him, not without Detective Quinn present, but I *would* find out what make and model car he was driving—and get the number off the license plate.

As I scanned the lot, I feared I'd lost him. There was no one in sight.

That was when I heard the gunshot.

Eighty-Five

~~~~~~~~~~~~~~~~~~~~~~~~~~~~~~~~~~~~~~

I couldn't figure out which direction the sound came from. But when a second shot echoed across the lot, a car horn began to blare—and didn't stop.

The noise came from a line of vehicles two rows away, and I soon found the sedan making the racket. I also discovered the reason the horn continued blaring.

Toby Mullins was slumped in the driver's seat. I only knew it was him because I recognized the tweedy brown sport coat. What was left of his head was jammed into the steering wheel, setting off the horn.

I saw something else, too. A left-handed woman's glove sat on the dashboard. It was tan leather and looked exactly like a match for my glove—the one with the bloodstain, the one the police took into evidence after I woke up on that park bench.

I stumbled backward, until my rear was pressed against another sedan. Then I looked up and saw a man staring at me. He was three car lengths away, and my fake glasses were dotted with raindrops, but I would have recognized *Stevens* anywhere.

The head of security at the Parkview Palace hotel stood frozen in place. Then our eyes met, and he bolted like a fat mouse who'd spied a hungry tigress.

"Stop!" I cried.

Of course, Stevens didn't stop. He didn't even slow down. And, really, why the heck should he?

I chased after him anyway, pushing aside the fact that he had a gun and had just shot a man in the head—twice. I was so outraged that I refused to see reason. I just *couldn't* let this man get away!

I didn't plan on confronting him, but I *did* intend to see what vehicle he used to drive off. The sooner the police apprehended him, the more likely he'd still have the murder weapon on him.

I ran as fast as I could. Huffing and puffing and jolting my wig crooked, I was happy to see my effort was paying off. Matt had been correct in his physical assessment of the guy. Stevens had packed on a few too many pounds for this sort of urban sprint.

In desperation to get clear of me, Stevens ducked behind a Driftwood Coffee supply van and I lost sight of him.

Certain I had gotten the best of the man, I circled the coffee truck and ran down a short alley that led to a hotel loading dock.

Abruptly, I stopped in my tracks. I was flanked by over-stuffed dumpsters on either side, and the smell was not pleasant. Other than garbage, the narrow dead end was empty.

I'd made a wrong turn. If Stevens came back, he would discover that I was the one cornered. Heart racing, I spun around and ran back toward the parking lot. As I circled that Driftwood van again, I ran smack into the strong arms of a tall man.

I was about to scream my head off when I realized the arms belonged to Detective Quinn. Mr. Dante was with him.

"It's Stevens!" I cried. "The head of security for the Parkview hotel. He shot a man named Toby Mullins, who was working for Tessa Simmons. I found Mullins dead in his car, shot through the head. Then I chased Stevens, but he got away."

I paused for a breath. "Listen. You can hear the horn. It's

still blowing! And a woman's leather glove was on the dashboard. It looked exactly like the one I lost during the abduction. I'm sure it's my glove! It's the evidence we need!"

The detective seized my shoulders. "Calm down, Clare. You're safe. It's over."

Quinn was right. I took some deep breaths, and my rapid heartbeat began to slow. My knees were still weak, but I was okay.

Quinn straightened my blond wig. "Do you feel faint? Should I grab my EMT bag?"

"No!" I firmly shook my head. "I'm fine."

"Good. Dante will get you out of here."

"What do you mean? Where should we go?"

"Back to the Village Blend, where you can hide in plain sight, just like we planned. Keep wearing your disguise. Use the back entrance and the service stairs, and you'll be fine."

"But don't you need me as a witness?"

"There are security cameras all over that parking lot. Those cameras are the witness. Now, go."

I hesitated. "But—"

"Dante, get her out of here!"

Then Quinn was off, calling in the murder while he ran toward the car with Toby Mullins's corpse.

EIGHTY-SIX

"**BOSS**, you're back!"

Esther Best had ducked into the Village Blend pantry for supplies when she saw the back door open and me and Mr. Dante walk through. Before I could utter a word, the barista poet was squeezing me like a Sunkist orange.

"Take it easy," Mr. Dante told her. "She just saw a guy get his head blown off!"

"What?! Omigod! Omigod!"

Pushing up her black-framed glasses, Esther went from completely freaked to mother-hen mode. Taking me by the arm, as if I were physically *and* mentally unstable, she insisted on "helping me" up the stairs.

"Esther, I'm fine," I assured her.

And I really was—which did little to douse my burning skepticism about Dr. Lorca's so-called diagnosis.

Seeing Toby Mullins shot to death had been highly disturbing. It had rattled my nerves, filled me with fear and dread, and sent adrenaline through my molecules. What it didn't do was make me woozy or forgetful. It didn't block any memories, either, at least no more than the original "emotional trauma" that Lorca claimed I'd experienced.

Traveling back here tonight with Mr. Dante, I recognized the streets of my West Village neighborhood and my beloved century-old Village Blend. But I still had no memories of living and working here—not *lately*.

In my mind, it had been a long time since I'd managed the place and roasted coffee in this basement. Though I was being told differently, I still felt as though I should have been returning to the suburbs of New Jersey, where I was a single mother raising my young daughter, Joy, and writing a column for the local paper.

"Do you want me to call Madame and let her know you're here?" Mr. Dante asked.

"Yes," I said, "but be careful."

"Don't worry," he said. "I won't use your name. I'll be cagey, like your boyfriend."

My boyfriend? I was about to ask, and stifled the question. He was talking about Detective Mike Quinn. To everyone around me, Quinn and I were a couple, even though it still felt as though we had met days ago, instead of years.

As Mr. Dante made his call, I climbed the back staircase with Esther, and waited as she unlocked the duplex door.

Madame's furnished guest apartment above the coffeehouse looked as elegant and tasteful as I remembered, though I had no *personal* memories of living here. When Matt and I were married and raising Joy, we lived in our own little apartment nearby.

But that was long ago (so everyone told me), and this was my home now. I barely had time to settle in, meet my two cats (whom Esther introduced as Java and Frothy), pull off my blond wig, and freshen up in the bathroom before I heard someone arriving at the front door.

It was Madame, thank goodness. She was here already, greeting me with open arms.

EIGHTY-SEVEN

ത~ത~ത~ത~ത~ത~ത~ത~ത~ത~ത~ത

"OH, my dear, welcome home!" Madame's hug wasn't as tight as Esther's, but her enthusiastic affection was just as touching.

I had so much to tell my former mother-in-law, and yet . . . I decided to keep the details of my crazy weekend to myself, including its awful, violent end in Long Island City. There would be plenty of time to fill her in. But not tonight.

Meanwhile, Madame informed me that she was going to help me make things right with the authorities. She said she knew about Detective Quinn's Monday meeting with a top law firm.

"And now that you're back, I'll be arranging for you to see a reputable psychiatrist. I have several recommendations from a professor I trust. Of course, the law firm Detective Quinn is hiring may want you to see their own doctors, as well, before they take you to the police."

I cringed at the thought of going through a grilling—and more physical and mental tests and diagnoses. But, given the way I'd left the hospital, I knew I'd have to endure the ordeal, sooner or later.

"May I see Joy now? Or at least talk to her by phone?"

"No, dear. Not yet. The police are watching her. She and

I have been in touch with careful conversations, but I don't think it's wise for you two to talk just yet. You don't want to give yourself away. Not when we're so close to resolving your legal tangle."

"All right," I said—but reluctantly.

"Don't be disappointed. You and Joy will be reunited soon. For tonight, try to relax, and see if anything comes back to you. I see your cats have no problem with their feline memories!"

Purring and brushing my legs with excited affection, Java and Frothy hadn't left my heels since I walked in the door. Their little paws suddenly reminded me of my ex-husband's words—*pussyfooting around*—and I couldn't help wondering what the next step would be for me and Mike Quinn.

"I assume Detective Quinn will stop by later," I said. "In the meantime, would you mind if I roasted some coffee in the basement this week?"

"Oh, my goodness, I would be delighted! And so would your baristas and all your customers. Guess who filled in for you while you were gone."

"Esther?"

"Esther?! Bah!" She waved her hand. "I filled in for you."

"You?"

"Of course! I asked Dante to help. That young man's arms are good for more than displaying body art. He did the heavy lifting, but I was the one roasting the coffee. Just like the old days."

"You're the one who taught me."

"Make a note, Clare. Dante's your boy if you want an apprentice roaster. He's quite interested in the process."

"That's good to know. What's his first name, by the way?"

"Whose?"

"Mr. Dante?"

"Oh, dear. I think it's time I tell you. The boy's full name is Dante Silva. There is no need to use Mister. To us, he's simply Dante."

"And nobody corrected me until now?! Did you think I was that far gone?"

"Let's just say that we were very worried about you. We still are."

With a frustrated sigh, I collapsed on the sofa—and my two feline roommates jumped all over me.

A short time later, Madame bade me good night, and I found myself puttering around the apartment's rooms, looking at the life I had been living. It was a peculiar way to spend an evening.

I riffled through unfamiliar clothes, examined curious collectibles, and admired pieces of jewelry that (apparently) I'd had the good taste to purchase. That was when I saw the pristine white ring box. I could guess what was inside. With anticipation, I opened the lid—

But the box was empty.

Hmmm, I thought. *Another mystery.*

In the kitchen, I found binders with recipes. In the living room, photo albums. I paged through the images, but they weren't anything I hadn't seen before. These were old photos of the life I remembered well—as a child and young woman. And then my time with Matt: our wedding day; our honeymoon; and plenty of photos when Joy was born.

Still too keyed up to sleep, I decided to cook something. I noticed a recipe on the counter and assumed I'd left it there.

"Chocolate Chip Coffee Cake," I read aloud, "brown sugar, white sugar, flour, egg, oil, vanilla, salt, leavening, chips . . ."

The cake recipe looked easy and tasty—and after what I'd just witnessed, I was in need of some home-baked comfort. So I mixed the simple batter and poured it into the pan. When I slid the cake into the oven, I noticed a broad-shouldered shadow leaning against the kitchen doorway.

It was Mike.

He'd entered the apartment so stealthily, I hadn't heard

a footstep. By now I had changed into clothes I'd found upstairs, a soft T-shirt and warm leggings. It must have reminded him of something good because his typical icy expression had melted into a puddle of sweet affection.

"Hi, Clare."

"Hi, Mike. Would you like some coffee?"

Eighty-Eight

~~~~~~~~~~~~~~~~~~~~~~~~~~~~~~~~

The coffee, it turned out, was more than a warm, invigorating beverage. My own house blend tasted comfortingly familiar, and the caffeine seemed to have a positive, head-clearing effect on my mind.

Could my own roasted coffee be the key to unlocking more memories?

Detective Quinn doubted it would be that easy.

He had brought up his EMT jump bag, just in case I relapsed and blacked out, but I was feeling fine and strong. Apart from my memory issue—and missing my daughter—I was glad to be here.

After I invited him into the kitchen, the detective pulled off his suit jacket and shoulder holster. He hung both on an empty chair, sat at the table, and stretched out his long legs.

I noticed Java and Frothy were glad to see him, enthusiastically depositing brown and white fur all over his slacks. I liked that he didn't mind, and he appeared to enjoy scratching their ears and petting their necks as much as they enjoyed the attention.

"So fill me in," I said. "What happened at the parking lot?"

"A small army of uniforms showed up from the local precinct and created a perimeter for the Crime Scene Unit. Then the Queens detectives arrived, and I told them what you would have—about Stevens's presence at the time of the gunshot, which they're going to confirm once they get a warrant for the security camera footage.

"I also let them know Stevens's connection to the Annette Brewster case. And, thanks to your sharp eyes, pointed out the glove on the victim's dashboard. I identified it as resembling a match to your glove with the bloodstain—the one we bagged for evidence last week."

"Did they find Stevens?"

Quinn nodded. "They caught up with him in his car, driving to his home on Staten Island. They're questioning him now. He claims he's innocent. We'll know more in the morning."

"I'm going to hope for the best," I said. "That Annette is still alive and Stevens knows where to find her—and who else was involved."

"It's a tangle," Quinn admitted, scratching the new growth of stubble on his jawline. "Let's hope it won't take long to straighten out."

I agreed. "There are still so many questions. Were Mullins and Stevens working together for Tessa? Or is Stevens working for Victoria? Was he trying to frame Mullins with that glove?"

Quinn drained his cup. "Good questions, Detective."

"Good answers would be more helpful, don't you think?"

"Yeah." He smiled. "But I'd say you gave us an excellent start."

I was about to thank him for sticking by me—when the kitchen timer went off. As I pulled my chocolate chip snack cake out of the oven, Quinn made a fresh pot of coffee, and we continued talking into the night.

Eighty-nine

~~~~~~

By the end of the evening, Detective Quinn and I had agreed that he would sleep in the guest room, and I would take the master bedroom. Then he went upstairs to settle in, and I cleaned up the kitchen.

As I passed the second-floor bathroom, I heard him starting a hot shower—a good way to dispel the night's chill. Moving down the hallway, I decided to do the same by starting a fire in my bedroom's hearth.

This old log fireplace would be more work to clean than my ex-husband's convenient switch-on/switch-off gas hearth. But I preferred the real thing—the outdoorsy scent of the wood, the uneven crackling, and unexpected pops. The authentic fire wasn't as safe or easy, but it gave more warmth to my body and excitement to my senses.

The smells and sounds also brought back a cascade of powerful memories. Romantic feelings came over me, and I got the strong impression that Quinn should have been here next to me, sipping coffee and relaxing, whispering sweet words before bed.

Just then I noticed something on the mantel. *A phone?* It was my smartphone, presumably, the one everyone said I'd left behind on the night of my abduction.

I turned it on and gazed into the glowing display with a

little trepidation. Matt had shown me a photo of Joy on his phone. Did I have photos, too? Would I be looking through the recent years of my life? Should I?

That was when I saw the thumbnail image titled *Mike's Proposal*.

Swallowing my nerves, I tapped the image, and a video began to play. It felt so odd, watching myself like a stranger, in a scene that I couldn't recall. Still, I had to smile, seeing the elaborate setup Mike had arranged, the mock arrest, and his cop friends showing up in uniform.

Then the line of blue parted like a curtain, and he was down on one knee . . .

"Clare, I love you," he began plainly, *"and I know you love me."* Opening the white box, he revealed a gorgeous blue diamond ring.

"I have something to ask you. And you'd better think hard about your answer. With these law officers as witnesses, it's going to be tough to change your story."

I watched myself nod, looking a little numb.

"Clare Cosi, will you marry me?"

I could see the deep affection on Detective Quinn's face—and on my own. And I knew I wanted that love back in my life. I didn't want to lose it.

Like this fireplace with real logs and real ashes, any recovered memories would have to include everything about our relationship, the exciting crackling and unexpected pops, as well as the bitter embers of anger and arguments.

Was I ready for that?

You'll have to be, I told myself, because that was what a true partnership required, a steadfast agreement to ride the ups along with the downs; to carry on through the stressful mess that was always a part of anything authentic, anything real.

Putting down the mobile phone, I considered my options.

Sensory reminders had helped before. And my ex-husband seemed convinced that making love with him would have been a powerful key to unlocking my memories.

You want to have sex with me for medicinal *purposes?*
I had asked Matt that question. Now I asked myself—
Are you willing to try?

"**MIKE?**" I called through a crack in the bathroom door.

"Are you all right?" he asked, pulling the door wide. A towel was wrapped around his hips. His hair was wet, his face full of shaving cream.

"I'm fine," I said, steeling myself from the sudden shyness. "When you're finished in there, can you come into my bedroom? I'd like to ask you a question."

"Okay."

He arrived barefoot, his long legs hastily shoved into sweatpants, T-shirt collar wet from his damp hair, face freshly shaved.

The attractive look of him made me think of our quiet talk last night. Sitting on the edge of his bed, I had wanted to kiss him. Not because I remembered our history, but because I felt an attraction to him—and not just his half-naked body. I admired the man he was, I enjoyed being in his company, and (most important to me) I trusted him.

Last night, he had kissed my palm. But he never tried to touch me, let alone make love. So what was he going to say to *this* proposal?

"I've been thinking," I began. "If I could remember our history, it would solve a lot for both of us, right?"

"Sure it would."

"Well, why don't you and I . . . you know . . . ?" I bravely gestured to the four-poster bed. "As an experiment, I mean."

Clearly, this was not the question he'd been anticipating. As I stood next to the bed, blinking expectantly, he stared thunderstruck in the middle of the room. He was so flabbergasted, in fact, I'm sure I could have knocked him onto the bed with a slight tap.

But that bewildered state didn't last long.

Stepping close, he searched my face. Then he lifted his

hand and brushed my blushing cheek. This time, I didn't back away.

Meeting his gaze, I took in the rugged, clean-shaven look of him, appreciating the square strength of his jaw, the creases, and crow's-feet. The scent of his aftershave was almost intoxicating. Swirling impressions began to flow over me, faint whispers of intimate moments in this bedroom, caresses and kisses and—

"Clare, before we go any further, I need to say something."

"Yes?"

"Whatever happens in this room tonight, I don't want you regretting it in the morning, because I'm not going anywhere. I'll keep loving you, whether you remember your love for me or not. Even if you decide to end us, and kick me the hell out of your life, I'll keep loving you, because I can't do otherwise."

It was at that moment, when he let go of all his expectations, that I felt a warmth blooming inside me. This wasn't a feeling from memory. It was brand-new. And I wanted nothing more than to show him what I felt.

I started slowly, with a kiss. Not a peck this time, but a long, lingering taste of him. It seemed so familiar, yet everything else was completely new—his body, his responses.

Clearly, however, I was not new to him.

Quinn seemed to know exactly what I liked. His fingers and lips knew how and where to touch. Soon, we were so turned on, we could hardly stand it.

Then something changed. The empty frames were filling again, repainting the blank walls in my mind with years of experiences.

All along, as we kissed and caressed, Quinn seemed to be struggling to keep himself in check—being careful to go easy, take his time.

"It's okay," I finally gasped, breathless and ready. "Don't hold back."

His blue eyes widened. "Are you sure?"

With a smile I told him the good news. "I remember you."

"What do you remember?"

"So much, Mike. And not just you. I remember us, and I remember the love."

He switched our positions so fast, I thought he'd performed a magic trick. Now I was flat on my back, and he was smiling down at me.

"Let's see what else you remember . . ."

ninety

~~~~~~~~~~~~~~~~~~~~~~~~~~~~~~~~~~~

I awoke in the bedroom I knew, inside the duplex I loved, reaching for the man I adored.

Sadly, the bed was empty—even Java and Frothy had abandoned me. But the stimulating aroma of fresh-brewed coffee told me that Mike was in the kitchen, feeding the fur balls and anticipating my need for a caffeinated pick-me-up after all our nocturnal activities.

I threw off the blankets and discovered they were my only defense against the chill of the autumn morning. I quickly covered myself with a robe and hurried downstairs.

I was hoping for a strong embrace and slow, sexy kiss from Mike but was doomed to disappointment. My fiancé was sitting at the kitchen table with a rough-looking guy in a flannel shirt, worn jeans, and work boots. The young man was solidly built with a shaved head and an outer-boroughs accent.

"Hey, Coffee Lady," the stranger called, smiling warmly.

"I know you, don't I?" I said. "You came to my hospital room, right?"

My question was said in a friendly manner—but the young man's face fell completely. I moved my gaze to Mike. He looked even worse.

"You don't remember Franco?" he asked, voice tight.

"No, I'm sorry. He's your sergeant, right? Sergeant Emmanuel Franco, isn't it? Nice to meet you."

Franco hesitated. He glanced at Mike, then back to me. "You and I have met before, Clare, many times. We're good friends."

Oh, no, I thought, dread gripping me. I looked at Mike.

His expression was close to stark fear. "Clare, do you remember me?"

"Yes! Of course! I remember everything about you—how we met and became friends, how you proposed. I remember *everything*. But I'm drawing a blank with Sergeant Franco. Why is that?!"

"What about your daughter?" Franco quickly asked. "What do you remember about Joy?"

I sat down at the table, closed my eyes. "She's still a little girl to me. But I *know* years have passed. This will sound far too simple, but it's like . . . I lost my front door key. I *know* I had it, but I can't remember where I put it!"

"Calm down, Clare. It's okay."

Mike got up, found me a mug, and poured me some fresh coffee. I drank it down like an ailing patient desperate for a magic cure. Suddenly, I realized I was wearing a robe and not much else.

"Do you two want to talk in private?" I asked. "I could go back upstairs—"

"Stay," Mike insisted. "Franco has been taking a hard look at Dr. Lorca. I think you should hear what he's found. Go ahead, tell her."

Franco nodded. "I started by looking at the other cases of sudden amnesia that Lorca treated, specifically Dana Tanner. Turns out, Lorca ordered one particular blood test, and then pulled the test results from her file. No biggie. It happens, I guess, but—"

Franco rubbed the back of his neck, suddenly sheepish. "Last evening, Tony DeMarco flirted with a nurse in the records department of a different hospital. He got a date *and* a peek at the files from another of Lorca's amnesia cases. Turns out, that same test was administered, and the results were also missing."

"Tell us more about this blood test," Mike said.

"It's a version of the Serum Serotonin Level test administered to detect a tumor or chemical depression. Not to treat amnesia."

My skin prickled under my robe. "Did he give that test to me, Sergeant?"

"We'll know soon enough. We're getting a warrant to grab your records along with a number of the other women who've reported similar symptoms. Those records will be reviewed by one of the medical forensic specialists who work with our OD Squad. If Lorca is trying to hide something, our guy will find it. Me and DeMarco have a theory but no facts to back it up yet."

"Don't make me guess, Sergeant. Tell me your theory now."

Franco and Mike exchanged another look. Mike nodded once.

"Tony and me, we think Lorca is hiding the presence of some kind of drug, and we think that drug was used on you."

"I was drugged?!"

"That's what it looks like," Franco said. "Hey, Coffee Lady, don't look so upset. If it's true, that's good news. At least you'll know you're not a head case."

ṅiṅety-oṅe

I downed a second cup of coffee while I absorbed Franco's revelation, too stunned to do more than listen as the two officers talked.

Mike asked Franco to keep quiet about my return to the city. He filled him in on his appointment with a law firm later today. "Once we secure Clare's legal protection, we'll consider our next step—and we need a little more time for that."

"My lips are sealed, but I won't be around anyway," Franco said. "Lorca is at his clinic upstate today. Me and Tony are going to take a drive and visit the doctor."

"What's your plan?"

The sergeant shrugged his big shoulders. "We're calling it an initial background interview."

"Good," Mike said. "Get some responses on the record. If he gives you contradictory answers or makes false statements, we'll have something to press him on—especially if the forensic evidence shows he's lying."

"Will do."

"Good work, buddy. Keep it up. And thank DeMarco for me."

"Sure." Franco rose. "Good luck with those attorneys today. I'll talk to you soon—"

"But not by phone. Check in when you get back, *in person*."

Mike escorted Franco to the door. On his way, Mike's phone buzzed and he answered the call. By the time he returned to the kitchen, the conversation was so intense that he hardly acknowledged my presence. Then the call ended and he faced me.

"I've got more upsetting news, Clare. I'm sorry. Stevens is being released."

"What?! Why would they let him go?"

"There was no evidence to hold him on. Stevens had no GSR on his clothes or skin—"

"GSR? That has something to do with firing a gun, right?"

"That's right. It means gunshot residue. Like I said, there was none on Stevens. No weapon in his possession when he was apprehended, and the Crime Scene Unit at the hotel has yet to find one in or around the parking lot."

"Stevens could have hidden it, or tossed it out the window of his car!"

"He didn't have a gun, Clare. The security camera footage from the parking lot clears him . . ." Mike continued to describe the footage, which showed a figure in a black rain poncho with the hood up approaching the dead man's car. It appeared Mullins rolled down his window and spoke with the stranger before the shooter fired twice. Then the shooter reached into the car.

A moment later the shooter fled the scene.

"This all happened a good thirty seconds before Stevens even appeared. His arrival was immediately followed by a woman with blond hair and big glasses wearing a green rain poncho. She peeked in the car, then saw Stevens nearby and raced after him."

"The police don't know the blonde was me, do they?"

"Not yet," Mike said. "And Stevens didn't recognize you, either. He described the woman who chased him as a 'nutcase.'"

"Great." I folded my arms. "Do you think he was lying? I mean, if Stevens honestly didn't remember me, that means he wasn't following me. So what did he claim he was doing at the hotel?"

"Following the dead man, Toby Mullins. Turns out, Mullins is a licensed private investigator. But Stevens didn't know that and neither did Victoria Holbrook. Both became suspicious of Mullins since he was lurking around the Parkview Palace, asking the staff questions. Victoria convinced herself that Mullins was involved in Annette's disappearance. She ordered Stevens to find out if Mullins was hired by Tessa—and whether Tessa was responsible for abducting and possibly murdering Annette, since her young niece is the principal beneficiary in Annette's will."

"What about the late Toby Mullins?"

"Mullins was hired by Tessa to find her aunt—"

"So that's why he was watching my hospital room?"

"Right. Tessa was highly suspicious of your loss of memory and asked Mullins to find a way to question you. Mullins was asking questions at the Parkview because Tessa was convinced *Victoria* was responsible for Annette's disappearance."

"Wait a second. If Victoria thought Tessa was guilty and Tessa thought Victoria was guilty, then it's unlikely either was behind Annette's abduction."

"It looks that way," Mike said.

"Here's a question for you. What about the leather glove? The one I saw on Mullins's dashboard. If it was mine, that's proof he was involved."

"We don't know yet if it's your glove. Forensics is testing for your DNA, but that takes time. And even if it is your glove, it proves nothing."

"How is that?"

"Remember, the shooter reached into Mullins's car. The police know he took the dead man's phone, but the killer might have also planted your glove on the dashboard—to set Mullins up."

"I understand. The shooter wanted to frame Mullins as a party to Annette's abduction, and by extension Tessa Simmons. That seems logical. Is that the theory of your police investigators? Do they suspect the shooter is involved in Annette's abduction?"

Mike shook his head. "The investigating officers are treating Mullins's murder like a smartphone robbery gone bad."

"But that's crazy!" I cried. "Can't the police pressure Tessa and Victoria? One of them must know something!"

"They've *been* questioned. Each suspects the other of being guilty. But there's no evidence, and you can't squeeze a square peg into a round hole."

Square peg into a round hole.

For some reason, my mind held on to that phrase and even formed a picture of that geometry. Suddenly something extremely disturbing emerged from my memory. *Square peg can't fit, round hole. Can't fit, round hole!*

"Clare?"

Like a punch in the head, this new memory was so powerful that I dropped my coffee, shattering the cup and scaring poor Java and Frothy into scampering away. Close to passing out, I sank into a chair—and started to slide off it.

Mike caught me before I hit the floor.

"Clare, what's wrong?!" he asked, alarmed. He was holding me so close, I could feel his heart beating under his T-shirt. I think my lips moved, but no words emerged.

Before I knew it, Mike was helping me lie down on the living room sofa. But I *had* to tell him! I had to get it out, even though it was difficult to form the words.

"The room," I rasped. "It had a *round* window, like a porthole, too small for me to fit through."

"What room, Clare?"

"The room they kept me in, for days."

"Who? Who kept you there?"

"The Grunting Men."

Ninety-two

∽∽∽∽∽∽∽∽∽∽∽∽∽∽∽∽∽∽∽∽

"**There** were two of them," I told Mike, ten minutes later.

By now I was sitting up, a fresh mug of coffee clutched in both hands. Mike was beside me, his EMT jump bag beside him.

"In my head I named them the Grunting Men because that's all they ever did to communicate with me. I don't know if they were hiding their voices, their accents . . ."

"What did they look like?"

"I never saw their faces. They wore ski masks and gloves when they first grabbed me. But later, while I was trapped in that room, each wore a bandanna draped over his nose and mouth."

"Anything else? Did they molest you? Assault you in any way?"

"No. They didn't touch me."

Mike nodded with relief. "That's in line with the physical exams you received after you came back to us."

"They were both big men and strong. I did make a rush to the door once, and the guy threw me on the bed with one arm, without even spilling the bowl of soup he was holding in the other."

"You had a bed? Can you describe more of the room?"

"It was small but well furnished. Blue wallpaper and a

tiny bathroom. It was a guest room, I think, because the dresser drawers were empty. One door led to a hallway. The Grunting Men were always struggling with the lock. And the only window was that tiny porthole."

"What did you see when you looked through the window?"

"Nothing. It was stained glass, too thick to see anything beyond whether it was day or night."

"And Annette?"

I shrugged. "I was alone. I only ever saw the Grunting Men."

Hands shaky, I drank more coffee. It strengthened my resolve to dredge up this memory.

"It was nighttime when I escaped, I remember that. I was feeling woozy, like I'd been drugged. I don't think I could even remember my name at one point. But I remember wanting to escape and testing that bedroom door ten or twenty times a day. One night that messed-up lock malfunctioned, and the door opened for me."

I closed my eyes and let the memories flow over me.

"I sneaked down a flight of stairs to the ground floor. The whole place was dark. One of the Grunting Men was snoring in the tiny living room. I was too afraid to pass him and go out the front door, so I went out the back."

"Where did you end up?"

"The woods, I thought, because I saw trees. But then I quickly realized I was in a courtyard. I wandered around until I found the gate and stumbled out. Then I was on a sidewalk and realized I recognized the street—Omigod!"

I jumped to my feet, dropping my mug again. Thankfully the porcelain hit the rug and didn't break. But my poor, long-suffering felines scampered away again, loudly mewing.

"That's it. The Mews!"

"What?"

"I remember where I was! They were keeping me in a town house at the Washington Mews, right here in Greenwich Village!" I faced him. "I think I can find the place again. The Mews is just one gated street, and that round stained glass window was pretty distinctive. Should we call in the police?"

"No police," Mike replied a little *too* quickly. "Let's see what we can find first."

I studied the man's stone face. He was holding something back. I was about to press him when he said, "We need hard evidence, Clare. Proof that your story is true. We need—"

I touched his arm. "We need to *find Annette*."

Ninety-three

∾◌∾◌∾◌∾◌∾◌∾◌∾◌∾◌∾◌∾◌∾◌∾◌

The Washington Mews, where I'd been held, was located on a gated cobblestone street, just one block from the park where I'd woken on a bench with a damaged memory.

Over a century ago, in the horse-and-buggy era, New Yorkers had built hundreds of mews like these—rows of two-story structures constructed to serve wealthy residents in larger homes. Typically the ground floor would hold stables for horses and carriages, with living quarters for domestics on the floor above. By now, most of New York's carriage houses have been demolished, but some have survived, becoming chic landmarked town houses for urban residents.

The majority of properties in this mews were used by New York University for programs on language and culture, but several of the buildings were still privately owned.

Unless my abductor was a raving-mad NYU professor of romance languages, I was looking for one of the private homes.

By one PM, Mike and I were walking slowly down the historic cobblestone street when I stopped dead and began to shiver—more from seeing that familiar stained glass circle than from the blustery autumn weather. I pointed to the town house a few doors away.

"There it is," I whispered.

Mike raised an eyebrow. "If you're sure, let's see who's home."

"Wait!" I called too late. He'd already pressed the doorbell. Mike rang three more times, without a response. Then he peered through the front window. Thanks to a gap in the curtains, we could see that the interior was all shadows and darkness.

"Let's try the back," Mike said.

The iron gate to the wooded courtyard was unlocked. Here the wind shook dying leaves loose as I led Mike into the private gardens behind the row of old houses. When we reached the right home, Mike approached the windowless rear door. He knocked loudly, then jiggled the knob and pushed with his shoulder. Finally, he took something from his jacket pocket.

"Watch my back," he whispered. "And if an alarm goes off, you run like hell out of here."

"What are you going to do?"

"Flash my badge."

"So, you really are breaking in, then? I thought we were looking for evidence—which will be useless if you enter the house without a warrant."

"And I thought we were looking for Annette."

Mike fiddled with the lock. After a moment, he cursed, and I figured he couldn't pick it. I wasn't sure if I was disappointed or relieved. Then I heard a click and saw his grin.

As he cracked the door, we both tensed—and didn't breathe again until we were sure no alarm would sound.

Mike shook his head. "And people wonder why they get robbed."

I pushed him through the door and into a narrow carpeted hallway. The town house was clean and neat, but the air was stuffy, as if no one had been here for days.

We passed the kitchen and a small bathroom. Both were empty. When we reached the living room, I recognized the couch where the Grunting Man had fallen asleep the night I escaped.

"I want you to stay down here while I check upstairs," Mike said.

He must be reading my mind, I thought, *because there is no way I want to see that room again.*

As Mike warily climbed the stairs, I took a closer look at the living room. My eyes were immediately drawn to a wall decorated with family portraits.

An old Rod Stewart song came to mind, "Every Picture Tells a Story," and I found a whopper.

Displayed in plain sight was the history of a family told in photographs. I recognized every person in these pictures, and that's what shocked me—because no one, including me, had ever guessed they were a family!

ηinety-four
∿∿∿∿∿∿∿∿∿∿∿∿∿∿∿

By the time Mike came down the stairs, I had it all figured out.

"Clare, I saw the room where they kept you," he said. "It's exactly like you described. I searched the other bedrooms, but there's no sign of Annette. We're back to square one."

"No, we're not. I think I found the key to what's going on—right here in plain sight."

He peeked over my shoulder.

"Let me tell you this story in pictures," I said, "starting with the photo of this very pretty, very pregnant woman. This is Victoria Holbrook, and she's standing in front of Schönbrunn Palace. That's in Vienna.

"I overheard Victoria tell Madame that she'd moved to Vienna, and Nora Arany hinted that Victoria might have moved there because she was pregnant. Right, and right."

I pointed to a second picture. "Here's Victoria standing with her child, a boy, maybe four or five years old. I heard Tessa Simmons wonder aloud if she had a first cousin adopted by an Austrian family, and this picture appears to answer that question. Victoria didn't give away her son. She decided to raise him herself."

I moved to the next picture. "A few years after that Vienna

photo, Victoria moved from Vienna to Venice—Venice, California. Here's Victoria and her nine- or ten-year-old son on the Venice Boardwalk."

Mike leaned close. "There's a man with them, but his head is turned, and I can't see his face."

"Don't worry. The next picture reveals all."

I tapped the glass. "That's Victoria, her son, and the boy's father. The event is the son's graduation from UC Berkeley School of Law. The graduate is wearing rimless round glasses instead of the horn-rims, and his hair is longer, but you can clearly see the boy is Owen Wimmer."

"And that man beside him?"

"Harlan Brewster. It looks to me like Owen was his only child, a bastard son who thought he was destined to inherit the Parkview Palace and the family fortune, only to be thwarted."

"Slow down, Clare. You'd better explain."

"Annette had breast cancer two years ago and beat it. But Owen probably expected her to die and leave everything to Harlan, who would then leave it to Owen. But it was Harlan who died, giving Annette control of the Parkview fortune, which she intended to pass on to her niece, Tessa."

Mike nodded. "And you think Owen snatched Annette. For what purpose?"

"A copy of Annette's last will and testament was taken out of the Gotham Suite. That's the will that names Tessa as the beneficiary. I think Owen wanted to coerce Annette into signing a new one, naming Victoria Holbrook as the beneficiary."

Mike Quinn smiled that smile he always displayed right before he collared a perp.

I removed the graduation portrait from the wall. "You can almost see Owen's resemblance to his father. I think Annette might have suspected who Owen was. And since there was no love lost between her and Harlan, there is no way Annette would leave a cent to his bastard son, even if it was her sister's child, too."

"This is pretty twisted," Mike said.

"As the Parkview's lawyer, Owen knew what was in the original will, and he also knew Annette intended to sell the hotel out from under his mother before Annette fled to France to be with her old flame, the painter."

"Could Victoria be involved with her sister's abduction?"

"It's possible. But then why would she ask Stevens to investigate Tessa? Unless that was part of an elaborate frame job."

"Everything you're saying makes sense, but we have no evidence," Mike said. "If the police picked up Victoria or Owen right now, they could deny all involvement and the NYPD would have to let them go in twenty-four hours."

"I know you found no evidence upstairs, but this property was obviously Harlan's 'love nest' with Victoria. Back at the Gypsy hotel, a friend of Annette's drunkenly mentioned there was such a place, though she didn't know where. Well, we found it. And if Owen hired goons to hold me here, he was probably holding Annette here, too."

"Yes, but once you escaped, he obviously moved her. The question is where?"

"Mike, if Owen used Harlan's property once, why not use it again? Hide her in plain sight, right? I think Owen is holding Annette on the Brewsters' estate in the Hamptons. And I think I know precisely where. So how about we notify the police, get a warrant, and have the Sandcastle raided?"

A shadow crossed Mike's face. "There's something I didn't tell you, Clare, but I think you'd better hear it now."

Oh, no. I braced myself.

"When Lori Soles called me last night at the Gypsy, she warned me the FBI was taking over the search for you. And right now members of the Major Case Squad are probably pushing a theory with the Feds that you're not innocent. That you were involved in either setting up Annette for abduction or taking money to be released in exchange for keeping your mouth shut."

I held my head. "I just got my life back, and now you're

telling me I'm facing Federal interrogation and maybe forced hospitalization—or worse?"

"It's decision time, Clare. Either we keep the appointment with that law firm, you turn yourself in to the authorities, and we try to convince them of our theory before Annette is either moved or killed. Or we go out to the Hamptons ourselves and find out if Owen is guilty."

Mike paused, his penetrating blue eyes gazing into mine. "This is your life, sweetheart. I'll go along with whatever you decide, but you have to make the call."

Ninety-Five

∽∾∽∾∽∾∽∾∽∾∽∾∽∾∽∾∽∾∽∾

Hours later, Mike and I were on those dark and dangerous roads again, but I took some comfort in my *nonna*'s old
saying. *Walking with a friend in the dark is better than
walking alone in the light.*

I was lucky in that regard. Michael Ryan Francis Quinn
was much more than a friend.

Good thing, too, because the road back to Long Island
was horrendously longer than usual. Multiple accidents on
the expressway turned a two-and-a-half-hour drive into a
four-hour ordeal, and the autumn sun was well below the
horizon by the time we reached the rural lane leading to the
Brewsters' Sandcastle estate.

While stuck in traffic, I told Mike my plan. It was a
desperate scheme that involved breaking in just like we had
at the Mews, but through a kitchen window instead of a
back door. I'd spotted that partially open window the last
time I'd crept around the property in the dark—not something I was looking forward to doing again.

"Heads up," Mike said. "Sandcastle is just around the
next bend."

"Mike! Look there!"

I pointed out a pickup truck parked on the shoulder of

the road. Mike slowed as we drove by, and I read the Ernest Landscaping logo on the door.

"Who landscapes at night?" I asked.

"Did you see anyone around the truck?"

"No."

"Then maybe the truck broke down, and Ernest is looking to have it towed. Unless he was one of Owen's Grunting Men and is inside the mansion right now."

"It's possible," I said, "although when you and I spoke to Ernest Belling, I didn't have one of my woozy memory reactions to him. And if he was involved, wouldn't Owen have opened the gates for him? Why would he want that truck parked on the road for all to see?"

"You might be right, Clare. But you could be wrong. Keep an eye out for Belling—and if he tries anything, use the Taser I gave you."

A moment later, we arrived at the tall wrought iron gates of the mansion.

"I can see lights through the trees," I said. "It looks like Owen Wimmer, Esquire, is at home."

Following my plan, I ducked under the dashboard while Quinn buzzed the intercom. A minute later, Owen's reedy voice answered.

"May I help you?"

"It's Detective Quinn. I have several follow-up questions about those letters you showed me."

"I've already turned copies of all pertinent correspondence over to your department."

"I know," Quinn said. "But I have new information."

"Very well, come in."

The gates to Sandcastle opened.

"It's your plan, Clare, so stick to it. He'll disarm the security system to let me in. I'll distract him with BS, maybe get him back to that study again. You're going to sneak around back and climb through the kitchen window—"

"If it's still open."

"Are you sure Annette is locked up where you say she is?"

"I'd bet my life on it. Which, if you think about it, I kind of am."

Mike cut the engine. "Good luck," he whispered.

"And you be careful. Owen's plan is desperate, even crazy. Maybe he's crazy, too."

Ninety-six

~~~~~~

IMPOSSIBLY, everything seemed to be going as planned.

Owen greeted Quinn with a handshake and invited him inside. The alarm system had been disarmed, and I found that the kitchen window was cracked enough for me to open it wider and crawl through.

There was a harrowing instant when I bumped an aluminum pasta strainer hanging under the window—but I managed to catch it before it clattered to the tiled floor.

Gingerly, I hung it up and proceeded.

As I moved through the house, I could hear Quinn and Wimmer talking, but I couldn't make out their words. The voices came from that messy study, far from the part of the house I was looking for.

Though this massive mansion seemed labyrinthine, it took me only a few minutes to locate the sterile, artless, all-white abattoir of a room with the glass walls facing the night-shrouded woods.

Though the recessed lighting was dim, I could still make out those five gargoyles on the room's wall, each one set in a decorative panel. As Madame had done in the Gotham Suite, I pushed on their grotesque heads, one after the other.

On my third try, the middle panel swung inward. Warily,

I peeked inside. The darkness made it impossible to see anything clearly, but I knew something was terribly wrong from the awful smell. Foul, stale air with the reek of human sweat and worse emanated from that black pit.

I pulled Quinn's flashlight from my pocket. The beam revealed a room about the size of the one I had been kept in, minus amenities like a window and a bathroom.

There was a bed, though, and I gasped at the emaciated figure lying on it. Annette was still wearing the black dress from the cake tasting. Now stained and torn, the garment was loose on her frame. Her blond hair hung in greasy ringlets.

"Annette, wake up," I whispered, gently shaking her. "It's me . . . Clare Cosi . . . I'm here to rescue you."

But she was dead to the world, and when I checked her pulse, I feared she was nearly dead.

I'd never considered this situation. I thought I'd find an incoherent but *conscious* Annette. It was going to be impossible for me to carry an unconscious woman out of here!

I discovered why she was so weak when I looked on the bedside table. There were legal documents stacked in a neat pile beside a pen. There was a handwritten note, too—

Sign your last will and testament and maybe I'll give you food.

I didn't need a signature to know who had written it: *A depraved monster named Owen Wimmer.*

I was glad to see Annette had resisted. Those legal documents were unsigned, which was clearly the reason Owen had continued to keep her alive. Thank goodness it was long enough for Quinn and me to find her.

As I set the papers aside, I heard a resounding clatter from the kitchen—the pasta strainer hitting the floor. I froze, cursing myself for not hanging it properly.

The dull murmur of conversation between Quinn and the lawyer ceased, too. Next I heard scuffling, then a crash, followed by more silence.

I waited a full minute before I left the secret room. Just

when I concluded that I was safe, the lights snapped on, and I blinked against the glare. When my vision cleared, Owen Wimmer was standing in front of me, a gun in one hand, a poker in the other.

I lunged with Quinn's Taser, but he struck it away with the poker. That's when I realized it was stained crimson. I had no doubt it was Mike Quinn's blood.

Ninety-seven

MIKE was alive!

For a moment that was the only thought my mind registered. At gunpoint, Owen had led me into the study, where I found the man I loved sprawled on the hardwood floor. He was unconscious, but still breathing. Owen had taken his gun—the same weapon he now pointed at me.

I didn't care about that. I didn't care about anything but Mike. I wanted to go to him, help him, but a maniac was threatening to shoot us both. He'd already struck me once, knocking my big glasses off my face. Then he tore my wig off, taking some of my own hair with it.

"So," he said smugly, "the drug finally wore off."

"What did you do to me?"

"Me? Nothing. Not personally, anyway. *You*, however, have been a royal pain. I saw through your flimsy disguise that day in the Gotham Suite, but I knew you were still experiencing memory loss, so I wasn't worried—until this afternoon, when my security app showed me video of you and the detective here breaking in at the Mews. I assumed you'd regained your memory, but you didn't call the police in, because *I've* been talking to the police and encouraging them to suspect your involvement in dear Annette's abduction. So you're a wanted woman now. And since you have no real evidence against me, I simply waited for you both to come here."

Suddenly, Mike groaned, and Owen aimed the gun at him. I loudly shifted on my feet so he would point it back at me.

"I understand why you took Annette that night," I said. "But why did your goons kidnap me?"

"I knew Annette planned to ask you to investigate Harlan's death, and I couldn't have that."

"Why not? Unless you murdered your own father."

Owen's eyes narrowed. "A part-time father is no father at all. My mother was fixated on Harlan—God knows why—but a paycheck is all that man was to me. After he put me through law school, he put me to work in his hotel. But as his only child, he owed me more. Much more. The Parkview and the family fortune should be mine. It's only right."

Owen leaned the poker against the cold fireplace.

"I'm surprised you and your cop friend were able to trace this all back to me. But then Toby Mullins was on his way to Sandcastle the night I murdered him."

"You shot Mullins?"

"*And* I successfully diverted attention from myself to Tessa by placing your missing glove in his car. That was my plan all along, to frame Tessa for Annette's abduction and murder. Then no one would be left to challenge the will. My mother certainly wouldn't, though she knows nothing about this. I couldn't trust her not to screw it up."

"What are you going to do with us?"

He gave me a sick smile. "A police detective who loves a woman wanted by the FBI? Why, it's the perfect soap opera, and in such a melodrama, they would run off together, simply disappear, never to be heard from again."

"You plan to kill us?"

"Not right away. I'll be torturing you both first, Ms. Cosi, a little fright show to persuade Annette to sign those papers." He sighed. "You know, my original plan was foolproof. Too bad it was compromised by those incompetent day workers I hired out from under Ernest Belling. They seemed bright enough. But the fools gave Annette too much of the drug, and they allowed you to escape. Frankly, they weren't worth the money I promised to pay them, so I didn't."

He shrugged. "After I had them move Annette out here, I convinced them to dig her grave on the estate's property. They never had a clue they were digging their own."

Suddenly, an angry roar filled the room, and a brawny figure in a bandanna rushed Owen Wimmer. The lawyer quickly aimed his gun at Ernest Belling. As the shot rang out, I leaped forward and grabbed the demented lawyer's arm.

Owen and I wrestled for the gun, while Ernest Belling staggered and dropped to one knee. As I continued my fight, Owen smacked me in the face with the flat of his free hand, and I saw stars. When he hit me a second time, I fell against the fireplace.

Through a swollen eye, I saw that Owen was about to execute Belling.

That was when Quinn made his move. Still on the ground, he wrapped his arms around Owen's legs. The lawyer teetered but didn't fall. Instead, he tried to aim his gun at Mike.

I was on my feet in an instant, snatching the poker. I swung it with all my might. The shock of the blow jolted my arms. God knows what it did to Owen Wimmer, who dropped like a rock.

I let go of the poker and knelt beside my fiancé. "Mike, Mike! Can you talk?"

He tried to sit up, but I stopped him to examine his wound.

"How bad?" he asked.

"You're going to need stitches, but that thick skull of yours seems to be intact."

Behind me, Ernest Belling groaned and sank to the hardwood floor. The bullet had struck his shoulder. I did my best to stanch the flow of blood while Mike called 911.

"He killed my cousin. He killed Tommy Cole," Belling gasped.

"Did your cousin help kidnap Annette?" I asked.

Belling nodded. "He bragged about a side job with big money. Then I heard the news about Mrs. Brewster going missing and possibly being abducted. When Tommy disappeared, I put two and two together. I thought Tommy might be in this place, doing secret work for Owen. I've been watching on the road for days. Tonight, when you guys came, I saw my chance. I hopped the fence, followed you in, and tried to stay out of sight. But when I heard him bragging about what he did to Tommy, I couldn't control myself."

Belling winced as I tied off his wound.

"Tommy was a lowlife who would do anything for a buck, but he was family."

Ninety-Eight

∽∿∿∿∿∿∿∿∿∿∿∿∿∿∿∿∿

A few weeks later, I gathered my coffeehouse family for a little talk.

Everyone had questions about what I'd gone through, and what *they'd* gone through. So—after returning from Washington for a tearful reunion with my daughter—I gathered everyone at the Village Blend for some answers, some coffee, and some good old-fashioned venting.

The first thing I wanted everyone to know was that my amnesia hadn't been caused by some hysterical emotional reaction. Against my will, I'd been injected with an experimental drug.

"It's called Nepenthe," I explained. "Dr. Lorca named it after the elixir of forgetfulness that Homer wrote about in *The Odyssey*."

Esther raised her hand. "Ms. Boss, if you're going to start this story three thousand years ago, I think we're going to need more coffee."

"And more of *these*," Sergeant Franco said, reaching for his third Goobers Cookie (our latest hit).

"I'll keep it short," I promised.

"Talk as long as you like, Coffee Lady. So long as you keep these outstanding cookies coming, I'll listen."

"We've got you covered, big fella," Tucker Burton assured him, "unless you plan on eating our *entire* pastry case."

I cleared my throat. "So, where was I?"

"Uh-oh, looks like the amnesia's kicked in again. Next thing you know she'll be calling me *Mister* Dante."

Beside the tattooed barista, Mike Quinn snickered, until I gave him a look. Bad enough he was wearing a bandanna to cover his head wound, which he probably thought was funny, too!

"You were talking about that experimental drug, Clare?" Madame prompted, sipping her espresso.

"That's right. The drug was developed by Dr. Dominic Lorca to treat victims of post-traumatic stress disorder. It sounds like science fiction, but researchers have been hoping to develop a pharmacological memory wipe for some time. The clinical goal is to eliminate the memory of the disturbing incident to alleviate the patient's distress."

I paused to sip my own cup of coffee—my elixir of choice for a very particular reason. "As it turned out, Lorca's Nepenthe was a bust. It caused wildly different reactions among people, and it eventually wore off. The traumatic memories began to return when the patient encountered memory triggers, especially when consuming natural stimulants like those found in coconut oil, ginseng, tea, and *coffee*."

"Huzzah!" Esther cried, lifting her cup and clinking it with Dante. "Coffee rules!"

"The drug's legacy could have ended there," I said. "But Sergeant Franco uncovered the rest of the story. Manny, do you want to fill us in on your investigation?"

Franco hurriedly brushed cookie crumbs off his flannel shirt.

"Yeah, well," he began, his voice a low rumble, "one of Lorca's assistants was a graduate student who summered in the Hamptons. He stole some of Lorca's stash and made big bucks selling Nepenthe to rich punks and frat boys as a reverse roofie—"

"You mean, roofer?" Madame said, puzzled.

"Roofie," Franco repeated. "That's the date-rape drug, flunitrazepam. When it's slipped into a victim's drink, they become drowsy, disoriented. The problem is, when the victim wakes up, they have a pretty good idea they'd been assaulted. But Nepenthe is different. Slip it into your victim's bloodstream, and they forget the assault ever happened, along with a lot of other stuff—enough to render the victim a useless witness."

Franco reached for another cookie but spoke before he took a bite.

"Dr. Lorca eventually found out what his graduate student was doing. He realized his drug was being sold on the black market. He was desperate to protect his reputation, and he began paying medical personnel in area hospitals to give him early tips on any case of memory loss that turned up in the ER.

"Everyone thought it was perfectly innocent. They figured the celebrity doctor was just seeking another subject for a book. But Lorca was actually covering up his employee's criminal behavior to protect himself. He pushed his way into each case, taking charge of the medical records, because he didn't want to risk other physicians detecting his drug, though their standard screens for alcohol, narcotics, and the like wouldn't have been able to reveal it. A unique serotonin test was what Lorca used to confirm his suspicions. That's why he always ordered it and was careful to bury the results."

Esther threw up her hands. "How in Buddha's name did Lorca's drug end up being used by someone at the Parkview Palace?"

"Harlan Brewster bought a stash in the Hamptons," Mike explained. "Harlan saw the drug as an income opportunity, a way for him and his son, Owen, to become fixers for some of the rich, famous, and misbehaving clients at the Parkview, which they monitored through the hotel's security cameras—including secret cameras set up in high-end suites."

"Peekaboo, I see you!" Tucker shook his head.

Esther shuddered. "No wonder Annette went goofy about turning off all the hotel cameras!"

"So Harlan was peddling this drug, too?" Dante asked.

"He was," Franco replied. "He sold the drug to clients at an astronomical price so they could 'erase' their misdeeds. And if they *didn't* buy it, Harlan found his payday the old-fashioned way—blackmail."

Quinn nodded. "Owen even created a fake Hamptons law firm to shield himself and Harlan from some of their dirty business dealings. Then Owen became resentful. If he was going to keep taking risks, he wanted more from Harlan. Lots more. And one night at the Sandcastle mansion, Harlan and Owen argued about it. In a fit of rage, Owen killed his father with a brass poker—"

It was Franco who snickered this time. "Wasn't that the same poker he whacked you with, boss?"

"Not pertinent to our narrative, smart-ass."

As the two detectives took good-natured jabs at each other, I explained how Owen had covered up Harlan's murder by staging a car accident, one the local police didn't question.

"After easily getting away with that murder, Owen set out to claim the legacy he felt entitled to. The plan was to snatch Annette Brewster, confuse her with the memory-wipe drug, force her to sign a backdated will leaving him and his mother the family fortune—and then kill Annette and frame Tessa for the crime."

"Did Victoria know about any of this?" Madame asked.

"No," I said. "Her son's scheme was an awful shock to her. She had convinced herself that Tessa was behind the abduction."

"What about that tree guy?" Matt asked.

"Ernest Belling is out of the hospital," I reported, "but he's unable to work due to his gunshot wound. So Annette arranged to cover all of Ernest's expenses, and she wrote him and Flora a giant check on top of that. It allowed him to hire a full-time nurse for Flora, and he's buying a local greenhouse to set up shop. After what Flora went through with her daughter's suicide, Annette felt justice was served by paying her the large settlement and letting her know the details of Harlan's ugly death."

"Ahem," Sue Ellen Bass interrupted. "If you want to see justice served, I'll do it right now by giving Quinn here a kick in the butt for what he put Lori and me through. We chased our tails across New Jersey and back while Clare was with him the whole time!"

"Listen, Sue Ellen," Mike said. "I'm sincerely sorry about that—"

"Is someone talking?" Sue Ellen asked. "Because I don't hear a thing!"

"Make up and play nice," Lori ordered her partner. "Quinn's covered our backs enough times. Cut him some slack."

"Oh, I'll cut him slack. I'm just not talking to him for the next six months!"

"Why don't you blame Allegro here?" Quinn said, gesturing to Matt. "He started the whole thing."

"Hold on a minute—" Matt protested.

"I *would* blame Allegro," Sue Ellen interrupted, looking him over like a juicy steak. "But his butt's a little too sexy to kick. What do you say, Matt? You used every credit card you own to buy fancy meals up the Eastern Seaboard. How about treating Lori and me to a nice dinner?"

"I'm not having dinner with him," Lori declared. "We all know his rep, and I'm married."

"Okay, then—" Sue Ellen winked. "I guess it's just you and me."

For the first time in his life, Matteo Allegro looked a little nervous about a woman's proposition.

"So what about that creep Wimmer?" Dante asked.

Quinn answered this time. "He's facing multiple murder charges, and because he's a flight risk, there's no bail. You won't be able to hire that lawyer to fix anything for the rest of his natural life."

"And Dr. Lorca?" Esther pressed. "Don't tell me he's going to get away with his cover-up."

"Lorca's facing obstruction charges, and that ain't all," Franco said. "He'll probably lose his medical license. And I suspect some former patients will be lining up with lawsuits, now that the story has gone public of how his drug was used and how he covered it up."

"What about Mrs. Brewster?" Dante asked. "Is she going to be okay?"

Madame smiled. "Annette's getting out of the hospital tomorrow. And a good thing, too. A painter named James Mazur arrives in the city this week. He's coming to escort her to Paris."

"I never heard of Mazur," Dante said. "What's his work like?"

"Give me a minute," I said, and retrieved a parcel that had arrived that morning.

It was Mazur's *Sunset Basket*. Tessa and Annette had gifted the gorgeous canvas to our collection at the Village Blend.

When I unveiled the breathtaking painting, everyone applauded, and I knew in the years to come, whenever I admired its romantic images—the picnic basket in the lush French countryside and the older woman riding her bicycle toward the silver-haired gentleman collecting wildflowers—I would think of Annette and James and how, in all their years of living, of good and bad and ups and downs, they had never forgotten their love.

I would think of them like this, spending their sunset years together, finally claiming the peace and happiness they deserved.

THAT evening, Mike came to my duplex after his work at the precinct was over.

He built a fire to dispel the chill of the autumn night, and we settled down in front of the crackling flames with hot cups of coffee, brewed from beans I'd roasted that morning, and a plate of maple sugar cookies I'd baked that afternoon.

While Java and Frothy faux-attacked Mike's feet, his tie,

and each other, we talked about our day, how we liked our dinner, and all the other seemingly trivial but ultimately beautiful things that made up our little lives.

Soon the conversation turned to the past few weeks and my brain fog, which was practically gone. I assured Mike that I was remembering everything now—Joy's growing up, my moving back to New York to take over the Village Blend, even that first morning when we met, right downstairs in this coffeehouse.

"I can't tell you how relieved that makes me," he said.

"There's only one problem. One thing I can't remember. I discussed it with Madame, and it all comes down to a single question that only you can answer."

"Go on, sweetheart." He leaned close. "What's the question?"

"Where the heck is my engagement ring?"

Mike smiled, as if he'd been waiting for this moment. Then he reached into his pocket, got down on one knee, and reenacted his proposal from memory.

RECIPES & TIPS
FROM THE VILLAGE BLEND

Visit Cleo Coyle's virtual Village Blend at
coffeehousemystery.com
for even more recipes including:

* Pistachio Muffins
* Crusty Italian-Style Rolls
* Easy Apple Cobbler Cake

RECIPES

∽∾∽∾∽∾∽∾∽∾∽∾∽∾∽∾∽∾∽∾∽∾∽∾∽

The Village Blend's Blueberry Shortbread

*This amazing shortbread, layered with blueberries, makes
an impressive addition to dessert plates and cookie trays.
These tender, delightful bars sell out quickly at the Village
Blend, but you can make them at home with this small-
batch recipe. To see a photo of these wonderful blueberry
shortbread treats, visit Cleo Coyle's online coffeehouse at
coffeehousemystery.com, where you can also download an
illustrated guide to this recipe section.*

Makes one 8x8 square pan of shortbread, 16 pieces

½ stick (¼ cup) unsalted butter, slightly softened
4 tablespoons (2 ounces) cream cheese, slightly softened
½ cup granulated white sugar
1 large egg yolk
½ teaspoon baking powder
⅛ teaspoon salt
1½ teaspoons pure vanilla extract
½ teaspoon lemon zest (grated peel with no white pith)
1½ cups all-purpose flour (spoon into cup and level off)
1½ cups fresh or frozen blueberries (see note*)
1 tablespoon granulated white sugar

*Note on blueberries: If using fresh blueberries, rinse and dry. If using frozen, do not thaw.

Step 1—Prep pan: Lightly grease an 8-inch square pan with butter. Create a sling with parchment paper by lining the bottom of the pan and allowing excess paper to drape over two of the sides. This sling will allow you to lift the pastry out of the pan to cut into bars. (Buttering the pan helps the paper to stay in place.)

Step 2—Mix the dough: Using an electric mixer, beat butter, cream cheese, and sugar until light and fluffy. Beat in egg yolk, baking powder, salt, vanilla, and lemon zest. Stop the mixer. Add flour. Blend on low speed just until dough makes coarse crumbs.

Step 3—Layer in the pan: Pour about ¾ of the crumbly dough into prepared pan. Using the bottom of a measuring cup, press the dough into an even base layer. Toss blueberries in 1 tablespoon of sugar and spread evenly over the dough. Finally, crumble remaining dough over the blueberries, distributing evenly. Place plastic wrap over the pan and chill in the refrigerator for 30 minutes. (Cold dough in a hot oven will give you a flakier crust.)

Step 4—Bake, cool, and cut: While pastry is chilling, preheat oven to 350°F. Remove pan from fridge, remove plastic from top of pan, and bake for about 30 minutes. Shortbread is done when crumbly top and edges have turned lightly brown. Remove from oven and allow pastry to cool in the pan for about 20 minutes (this time is needed for pastry to set properly and to avoid breaking or crumbling). Use handles of your parchment paper sling to lift pastry slab onto a flat surface and carefully cut into 16 squares. Store completely cooled bars in an airtight container in refrigerator. If stacking in the container, be sure to use wax paper between the bars.

The Village Blend's Strawberry Cream Cheese Scones with Strawberry Glaze

A romantic breakfast or afternoon treat, these gorgeous scones are not to be missed. No wonder they practically seduced Clare from the mere description in Mike's memory. The cream cheese in the dough is the secret to making the pastry melt-in-your-mouth tasty. And the reserved strawberry juice (from the first step) not only flavors the glaze, but also blushes it a lovely light pink color. To see a photo of these wonderful scones, visit Cleo Coyle's online coffeehouse at coffeehousemystery.com, where you can also download an illustrated guide to this recipe section.

Makes 8 scones

For the strawberries

2 cups chopped strawberries
1 tablespoon granulated white sugar

For the scones

3 tablespoons cold heavy cream, plus a little more for baking
1 large egg, lightly beaten with fork
1 teaspoon pure vanilla extract
2¼ cups all-purpose flour (spoon into cup and level off)
1 tablespoon baking powder
½ teaspoon salt
½ cup very cold unsalted butter, cut into cubes
4 ounces very cold cream cheese (block not whipped),
cut into cubes
⅓ cup granulated white sugar
Strawberry Glaze (recipe follows)

Step 1—Prep the strawberries: Hull strawberries, wash well, and *loosely* drain (they should remain very damp). If using frozen, do not thaw. Roughly slice the berries over a bowl, into small pieces. You want about 2 cups of these pieces. Toss them well with 1 tablespoon sugar. Cover the bowl with plastic wrap and set aside on the counter for 60 minutes. As the berries macerate, the sugar will draw out some of the *strawberry juice*, which you should drain off and *set aside for use in the scone glaze* (recipe follows). After the chopped berries are well drained, measure out exactly 1½ cups of the strawberry pieces, set them aside in the refrigerator to chill, and begin to make your scones.

Step 2—Make the dough: In a small bowl, whisk together these three wet ingredients: 3 tablespoons cold heavy cream, egg, and vanilla extract. Set aside *in refrigerator.* (Keeping things cold is key in this process.) In a large bowl, whisk together your 2¼ cups flour, baking powder, and salt. Using clean hands, work the *very cold* cubes of butter and cream cheese into the flour mixture. Rub and squeeze until all the mixture resembles coarse crumbs— there should be no large "lumps" of butter or cream cheese left. All crumbs should be no larger than a pea. Now stir in the sugar with hands, combining well, and gently fold in the 1½ cups of strawberry pieces from Step 1. Finally, pour in the chilled wet ingredients. Gently mix with hands until dough forms.

Step 3—Form and chill: Generously flour a flat surface and turn the dough out onto it. Flour your hands well. Gently work with the dough, forming it into a ball. Pat the ball into an even circle of about 7 or 8 inches in diameter and ¾ inch in thickness. Use a sharp knife to slice the circle into eight wedges—do not fuss with the wedges or try to perfect the edges, handle very little. Chill the wedges in the refrigerator for a full 30 minutes while preheating your oven to 425°F. (The cold dough going into the hot oven will help give you nice, flaky scones.)

Step 4—Brush and bake: Line a baking sheet with parchment paper and place it into the oven to heat it. After the dough has chilled, brush the tops lightly with cold heavy cream and place the wedges on the hot pan, allowing space between the wedges for rising. Bake for 20 minutes at 425°F, rotate the pan, reduce the temperature to 375°F, and continue baking for a final 5 minutes. Cool and ice with **Strawberry Glaze** (recipe follows).

Strawberry Glaze

*1½ cups (or so) confectioners' sugar
3 tablespoons heavy cream (do not substitute)
1 tablespoon strawberry juice (reserved from scone recipe;
or see note*)
1 to 3 teaspoons water (for thinning the glaze)*

*Note: If you need a substitution for the 1 tablespoon of strawberry juice, try this. Stir 2 teaspoons of strawberry jelly or jam into 1 tablespoon of water. Like the strawberry juice, this will blush the glaze a pretty pink color while also adding a hint of strawberry flavor.

Sift 1½ cups of powdered sugar into a mixing bowl. Add 3 tablespoons of heavy cream and 1 tablespoon of strawberry juice (or use the substitution described in the note above). Whisk well to create a glaze. If the glaze is too thick, whisk in water, 1 *teaspoon* at a time, until you have your desired consistency. Test the glaze by drizzling on a plate. If the glaze is still too thick, add more water. If it becomes too thin, whisk in more confectioners' sugar. Finally, finish the scones by drizzling the glaze on with a fork. Or, if you create a glaze with a thinner consistency, you can simply dip the top edges of your scones into the glaze. Be sure to quickly set the scones upright on wax or parchment paper, allowing any excess glaze to drip decadently over the sides before setting.

The Village Blend's Pistachio Muffins

These pistachio muffins are outstanding. The batter tastes like pistachio ice cream, but they're more nutritious because of a secret ingredient in the muffin recipe: ricotta cheese. Ricotta adds protein and substance without heaviness and it provides moistness without the high calories of extra butter or oil. Try these babies warm, right out of the oven, split open and slathered with butter or cream cheese. Just like the hospital staff, lured away for a break by the Pied Piper of Village Blend pastry, you will absolutely eat with joy! To get the recipe for these muffins with photos illustrating each step, visit Cleo Coyle's online coffeehouse at coffeehousemystery.com, where you can also download an illustrated guide to this recipe section.

Cacio e Matteo

(A QUICK & EASY PASTA DISH)

Behold Matteo Allegro's very loose interpretation of the classic Italian dish Cacio e Pepe. When made the traditional way, this Roman pasta dish would not include oil or herbs, simply a toss of the pasta with cheese and plenty of black pepper, using a bit of the pasta cooking water for velvety smooth results. During their marriage, Clare was the one who made the Cacio e Pepe and her technique was flawless. After their divorce, Matt's attempts to re-create her meal always resulted in a gloppy mess. But if there was one thing Matt had mastered, after years of sourcing coffee in developing countries, it was the art of adaptation. Adding garlic-infused olive oil to the mix, along with some classic Italian herbs, gave Matt a quick, easy, and foolproof bachelor dinner with no glop in sight, and no need for sauce. So here it is: Cacio e Pepe *made* Matteo's *way.*

Makes 4 generous servings

> 6 cloves of garlic, peeled and smashed
> ½ cup extra-virgin olive oil
> 1 tablespoon coarse sea salt (or 1½ teaspoons fine salt)
> 16-ounce package of spaghetti
> 1 cup grated Pecorino Romano cheese
> 1 teaspoon coarsely ground black pepper
> 1 tablespoon Italian herb seasoning mix (see note*)

*Note: Using a premade Italian seasoning mix is the fastest way to create this dish, but feel free to mix your own using equal parts dried oregano, basil, marjoram, thyme, and rosemary.

Step 1—Infuse the oil with garlic: Peel garlic cloves and smash the cloves a little to release the flavor. Place the crushed cloves in a small pot with olive oil and heat to a simmer (do not boil). As soon as the oil begins to simmer, remove it from the heat, cover with a tight-fitting lid, and keep warm until the pasta is cooked.

Step 2—Make the pasta: Add salt to about 4 quarts of water. When a rolling boil is reached, add pasta and cook according to package instructions, to desired tenderness. Drain pasta well and return it to the original cooking pot (which now should be completely drained of water).

Step 3—Garnish: Quickly pour the warm garlic-infused olive oil over the pasta (you can strain out the chunks of garlic, if you wish, but Matt doesn't bother). Toss to coat. Evenly sprinkle on the cheese, pepper, and herbs and mix well to distribute the flavors through the pasta. Serve warm with an extra bowl of grated cheese on the side (for garnishing). Red pepper flakes also make a nice optional top-ping, for those (like Matt) who always fancy a little heat.

Matt's Coffee Beef Stew

The day coffee hunter Matt whipped up this amazing beef stew for his ex-wife Clare, he was stewing over Detective Quinn's visit to the Hamptons, but his foul mood did nothing to temper the satisfying flavor of this hearty dish. Many chefs will tell you that coffee works wonderfully as a meat tenderizer and flavor booster, which is exactly how Matt uses it in this recipe. The brewed coffee not only helps to tenderize the tough stewing meat before cooking, but also deepens the umami flavor of the beef. As Clare deduced upon her first spoonful, this stew was inspired by another meal, one Matt often made during their marriage—a more elaborate dish with Mayan roots, which Matt discovered while sourcing beans in El Salvador. You can find that recipe (Carne con Coffee) in the appendix of Cleo Coyle's fifth Coffeehouse Mystery: Decaffeinated Corpse.

Makes 4 large servings

2 cups black coffee, divided
2 teaspoons kosher or coarse salt, divided
1½ to 2 pounds beef stewing meat, cut into 2-inch cubes
½ cup all-purpose flour
1 teaspoon freshly ground black pepper
2 to 4 tablespoons vegetable oil
2 teaspoons cider vinegar
4 cups beef broth (or mix 2 cups broth with 2 cups water)
3 bay leaves, whole
2 medium onions, chopped
6 carrots, cut into ¼-inch rounds
10 to 12 small new potatoes, cut in half

½ cup frozen corn kernels (optional)
1 tablespoon butter

Step 1—Prep meat: In a shallow container, whisk together 1½ cups of the coffee with 1 teaspoon of the coarse salt. Add the cubed beef. Toss to coat. Marinate at room temperature for 1 hour. When the beef is ready, remove the cubes from the marinade and discard the liquid.

Step 2—Brown the meat: First season the flour with the ground black pepper, and remaining 1 teaspoon salt. Toss beef cubes in the seasoned flour to coat. Heat 2 tablespoons of the oil in a deep pot or Dutch oven. Sauté the beef in batches, 5 minutes per batch, turning the beef cubes until they are browned on all sides. Add more oil between batches as needed.

Step 3—Start the stew: Remove beef cubes from the pot but leave the juices. Add the vinegar and the remaining ½ cup of coffee to the pot. Cook over medium-high heat for 3 minutes. Return the beef cubes to the pot. Add the broth and the bay leaves. Bring to a boil, and then reduce immediately to a simmer.

Step 4—Simmer and serve: Cover and cook until the beef is tender, about 90 minutes. Add the onions and carrots and simmer, covered, for another 15 minutes. If liquid seems too low, add a little more broth. At this point add your potatoes and simmer, covered, until vegetables are tender, about 20 more minutes. Finally add corn (optional) and butter and simmer for 10 more minutes. Serve stew hot with crusty bread or rolls (see next recipe) or with flour or corn tortillas. As with many stews, this one tastes even better reheated the second and even the third day, with the flavors deepening and developing.

To store: Wait for the stew to cool completely, then pour into an airtight container and keep in the refrigerator for up to 3 days.

Clare Cosi's Crusty Italian-Style Rolls

Some of Clare's fondest childhood memories took place in the kitchen with her grandmother, where she helped bake rolls like these, pans and pans of them, to sell in her nonna's little Italian grocery store. These golden crusty rolls are amazing right out of the oven, smeared with plenty of butter. Heap them into a basket for service with dinner. Or slice them in half and layer on salami and provolone (or your favorite cold cuts). This is an easy recipe to follow. No bread or pizza stone needed. You'll bake the rolls on a simple sheet pan. To get the recipe for these rolls with photos illustrating each step, visit Cleo Coyle's online coffeehouse at coffeehousemystery.com, where you can also download an illustrated guide to this recipe section.

Parkview Palace Salad

This festive, elegant salad was based on the famous Waldorf salad, but with its own delicious twists. Serve it for a spectacular start to a holiday dinner or make it a stand-alone lunch salad by adding chopped chicken or turkey. To see a photo of this salad, visit Cleo Coyle's online coffeehouse at coffeehousemystery.com, where you can also download an illustrated guide to this recipe section.

Makes 2 servings

> 1 pear (or apple), diced
> 1 stalk celery, chopped
> 1 tablespoon mayonnaise
> 2 tablespoons crumbled Stilton (or blue cheese)
> 2 tablespoons dried cranberries (e.g., Craisins)
> 2 tablespoons candied chopped pecans (recipe follows)
> Optional: ½ cup chopped chicken or turkey

Combine diced pear (or apple) and chopped celery in a bowl and toss with mayonnaise until coated. (If adding chopped chicken or turkey, do so now, adding a bit more mayonnaise to coat.) Divide into the serving bowls or plates and top with crumbled Stilton (or blue cheese), dried cranberries, and candied pecans. (The recipe for candied pecans follows this one.)

Candied Pecans

Wonderfully crunchy with a baked-on sweet-and-salty crust, these candied pecans make an excellent snack for parties as well as a fabulous topping for ice cream, yogurt, and salads, including the Parkview's famous signature salad (see the recipe before this one).

Makes 2 cups

1 egg white
1 teaspoon maple syrup
2 cups roughly chopped pecans
¾ cup Sugar in the Raw (aka turbinado sugar)
½ teaspoon coarse sea salt

In a large mixing bowl, combine egg white and maple syrup and whisk well. Pour in the nuts and stir them gently until well coated with the egg white mixture. Set aside. In a separate bowl, whisk together Sugar in the Raw (turbinado sugar) and coarse sea salt. Pour the sugar-salt mixture over the wet nuts and gently fold until well coated. Dump the bowl's contents onto a baking sheet that's been lined with parchment paper. Spread the nuts out in a single layer. Bake at 300°F for about 30 minutes. Using a spatula, gently flip the nuts and cook for another 10 minutes. This flipping ensures that any dampness on the underside of the nuts will be cooked. Nuts are done when the outside coating becomes crisp. Cool completely before storing in a plastic bag or airtight container.

Champagne Chicken Paprikash

When Clare celebrated her young daughter's birthday at the Parkview Palace hotel, she enjoyed this regal champagne-infused dish. A fusion of French and Eastern European cuisines, this simple yet sophisticated version of classic chicken paprikash was not invented by the Parkview, however. The credit goes to New York's famous Four Seasons restaurant. This recipe is Clare's adaptation of the Four Season's dish. To see a photo of the finished chicken, visit Cleo Coyle's online coffeehouse at coffeehouse mystery.com, where you can also download an illustrated guide to this recipe section.

Makes 4 servings

4 tablespoons sweet paprika
¼ teaspoon finely ground sea salt
⅓ teaspoon ground white pepper
4 skinless, boneless chicken breasts
3 tablespoons fresh or dried shallots (do not substitute)
⅓ cup butter
2 cups (16 ounces) champagne
2½ cups (20 ounces) heavy cream
1 teaspoon cornstarch + 2 teaspoons water (for thickening)

Step 1—Prep the chicken breasts: Preheat oven to 350°F. In a shallow bowl, blend the paprika, sea salt, and white pepper. One at a time, roll each chicken breast in the mixture.

Step 2—Poach the chicken: Place the breasts in a Dutch oven or flame-proof casserole dish and add the shallots (do not substitute), butter, and champagne. Cover and poach in the 350°F oven for 35 to 40 minutes, depending on the size of the chicken breasts. The breasts are done when the chicken meat springs back when pressed. If you have a meat thermometer, internal temperature should be at least 165°F. Remove breasts from the pot and hold in a covered dish to keep warm. Meanwhile, make the sauce.

Step 3—Create the sauce: Place the Dutch oven, uncovered, on your stovetop and bring the liquid inside to a simmer, over medium heat. Continue to simmer uncovered for 10 minutes or until the liquid is reduced by two-thirds. Add the cream and continue simmering and occasionally stirring until the sauce is thick enough to coat the back of a spoon (without running off like water). To hasten this process, create a thickening paste by whisking together 1 teaspoon cornstarch with 2 teaspoons cold water in a small bowl or measuring cup. Pour this paste into the cream sauce while stirring constantly for the next few minutes. The thickness should now be perfect. Pour the sauce over the warm chicken and serve immediately.

KFC-Style Fried Chicken

While sourcing coffee in El Salvador, Matt made a friend who confided that a meal of fast-food fried chicken was always shared before peace talks between rival gangs. The fried chicken of choice came from Pollo Campero, *the KFC of the region. When Matt's divorce turned ugly, he decided to bring the tradition north—with actual KFC chicken. Clare took the bait, along with the challenge of guessing all of the colonel's famous eleven herbs and spices. While KFC has never divulged its secret fried chicken recipe, many Sherlock chefs have attempted to deduce it. This adapted recipe serves as Clare Cosi's preferred solution to that particular culinary mystery with the help of the* Chicago Tribune, *which originally shared the most famous copycat recipe. Clare made several adjustments for the very best flavor (in her opinion, of course).*

Makes 4 servings

> 3 to 5 pounds chicken (10 pieces: wings, drumsticks, thighs, breasts; or whole chicken cut up, see directions*)
> 1⅓ cups buttermilk
> 1 large egg
> 1½ teaspoons dried basil
> 1½ teaspoons dried oregano
> 1½ teaspoons dried thyme
> 1 teaspoon black pepper
> 1 teaspoon celery salt
> 1 teaspoon garlic salt
> 1½ teaspoons ground ginger
> 1½ teaspoons mustard powder
> 1½ teaspoons sweet paprika
> 2 teaspoons white pepper
> ½ teaspoon salt
> ½ teaspoon Accent seasoning (optional)
> 2 cups all-purpose flour
> 3 to 5 cups vegetable oil

Step 1—Prep the chicken: Rinse the chicken pieces thoroughly and pat dry. *If using a whole chicken, cut the bird into 10 pieces: 2 wings, 2 drumsticks, 2 thighs, and 4 breast pieces. (Cut breast in half, then in half again. Do not attempt to fry a whole breast.)

Step 2—Marinate the chicken: Whisk together the buttermilk and egg in a large bowl or plastic container. Add the chicken pieces to the mixture and marinate at room temperature for 45 minutes.

Step 3—Prep the coating: While the chicken is marinating, combine the herbs, spices, and salt in a bowl, along with the Accent (if using). Because basil, oregano, and thyme leaves are larger than the other powdered ingredients, you will need to pulverize everything together. Pulse them in a food processor, or a nut grinder, or place all your herbs and spices in a plastic bag and pulverize them with a meat hammer or rolling pin. Next measure out the flour and whisk into your pulverized spice mix.

Step 4—Coat the chicken: When marinating is complete, remove the chicken pieces from the bowl one at a time, shaking off the excess liquid. Dredge each chicken piece in the flour-spice mixture, turning and rolling until thoroughly coated. Place the pieces on a sheet pan and allow them to rest for 30 minutes more at room temperature.

Step 5—Heat the oil: While chicken is resting, prep the oil for pan-frying. You'll need to submerge the chicken as much as possible during frying, so choose a deep skillet or sauté pan, one that will allow you to pour the oil about 3 to 4 inches deep. Once poured, preheat the oil to 350°F.

Step 6—Fry the chicken: When the oil is hot, fry the chicken in small batches of three to five pieces. Don't crowd the pan. Fry for 15 to 20 minutes, turning about every 3 minutes. Be sure to reheat the oil between batches. Do not place finished fried chicken on parchment paper or paper towels—the pieces will become mushy. Instead, keep the freshly fried chicken crisp by placing the pieces on a rack with a sheet pan beneath to catch any dripping oil. Set the rack inside a low-heat (225°F) oven, where your newly fried pieces will stay warm until all of your chicken is done, and you're ready to serve it up!

Coffee and Cream Cake

This light chiffon cake, kissed with the flavor of sweetened coffee, makes a wonderfully sophisticated dessert. No wonder Clare chose it as her favorite among the cakes she sampled for her wedding day. To see a photo of this finished cake, visit Cleo Coyle's online coffeehouse at coffee housemystery.com, where you can also download an illustrated guide to this recipe section.

Makes two 8-inch round layer cakes

For Step 1

> 4 extra-large egg yolks, room temperature
> (reserve whites for Step 2)
> 2 teaspoons instant espresso powder (not instant coffee; see tip*)
> ⅓ cup brewed coffee
> ¼ cup canola or vegetable oil
> ½ teaspoon vanilla extract
> ½ teaspoon kosher salt (if using fine salt, reduce slightly)
> ⅓ cup granulated white sugar
> 1½ teaspoons baking powder
> 1¼ cups sifted cake flour (sift before measuring)

For Step 2

> 4 extra-large egg whites
> ¼ teaspoon cream of tartar
> 6 tablespoons granulated white sugar

Prep step: First, preheat oven to 350°F. Line the bottom of two nonstick cake pans with parchment paper, and coat the paper lightly with nonstick spray. Separate the eggs. You will need both the yolks and whites in this recipe.

Step 1—One-bowl mixing method: In a large bowl, dissolve the instant espresso powder into the brewed coffee (if the coffee is very hot, wait until it cools before proceeding). Add the egg yolks, oil, vanilla, salt, sugar, and baking powder. Beat well with an electric mixer, at least 3 minutes.

Stop mixer and add the sifted cake flour. On a lower speed of your mixer, blend until a smooth batter forms, but do not overmix at this stage. Set bowl aside.

Step 2—Lighten batter with whipped egg whites: Choose a very clean glass, ceramic, or metal bowl for this next step. (For best results do not use plastic. Grease clings to plastic and this will prevent you from properly whipping the whites.) Using an electric mixer, beat egg whites and cream of tartar on high speed until frothy. Gradually add in the sugar and beat until you see stiff, glossy peaks. Very gently, fold these glossy, sweetened egg whites into the batter mixture from Step 1. Divide your final chiffon batter between your two cake pans.

Step 3—Bake: In your well-preheated oven, bake for 25 to 30 minutes or until tops spring back when lightly touched. Remove cake pans from oven and cool on wire racks. To remove the cake layers from their pans, wait until *completely* cool (at least 1 hour). Then cover two plates in plastic wrap. Carefully run a butter knife around the insides of each pan, loosening any areas of the cake that might be sticking. Gently place the plastic-covered plates over the tops of each pan and invert. The cake layers should fall out easily. If not, gently tap the bottom of each pan. Remove the pans and peel off the circles of parchment paper from the cake bottoms.

To finish: Ice these cooled chiffon cake layers with an amazing **Mocha Buttercream** (see the next recipe). If you have time and really want to make a showstopping cake, chill the layers well, then carefully slice the two 8-inch rounds in half, creating 4 thin layers. Between each layer, slather on a filling of "Cream" by making the **Stabilized Whipped Cream** (recipe on page 371) and ice the entire "Coffee and Cream Cake" with the Mocha Buttercream, as suggested. Garnish the top of the iced cake with chocolate-covered coffee beans or chocolate curls. For instructions on how to create **Chocolate Curls**, turn to page 372.

Cooking tip: Espresso powder (or instant espresso) is not made of ground espresso beans. It is freeze-dried espresso that dissolves quickly in liquids. A good-quality brand to look for is Medaglia d'Oro. You can use any brand of instant espresso in this recipe, but do not substitute instant coffee. It gives a harsher and more sour flavor than instant espresso, which brings a richer, earthier note.

Mocha Buttercream

This beautiful buttercream icing makes a fabulous finish to the Coffee and Cream Cake that Clare sampled in preparation for her wedding day. This is an outstanding icing that's very easy to spread. Fluffy and light, it delivers gentle chocolate flavor, kissed with coffee, of course. (You may want to eat it with a spoon.) It pairs wonderfully with other cakes, as well. Try it with chocolate cake or a plain yellow cake or cupcakes. To see a photo of the finished icing, visit Cleo Coyle's online coffeehouse at coffeehouse mystery.com, where you can also download an illustrated guide to this recipe section.

Makes approximately 2½ cups frosting

2½ teaspoons instant espresso powder (not instant coffee)
4 tablespoons hot, freshly brewed coffee
2 teaspoons pure vanilla extract
⅓ cup natural, unsweetened cocoa powder, sifted
1 cup (2 sticks) unsalted butter, softened
3½ cups confectioners' sugar
Pinch of salt (to balance sweetness)

Step 1: In a small bowl, hand-whisk the instant espresso powder into the hot coffee until dissolved. Add the vanilla extract and whisk in the cocoa powder. Set aside this coffee-cocoa mixture to cool.

Step 2: In a large mixing bowl, beat the softened butter until light and fluffy. Reduce the mixer speed and add your confectioners' sugar a little at a time, while scraping down the sides of the bowl. After all of the sugar has been added, move to the next step.

Step 3: Beat in the *cooled* coffee-cocoa mixture (from Step 1) until your frosting is beautifully fluffy. Finally, add a pinch of salt to balance the sweetness. Sample the frosting and adjust to your own taste. After frosting your cakes or cupcakes, try garnishing the tops with chocolate curls or chocolate-covered espresso beans.

How to Make a More Stable Whipped Cream Filling or Frosting

Fresh whipped cream is a fluffy delight when used as a frosting or filling for cakes and cupcakes. But a special step is needed to keep it from quickly deflating or becoming watery on your cake. Follow these simple directions, and you'll see how easy it is to make a more stable whipped cream frosting.

> 5 tablespoons granulated sugar
> 2½ teaspoons cornstarch
> 2¾ cups heavy whipping cream, well chilled
> 1 teaspoon vanilla extract (use clear vanilla for whiter results)

Prep step: Place a large bowl and your electric mixer's beaters into the freezer to chill.

Step 1—Create the stabilizer: Into a small saucepan, combine the sugar and cornstarch. Pour in ½ cup of the cream. Bring the mixture to a simmer over medium heat, whisking continually until the mixture thickens (about 2 minutes). Remove from heat and whisk in the vanilla. Transfer mixture to another container to cool to room temperature. You can place the mixture in the fridge to accelerate the cooling, but *do not* allow it to harden.

Step 2—Whip up frosting: In your large *prechilled* mixing bowl, whip the remaining 2¼ cups of cream with your electric mixer until frothy and slightly thickened. Slow the mixer and beat in the (room temperature) stabilizing cream from Step 1. Increase the speed to high and whip until firm peaks form.

Cooking tip: Before frosting any cake, be sure it is completely cooled or the frosting will melt. Store any unused frosting or uneaten cake in the refrigerator.

How to Make Chocolate Curls

Chocolate curls make a festive topping for cakes, cupcakes, puddings, and ice cream, as well as coffee drinks, and hot cocoa. You can even combine chocolates for a striking effect, garnishing with a combination of white and dark chocolate curls. To make them, you will need . . .

1 block chocolate (white or dark)
Vegetable peeler

To create chocolate curls, start with a block of room-temperature chocolate. Using a vegetable peeler, scrape down the block and you'll see curls of chocolate peel away. Chill or even freeze the curls for more sturdiness and longer life.

The Daisy Fay

Quite a few bartenders have paid homage to F. Scott Fitzgerald's The Great Gatsby *by naming their creations after the much-mooned-over character of Daisy Fay Buchanan. The Nostalgia bar at Long Island City's Gypsy hotel included its own "Daisy Fay" cocktail for good reason. Not only does the Fitzgerald novel take place on Long Island, New York, but the shocking traffic death near the end of the novel, with Daisy at the wheel, occurs less than a mile from the hotel's Queens location. How appropriate that Clare should order a version of the cocktail, mere minutes before her own shocking discovery in the hotel's parking lot.*

The Nostalgia's Gin Daisy Fay

The Nostalgia's bartender gives you several options to tailor this beautiful, refreshing cocktail to your own taste. His original inspiration for the drink is not only Gatsby's iconic Daisy but the pretty pink "Gin Daisy," an American cocktail that's been enjoyed, in one form or other, since the 1850s.

Makes 1 serving

> 2 ounces gin
> 1 wedge of lemon (for juicing)
> 4 ounces pomegranate juice
> Ginger ale (or seltzer or champagne)
> Maraschino cherry
> Thin slice of lemon (for garnish)
> Sprig of mint

Add a few ice cubes to a glass. Any glass will do, but a tall glass (Highball or Collins) will show off the drink's bubbles. Pour in the gin, squeeze in the juice from one lemon wedge, blush the gin with the pomegranate juice, and stir. Top with ginger ale (or seltzer or champagne), gently stir again, and garnish with a maraschino cherry, a lemon slice, and a sprig of mint. Add a cocktail straw if you like.

The Village Blend's Latest Hit
Goobers Cookies

Inspired by the beloved retro candy of the same name, these cookies feature a satisfying combination of peanuts and chocolate. In fact, they're so satisfying, you may find (just like Franco and the Village Blend's happy customers) that they're hard to stop eating—not unlike the candy after which they're named. A bit of peanut butter and brown sugar in the dough add to the flavor, and a classic baker's secret provides a beautifully chewy texture. To see a photo of these delectable cookies, visit Cleo Coyle's online coffeehouse at coffeehousemystery.com, where you can also download an illustrated guide to this recipe section.

Makes about 40 cookies

1 stick (8 tablespoons) unsalted butter, softened
½ cup creamy peanut butter*
¾ cup granulated white sugar
1 cup light brown sugar, packed
1 large egg, room temperature
1 teaspoon lemon juice (promotes chewy texture)
1½ teaspoons pure vanilla extract
½ teaspoon baking soda
¼ teaspoon baking powder

¼ teaspoon salt
1 cup all-purpose flour (spoon into cup and level off)
¾ cup finely chopped unsalted roasted peanuts
1 cup mini chocolate chips, semisweet (if using larger chips, chop into small pieces)

*For best results do not use a natural peanut butter that easily separates.

Step 1—Make the dough: Using an electric mixer, cream together butter, peanut butter, and white and brown sugars in a large bowl until light and fluffy. In a small bowl, whisk together the egg and lemon juice and blend into the dough. Measure in your vanilla, baking soda, baking powder, and salt and mix well. Turn mixer to low and blend in flour. Do not overmix, but be sure that all of the flour is completely incorporated. Finally, fold in the finely chopped peanuts and 1 cup mini chocolate chips. Dough will be very soft and sticky, which is why you need to be patient and chill it.

Step 2—Chill and preheat: Cover the bowl with plastic wrap and chill for 30 minutes (so you'll be able to roll it properly) for the next step. While you're waiting, preheat your oven to 350°F and line a cookie sheet pan with parchment paper or a silicon mat.

Step 3—Bake: Break off pieces of dough and gently roll into balls of about 1 inch in diameter. Place dough balls on lined pan, allowing room in between for spreading. Bake about 13 to 14 minutes. Cookies should be slightly underdone. Remove pan from oven and *allow cookies to sit on the hot pan and finish cooking for another 8 minutes*—this is a part of the process that will give you an irresistible chewy-on-the-inside, crispy-on-the-outside cookie. Enjoy!

Cooking tip: When baking cookies, never put raw cookie dough on a hot pan. Your pan should be no warmer than room temperature. A hot pan will make your dough spread too quickly and too much during baking. If you need to reuse a pan quickly after it comes out of the oven, simply run it under cold water and dry it off, and you're good to go.

Clare's Cozy Maple Sugar Cookies

These tender sugar cookies with lightly crispy exteriors yet soft and chewy interiors are beautifully flavored with maple syrup, vanilla, and a secret ingredient. While they may look like simple, Mom's-cookie-jar snacking cookies, their complex flavor profile makes them delightfully satisfying treats to pair with coffee or tea for after-dinner dessert plates or holiday party trays. For best results, be sure to use real maple syrup and not "pancake" or "waffle syrup," which is simply corn syrup with maple flavoring. When in doubt, check the ingredients. The real stuff lists only one ingredient: maple syrup. To see a photo of these cozy cookies, visit Cleo Coyle's online coffeehouse at coffeehousemystery.com, where you can also download an illustrated guide to this recipe section.

Makes about 2 dozen cookies

12 tablespoons (1½ sticks) unsalted butter, softened
½ cup granulated white sugar
1 large egg
⅓ cup pure maple syrup (not "pancake syrup")
½ teaspoon salt
½ teaspoon pure vanilla extract
1 teaspoon baking powder
½ teaspoon baking soda
1 teaspoon fresh lemon juice (do not omit)
2 cups all-purpose flour (spoon into cup and level off)
1 cup granulated white sugar (to coat before baking)

Step 1—Make the dough: Using an electric mixer, cream the butter and ½ cup white granulated sugar in a large bowl. Add the egg (whisk lightly before adding), maple syrup, salt, vanilla, baking powder, and baking soda, and beat well. Blend in the lemon juice (an important part of the flavor profile; do not omit). Finally, turn the mixer to low and mix in all of the flour to create the silky dough. Do not overmix, but be sure all flour is incorporated and bowl is scraped clean. Dough will be soft and sticky and hard to handle, which is why you need to be patient and chill it. If you sample the dough at this stage, don't worry about the lack of sweetness. This dough is designed to balance the addition of sugar before baking.

Step 2—Chill it, baby: Cover the bowl tightly with plastic wrap (to keep it from drying out) and chill the dough for 2 hour in the refrigerator to firm it up *and* allow the flavors to develop. If you'd like to store the dough longer than 2 hour, scrape it into an airtight plastic container and keep it chilled in the refrigerator. Do not store longer than 2 days before baking.

Step 3—Prep for baking: When you're ready to bake the cookies, preheat your oven to 350°F and line a cookie sheet pan with parchment paper or a silicon mat. Pour 1 cup of granulated white sugar into a shallow bowl or pie plate. To form each cookie, dampen your hands and dust them well with sugar. Break off a piece of dough and form a ball, about 1 inch in diameter. Roll the ball in the bowl of sugar, generously coating, and place it on your lined baking sheet, allowing room for spreading.

Step 4—Bake: Bake in your preheated 350°F for 11 to 13 minutes (the time will depend on your oven). Finished cookies should be creamy on top and golden brown around the edges. That golden brown caramelization is important for flavor, but do not allow the bottoms to turn

overly brown or burn. Remove pan from oven and allow
cookies to cool a few minutes to set before carefully sliding
the parchment paper of baked cookies onto a rack to finish
cooling. As the cookies cool, they will harden, becoming
lightly crispy on the outside yet soft and chewy on the inside. Eat with joy!

Clare's Chocolate Chip Coffee Cake

*No better cake could welcome Clare home to her beloved
Village Blend better than this easy single-layer coffee (or
tea) cake. This is an absolutely delicious and satisfying
snack cake, layered with amazing flavor—no frosting required. Just mix up the ingredients in one bowl, slip the
cake pan in the oven, and start the coffee brewing!*

Makes one 9-inch round cake (12 servings)

2 large eggs
½ cup vegetable oil
½ cup 2% milk
½ cup granulated white sugar
½ cup light brown sugar, packed
2 teaspoons pure vanilla extract
½ teaspoon salt
2 teaspoons baking powder
2 cups all-purpose flour (spoon into cup and level off)
2 teaspoons cornstarch (for better cake texture)
½ cup mini chocolate chips, semisweet (if using larger chips, chop
into small pieces)

Step 1—Prep oven and pan: Preheat your oven to 350°F.
Prepare your 9-inch round cake pan by greasing the bottom
and sides with *butter* (*do not use* oil or nonstick spray,
which will overly toughen your cake's bottom and edges
and impart unappealing flavors in the crust). Also *line the*

bottom of the pan with parchment paper (the butter will help the paper stay in place).

Step 2—One-bowl mixing method: Using an electric mixer, beat eggs, oil, milk, sugars, vanilla, salt, and baking powder for a full minute. Stop the mixer and measure in the flour. On top of the flour, sprinkle on 2 teaspoons of cornstarch (which will help create a more tender crumb), and lightly stir the cornstarch into the flour. With your mixer on low, fully blend in the flour-cornstarch mixture, but do not overmix, or you will develop the flour's gluten and toughen the cake's texture. Finally, fold in the mini chocolate chips. If using larger chips, be sure to chop into small pieces.

Step 3—Bake: Scrape the batter into the prepared 9-inch round cake pan. Gently shake the pan to spread the batter out evenly. Bake in your preheated 350°F oven for about 30 minutes. Cake is done when a toothpick, inserted into the center of the cake, comes out with no wet batter clinging to it. Remove the pan from the oven and allow it to set by cooling on a rack for *at least 20 minutes* before serving slices directly from the pan or (better yet) de-panning the entire cake (see how below). Note that the center of this cake will fall slightly as it cools, and that's expected.

To store: Place completely cooled cake in an airtight container (like a cake keeper) or you can wrap the cake snugly in plastic wrap. If you live in a warm climate or wish to store the cake longer than 24 hours, move the airtight container (or plastic-wrapped cake) into the refrigerator.

To de-pan: Run a butter knife around the edge of the cake to release it from the pan. Place a plate over the pan's top and turn everything upside down, flipping the cake onto the plate. Remove the parchment paper from the bottom of the cake. Use the same plate-on-top method to flip the cake again, turning it right side up. Now you're ready to cut the cake and start that fresh pot of coffee!

To see a photo of this marvelous little cake, visit Cleo Coyle's online coffeehouse at coffeehousemystery.com, where you can also download an illustrated guide to this recipe section.

**From Clare, Matt, Madame, Quinn, Franco, Esther, Dante, Tucker, and everyone at the Village Blend . . .
May you eat and drink with joy!**

**Don't Miss the Next
Coffeehouse Mystery
by Cleo Coyle**

HONEY ROASTED

**For more information about the Coffeehouse
Mysteries and what's next for Clare Cosi and
her merry band of baristas,
visit Cleo Coyle at her website:
coffeehousemystery.com.**

ABOUT THE AUTHOR

CLEO COYLE is a pseudonym for Alice Alfonsi, writing in collaboration with her husband, Marc Cerasini. Both are *New York Times* bestselling authors of the long-running Coffeehouse Mysteries—now celebrating eighteen years in print. They are also authors of the national bestselling Haunted Bookshop Mysteries, previously written under the pseudonym Alice Kimberly. Alice has worked as a journalist in Washington, D.C., and New York, and has written popular fiction for adults and children. A former magazine editor, Marc has authored espionage thrillers and nonfiction for adults and children. Alice and Marc are also both bestselling media tie-in writers who have penned properties for Lucasfilm, NBC, Fox, Disney, Imagine, and MGM. They live and work in New York City, where they write independently and together.